THE KING'S CAPTIVE

Gate of Myth and Power Book 1

K. M. SHEA

THE KING'S CAPTIVE

Cover Art by Trif Book Design
Edited by Deborah Grace White

ISBN: 978-1-950635-20-7

www.kmshea.com

For cats everywhere, for putting up with getting their toe beans squished, their bellies rubbed, and being cuddled to death. We're sorry, you're just too adorable!

CHAPTER ONE

Chloe

I clutched the waxy, white paper bag that held my donuts—which would be my breakfast once I finished my shift—and stepped around a puddle.

No wet shoes. I'd decided that when I started my walk to work. *Wet shoes are gross, but—more importantly—I don't want to risk any of the books.*

Not that I had a habit of dropping the books I was supposed to be stocking and selling on my feet, but I was enough of a book lover that the idea of besmirching the bookshop I worked at was horrifying.

I flicked the hood of my raincoat back, and swung my donut bag.

Magic brushed my senses, and I froze.

Magic was a difficult sensation to pin down because individual supernaturals experienced it differently. To me, magic was a physical sensation—one that bloomed across my body.

I waited a moment, and the feeling solidified into a delicate, silken sensation that tickled my elbow.

Fae magic.

The trace was weak, but that didn't mean the fae were far away. It meant whoever was using magic was weak. Which was good news! Weak fae were much easier to escape. However, I was currently in the middle of a park—which was the worst spot to face a fae since they did best when surrounded by nature.

Maybe I can avoid them—or at least avoid being seen.

If I excelled at anything, it was going unnoticed, which was a great self-defense skill for a lone supernatural like me, even if it was a total confidence killer.

I started walking again, tilting my head down as I tried to discreetly peer around the block-sized park that hugged Fairy Lake's shore.

On the opposite side of the park, three fae strutted past a set of green mesh garbage cans.

The naiad, a water nymph, was easy to spot. He was wearing wet-looking fabric fashioned like pants and a t-shirt, and veered toward every wet spot on the sidewalk. Most obvious, though, was the scale-like pattern on his neck and hairline that glimmered in the fading sunlight when he moved.

His companions both looked soggy and grouchy—probably from the long day of rain. The shorter one was most likely a brownie, going by his height. A brownie was a kind of household fae who was roughly waist high to the average human, with thin, delicate limbs and large, mischievous eyes. They were easy to recognize, but this one was wearing a kid's raincoat—a bright blue one that was adorned with yellow duckies—draped over his frame, so I couldn't be sure.

My stomach dropped when I studied the last fae—a troll who was nearly as wide as he was tall.

The brownie would be easy to evade if I didn't get too close, and the naiad is so excited by the water he wouldn't even notice me...but trolls...

Trolls were a little more predatory than the common fae—who already ran way more bloodthirsty than your typical human.

Time to make a speedy departure.

My heart picked up a little as I swung my gaze from the lake—a terrible choice given the naiad—to the busy street that ran parallel to the park.

I should cross the street. I can lose them between the traffic and all the humans who are out for dinner.

When I reached one of the branching woodchip paths I turned off, following it toward the street.

Despite the increasing pitter patter of my heart, I kept my posture relaxed, and I swung my donut bag. I didn't keep my cool because I was kick butt or anything—quite the opposite. I had to stay calm, because I'd be much more noteworthy to the fae if they realized I was afraid. I needed to swindle them into thinking I was a human who didn't know better.

The three fae—and any supernatural in their right mind—would never harm a human.

That was the one thing that united the supernatural community—our collective need to make the humans think all supernaturals were relatively harmless on average and dangerously beautiful at most.

Humans outnumbered us supernaturals, by *a lot.* Combine that with the death rattles magic had been giving for the past few decades, and we would never survive if humans attacked us. Thankfully, humans were very taken by supernaturals—which I'm sure wasn't at all influenced by vampires' easy charisma, or the magic-induced beauty of the fae.

Still, my ability to pass as a normal human had been a key survival technique for me since I was little. Fae, wolves, and other supernaturals would leave a human alone. But a supernatural with no Pack, Family, House—no kind of protection from any magical entity?

Let's just say it was open season all day, every day on me.

The instinct to run rammed around my head like a ping-pong ball, but I kept my steps to a trudge and my shoulders hunched against the chill the rain had left in the air.

I listened, my heart falling when I heard the heavy thud of the troll's steps as the trio turned off the sidewalk that cut through the park, and followed me up the woodchips path.

The mathematical chances that this is a coincidence are very low.

I stepped off the woodchips and onto the street sidewalk, wavering for a moment as I tried to decide if I could still head toward Book Nookery, or if I needed to take a convoluted route to ditch the fae.

Although it had stopped raining about an hour ago, the pungent scent of wet asphalt still filled the evening air, and the clouds hadn't cleared from the sky, so only a sliver of the pink sunset was visible from the leftover gloom of the weather.

They've realized I'm a supernatural. Run. The instinct—forged by hundreds of nerve-wracking experiences—gnawed at me. I had survived this long by trusting that instinct.

I bolted in the opposite direction from Book Nookery, walking fast as I searched for a narrow alley or inlet that would be suitable to disappear down along the rows of brick stores, cafés, and restaurants that crowded the street.

The heavy step of the troll followed me, and I sped up into an almost jog as I dodged the cheerful humans who clogged up the sidewalks. The angry mutters of the fae behind me made me hope they were having a hard time keeping up.

Running isn't going to shake them—they're being too persistent about this. I'll need to be proactive.

I peered down the street and saw the perfect place to act—an Indian restaurant named The Flying Curry. I lurched closer to the brick building—almost smacking my arm on a window flower box —and positioned myself so I could dart down the alley next to it. I risked glancing back over my shoulder, briefly meeting the naiad's sharp and intelligent eyes.

"There!" He pointed to me and hurried ahead, abandoning his friends.

Now, real fear was starting to simmer in my belly. I darted down the alleyway, shimmying up and over the locked iron gate without even wrinkling my collared shirt. (Fleeing for your life is an excellent motivator for a lifetime of general physical fitness.)

The supernaturals had invested heavily in downtown Magiford —one of many attempts to extend the delusion that supernaturals were all very kind—so the alleyway was unfortunately empty of trash cans or anything I could hide behind. Instead, it had a little stone path with glowing strands of light crisscrossing above my head, and a bunch of outdoor tables and chairs for The Flying Curry.

But I wasn't looking for what anyone normal would consider a safe hiding place. I was looking for something uniquely suited to my...magic. That was why I'd chosen The Flying Curry.

I dove past the restaurant's side door that opened into the alley and crouched behind a table. Sweat dotted my forehead as I prayed I'd been fast enough that the naiad hadn't reached the alley. Then, I tapped my magic.

Faster than I could breathe—faster than I could *blink*—I was no longer a human holding a donut bag.

Instead, I was a black housecat. My fur was medium length, my eyes an average yellow, my build unremarkable from any typical household pet.

My fur used to be thick and shiny, but it had become a little thinner over the past few years due to the stress that came with living in Magiford as a lone supernatural.

I hurriedly jumped onto one of the tables, stuck a front paw out, and started calmly licking my leg despite the pounding of my tiny heart.

The naiad ran into the alley so fast he slammed into the iron gate, shaking it. The troll and brownie were a step behind him.

The naiad studied the fence for a moment, then glanced down at the brownie.

"Fine, fine." The brownie—with his smaller body—squirmed through the gate, popping out by the tables and chairs.

"Do you see her?" The troll's voice was so deep and booming, it rattled my cat bones.

"No..." The brownie took a few steps into the alley, his eyes flicking back and forth. His eyes settled on me.

I forcibly kept my body relaxed, though the impulse to puff up my fur was terrible. But I had an act to sell. So I scrubbed at my face with my paw as the fae took a few uncertain steps closer.

There was something about the magic of my cat form that made me hard to recognize, even if they *knew* I could shift into a cat. It was a wonderful survival technique, but I didn't like to lean into it too much because there was always a chance it could fail.

The brownie was almost to the first restaurant table, and I'd have to start thinking about running if help didn't arrive shortly.

The cat door built into the bottom of The Flying Curry's side door twitched open, and a brown and gray tiger striped cat stuck its head out.

It growled at the brownie, stepping into the alley as the hair on its back puffed up. When it caught sight of me it meandered in my direction, audibly purring.

When the tiger striped cat jumped on my table to join me, it snuggled in and started licking my ear. It was a weird sensation—something scratchy and wet scraping my ear—but I'd been thoroughly groomed by *a lot* of cats in my days of running and hiding.

I'd also been swiped by animal services more times than I cared to admit, but that hadn't happened since I'd moved to Magiford. So far.

The brownie stopped short of my table. "Definitely not her," he declared. "Must be the restaurant cats."

There was only one cat that belonged to The Flying Curry, but I'd made a point of hanging around several of my safe havens, like this particular restaurant, on my days off. If my efforts had paid off, most Magiford citizens mistakenly believed there were a dozen black cats that belonged to local businesses.

"Obviously the cat isn't her," the naiad said. "No transformation can be completed that fast. She had, what, three seconds before you were on her?"

The brownie peered down the dead-end alleyway. "She must have used magic."

I twitched my long black tail and stood up. While I stretched my front paws out in front of me, the tiger striped cat—his name was Rajiv—hissed at the fae again.

"Are we even sure that was cat girl we were chasing?" the troll rumbled. His voice sounded like boulders colliding.

It's reassuring that my magic of forced doubt is still working, but they have a nickname for me? That's terrible news.

I wanted to go unnoticed. My dream was to be ignored and viewed as a swirl in the mass of Magiford citizens despite my unusual magic.

Being called *cat girl* by fae didn't bode well for that goal, but the naiad had the Seelie emblem—a glowing purple flower—painted on a leather bracelet that dangled from his wrist, so if I was lucky only the Seelie Court was aware of my presence.

The Seelie Court and its counterpart, the Unseelie Court, were the smallest, least powerful fae Courts in Magiford. It was usually the Seelie and Unseelie Courts that bothered me—they were constantly warring over territory lines downtown. The other Courts were too big and powerful to care about Magiford itself.

Although human stories painted Seelie fae as kinder and less prone to violence than Unseelie fae, the truth was both Courts were under the control of temperamental, power hungry rulers, and there wasn't much difference between the two of them.

"I'm reasonably sure it was her," the naiad said. "She seemed scared. Cat girl is always scared."

Yes, because I'm a scaredy cat, not because I'm forever being chased.

Definitely not.

The trio didn't react when I jumped off the table, Rajiv following me.

"Such a shame." The naiad sighed, his scale pattern glowing in the dim string of lights. "We could have killed a few minutes playing with her."

I kept my pace slow and languid as I traveled along the side of The Flying Curry with Rajiv and ignored the threat. It was something I'd lived with all my life—a byproduct of having no supernatural allies or friends, because no one knew what I was.

I was a supernatural, but I was human. Probably.

Most supernatural humans were wizards. Wizards used magic to control water, fire, and the elements. There were a few other subsets—like werewolf hunters, vampire slayers, and oracles. But I wasn't any of those.

Humans—magic or not—weren't supposed to be capable of shifting—that would put me in shifter territory. Except I'd been put through dozens of blood tests that had all testified to my human DNA, and my ability to instantly shift from human to cat was an impossibility for shifters. They typically took a minimum of forty seconds to shift, and they turned any clothes they were wearing into tatters in the process.

Meanwhile, when I shifted back to my human body I'd still be wearing my clothes and holding my donut bag.

No one from the Curia Cloisters had heard of a human supernatural who could shift into a housecat, which meant there was no one I could register with—not a wizard House, a shifter Pack, nothing.

I'd been living as a lone supernatural my entire life—a very dangerous position to be in these days, as it made me an easy target to bully.

"By now she's probably in Unseelie territory," the naiad said. "Our king would not be pleased if we ventured there just to play with a mongrel."

Rajiv stopped long enough to growl at the fae one last time, then ran to catch up when I rounded the corner of the building, stepping onto the sidewalk.

He followed me all the way to the front step of The Flying Curry, where I stopped to touch my nose to his in my thanks.

Once I was certain he wasn't going to follow me, I continued on my way, sticking to the growing shadows, while Rajiv sat down on the front stoop and waited for someone to open the door for him.

I picked my way to Book Nookery as a cat—it was safer in the growing twilight as fewer people would notice a black cat. It was also faster as I could walk across yard fences and cross the city by rooftop in this body—cat athleticism was crazy fun to have when I wasn't worrying about getting chased.

I used the giant clocktower that had recently gone up downtown as a convenient marker while I created my winding trail.

The tower was gorgeous, and the clock face was illuminated in the darkening sky. I hadn't dared to go near it as a cat, and it wasn't yet open to the general public since construction had started late last fall/early winter. Supposedly some big city donor had built it for tourism purposes and to foster new businesses in the base of the tower. I liked it, because it stuck above most of the other buildings and was an easy landmark as I scrambled from rooftop to rooftop in my cat body.

Using rooftops—and cutting through some backyards—it took me about ten minutes to arrive at my workplace.

The bookstore squatted in the streets between the downtown shops and a residential section of Magiford. (More specifically, a neighborhood that held several particularly powerful Wizard Houses.)

Housed in a sprawling, brick Victorian house with white ornamental trim and gables that had fairy tale creatures carved into the design, Book Nookery was a twenty-four-hour bookstore.

I passed underneath the newly varnished, wooden sign that

hung off the front gate, walked past the lamppost that had been sputtering since the day I first started working here over three years ago, and made my way up the stone path.

I paused when I heard the coo of a pigeon and the loud sound of flapping wings, then peered up at the sky, narrowly avoiding getting pelted in the face with a french fry.

Sitting on the Book Nookery sign was one of my few "friends" in Magiford, a trash griffin.

Trash griffins were pint-sized griffins with the head, chest, and front feet of a pigeon, and the body, back legs, and tail of a raccoon. They typically could only be found in their home in the fae realm, but I'd been running into this particular trash griffin—he had a distinctive green and purple feather pattern on his shining dome of a head—since I'd moved into Magiford and had come to think of him as a friend.

I called him French Fry, because he somehow always seemed to be carrying a couple of old fries, and he was about as smart as the paper bags they came in.

Despite his stupidity, he was the only creature alive who could recognize me in my cat and human form, so take that as you will.

I meowed a greeting to French Fry—who was chewing on a blackened sample of his namesake as he balanced precariously on the sign. He whipped his raccoon tail at me, which made him fall over the side of the sign and crash into the marigolds planted beneath it.

I curled my tail in a question mark shape, but French Fry was fine. His furry rump stuck out of the flowers like a plant, but he cooed into the roots.

I purred, then headed in to work. Instead of climbing onto Book Nookery's porch, I followed a row of lilac bushes along the side of the house. Once hidden by the overgrown bushes—which hadn't yet bloomed despite it being April—I tapped my magic. Immediately, I was human again. My khakis weren't even wrinkled, and I still clutched my donut bag.

By the time I tugged my clothes straight, French Fry had popped out of the marigolds and taken to the air. He did one drunken lap over my head, then followed me when I hurried around to the back employee entrance that opened into the kitchen.

"See ya, French Fry. I'll throw you a snack during my lunch break if you stick around," I called before I disappeared inside.

French Fry cooed, then slammed into one of the kitchen windows and skidded down it, leaving a few tiny purple and green feathers on the glass.

I laughed as I wiped my shoes off on the rug, then took a proper step into Book Nookery's impressive kitchen.

An enormous oven and stove range took up one wall all by itself. Windows filled the entire opposite wall, and the rest of the wall space was covered in an erratic assortment of gorgeous wooden cupboards and cabinets in all shapes and sizes. The ceilings were so high I could stand on the counter and I still wouldn't be able to touch either of the two chandeliers, and the marble floor was so clean I could see my own reflection in it.

My boss, Mildred Booker, stood next to the island, two of her fingers wrapped around the delicate, porcelain handle of a teacup.

Ms. Booker had shoulder length brown hair with natural streaks of gray that gave it a frosted appearance. I wasn't sure how old she was, but if I had to guess I'd say she was in her mid-fifties from the set of her smile lines, the kind crinkles at the corners of her eyes, and the powdery appearance of her skin.

She was always the picture of elegance with her demure smiles and the graceful way she moved. I hadn't seen her in anything besides a skirt, dress, or a rare pantsuit, and she was never without a string of pearls.

She pushed her delicate glasses up her tiny button nose as she peered up at me—I was average height, but Ms. Booker was tiny and delicate. "Good evening, Chloe, dear."

"Good evening, Ms. Booker." I shouldered off my coat and

hung it in the closet before tucking my donut bag, wallet, and keys in the kitchen cupboard Ms. Booker let me use during my shifts. "Busy day today?"

"Not during the day shift." Ms. Booker stirred her tea with a tiny gold spoon. "I imagine everyone was out and about, trying to learn more about the fire over at House Rothchild."

I was so surprised I stopped trying to rearrange the gauzy scarf I wore to try to dress up my plain navy shirt. I wasn't very good at fashion, but for the sake of Book Nookery, I'd try. "There was a fire? Why didn't the House immediately put it out?"

Wizard Houses were magical entities unto themselves. They bonded with the Wizard family leader—the Adept—and could do everything from rearrange rooms to make flowers bloom out of season.

That a *fire* ripped through a House, and the House didn't immediately tap into the water line to put it out...it wasn't good.

"Josephine Clifton came in this afternoon," Ms. Booker said. "She heard it was a bad artifact. The Adept bought it because he felt the House wasn't giving him the power he deserved—never mind only fae can actually use magical items and artifacts, the loon, and all it did was splinter the Adept's relationship with the House. The artifact blew up while most of the Rothchild wizards were gone at work. The fire department got it before it spread outside the kitchen, though, and the House is fine, if not angry about its ruined kitchen flooring."

"A bad artifact did it?"

Ms. Booker nodded. "A brand new one." She sipped from her fancy teacup. "I say it's all because of magic dying out—makes any new artifacts hitting the market unstable. Though I also think the Adept was an idiot for believing he could even *use* an artifact. That sort of magic is limited to the fae."

"Maybe." I took a few steps toward the hallway, then paused. "Do you think we have anything to worry about? Book Nookery isn't..." I trailed off, hoping Ms. Booker would say something.

Book Nookery was a mystery, even to longtime Magiford residents.

Ms. Booker was a wizard, but she had never pledged to a wizard House. Rumor had it Book Nookery used to *be* a wizard House, and Ms. Booker was its Adept, but the rest of the family had died out or left and it went defunct.

Others said Ms. Booker built Book Nookery herself and put some wild magic into the building.

Ms. Booker never gave any indication if either of those urban legends were correct, but I'd been around the shop long enough to know the house had too much magic floating through it for it to be completely normal.

Ms. Booker flapped a hand at me. "Don't you worry your head," she said. "Book Nookery is completely safe."

"Of course." I smiled and tried to stand straighter—Ms. Booker was always after me for my posture. "I'll use the restroom, then start my shift."

"Indeed," Ms. Booker said. "You know to call me if you have any difficulties."

Only the bottom floor of the building was used for the twenty-four-hour bookshop. Ms. Booker lived in the upstairs floor by herself.

"Yes, Ms. Booker." I slipped into the bookstore bathroom—a beautifully wood paneled room with a fancy mosaic tiled floor and a window of swirled glass.

I shut the door and leaned against it, then turned to peer at my reflection in the giant, gilded mirror.

I hadn't forgotten how easily the fae had spotted me, which was odd.

I was...unremarkable.

I was average. Maybe I could be considered pretty, but only in a next-door-neighbor way that made me completely forgettable with my wavy brown hair—which I currently had tucked into a braid because Ms. Booker liked tidy appearances—and common brown eyes.

Despite a childhood of wishing I was taller, I was only average height with an average build, though I had runner legs from all the sprinting away from other supernaturals I did. I was just...normal.

My chin was maybe a little too angular, but the only thing that was striking about me was the beauty mark under my left eye that added a little sophistication to my otherwise normal features. But I'd covered the mark up with concealer—as I did every day—precisely because I didn't *want* to be memorable.

"It's still covered." I tilted my head up and down as I studied my reflection, making sure the rain hadn't uncovered the hidden beauty spot.

Being unremarkable made me that much harder to notice, single out, and beat up. It was another survival technique—one that was necessary for me to survive in Magiford, since it was the supernatural center of the Midwest.

Have I just been in Magiford so long that other supernaturals are getting better at recognizing me?

I uneasily backed up until the backs of my calves brushed the clawed foot bathtub.

I'd originally come to Magiford with the hope of getting hired at the Curia Cloisters.

Since no one knew what kind of supernatural I was, working in the Midwest's supernatural headquarters would be the safest place for me, because the Curia Cloisters took care of its employees.

But I'd been in Magiford for over three years, and I still hadn't been able to secure a position.

Maybe it's time to think about changing my strategy.

The idea sat in my belly like a rock. I briefly hunched my shoulders, then shook my head.

But I'll have to think about it later—when I'm not at work.

CHAPTER TWO

Noctus

"The mantasps are this way, Your Majesty." Charon pointed to a rock path that wound around the side of a mountain.

I held the hilt of my sword, steadying it as I started the climb. "Ker and Aristide?"

"Are waiting at the bottom of the mountain, with your people," Charon said. "At the last report, I was told Aristide had harassed several guards into producing a lawn chair and an umbrella for him."

"How very on brand for him," I said.

A wide gap swallowed up part of the trail, carving a gorge between the two sides, likely from when the winter snows had started to melt. I jumped it, then stepped off the trail and waited for Charon to catch up.

Charon climbed down the gorge—which was only about eight feet deep.

While I waited for him, I studied the rising moon. The sky was starting to turn a rose color as the sun sank on the horizon. It was a mantasp's preferred time to hunt.

Charon crossed at the bottom of the gorge and climbed the other side, joining me once again. "There are only two reported mantasps, though there could be more," he said, launching into the details of my mission. "They haven't broken through the wall —I don't think they *could* even if there were a thousand of them— but their presence has alarmed your citizens greatly."

Everything alarmed my citizens greatly.

They were elves, in a world where elves had been killed out after losing a war. They survived only because they were able to hide in the shadow of my magic. I was fairly certain anxiety settled upon them at birth.

"Is there anything else that is *alarming* my citizens?" I asked.

"Within your realm? No," Charon said. "Within Magiford? Yes. King Harel and Queen Darina are battling over territory lines."

I blinked as we rounded a bend in the mountain, and the immense wall of breathing magic that marked the boundaries of my realm stood immovably in our path. "Who are Harel and Darina?"

"The King of the Seelie Court and the Queen of the Unseelie Court in Magiford," Charon supplied. "They are the only Seelie Court and Unseelie Court in Magiford, as they have eliminated all other rivals."

"I see," I said, his words stirring my memory.

Earlier in the year, Darina overthrew the last competing Unseelie King in Magiford, effectively splitting the city between herself and Harel.

I didn't bother myself with the politics of the paltry, but in this case I had taken note. Magiford had historically been home to multiple Seelie and Unseelie Courts. It was highly unusual that Harel and Darina had been able to solidify their power base.

I turned to Charon in my surprise and near disappointment with those in my realm. "What could my people possibly fear from *fae?*"

The Seelie and Unseelie fae were both local fae Courts—the smallest in the area. There were Seelie and Unseelie Courts in every major city of America—they were like common goldfish, and roughly as frightening as a goldfish as well, though their monarchs were frequently pompous tyrants who ruled through fear.

"King Harel and Queen Darina are fighting for territory," Charon said. "There have been open battles between them. Nothing that has harmed any humans—they know better than to attract the Curia Cloisters' attention. But it has started to affect some of the less powerful supernaturals."

"Have they harmed any elves?"

"Not at this time, no."

"Then we'll leave it as it is for now. The Seelie and Unseelie have been sniffing around the house ever since the Paragon started showing up on my doorstep. I am not involving myself in their petty fight."

They're so incompetent, they'd destroy everything I've worked to protect in Magiford.

We were close enough to the magic wall that I could hear the hum of the magic—a low, contented sound that testified to the strength of the barrier. I could also see the wasteland that stretched beyond the wall.

The fae realm was riddled with a toxic miasma that had consumed almost everything livable. Elf magic could hold it back—that was how places like the Summer Court and Winter Court still had their lands in the fae realm. But that power came at a premium, considering supernaturals were under the mistaken belief that all the elves had died out in the catastrophic war centuries ago.

I seek to keep it that way.

The shadowy figures of the mantasps were visible through the haze of the magic wall, so I pulled my sword free from its scabbard.

Charon stopped by the barrier and peered back at me with his placid expression. "What will you do if King Harel and Queen Darina *do* harm an elf?"

I stared at Charon. "They don't even know any of us exist."

"Perhaps, but they're starting to suspect something of you."

"That would imply they still know nothing of my people."

"But if you catch their attention, they might find out."

"Unlikely—that is heavily overestimating their cognitive abilities," I said. "But if the worst does come to pass, and they realize there are other elves, I'll take care of it."

"How?"

"If there is no king or queen of the Seelie and Unseelie Courts, the news won't spread, will it?" I stepped through the wall, and the humming of the magic buzzed in my bones.

Since it was my magic, I was the only being the walls would allow past, but it didn't matter. I didn't need backup to deal with two measly mantasps.

I emerged on the other side of the wall, sighing in annoyance at the acidic taint to the air. The ground was blackened—as if it had been burnt—and not a blade of greenery survived the all-consuming miasma. It sucked the magic out of the living.

The only reason I was fine was that I could replenish magic faster than the miasma could eat it, even with the magic-binding shackles fastened around my wrists.

It's still a nuisance, though. I stepped on a stone, which crumbled like a husk of a chalk, and vaguely noticed the pain that started to burn my lungs from the poisonous air.

"Your Majesty?" Charon called through the wall; his voice warped by the magic.

"I'm fine, Charon." I studied the mantasps with a frown as they scuttled closer.

A gross combination of a wasp and a praying mantis, mantasps were wingless insectoids with six sapling sized legs, a grayish-brown exoskeleton, and a stinger the size of a small dagger adorning their abdomens.

Roughly the size of an average human, mantasps stood upright on their back legs and used their remaining four limbs like arms to grasp, or like daggers, since each leg was tipped with scythe-like claws.

These two particular mantasps ground their beetle-like, serrated jaws, creating a clicking noise that was almost as annoying as the acidic air.

I kept my sword lowered and waited as the pair lunged toward me.

At the last moment I dove to the side, and they nearly slammed into the magical barrier.

I extended my sword, and it felt like time slowed down—though I knew it was actually that I sped up. A flick of my sword, and I beheaded the first monster.

The remaining one started to click its jaws and turn around, moving as slowly as a snail. I leisurely stabbed it through the abdomen, killing it.

I waited for a few moments to make sure they were dead, and listened to the howling wind as it kicked dust into the air.

Faintly, there was another click.

I drew a hunting dagger from my belt and threw it into an ashy cloud.

The crunch of an exoskeleton hitting the unforgiving ground filled the suffocatingly silent landscape. A moment after, the wind whisked the ashy cloud away, revealing the slumped—and dead—third mantasp.

There were three of them? Interesting.

I retrieved my dagger but didn't put it away—I wanted to clean it first. I returned to the wall and listened for a few minutes longer, but I didn't hear anything.

If I took the shackles off, it would take me only a breath to use magic and be certain there were no more monsters, but the shackles were a necessary evil.

Reluctantly I stepped through the wall, re-entering my realm, where the elves I ruled over so feared me that they were reluctant to follow me to exterminate creatures they had personally requested I kill.

All hail the last king of the elves. It's such fun.

CHAPTER THREE

Chloe

Several days after I was chased by the Seelie fae, I slid the paperback copy of *Pride and Prejudice* back into its spot on the shelf, carefully lining it up with the other Austen titles we had in stock.

I'd grabbed it for a customer—a fae noble who was probably from the Night Court based on the crescent moon brooch pinned to her blouse—but she'd bought the special edition leatherbound copy we had on display by the front desk.

I need to wipe down these shelves; they're starting to look dusty. I glanced out of the nearest window, admiring the morning sky—which was paling from the deep black of night to the navy of morning as the horizon barely started to brighten.

It will have to wait until next week. My shift is almost done, and I get the next two nights off!

I wove my way between the labyrinth of bookshelves, passing by brightly covered cookbooks that I swear smelled like basil, cinnamon, and other cooking spices.

When I reached the geography section, I walked under a

globe light that hung from the ceiling and paused just long enough to check the frame on the enormous, glass-covered map of Magiford that hung on the wall. (If Ms. Booker ever found any dust on it, I'd hear about it.)

I stepped out of the geography section—which was housed in what was supposed to be a formal dining room—and into the main section/entry of Book Nookery.

The checkout counter—an antique wooden desk that weighed about a thousand pounds—was pushed against the winding wooden staircase that led to Ms. Booker's residence upstairs. I made my way over to it, turning when the front door creaked open. "Mr. Gleevers, good morning!"

Mr. Gleevers was a portly human—a normal one, not so much as a drop of magic in his family. He never went anywhere without his newsboy cap, tweed jacket, and distinctive mutton chops.

"Chloe, good morning to you!" Mr. Gleevers beamed at me. His ruddy complexion made his smile extra jolly. If he grew a beard, he'd be a shoo-in for the role of Santa.

"Good morning." I moved behind the counter and grabbed the tablet that was connected to our catalog—Mr. Gleevers always had specific book requests, so it was best to prepare. "You're here bright and early. It's nearly five in the morning—I usually see you closer to midnight hours."

"I finished my latest research topic just an hour ago, a paper on selkies!"

Despite being human, Mr. Gleevers loved researching supernaturals. He lived on the same street as Book Nookery, and had purchased a library's worth of books about supernaturals since I'd started working here.

He described himself as an armchair scholar, but I was pretty sure he was more familiar with pieces of supernatural society than I was, and he posted his research online.

"Congratulations on another finished project," I said.

"Thank you. Here—I brought you this!" Mr. Gleevers set a

paper carton of chocolate milk on my desk—just like the ones kids got with school lunches—getting a laugh out of me.

The night patrons of Book Nookery knew I had a thing for milk—which was kind of funny considering I could turn into a cat, and cats, despite the popular belief, are lactose intolerant and drinking milk can make them sick.

I'd been obsessed with drinking milk as a kid. My adopted family were all model/basketball star tall. I was average height, but I felt short and squat next to them. When I was in elementary school I was convinced milk with its calcium would be my magic key to growing taller.

It hadn't worked, but I still loved the drink—be it cow milk, coconut milk, oat milk, or cashew milk.

"That's very thoughtful of you, thank you!" I picked up the carton and toasted him with it.

Mr. Gleevers chortled. "Gotta treat my favorite reference helper!"

"I'm always honored to help in any way I can." I opened the chocolate milk and took a few sips, nostalgia for my school years hitting me hard, before I set it down and put on my work mode. "I'm guessing that since you're here so soon after finishing a paper, you've been bitten by a new project?"

"Indeed, I have!"

"Then what can I help you look for?" I moved my milk carton to a lower shelf of my desk, then set up the tablet and its keyboard, my fingers hovering over the keys.

"I'd like any books you might have on elves!" Mr. Gleevers declared.

I froze. "Elves?" I repeated, my voice cracking with tension.

Elves were a delicate topic for supernaturals.

We'd led the humans to believe they'd died out several centuries ago—which was true. What we refrained from explaining was that they'd died out in a massive war, one between the elves and every other supernatural race in existence, and that they'd been eradicated after losing.

It was a dark chapter of our history, but it had been necessary.

Real elves weren't the silk-wearing, poetry-writing scholars we'd led humans to believe.

Elves were cruel, ruthless beings who had ruled over our society with an iron fist and vast magical powers that couldn't be matched by any supernatural, except maybe the dragon shifters.

The elves had done everything they could to subjugate other supernaturals, keeping werewolves as pets and fae as servants. Supernaturals had allowed it for centuries because elves created magic by existing—it was theorized that their extinction is what was leading to magic slowly dying out in modern generations.

The end of the elves had come when they'd turned their power-hungry gaze upon humans with the intention of revealing themselves and enslaving humans as well—an impossibility given the vast numbers advantage humans have. The rest of the supernaturals revolted, and war erupted.

But I can't tell Mr. Gleevers that!

I cleared my throat and forced a smile. "I'm afraid we don't have any books on elves here in Book Nookery."

I knew for a fact Ms. Booker had a few in her private collection, but she rarely let anyone see them, and we didn't carry any that were purchasable.

"That's understandable. Just tell me what you can order, in that case," Mr. Gleevers said.

I strained my mind, trying to remember the script Ms. Booker made me memorize for instances like this one. "There actually aren't any books about elves within the supernatural community," I said. "Out of respect. Given how they walked the earth, it is the most honorable thing to do."

It wasn't a lie—if the humans knew elves were bloodthirsty and that we'd killed them, they would freak.

Mr. Gleevers slouched so much; I swear even his muttonchops

drooped. "Is that so—that's a shame. Though I don't wish to be disrespectful to them."

"There are several pieces of elven made art at the Magiford Curia Cloisters," I said. "You'll need to call ahead to arrange for a visitor's pass, but the art is open to the public. Otherwise, I would suggest researching the higher fae Courts. They're said to be the closest things to elves that we have left, given that the elves passed on some of their knowledge of magic to the fae."

Mr. Gleevers perked up, his eyes bright once again. "Really?"

"Yes. Actually, the queen of the only Night Court in the USA lives here in Magiford, and she's been rallying the other fae Courts. She's a wonderful example of fae power."

The Night Court Queen was also famously half human, but Mr. Gleevers didn't need to know that—I just needed to get him distracted from the topic of elves.

"How interesting. You said she rules the Night Court, eh?"

"Yes. I happen to have a new book about their history if you're interested."

"Indeed, I believe I am!"

Within five minutes I'd located the book, settled Mr. Gleevers's payment, and escorted him out the door.

"Enjoy your new read!" I waved as he shuffled down the stone path.

"I shall! Have a good day, Chloe!"

"Thank you—you too!"

I waited until Mr. Gleevers made it to the sidewalk out front before I released the breath I'd been holding in and closed the door.

I turned back around just in time to see Ms. Booker come down the staircase, her dress flats quiet on the carpeted steps. Her hair was carefully set in loose, perfect curls, and a string of pearls hung from her neck even though it was just past five in the morning.

"Good morning, Chloe dear." Ms. Booker delicately stepped off the last step and set her hand on the desk. "Your shift is over."

"Thanks, Ms. Booker."

Ms. Booker turned a page in the daily calendar placed on the front of the desk. "Were there any problems last night?"

I shook my head as I slipped past a bookshelf of plant books, pausing just long enough to replace an ivy tendril on the shelf as it was making attempts to climb across the gaping space between two bookshelves. "No. It was a slower night—maybe only a hundred customers—so I was able to finish payroll."

Although I worked the night shift of the twenty-four-hour bookstore, it was popular given the nocturnal nature of several of the more populous supernatural races. I filled any free hours by helping Ms. Booker with her accounting and payroll since I'd gotten a college degree in finance. (Another bid to make myself more favorable to the Curia Cloisters since supernaturals weren't historically interested in subjects like accounting.)

Ms. Booker adjusted the enormous—fake—emerald ring on her tiny finger. "Slow nights are bound to happen."

"Mr. Gleevers just left," I said. "He's onto a new research topic."

"I would expect nothing less from such a curious and diligent man. What is the topic this time?"

I started to slide my hands into my pockets, then stopped—Ms. Booker didn't like fidgeting or slumped posture. "Elves."

"Elves?" Ms. Booker's penciled in eyebrows flew up toward her hairline.

"I followed protocol. I think I've managed to distract him with the fae. He bought a book about the Night Court."

"I see. In that case, you did well," Ms. Booker said. "But, as I said, your shift is over. You take care and run along home."

"Yes, Ms. Booker. Have a great day." I darted behind the desk long enough to grab my carton of milk, then exited the maze of bookshelves and slipped into the kitchen where I grabbed my wallet, keys, jacket, and my bakery bag that held my breakfast.

I'd gotten donuts again—a donut shop called "Magiford Donuts" had opened downtown a few months before, and I was ridiculously hooked.

I finished my milk and tossed the carton before I slipped outside and put my jacket on, shivering a little in the morning chill. Spring was settling into the ground—we weren't getting frost anymore, and daffodils were starting to bloom. But it still got really cold at night, which made for a brisk walk back to my tiny studio apartment as the sky was still a pale navy blue and the sun hadn't even started warming the horizon line.

My phone beeped when I was heading out of the neighborhood, and I almost strangled myself with the gauzy scarf I wore more for fashion than warmth—it was white with a flower pattern—as I juggled my donuts and my wallet until I could see who had messaged me.

It was my sister—my adoptive sister—Joy. Every morning she texted a picture of a cat to me and our brother, Pat, which was short for Patience. (I'd already been named Chloe when my parents adopted me—or at least, my name was Chloe according to the letter pinned to my baby blanket when I'd been abandoned at a hospital—so to match Joy and Pat/Patience, my parents gave me the middle name of Grace.)

Today's picture was of an adorable gray colored cat wearing glasses and posed next to books—what could I say, Joy knew her audience.

I was about to type out my response when fear slammed into me, turning my spine into ice. A presence—oppressive and frightening—hung in the air.

I convulsively tightened my hold on my phone and looked around, peering up and down the empty street.

Squinting back into the residential area, I could see one or two people out walking their dogs in the dim morning light.

The downtown district was still relatively quiet. No one was out on the sidewalks and stores weren't open, but lights were on, and I knew closer to main street all the cafés and coffee shops would be open.

Even though I didn't see anything, the feeling didn't go away. It curled around me, eating at my senses as the impulse to run rippled through my body. It felt like a sword at my back—or maybe claws digging into my throat.

I had to be missing something.

There was no magic—I would have felt it. Straining my ears, I couldn't hear anything besides the faint hum of traffic. My heart beat in my eardrums, but not so loudly that it could be covering up any other noises. *There should be birds singing, even this deep in the city.*

I picked at my phone's plastic case in my nervousness, but I couldn't see anything that would explain the sudden...*pressure*.

Although my breath wanted to come faster, that would only move me closer to hysteria, so I kept it measured as I started walking again. My instincts screamed that I needed to run, but sprinting through the neighborhood in business casual clothes was a surefire way to make myself stick out.

I don't know what the threat is—or if it's even real. I need to be careful.

My walk was too fast to fit a normal pace, but I didn't think I could slow down even if I wanted to. My hands were clammy, and the instinct to run was so overwhelming, I could feel it in the back of my throat.

I veered off the regular route to my apartment and instead pointed myself in the direction of downtown, trying to get closer to human life. There had to be a coffee shop or café I could get to.

I was hurrying up a side street when I thought I heard the tap of footsteps behind me.

I angled myself toward a store window—a real-estate agent's

office—as if I was looking at the hours, and glanced down the street.

It was empty.

Not a single person was there. But that dark, heavy feeling grew stronger, and sharper, by the second.

I bolted. I wasn't concerned anymore about fitting in. Whatever this was...it was too dangerous.

I ran for the nearest café, my heart pounding louder and louder as I realized there were no cars, no movement of any kind on the streets.

What's going on?

I was about two blocks away from the closest café before I finally heard something, voices. A note of sharp laughter, followed by a high-pitched yip.

A silken sensation tickled my elbow: *fae.*

Do I run to the café and hope it's open despite whatever is going on? Or do I throw myself at the fae and hope that whatever is following me isn't willing to mess with them?

I wasn't too concerned about what the fae would do to me. They'd rough me up as part of whatever power/mind games the supernatural community thrives on. But eventually, I'd get away. I *always* got away.

Whatever was following me...it was on a totally different level from what I was used to dealing with. I couldn't make a mistake.

I glanced back over my shoulder, and in the shadows of a shop awning, I thought I saw something stir.

Magic grated against me. It was prickling and painful—like the dulled edge of a dagger that had never been sharpened.

Fae it is.

But I needed to be crafty about it. If I ran to the fae and asked for help they would never risk it. I needed to *trick* them into helping me.

I changed directions, turning off the main road I'd been

following, and ran down a smaller street, heading toward the fae laughter.

I popped out of the side street, almost staggering onto the road before I corrected myself.

The heavy feeling had followed me, digging into my back as I studied the tiny green space in front of me. It wasn't even the size of a city block. It just had a fountain and a few beds of greenery that would bloom into flowers as spring continued to thaw, and was lit up by an abundance of bright streetlights.

The naiad, brownie, and troll who had chased me downtown a few days earlier were walking through the green space, angling back toward a residential part of town. A dryad and a pixie—at least I assumed it was a pixie; it fluttered around on glowing wings, moving so fast it resembled a bouncing ball of light—had joined them for today's outing.

Seelie fae, that's fine. Seelie or Unseelie doesn't matter right now.

I sprinted up the sidewalk, running parallel with them until I managed to get ahead of their group. I waited impatiently at a stop light, and the heavy feeling drew closer. I twisted around—the weird shadows I'd seen earlier now lingered behind a flower bed.

This light isn't going to change in time. It's getting closer.

A quick glance up and down the street confirmed there was no traffic, so I bolted across the crosswalk. I slowed down, however, when I reached the sidewalk that intersected with the Seelie fae's path.

I tried to make it look like I was in a hurry—not that I was spooked because something—possibly a portend of death—was chasing after me. I resembled a shaken chihuahua on the best of days, so it was doable.

I purposely didn't look at them as I scuttled past, still clutching my donut bag.

"Hey!" the naiad shouted.

I jumped—dropping my donuts—and turned toward them, as if they'd caught me off guard.

The brownie tilted his head back and forth as he studied me, showing no signs of recognition, and even the naiad looked confused as he studied me.

Oh, sure. Now *they don't recognize me. Thanks, magic.*

I tapped my magic so I shifted to a cat in front of them, then made a wild scramble—as if I'd lost control of myself in my fright.

"Oh, it's cat girl!" The naiad pointed at me—as if the others could have missed my transformation.

Yes! They're buying it!

He jumped forward and scooped me up.

This I was considerably less excited about. Being held is not a fun experience, much less the process of getting picked up.

"That's cat girl?" the troll rumbled.

My temperamental magic must have been working overtime, because he sounded doubtful and uncertain despite my show.

"She changed right in front of us...didn't she?" The pixie darted forward, hovering a foot above me. Her wings shed little sparks of light, but I focused on wriggling—pretending to try to escape.

The naiad held me under my armpits and dangled me out in front of him. "Don't blame yourself, my fellow. She looks so...catlike."

"What are you going to do with her?" The brownie slipped his long, slender hands into the pockets of his corduroy vest. "We're supposed to go see *that guy*. Orders of the king."

The naiad shrugged. "She'll come with. It's not like she can escape us—she's a cat."

The dryad tucked an ivy tendril woven through her hair behind her ear. "She could be a risk."

"Or, she could save our skins when *he* inevitably refuses our offer, and we're forced to return empty handed to King Harel."

I tensed in the naiad's grasp. *Take me back to King Harel himself? That can't happen, I'll have to escape before then.*

I twisted in the naiad's hands, not liking the way I hung helplessly. He ignored me—too focused on his comrades.

But when I felt the heavy, shadowy presence, and spotted it across the street, I reflexively sank my claws into the scaled skin between the naiad's fingers.

How are they not freaking out! Can't they sense it—or see it?

The naiad was mostly bothered by me. He hissed as he dislodged my claws, totally oblivious to the danger.

As a cat, the shady presence painfully brushed my whiskers, and my hair was standing up against my control—I was probably going to lose another patch of fur after this.

Maybe I messed up. I should have gone to the Curia Cloisters. But that's a long run from downtown. It probably would have caught up with me before I reached the Cloisters, whatever it is.

"I suppose she would be something the king could work his aggression out on besides us," the brownie thoughtfully said.

The dryad shrugged. "We need to keep moving. King Harel won't accept excuses if we're late."

The fae ambled off, zigzagging south—back to the more residential area of Magiford, where I'd just come from—and east.

*This isn't going to put me any closer to home, but is that...*thing *still tracking me?*

The fae casually crossed the street, without looking of course. Supernaturals weren't the greatest with traffic laws, which led to frequent fender benders downtown no matter how much the human police had tried educating the public.

The naiad switched to holding me by my stomach—though he pinched my legs together so I couldn't claw at him again. I was still able to twist—cat bodies are very bendy—so I could watch behind the group.

My blood thickened in my veins when I saw the shadow lurking at the edge of the green space.

It kept pace with us for several streets, hanging approximately a block back.

It's not getting closer, so it's definitely me it was after, not supernaturals in general. But why?

While some supernaturals considered picking on me cathartic, there wasn't really a *point* to messing with me besides sheer malice or making a show of power. I couldn't do anything for anybody, and no supernaturals cared about what happened to me.

The naiad turned, and my vision swirled as he laughed at something one of his friends said. When he straightened up, the shadow was gone, but I could still feel its presence linger in the air.

Did it give up?

I wasn't going to start my escape attempts until I knew for sure.

I need to get a better look.

I yanked one of my front paws out of the naiad's grasp as we turned into what appeared to be some kind of cul-de-sac.

The brownie shivered. "I still can't believe one of *them* lives...here."

The troll peered up and down the road—which was as silent as a graveyard this early in the morning. "It's strange," he agreed. "Like a wolf living among sheep."

"We don't for sure know that he really is one," the naiad said.

I managed to peer down the street again—no shadow. The heavy feeling was gone, too.

Whatever it was that had been following me, it had given up.

For now.

Shivering, I looked around, trying to figure out where I was.

The horizon had turned a water gray as night retreated, with the roots of the sky blazing red—a sign that sunrise was on its way. This—combined with the still bright streetlights—illuminated the neighborhood in a dullish light, revealing that we were in one of the many human neighborhoods in Magiford.

The houses were modest sized with front yards that were green but sported the occasional dandelion. A few driveways had sidewalk chalk drawings that were clearly the work of kids, and one of the houses had so much lawn furniture piled on it, it was a wonder anyone could get to the front door.

The fae stopped outside a small sized, Cape Cod-styled house that was white with blue flower boxes and blue shutters. It was one of the few houses on the street that had a fence—an ornamental one made of wrought iron that was about hip high.

My fae escort stood awkwardly on the sidewalk, all of them staring at the house.

"Is someone going to go ring the bell?" the pixie finally asked.

"I'm not passing that property line," the brownie flatly said. "No way."

The dryad pressed her lips together. "I heard the last fae who attempted stepping onto *his* property woke up a week later."

"Rumors," the pixie said. "Probably started by the Unseelie because they want him as an ally."

"Maybe," the naiad said. "Or maybe it's the truth given the history of his people."

This whole conversation had me a lot less excited about being with the fae. The shadow's retreat didn't have me too hopeful that it was entirely gone, but as a cat I'd be able to trot off between homes at the end of the cul-de-sac and head out in a different direction, making me harder to track.

Now seems like a good time to slip off—because if they *don't want to talk to this supernatural, I definitely don't.*

"If we don't ring the doorbell, how are we supposed to talk to him?" the brownie asked.

"I vote we wait," the pixie said, her voice shrill.

The naiad was distracted, so I tugged my other front paw from his grasp—my cat agility was the only thing that kept me from slumping forward and hanging from his hands by just my back paws.

I didn't inherit all of a cat's senses—my sense of smell and hearing were slightly better than a typical human's, and my night vision was excellent, but not equal to a cat's. The biggest boon I had—as both a cat and myself—was my catlike reflexes, which kept me from face planting despite all the mad scrambling I did for survival. They gave my human form a hefty boost, too, which was nice for climbing trees, walls, and houses when escaping other supernaturals.

"We could throw something at the house," the troll suggested.

The naiad shivered. "That's even worse than ringing the doorbell!"

As I set to work trying to pull my back two legs free so the naiad would only be holding me by my belly, the front door of the quaint house swung open.

Someone stepped onto the cement porch, but I didn't initially notice because of the raw power that electrified the air.

Magic pulsed through my body—a foreign kind of magic I'd never encountered before. It was overwhelming and sharp—like a knife in your ribs.

The fae must have felt it, too. The naiad almost dropped me before he caught himself and clutched me to his chest.

For once, I didn't mind. I wanted to get away from whoever had just stepped outside and brought the strange magic with them.

I hunched, trying to make my cat form as small as possible while I peered through the morning light at the feared homeowner.

He was tall—taller than a typical fae, and he even had tapered ears to match, though the tips of his were longer than usual. Instead of the willowy grace of the noble fae, he was a solid presence. Too solid, in fact. Looking at him burned my eyeballs.

He was almost as broad shouldered as a werewolf, and his strong jawline and the planes of his face were like a carved marble statue—the kind of perfection that humans put in their art but never showed up naturally.

His hair was a rich, dark gold color, and just long enough that it looked like he could comb his fingers through it when he was contemplating lesser creatures—as he was now, staring at us with hazel brown eyes that had black spirals circling through the iris, giving him a hypnotic look.

He was wearing what could loosely be called human clothes—loose linen pants and a black shirt—but he was a pinnacle of supernatural beauty. It was terrifying.

Ooohh, I think he's worse than whatever was following me. This was a bad idea. A very bad idea. My gut steered me wrong on this one!

I shrank back from the...being. (I didn't know what else to call him, because he definitely wasn't human, vampire, or fae!)

He studied the Seelie crew lined up on the sidewalk. "What do you want?" His voice was deep and sharp.

The brownie trembled and seemed to curl in on himself. "Honorable sir," he warbled. "King Harel of the Magiford Seelie fae wishes to extend an invitation of alliance—"

"I'm not interested."

The brownie gulped audibly. "W-we understand, but, perhaps you would h-hear King Harel's terms?"

"No." The supernatural sighed—the troll winced so hard he almost fell off the curb at the noise—and ran his fingers through his golden hair. The growing morning light caught on the shackle-like metal bracelet that was fitted around his wrist and made it glint.

Okay, he said no. Now we can leave!

I squirmed in the naiad's arms, hoping he'd start moving.

He didn't.

"King Harel will give you anything your heart desires—" the brownie made one last, vain, effort.

"If I ever fall so low that a Seelie fae king is in a position to help me, it is a sorry day," the being said.

Seelie and Unseelie fae were among the weakest Courts because they weren't landed—they had no connection to the fae realm. They were small and very localized, typically sticking to one city.

But for a supernatural to talk so dismissively about a fae *king* —Seelie or otherwise? This guy was in a league I aspired to never encounter in my whole life. If I stuck around, it was definitely going to use one of my proverbial nine cat lives.

Apparently, these fae have a death wish. Good for them, but I don't. I wriggled, loosening the naiad's grasp on me with the goal of freeing myself.

A gurgling noise leaked out of the brownie, and the naiad quivered as he struggled to hold me.

The intimidating supernatural had been studying the troll—who was so curled up he was almost huddling on the ground—but he flicked his eyes down the motley lineup.

I was almost free, the naiad's fingers were starting to loosen up. *Just a little more and I'll slip away before he smites us...*

"The cat," the supernatural said.

The pixie's wings spasmed. "The cat?" she repeated, her voice so high from fear I could barely understand her.

The supernatural extended his hand—like a king of old. "Leave the cat here."

CHAPTER FOUR

Chloe

I froze. *No...they wouldn't.*

The naiad exchanged looks with the brownie before he took a step closer to the front gate. He paused at the threshold, then held me over the edge of the property line, dangling.

It seemed like not only would they be willing to toss me to this unknown supernatural, they were going to!

I wriggled wildly, scratching at the naiad's hands as I hissed.

The supernatural glided down the front sidewalk and reached us faster than he should have. He slipped his arms around my body, taking me before the naiad dropped me from the scratch-fest I was doling on him.

The supernatural glanced imperiously at the fae as he adjusted his grasp on me. "Go away."

The pack of Seelie fae took off, sprinting down the sidewalk without even looking back at me.

Traitors!

I howled in my little cat voice, but the powerful supernatural swung around and strode back up to his house.

A little factoid about being carried: it's terrifying.

Being carried is like being loosely secured to a track-less roller coaster that has broken seatbelts that could unbuckle at any moment.

So as the supernatural approached his—house? Lair? I wasn't sure which it was—I pressed against his chest, digging my claws into the neckline of his shirt, and propped my back paws on his side as I hung on in what could be interpreted by a doting human as a cat hug, but was really just me doing my best to hold on for my life.

The supernatural paused on his cement porch. He had one hand on my rump and the other on my upper back, which he briefly removed to pet the top of my head. "You're safe now," he informed me.

No I'm not. I am the opposite of safe! I need to get away as soon as—

He opened his front door and stepped into a doorway of magic.

Power crackled through my body, and for a head spinning moment I couldn't tell up from down as I was surrounded by darkness.

When the sensation cleared and I could finally see straight, I was being carried down the long hallway of a house whose floor plan did *not* match the little Cape Cod home.

...*What?* What? *Where are we?*

The hallway's ceiling was so high, it made Book Nookery's vaulted ceilings seem cramped. Huge doors the size of the fae trolls lined the wall, with white carved rock arching over each one of them.

I hauled myself high enough up the supernatural's chest that I was able to peer over his shoulder.

Behind us was a golden gate that swirled with white magic.

What?

Magical gates existed—obviously the fae had to be able to get to the fae realm *somehow.* But they weren't just...standing around, and it took the cooperation of magical animals to produce them.

Who is this guy that he has a gate *in his house?*

"Your Majesty."

Your Majesty? He's a KING?!

A shape emerged from the shadows. Tall and lean, he had a similar feel to the guy carrying me, but the impression of power was much weaker. He had the same tapered ears, and his hair was blond—but a shade so pale it was closer to platinum.

My supernatural kept walking but flicked his hazel eyes in the shadow guy's direction. "What is it, Charon?"

"Are you sure you don't wish for me to pursue the...unwanted visitors?" The new guy, Charon, fell into step behind my supernatural, his head bowed in homage.

He's a king with bloodthirsty minions. This is getting better and better. He must be some kind of high ranking fae.

"It's unnecessary," my supernatural said. He adjusted his hold on me, better supporting my back.

I twisted so I could peer back at the gate, trying to fix its appearance and location in my mind and ignore the nausea-inducing sensation of being carried *and* looking backwards at the same time.

"They dared to make requests of you." Charon adjusted the gray hood that was only half on his head, pulling it all the way up so it covered his pale blond hair and gave him a brooding appearance.

"They have no idea who I really am," my supernatural said. "Or they wouldn't ask—obviously. I'm not certain they even know what I am—all they know is the Paragon visits, which is enough to make them assume I have power."

Charon bowed his head in response.

We rounded a corner, and since the gate was no longer within sight, I swapped goals to memorizing the route so I could retrace my path when escaping. So I switched to pressing my side against the...fae king? (No other supernaturals had recognized kings—leaders, sure, but monarchy systems were strictly fae-only.)

I was busy trying to commit the route to memory, but I did take note of the art—the life-sized marble sculpture of a charging unicorn, a jade carving of a dragon that was the size of my torso while in my human shape, and a brightly colored wall weaving of a phoenix that I was pretty sure was from South America.

All of it was pricey—and *old*.

He's a king, he has minions, and he's rich. I am going to die.

Charon's eyes settled on me as the duo started up a beautiful spiral staircase—which was probably made of granite or some fancy rock I didn't know in my peasant-human upbringing. "The cat?"

The fae king shrugged, rocking me with the motion of his shoulders. "I thought it might be fun to have a pet, and a cat would be a better match than a dog, given Ker's presence."

At least he hasn't figured out I'm a human. Yet. I will have to escape before he realizes it.

Charon fell silent, but he studied me with his unnerving eyes—a light gray that was nearly colorless, but still had the same dark spirals as the king.

They must be some offshoot of fae. Maybe they're European, and that's why they feel so different?

When we reached the top of the stairs, I was shocked to discover this floor was even more opulent than the previous, with impossibly long and thick rugs padding the floor, antique furniture that was veined with magic, and priceless pieces of art that were arranged better than some of the art museums I'd visited.

The walls were made of an alabaster stone and were adorned with designs, though most of them featured warriors in fancy armor sets. There were even entire battle scenes with armies marching against one another.

The carvings made me uneasy—fae armies weren't so uniform

given that a Court's citizens varied vastly. Only elves had maintained armies like that.

The other thing that bothered me was that for all the luxury, there was only one tea set among the art and furnishings—a set that appeared to be made entirely of silver.

It was unsettling because fae were famously obsessed with tea and integrated it into their decor. It was starting to seem like my supernatural being a fae king was quite possibly the *least* threatening option.

As I clung to my supernatural, I saw only a few doors on this very large wing. My ride strode up to the biggest—of course—and opened the door to what I think was supposed to be a bedroom, but all my attention was taken up by the two supernaturals waiting inside.

The first was a woman who was stooping over a marble fountain that spilled into a reflective pool.

She was a werewolf—I could tell by the way she stood and tilted her head back and forth, the tip of her round nose scrunching as she scented us. She was also probably the "Ker" they'd referred to earlier.

Her eyes were dark brown—surprising as werewolves typically had anything from yellow to blue—and her hair was earthy black and pulled into two loose braids. She had that werewolf intensity that made me supremely uncomfortable as a human, much less as a cat. It was like she was memorizing everything about me, and would be able to find me no matter where on earth I hid—something I'd believe given how powerful werewolf noses were.

Like the other two, she was also very tall. *Why is everyone here so tall?!*

She blinked at me, and I huddled into the smallest shape I could manage while still safely anchoring myself.

"Why," started the second supernatural, who was sitting on a frosty blue, velveteen chaise lounge, "is there a *third* heartbeat, that sounds like it's going to explode, when only Charon and

Noctus have entered the room?" The supernatural stood up and turned around.

He was surprisingly slender in build and was probably the least threatening supernatural in the room...until I saw his red vampire eyes and over-pronounced fang teeth.

Unlike the others, who were all dressed in comfortable, movement friendly clothing, he was wearing a charcoal suit with a purple tie. His light brown hair was precisely cut and threaded with gray, but there was something about his red eyes. They didn't focus right—he seemed to be looking more in our general area than at me, Charon, or my supernatural ride.

"Noctus has a cat," Ker said.

"A cat?" The vampire frowned, still looking past us. "I guess that explains the heartbeat. But why in the blazes do you have a cat?" The vampire tapped the rim of the wine glass of red liquid he was holding—I was pretty sure it was blood—then took a careful, measured sip.

As my ride walked deeper into the room, I noticed the vampire's pupils were shaking.

He's blind, I realized—so baffled I almost forgot to act like a cat. *But vampires have heavy duty healing powers. What could possibly have made him blind?*

Ker skirted around the reflective pool. "I would like to hear the story as well."

When the werewolf drew close to us, she bent over so she was eye level with me.

I didn't have to channel my cat acting skills—her raw, werewolf intensity made me quake in my little feline body.

Ker smiled at me and made a cooing noise that was probably meant to soothe me, but it was her smile that stopped my shivering. It pronounced the roundness of her cheeks and lit up her dark eyes with a brightness that seemed to come from her soul.

She's not cruel—she's kind. Gentle, even. That's rare for a werewolf.

When she offered her hand, I cautiously sniffed it. I didn't possess the cat sense of smell, so I could only smell the fabric softener she used on her clothes, and the faint musky scent that most werewolves had.

While I sniffed, my supernatural—Noctus, apparently—spoke. "The narcissistic Seelie King made another attempt for an alliance."

The vampire scoffed. "Of course he did. Neither he nor the Unseelie Queen will stop pestering you now that they've half figured out you're an elf."

AN ELF?

"They suspect," Noctus said. "They haven't asked me to confirm it, yet."

He moved me a little, and I was so shocked by the revelation that he was an *elf* that I didn't protest.

An elf.

He's an elf?! But how? What—this can't be real!

I had to concentrate on fighting all my instincts to puff up, hiss, or claw my way free—all of which would potentially reveal I could understand what they were saying—and just sat stiffly in the elf's arms, putting the pieces together.

Wait...that means he's an elf king? *How? They all died!*

Obviously, he'd survived. And if I had to guess, I was pretty sure Charon was an elf as well due to the similar build—and the ears.

Ker took my lack of movement as an invitation to scratch my cheeks. "Aristide, you need to come feel this cat—his fur is so silky!"

"It's scared," Noctus said. He didn't sound concerned—it was more of an observation.

"That's normal," the werewolf said. "Though I am probably crowding him—but he's accepting pets very nicely, and his fur is well kept. Do you think he was their pet?"

I wasn't bothered that they kept calling me a he—most people guessed, and I'd stopped being offended about it after my third stay at the animal shelter when I was a kid. But I did meow when Noctus shifted his hold on me.

"No," Noctus said. "The whole time they stood out on the sidewalk it was trying to get free. It was not pleased with its situation." Noctus scooped me up and held me up to eye level, staring at me with his strange, intimidating eyes.

I didn't like dangling in the air, but now that I knew he was an elf king I didn't dare claw him. *But I* must *act like a cat, or they'll get suspicious!* I meowed pitifully and twitched my tail.

"If the fae had him, how did you end up with him?" The vampire, Aristide, moved across the room with slow but certain steps. He avoided the raised edge of the reflective pool and the arm of the chaise lounge without bumping into either.

"I took it," Noctus said.

"Took?" the vampire repeated. "By force?" When the vampire drew closer to us he had to tilt his head—listening to us with his vampire hearing, probably picking up on the thud of our heartbeats or even the smell of the blood in our veins—and positioned himself next to the werewolf.

"I didn't use my magic if that's what you're asking," Noctus said. "I'm avoiding attention, not actively attracting it."

The vampire's brow turned stormy. "You took a *gift*, from the fae?"

"I made certain not to say it was a gift," Noctus said.

The vampire groaned and rubbed his head. "Noctus! You should know better!"

"Peace, Aristide," Noctus said. "It was a calculated risk. At worst, the fae are a nuisance and would mean more work, but they could never do anything to me or my household. Besides, even as a cunning fae, there's no possible angle for them to construe the cat as a gift. They didn't offer it to me. Whatever they had planned for it, they intended to see to it later."

"Poor little guy," Ker said.

Aristide frowned. "What does it look like?"

"The cat? All black," Ker said. "He's fluffy—not longhaired, but pretty close."

"Does it have weirdly colored eyes or weird markings?" Aristide asked. "It might be a trick to get you to bring a fae inside your domain."

I had to force myself to keep breathing as I sat stiffly in Noctus's arms. *Don't react, don't react. A blink could get me killed right now.*

"It's just a cat," Noctus said. "Even with my powers leashed as they are, I'd sense it if he was a disguised fae."

"He doesn't even smell like magic," Ker said. "You're probably right, Noctus. The fae picked it up just to torture it, the sickos."

Aristide finally petted me, scratching the spot under my chin that most cats like, and I couldn't help but purr from sheer relief —I hadn't been caught.

I already knew werewolves and vampires couldn't tell me apart from a normal cat even with their enhanced senses, but it never occurred to me I would have to fool an elf. I might possibly, hopefully survive this—if I don't die of a heart attack before I can get out.

"What do you intend to do with it?" Aristide asked.

"I'm going to keep it as a pet," Noctus said in the most unaffectionate tone possible.

The idea gave me indigestion, but I kept on purring as Ker brushed the top of my head.

"Oh," Ker said.

Aristide nodded. "Ah. Well. I should have known you wouldn't have the typical elf superstition against cats. Good for you."

It felt a little odd that they accepted such a terrible reason so easily given the cross examination I'd witnessed, but I was more uncomfortable by the way Ker and Noctus were looking down at me.

This feels like the punchline of a really bad joke, I thought as the trio petted me. Or rather, Ker and Aristide petted me as Noctus watched. *A werewolf, an elf king, and a vampire find a cat—HEY!*

"What gender do you suppose it is?" Noctus lifted me up into the air and twirled me around so my rear faced him.

I tucked my tail and curled my entire butt up, doing an extreme cat version of a gym bro's calisthenic leg raises.

"Ker, hold its tail," Noctus said.

No, no, Ker, don't do that. I curled my tail even more tightly against my body as the werewolf tried to gently tug it up. *There's a lot of things I'll suffer through—this is not one of them!*

I yowled, and Aristide raised an eyebrow. "Judging by the joyous noises your new pet is making, you're inspecting his rear?"

"Attempting to is more correct," Ker said. "He's got a tail made of iron, and I don't want to hurt him."

I yowled again as Ker tried to maneuver my tail.

"At least you can confirm he has an impressive set of lungs," Aristide blithely said.

"Can you see yet?" Ker asked.

"No," Aristide said.

"It's being difficult," Noctus said.

He's the only one calling me an it, and he's the one that wants a pet. That is weird.

Noctus jiggled me, throwing my rear high in the air.

Suitably freaked out, I hissed, and out came my claws.

"It is a girl cat," Noctus announced.

Absolutely mortified, I wailed even more loudly and dug my claws into his arms.

As he lowered me, it occurred to me that elves were famous for their cruelty, and now I was probably going to experience it firsthand.

I went rigid, my heart wildly thumping as he set me on the ground.

"What are you going to name her?" Ker asked.

I cranked my head back to peer up at the trio, trying to figure out if the punishment was still incoming, or if I was forgiven because they were all under the impression I was an animal.

"I don't know," Noctus announced.

I, I don't think I'm going to get punished for the claws, which means I better act like a cat if I want to keep this ruse up!

I bolted—like any cat in a strange environment would do—shedding little tufts of hair from the anxiety of it all.

I made for what I assumed was a giant bed. It was settled on top of three onyx stairs, and was bigger than any mattress I'd seen, and was covered in mounds of white and light blue pillows.

I hid at the foot of the bed, crawling between two pillows that had been carelessly thrown there, and peeked out from my cave.

"I hope she doesn't become a tripping hazard for Aristide." Ker shifted her weight back and forth, then glanced at the vampire.

Aristide shook his head. "It won't be an issue. At the rate her heart pounds, I'll be able to pinpoint her location in any room with ease. She is an anxious creature."

Anxious doesn't even begin to describe how I'm feeling!

This was, by far, the worst-case scenario I could have ever wandered into. A king of a long dead race was infinitely worse than the shadow that had been stalking me.

I couldn't even fully wrap my head around the situation. *How did this happen? And what the heck is an elf king doing in* Magiford*?*

Charon dug a tiny notepad and pen from a pocket on his hooded, cloak-like shirt. "I will need to purchase items for her." He paused, his pen resting on his notepad. "That is...what exactly does a cat need besides moisture and nutrients?"

"Maybe cat toys?" Ker suggested. "Probably a collar."

"I'll take care of the collar," Noctus said. He was the only one actively watching me, and he narrowed his eyes. "She doesn't seem to care about me."

Vain, much? Of course I don't!

"I imagine the new location has her frightened," Ker said. "I might also be part of the problem—most cats aren't fond of werewolves. I think they can tell we're basically big dogs." She twisted so she could glance guiltily at me.

Noctus tilted his head maybe a fraction of an inch, but there was something about the way he watched me that made my nerves tingle. "Perhaps, but animals adore elves."

They what?

I didn't know that. *Why* would I know that? Any common knowledge about the elves, besides their bloody history, was lost. The fae had the best idea about the elves as they'd learned a lot from them, but I couldn't ever recall hearing that the elves were particularly good with animals.

This just keeps getting better and better. I swear I can feel the hair falling out of my coat from the stress.

Aristide folded his arms across his chest. "As I said before, her heart sounds ready to bust out of her chest. She's terrified. I imagine once she calms down your animal magnetism or what-have-you will sink into her."

I hope not! It can't, right? I'm not a real cat.

I was also immune to nearly all types of magic. So that would automatically mean any weird magic King Noctus had wouldn't work on me...right?

But...that means that then I'll have to pretend *it's working on me.*

CHAPTER FIVE

Chloe

The realization hit my gut like a bad burrito.

How was I even going to pull that off? Purr and sit on his lap—the lap of an *elf king* who should be dead and had probably killed more people than I'd ever see in my entire life?

Ker nodded. "In the meantime, she should stay in your room for a day or two—until she's comfortable with her surroundings."

What? No! That's a terrible idea!

Years of experience and a strong sense of self-preservation kept me from poking my head out of the pillow cave and hissing. My life depended on my acting abilities.

Charon finished writing in his notepad. "I will notify our people of the new member of your household, Your Majesty."

Our people? There are more elves than just the two of you?

I mean, I guess it made sense if Noctus—a king—survived...

Noctus finally looked away from me long enough to nod to Charon—who I was starting to suspect was his right-hand man, or steward or something. "Why should they need to know?"

"If the cat is allowed to run freely, they'll need to be made aware—to make certain there aren't any accidents," Charon delicately said, which made me feel peachy about the friendliness of Noctus's "people".

"Charon's got the right idea," Aristide said. "Most elves don't associate cats with good things—even all these years later. It's better to warn them."

Why would they have a thing against cats?

Noctus's gaze flicked back to me. He studied my pillow fort for a moment, then strode across the room, approaching the bed. "There will be consequences to anyone who harms her." He climbed the stairs to his bed and held out his fingers for me to sniff. "Violent consequences."

Great, so I only have to worry about you killing me before I can get out of here. That's wonderful.

I poked my head out of my silken cave—I needed to start the ruse that his animal powers or whatever worked on me—and sniffed his fingers just like I had for Ker.

I glanced up at him and was a little unnerved by his gaze, but my all-consuming need to live was stronger than my fear, so I set my chin on his fingers and purred.

The right corner of Noctus's lips twitched up the smallest bit in what was maybe the start of a smile. It didn't soften his face at all—if anything, it amplified the cold perfection of his looks, making him even harsher.

Every instinct in me screamed that I needed to back away and run. But I stayed where I was, and Noctus smoothed the fur on the top of my head.

Keep calm and survive—that's my motto.

Noctus gave me one last pat, then he stalked down the stairs and headed for the bedroom door. "We should leave her to get settled."

"Ah, yes," Aristide said. "Of course I can vacate the premises to make a housecat comfortable. Why not?"

Ker chuckled as she opened the door and slipped out.

Charon was right behind her. "There are some things that require your attention, Your Majesty."

I sprang off the bed and ran for the door—hoping I could maybe slip out after them.

Noctus—who was last to leave—was too quick. He closed the door behind him—before I could even make it halfway across the room.

I tried meowing pitifully, but the muted hum of their voices faded away. They were gone.

That means it's time to make an escape plan.

Standing on my hind legs, I stretched to reach the round doorknob—I was too short. I jumped and managed to latch on to the knob, then swung my body to turn it. It didn't turn far, and it made a clicking noise.

It's locked? I can't get out?

That complicated things.

I didn't dare turn into a human. Since Noctus was an elf, I had no idea what kind of magic he'd cast on the place. Elves were capable of some of the most complex kinds of magic there were—entire strains of magical arts had died with them.

For all I knew his reflective pool was magic and he was using it to keep an eye on me.

That meant I had to stay in my cat form and act like a cat.

Keeping that in mind, I started my grand plan by making a thorough inspection of my surroundings.

I made a circuit of the bed—the one little sliver of daring I had made me brave enough to walk over all of Noctus's pillows, hopefully I shed cat fur on them—and inspected the giant marble fireplace at the far end of the room. I even rested my paws on the edge of the reflection pool and peered in—it was a weird depth, so I couldn't tell how deep it went—all so I could eventually make my way over to the giant, floor to ceiling windows.

Those windows were my best chance for freedom. At least

they'd give me an idea of what was up with the weird, magical house.

I tried to be casual as I approached one of the giant windows, batting at the heavy, brocade curtains that were tied to the side.

But when I saw the outside, my heart stopped.

I'd known some weird magic was at work—there was no way a house this huge fit in the little Cape Cod home I'd seen on the street. That hadn't prepared me, however, for the *city* outside the bedroom windows.

It seemed Noctus's home was built into the side of a small mountain.

An entire city occupied the lower half of the mountain. The city was built in semi-circle tiers, with smaller levels at the top and larger levels at the bottom.

The roads and walls of the levels were all constructed with a shining white stone, and there were a few blocks of buildings made of milky rock, too, but there were splashes of color where buildings were constructed with timber and red brick.

Two huge waterfalls gushed down the mountainside, jutting out on either side from Noctus's cliffside quarters and cascading down, falling through the tiers of the city in cleverly constructed pools and aqueducts.

People in colorful clothing filled the streets. About half of it seemed modern with flowered sundresses, jean shorts, and cotton shirts, and the other half was...I didn't know what to call it except to guess that tunics, leather jerkins, and chain mail were possibly elf fashion.

Charon said Noctus had people, but I didn't think that meant an entire kingdom!

We had to be in the fae realm—which wasn't impossible given that the fae realm was an uncrossable wasteland except for the land the higher fae Courts had staked out using ancient elven spells centuries ago.

As an elf—with a *city* of elves at his disposal—Noctus wouldn't have a problem carving out his own piece of the fae realm, creating a hidden city of a supernatural race that was supposed to have been safely dead for centuries.

I sat down and leaned against the glass window, trying to fathom it all.

The windows were a dead end—there was no way I was going to try to jailbreak my way out of Noctus's rooms to escape into the even greater danger of the city.

I was going to have to leave this place the same way I'd come in—through the front door.

In the meantime, I was stuck in the city—fortress?—of a long dead race, and their entrance to the human world was a tiny Cape Cod house in Magiford.

That's it. As soon as I get out of here, I'm moving to a different state.

NIGHT FELL—AT least, I *thought* it was night. Since the city was in the fae realm, its day and night could be off compared to the human world. I wasn't at all sleepy, but that most likely was my finely honed survival instincts—they'd keep me wide awake rather than risk sleeping in an elf's bedroom.

I stared out at the white city, which was bathed in the silvery light of a full moon.

I'd been too distracted to see it the first time I'd looked, but beyond the city was a sandy beach that sank into a huge lake, a forest, and more mountains.

Although the sky was a swirl of black and blue and spattered with glittering stars, there was a faint flickering of the horizon line that swirled with rainbow hued colors. That had to be the magic-forged wall that held back the miasma that was slowly eating the rest of the fae realms.

I curled my tail around my paws as I watched small waves crash onto the sandy beach.

Maybe they'll let me out soon.

I had tonight and tomorrow night before my next night shift at Book Nookery, but the less time I spent in this place, the better.

The bedroom door swung open with a whisper.

I stood and turned around, hopeful, but Noctus was already closing the door behind him.

He was still dressed in his casual clothes, but he carried a wooden box that was about as big as my cat form.

Noctus glanced at me, then sauntered across his room, pausing next to my bowls that had been arranged near the reflection pools.

I didn't know if it was because the king had never had a pet before, or if the elves were just that rich despite being in hiding, but my water dish was a porcelain bowl with pink flower blossoms that were edged with real silver, and my food dish was silver and had pink jewels fashioned into flower-like shapes encrusted on the rim.

The food bowl had a glop of raw meat—which I wasn't eating. Despite my cat shape, it would still make me sick, and that was the last thing I needed while trying to escape.

"You haven't eaten," Noctus said to me.

I sat down again and twitched my tail back and forth as I watched him from halfway across the room. *Thank you, but no. Though if you offered me some milk I'd really appreciate it.*

I'd gotten myself into situations a time or two before that meant I had to keep my cat shape. I'd been able to survive off milk because the humans caring for me hadn't known any better. With a little luck, the same would happen here.

Noctus stared at me for another moment, his gaze so intense I almost cracked and hid behind one of the thick drapes.

Eventually, he turned away from me and approached the chaise lounge positioned in front of the fireplace.

He sat in it, dropping with an unnatural grace that came with having perfect control over his entire body, and set the box down. When he moved his hazel eyes to the fireplace, it roared to life, flaring with ghostly blue and white flames.

That's not creepy at all.

Noctus stared into the flames as silence stretched through his room.

I wonder...based on what he and Charon were talking about with animals liking elves, do I need to approach him to be a believable cat?

As if he could hear what I was thinking, Noctus again glanced in my direction.

I guess that's my cue.

I padded toward the chaise lounge, pausing cautiously with one front paw in the air as I peered up at him.

Cats were logical creatures. Magic or not, any housecat with a shred of self-preservation instinct would be reluctant to approach Noctus. The magic coming off him was nearly tangible, and it brushed my whiskers like a shock of static electricity.

I sat down next to the chaise lounge, leaning against one of the wooden feet, then positioned myself so I could peer up at him.

Noctus leaned over and scratched my cheek. It took a few false starts, but I got myself to purr.

This seemed to please him, because he leaned back in his seat again. He stared at the pale blue flames of the fire and absently rubbed at the metal, shackle-like bracelets that were clamped around his wrists.

Okay. Step one is complete, but if I want to keep up the act, I need to get up on the chaise and...sit with him.

The idea was as appealing as the raw meat in my food dish, but I needed to keep Noctus convinced I was a plain housecat.

I crouched down, then made the jump onto the chaise lounge's arm, balancing easily with my cat-given agility.

Despite my status as a pariah by supernatural standards, I did like my powers. It was fun to see how far I could jump as a cat, and my magic-granted sense of balance had saved me multiple times in both of my forms.

Cheered by my success, I hopped into the open space next to Noctus, smashing myself as close to the arm as I could to avoid touching the elf. (I was pretty sure I was immune to his animal powers, but I didn't want to test the theory.)

Noctus petted me, then leaned forward and grabbed the elegant coffee table positioned a few feet away from the chaise lounge.

He tipped the coffee table on its side, revealing two rows of daggers and an ax Velcro-ed to its underside.

Does he have random weapon storage spots everywhere? Maybe I'll have to start exploring under his furniture.

Not that weapons would do me any good. I was a runner. Pat made sure both Joy and I were familiar with a handgun and basic self-defense moves because of his work background, and Joy kept me stocked with pepper spray, but my greatest assets were the physical abilities that came with shifting from human to cat, not fighting.

Noctus pulled daggers out from behind the laces of his boots and swapped them out with a belt knife that clipped to the buckle of his leather belt.

He rolled up the sleeves of his dark, aqua colored shirt, where two small daggers and sheaths were strapped to his forearms. He unbuckled the sheaths and exchanged them for a larger set.

Before he strapped the larger daggers to his forearms, he removed them from their sheaths and studied the edges.

He balanced one of the daggers on a fingertip, then flicked it into the air and gracefully caught it without even looking at it.

So the elf king is good with weapons. That's an important lesson to learn rather than experience.

Noctus strapped the daggers in place, rolled his sleeves back down, then stood up and flipped up the back of his shirt to reveal a knife sheath at the small of his back. He compared that one to the rest of his coffee table arsenal before seemingly deciding nothing else would suit, and slid his knife back in place.

Finished—or at least I assumed so, unless he had knives hidden in places I didn't want to see—Noctus sat back down and stared at me. As if *I* had something to contribute.

Sorry, I didn't know this was the "little free library" of weapons.

He petted me, but a troubling furrow burrowed between his eyebrows. He picked up one of my paws—daring to touch my toe beans—and pressed, making one of my claws pop out. "You are relatively helpless," he said.

Obviously, you've never had a housecat claw at your eyes. I was a runner, but I *did* know how to inflict damage if needed for my escapes.

"I should get a protective spell for you."

No, that's not necessary, but thank you for being a conscientious pet owner.

Noctus reached again for his coffee table arsenal, this time grabbing the ax. He turned it round and around in his hands, a frown forming.

Without any warning, he slammed the ax down on the edge of the coffee table, cracking it. Not just a little crack—the jagged mark ran down the length of the coffee table. He hadn't split it in half, but if it tipped over it would break apart.

My fur fluffed up around me, and my whiskers tingled as I stared at the cracked coffee table. *He did that with an ax. Without magic. How were the elves* ever *defeated? What the—*

"Too dull," Noctus announced. "It needs to be sharpened. I'll have to add it to the armory stash and take care of it later."

I gulped. *That's dull?*

Using the toe of his boot, Noctus righted his nearly broken coffee table—which groaned and buckled as he settled it into place and placed the ax on top of it.

He then reached out to pet me again. Despite the need to

keep up the act, my instincts won, and I flinched, shrinking back so I pressed myself into the back of the chaise lounge.

Noctus paused, his fingers outstretched, and there was something about the look in his eyes. It wasn't hurt, but something closer to resignation.

"I forgot, something like that would scare you," he said. "A loud noise would be frightening to a cat. You can go off—I'm sure the only thing keeping you here is my magic."

He stood up and walked over to the immense windows, staring out at the city like the ruler he was.

I sat on the chaise lounge—half held in place by fear, and the other half by my own plotting.

At least he knows he's scary.

I shook my head, trying to rid my whiskers of the tingly feeling that hadn't completely left.

Now what? Do I go hide? Or do I need to sit here and be casual and catlike?

I'd spent years as a kid studying cat behavior so I could believably act like one—I needed to, in order to survive. But I had no idea how a cat would react to an ax ruining a coffee table.

Hiding would probably be the natural behavior...but I get the feeling that's not the kind of cat King Noctus wants.

He said he wanted a pet, and every action he'd done so far had indicated it was true. I couldn't understand why he wanted a cat, but I needed to act based on what was, not what made sense.

Escaping is still the goal, but I don't think my usual tricks—like slipping out the door and running like mad—are going to work. I'll need to switch my focus to getting him to like me enough that he lets me out of his room. That means I can't just be a believable feline, I need to start winning points with him.

Mustering my courage—and trying to keep my hair from puffing up any higher—I stood up and leaped off the chaise lounge.

I meandered over to Noctus, taking the opportunity to stop

and rub my face against the occasional piece of furniture along the way. When I reached Noctus I meowed and circled around his legs.

Noctus looked down at me.

I quirked my tail, opened my eyes wide, and did my best to look cute.

It worked too well. Noctus picked me up, propping me against his chest.

I wriggled until I could dig my claws into either side of the V-neck collar of his shirt, then propped myself against him as best I could.

Noctus let me get comfortable before he scratched under my chin.

I mustered a few purrs to satisfy him, and I swear I felt his posture relax.

He stared down at his moonlit city, and together we watched the few citizens who were up as they hurried down the streets, heading home for the evening.

The sleepy city was soothing to watch. Ivy covered sections of the walls, and its tendrils swayed in the breeze. Out on the lake, a few waves were big enough to be capped with white foam.

My fur finally returned to normal, and while I still thought it was best for my health to be far away from the elven king/arms dealer, I was calmer.

I'm surviving it. That's the important part.

Noctus managed to tease another purr out of me. "In the future I will endeavor not to frighten you," he said.

I flicked my tail back and forth.

"I will," Noctus said. "Though it might take me some time to discern what frightens you."

Whatever. Could you just put me down?

"You will only get the best treatment. Which, Charon discovered after some research, will require a trip to the human veterinarian."

Yeah, yeah, get me my shots, sure, but can't you put me back on the ground?

Since I'd been picked up by animal services way more often than my parents ever knew—Joy, Pat, and I had pooled our allowances for an "adopt Chloe back slush fund" that they'd had to use numerous times in my childhood—I already knew that cat shots didn't affect me. Thank you, magic!

Noctus met my gaze. "He mentioned I should consider getting you microchipped and fixed."

He WHAT?

I almost puffed up again, and I barely managed to hold back from hissing. The next time Charon came to the room, I was going to do my best to trip him. Or maybe throw up on an expensive carpet and push some priceless art off some tables.

Microchipped and fixed? No! No way!

I was so horrified I could only gape at Noctus in total, absolute horror.

Microchipped and fixed!

Noctus tried to scratch my chin again, but I was as stiff as a board.

Microchipped. And. Fixed.

"There are magical methods of keeping tabs on you, so I don't feel at this time it will be necessary." Noctus turned away from the window and walked across his room, though he glanced down at me when a mewl of relief escaped from me.

New plan—no—same plan, but it's even more important! I need *to suck up to Noctus, no matter how scary he is, for my survival* and *to save my dignity!*

Noctus set me down on his bed.

I collapsed on it, too tired for my legs to hold me.

Noctus held his hand out to me, his palm vertical as if he were trying to motion to me to stop.

I looked from his hand, to Noctus.

Noctus stared at me with expectation.

I tucked my paws in underneath me. *I'm sorry? I don't understand what you want. Are you trying to use animal magic on me? Or am I supposed to do something?*

Before Noctus could give me any kind of verbal hint about what he was doing, the door creaked open, and Charon slipped inside. He wore fitted linen pants, but still had his hooded, cloak-like shirt on and was holding his tiny notebook. "Your Majesty?"

Noctus petted me one last time, then sauntered down the stairs of his bed. "It's late, Charon. Why are you still working?"

Charon's expression didn't change—he only slightly lowered the lids to his eyes, but somehow it managed to make his whole face look wry. "I'm still working because *you're* still working."

"I'm not working." Noctus frowned at my bowls again on his way over to the giant fireplace. "I'm merely going to slay the rock monster that keeps bouncing into the mountain barrier." He removed a sword—an enormous one that was surely way too big to be of any use in actual battle—from a decorative placard, then glanced at the oddly colored fire in the fireplace, which immediately snuffed out.

"For you, Your Majesty, that *is* working," Charon said. "For everyone else it would be lunacy."

"You're always so charming, Charon."

"It is Aristide's role to be the charming one among your comrades," Charon said. "And I see I will need to bring out one of the replicas of your coffee table from the furniture storage?"

"The ax is dull."

"Of course, Your Majesty."

"Make sure you place it on the marks in the carpet, so it is in the exact same position and Aristide doesn't run into it." Noctus was already to the door when I realized he was leaving. By the time I jumped off the bed and hurried down the stairs he was in the hallway, twirling the oversized sword with one hand with Charon right behind him.

"I have replaced your furniture before, Your Majesty. I am well acquainted with the custom." Charon pulled the door shut behind him while I was only halfway across the room.

I skidded to a stop and plunked my rear down, disappointed I'd missed a chance to flee, but also too bewildered to really comprehend it.

I thought being a solo supernatural was stressful, but this takes the cake. By the time I get out of here, I'm going to be one bald cat.

CHAPTER SIX

Noctus

I studied the black collar wrapped around my fingers, and wondered if I really should perform this magic.

Yes, I should protect my new pet, but what I had planned went beyond what was necessary. Using it would be impulsive, foolish, and brash.

If any of my friends knew, they'd discreetly question my sanity. And yet...

Magic hummed around me, pleased with the idea. Even the shackle that held back a major portion of my power couldn't hide the musical chord magic produced at the thought.

All supernaturals wielded magic differently.

Humans—magic's absolute favorites—didn't need anything. Wizards could pull wild magic from the air and filter it through their blood into a usable, elemental form.

Fae used magical tools and artifacts to bend wild magic to their will.

Elves were somewhat similar in that we worked best if using an artifact or tool, but it wasn't fully necessary. The check to our power, however, was emotions. Our mood and emotion drastically affected our ability to wield magic.

An emotionally unstable elf wouldn't be able to summon even a flicker of magic, no matter what item they were using to bolster their power. A raging elf might be able to use huge amounts of power, but it made them sloppy, imprecise, and *very* easy to kill.

That the wild magic—which I couldn't see but could hear—was so *pleased* at the idea of what I was considering was puzzling.

Magic hadn't had an opinion about my actions since the elven war.

Curious, I got off my bed and strode across my room, looking for my cat. She'd proven to *hate* sleeping on my bed with me despite her otherwise affectionate manners. But I had a good idea of where she was.

I entered my bathroom and flicked on the lights.

My cat was curled up in the sink, her long tail wrapped around her.

I leaned against the doorframe as I watched her, trying to discern what it was that had magic stirring.

She blinked in the abrupt light, then stretched, arching her back, before she jumped off the counter and started purring.

I picked her up, and she immediately latched on to my shirt, setting her small head on my shoulder as her purr sputtered in her chest.

I know better than to be brash and emotional. It is why I was so much more powerful than my own family, who were already at an impossible strength. Being in control is what has gotten me this far. Breaking that control for a small cat is stupid, no matter how pleased wild magic is about it.

But I was tired. Tired of the endless control, the endless strength, the endless power.

Power was not the gift humans and supernaturals alike were convinced it was. Power was a *curse*. One I'd keep on bearing.

And there was something about this cat. In holding her...I

couldn't identify the feeling, except that it was peaceful. As a Mors elf, peace wasn't something I often experienced.

Couldn't I—for once—allow myself this instance of impulsiveness?

There's no reason to do it, though. She's a cat. Aristide, Charon, and Ker have been with me through darkness and back. Why bend this rule for a cat?

I could use magic as an excuse, of course. But in reality, I was considering this only because a cat—even one as intelligent as this one—was the sole safe possibility for me. She didn't know I was a king. She couldn't comprehend my power, or ever understand the dark and terrible things I'd done.

She was a cat. She purred when I petted her, and she slept in my bathroom sink.

My mind made up, I strode toward the door. I'd need to go far away to perform the spell, or Charon would realize what I was doing.

It's safe enough, and magic approves. Peace is special and sacred. It should be acceptable that I protect her to give myself even this momentary illusion.

I knew the reality: peace was something I could never have.

CHAPTER SEVEN

Chloe

I pawed at my reflection in Noctus's pool, sending ripples across it, but I still couldn't judge how deep it was.

Is it deep enough to swim in? Or is it just for show?

I wasn't going to jump in. Although I could swim as a cat, I had no idea if this was even normal, safe water. With my luck, it had magic in it.

I flicked my tail back and forth before I stalked back over to the windows.

I'd studied the city for hours, trying to figure out if it operated on a similar time pattern to the human world or not.

I wasn't certain, but I was pretty sure it was close. If it was, that meant tonight would be my first shift back at the Book Nookery, and that I'd missed two of my good morning check-in texts with Joy and Pat.

They probably haven't started freaking out yet...but if I don't get out of here soon, Pat might drive down to Magiford to look for me.

Now that I knew there was a hidden *elf city* within Magiford, it was the last place I wanted my family to come.

I needed to get out—to assure them, to get to my job, and to *eat*.

I was absolutely starving, and I was nearly to the point where I'd let the elves look at my rear again if it meant I could get a donut or a sandwich—anything edible, besides the cat food they kept trying to feed me.

They haven't even offered me milk! Have they never seen a human movie with a cat in it?

I also badly needed to sleep. I'd dozed occasionally, but I hadn't deeply slept since Noctus had forcefully adopted me—it was too risky. I could survive on less sleep than the average human, but this was pushing my limits.

Still aware that Noctus might have some weird spells on his bedroom, I made a show of licking one of my front paws and rubbing my furry face before I glanced outside the window again.

I was watching the flying seagulls and wondering how they'd gotten inside the realm, when I heard the faint murmur of voices and immediately abandoned my window post to run for the door.

I positioned myself next to it, just out of kicking range, but close enough that as soon as it opened I'd be able to dart out.

No one had come in the rooms much besides Noctus.

He'd delivered the water and food dish and come back occasionally to pet me. He'd slept here for a few hours—I'd sequestered myself in the bathroom during that time because being around a sleeping elf was one giant nope I was going to avoid—but he was too fast, so all my escape attempts had been thwarted.

I crouched down as the voices got closer, and my heart beat faster.

The door cracked open, and Aristide's voice slipped through the space. "Your little pet is right by the door—I can hear her frantically pumping heart."

Well. There went my element of surprise.

"Are you sure she's not sick? I've never met a creature who spends the majority of their time in a near-constant state of terror."

The door swung open, and I sprang, my front paws hitting the woven rug just outside Noctus's room.

Noctus caught me before I could get any farther, propping me up against his side as he stepped back into the room.

Do I risk clawing him to get him to put me down?

Aristide and Ker followed him inside and closed the door before I could analyze the pros and cons of the situation.

Discouraged, I hooked my paws into the neckline of his black, collared shirt in a makeshift cat hug as my belly flopped in my gut from the movement as he trekked across the room.

Noctus caught sight of my bowls. "She still hasn't eaten."

Charon had cleaned my dish yesterday before putting out canned cat food—which was even less appetizing than the raw meat.

Ker sniffed the food. "It doesn't smell off. But neither did the raw steak you tried feeding her yesterday."

Steak? Who feeds a cat steak? How much money does he have? I know the elves were the top of the supernatural food chain, but he's in hiding*! He shouldn't have this kind of cash.*

"Hunger strike, perhaps?" Aristide suggested. "Cats are temperamental creatures."

That's pretty hypocritical coming from a vampire.

"You could try giving her milk," Ker suggested.

"That's a human-created myth," Aristide said. "Cats are lactose intolerant for the most part. It'd make her sick."

I stared at the vampire, half impressed and half desperate. *You! You're why I haven't gotten any milk!*

Noctus glanced down at me, the odd spiral of his eyes almost hypnotic. I stared back at him, until he raised an eyebrow.

I better make a move.

I purred so loudly my whole body vibrated and rubbed my cheek against his chest, displaying my (fake) affection for him.

Pacified, Noctus cradled me with one arm and scratched my cheek with his free hand. "She's not upset. I just haven't found the right food yet."

"She's a cat," Aristide said. "Cat food is the *definition* of the right food."

Noctus set me down on his plush bed. "Not for my pet."

I purred some more and twitched my tail left and right, staying where I was when I really wanted to bolt away from the rich, scary-powerful elf king.

There was an intensity to Noctus that burned when I was close to him. It felt...*wild*, and not at all safe. Given that I had spent most of my adult life scrabbling to survive, hanging out with that kind of vibe was not my idea of a pleasant time.

But Plan Suck Up is still the best option, so off I go!

I purred some more as Noctus balanced me and watched Ker as she sidled up to the reflection pool.

Aristide stayed by the door, holding a white cane. "Has she moved anything?"

Noctus glanced around the room. "It seems she played with the curtain, but no. She hasn't moved anything besides the blankets on my bed."

Aristide confidently made his way across the room, using his white cane as a guideline as he set it on the lower edges of furniture, then scooted around it. "Despite her strange eating habits and dubious origins, it seems you have found yourself quite the nice pet."

Noctus looked down at me again. "I agree."

Good. You keep on thinking that.

Judging I could finally stalk off, I started sauntering across his bed, making sure I didn't put my back to him.

Before I took more than a few steps, Noctus picked me up again. This time, he sat down, and placed me on his lap.

Oh. Oh, wow. This is weird.

Perched on his legs, his intensity and...*him-ness* surrounded me like an overwhelming cloud.

My heart catapulted itself into double-time as I sat frozen, not sure what to do.

I'd sat on laps before as a cat, but it had always been my family. This was a new—and unwanted—experience.

While I was frozen, Noctus pulled something from his pocket —a tiny loop of black fabric accented with black lace, beading, and three jewels that were a deep ruby red, each roughly the size of a pomegranate seed.

The jewels were clustered together, giving the contraption a sort of crown-like appearance.

Wait—that's not a collar, right? I glanced up at Noctus. *Then again, he did give a cat a silver food dish. I can't tell if it's because he's excited about the idea of owning a pet, or if it's because that's the kind of lifestyle he lives. Either way, a jeweled collar would be utterly—*

Noctus slipped the collar over my head—the fabric stretching for a comfortable fit. He straightened it, adjusting it so the jewels glittered at my throat.

Ker stirred from her spot by the reflection pond. "How does she like her collar?"

"She doesn't seem to mind it." Noctus scratched under my chin.

"Won't it come off easily?" Ker asked. "It didn't buckle into place."

"It doesn't need to buckle," Noctus said. "I enchanted it. It will stay on her."

Did he mean the collar itself is enchanted, or he enchanted it to stay on me?

If it was the latter, it wouldn't be much of a problem, I'd just get someone to pull it off me when I was in my cat form. If it was the former...

It shouldn't matter too much. When I turn into a human it will disappear no matter how he enchanted it.

Before I could further ponder it, Noctus picked me up again, tilting me against his chest. "Her name is Ama," he said.

Aristide leaned against a sideboard. "The elven word for sweet? How...surprisingly adorable."

Yeah, it's surprising alright. I figured he'd just keep calling me "cat" until I escaped.

My stomach growled as I peered up at the elven king, both worried and fascinated by his cold, almost cruel beauty.

Noctus slightly narrowed his eyes, and my heartbeat automatically picked up.

What, did I do something wrong? Is he questioning if I'm really a cat?

"It's a good name," Ker said. "I'm sure she'll live up to its meaning."

Still holding me, Noctus stood up and descended the stairs of his posh bed. Going down the stairs in his arms was a jarring, bouncing experience that had me digging my claws into the neckline of his shirt for balance.

Noctus absently petted me as he headed for the door.

Wait—is he taking me out?

I couldn't stiffen any more than I already had from the stairs ride, but I wildly turned my head, my glee building as he pulled the wooden door open.

"You're leaving?" Ker asked.

"I have work to do," Noctus said. "But first, I'm taking Ama to the kitchens. She needs to eat."

Noctus gently stroked my head, so I let myself purr.

I was pretty excited about the idea of eating, but I wasn't totally certain eating *elf* food was a good idea. Who knew if they cast enchantments on it? No, what really had me excited was that I was *outside his rooms*!

Maybe I'd even make it to his weird gate!

The important question is if I can get to the door, do I risk turning into a human so I can open the gate? It would reveal I'm human when there's no guarantee that the gate will work without Noctus.

Ker poked her head out of the bedroom to shout down the hallway after us, "We'll meet you in your study after you feed her?"

"Fine," Noctus said.

We reached the spiral staircase, and I meowed in dread, hooking my claws in his clothes again before he started our descent.

The roller coaster feeling that accompanied being carried took on a bone jostling twist, but Noctus didn't seem to pick up on my terror.

In fact, once we reached the bottom floor and I set my chin on his shoulder to help fortify myself, he moved his hand so he held me closer, his fingers stroking my fur.

I was disappointed to see that we moved in the opposite direction from the gate/front door.

We passed by a giant portrait that was nearly as big as Noctus's bed, of an elf wearing plated armor that glowed with magic. The elf was carrying a massive, jeweled scythe, which dripped with blood, and around him was rubble.

Positioned below the immense painting was a golden plaque with fancy letters—which were at odds with the stark horror of the portrait—that simply read "Destruction."

Does he keep this portrait as an intimidation tactic, or is that just how elves are, so to him it's like a regular painting? Or is the elf in the armor Noctus?

I couldn't tell—the elf wore a helm, so only their mouth and chin were visible.

Noctus turned up a side hallway, which was smaller and less opulent, with white and black tiled flooring and only fresh flowers in crystal vases to serve as decorations.

There were only two doors—one on the left and one on the right. Noctus chose the door on the right, pushing it open and revealing a sunny, oddly shaped kitchen.

Arranged like two squares merging together in the corners, the room was almost diamond shaped with the extra walls and angles.

The floor was made of stone that had been smoothed with decades—perhaps centuries—of feet crossing over them. A giant stone fireplace presided over one wall of the lower rectangle, and it had a fire pit inside it.

A huge range oven took over the upper square area of the kitchen, along with a copper sink, and endless cabinets crafted out of a warm golden wood that made the room feel extra cozy.

Strings of garlic bulbs, dried chilies, and herbs hung from the ceiling and coiled around the fireplace chimney. Copper pots hung from nails on the wall, and two island countertops were covered with finished dishes, presented on shining silver platters.

My nose twitched at the rich scent of basil and garlic that wafted off the food, and my stomach twisted angrily in my belly.

Do they just have steaming, hot food available all the time, or is this some kind of preservation spell?

Noctus had been going toward the fridge in the upper rectangle of the kitchen, but he glanced down at me and paused next to the food. "Is there something you want?"

Two days. I haven't eaten in two days. *And I didn't even get to eat the donuts I'd bought from Magiford Donuts.*

But it was *elf food.* Who knew if it'd be safe to eat—or if I'd suffer any consequences for giving in?

But I'd been drinking the water since I arrived, and nothing bad had happened...

Noctus set me down on the counter, further weakening my resolve. My black nose twitched as I sniffed, the delectable scents making my stomach growls sharp and painful.

There were three loaves of steaming bread, a platter of potatoes cooked in butter, corn on the cob—which was definitely out of season considering it was April—a bowl of fruit that was so beautiful and perfect they almost looked like jewels, and several trays of meat.

I hunkered down next to a roasted chicken and meowed. The delicious scent made my mouth water, and the food didn't stir any sensations of magic in me. I didn't even feel it in my whiskers, so it was probably fine...

No, it's too risky.

I turned around and walked back to Noctus, feeling downcast with every step of my paws.

Noctus watched me for a moment, then produced a giant knife from one of his pockets.

I watched as he reached over me and cut a bite sized chunk out of the chicken.

"You have to eat." He held it under my nose, and steam laced with the tangy scent of spices brushed my whiskers.

Aw, what the heck. I'm already in deep trouble. It can't get any worse than this!

Hunger knifed through my belly, and I gave in, devouring the piece of meat.

Noctus had another piece cut for me before I could finish chewing what he gave me, and hand fed me the next piece.

This went on for about five minutes, until I'd filled my tiny cat stomach.

As I ate the last piece of chicken, I peered up at Noctus and was struck by the utter ridiculousness of the situation.

Noctus—a deadly and dangerous elf king—was hand feeding his pet cat freshly cooked chicken.

Bro, you should have gotten a pet ages ago if you were going to be this dedicated. I'd feel bad for you, if you weren't a figurative nightmare from supernaturals' past.

Full, I turned my nose away when Noctus offered me one last piece.

He ate the chicken himself, and a thoughtful expression flickered in his eyes.

I purred my thanks to the elf king—I even rubbed against his hand when he scratched my chest.

Noctus picked me up—being careful with my bulging belly—but positioned me so I could look up at his face. "Everyone else will call you Ama," he said. "But to me, you are Amalourne."

CHAPTER EIGHT

Chloe

I didn't know a lick of Elvish, so for all I knew he'd just renamed me "sweet bottomless stomach", but he seemed happy, and I didn't really care what he called me as long as I survived, so I purred my agreement.

Whatever you want, elf king. But I'd like it very much if you'd please put me down, preferably near that weird gate of yours, thank you.

Noctus carried me out of the kitchen and back into the hallway. To my delight, we walked toward the golden gate.

I could actually *see* it—it was beautiful with intricate flowers and delicate leaves sprouting off it. There was no mistaking it!

We were two doors away from it when Noctus made an abrupt turn into a darkened room.

Judging by the enormous desk and all the bookshelves stuffed with books that were leatherbound and looked old enough to predate the founding of the USA, it was probably Noctus's study.

It was just as showy as his bedroom, with three stained glass windows that decorated the room with dapples of colored light.

The near wall to wall bookshelves didn't stretch all the way up to the ceiling. Instead, there was a shelf that fit snugly against the ceiling and edged the entire room. Judging by the way my whiskers tingled when I looked up there, I was pretty sure the more potent magical books—which could also be more volatile—had been placed up there, out of reach.

Two enormous ladders were tucked against the bookshelves so you could reach the top shelves—the ceiling was again insanely high.

Things that I was starting to consider standard signs of elven lavishness—a plush dark aqua colored rug with a golden phoenix pattern, a porcelain vase of flowers that looked like they were spun from glass but glowed with magic, a globe that didn't look *anything* like Earth—were precisely placed around the room to create a seamless blend.

But what I found most interesting about the place was the only window that wasn't made of colored glass—which was also much smaller and had the same flower box outside it that the Cape Cod home had—and the glowing night sky that the ceiling opened into.

The ceiling had to be magic of some sort—I knew there was a second floor over the study, so it wasn't showing me outside the castle. As I watched I could see the stars move, as if it was a time lapse of the night sky.

It's gorgeous...but that window. Is it looking outside into the human neighborhood?

Noctus approached his desk, then paused to set me down on a cream-colored cat bed that had to be handmade, if the gold roses embroidered into the sides were any indication.

The bed was positioned near a fireplace—I was starting to think every room in this castle-home had one—which roared to life with blue and white flames when Noctus sat down at his desk.

I immediately hopped out of my bed and began exploring, slowly making my way toward the wall of windows.

Noctus pushed a button on his desk, then glanced at me as a sleek computer screen and keyboard popped out of the desk—a bizarre display of technology in a room that felt as old as magic.

Feeling bold after being hand fed, I hopped up onto his desk, swinging my tail back and forth.

Noctus pet me, then returned his attention to the computer screen, opening what appeared to be his email.

I almost fell off the desk when he also opened an Excel document—who knew kings actually had to do *work*?

But I didn't care about his work—the less I knew, the better. So I made the jump to the shorter, approximately thigh high shelf of books and papers that was positioned against the wall of windows, fitting neatly below them.

I peered through the closest stained-glass window. There were diamonds of red, blue, and yellow glass. When I looked through the yellow ones, I could see the tiered elven city—which was a little odd because I didn't think we were facing the right direction for it.

But as I watched, I saw people scurry about, some of them as small as ants in the lower tiers of the city.

I glanced at the next colored window and was treated to the same view. When I reached the clear window I had to stand on my hind legs and rest my paws on the edge, because it was so much smaller than the other windows, then poked my head up over the window frame.

Outside was a lush green lawn, a fence, and a human neighborhood of modest sized homes.

That's it! That's Magiford!

I scrambled onto the windowsill, using my catlike balance to sit on the narrow surface.

Across the street and one house down, a girl with dishwater blond hair was battling with a push lawnmower, trying—and failing—to get it started as she yanked on the cord.

Directly across the street, three old men were seated on a

porch crowded with lawn furniture, sipping at something in frosted glasses.

Can I get out there through this window?

It had to be a portal of some kind—unless the stained-glass windows were portals?

We were directly next to the house entrance, and going off the location of Noctus's bedroom, it seemed like we technically should be facing into the mountain the city was built against.

I didn't feel any magic coming off the plain window—not even with my bottom planted on the window sill—but the rest of the study tingled with it.

Maybe I can pull this off...

I studied the window, pleased to see it had a regular window lock, and appeared to swing out instead of push up.

The door clicked open, and Ker strolled inside, Aristide following behind her.

Aristide pointed his face in my direction. "The cat is by the windows?"

"If by 'the cat' you are referring to Ama, yes. She's sitting on a window sill," Noctus corrected.

"Yes, yes. Ama." Aristide confidently strode into the room and extended his hand, slowing down when he touched the back of an embroidered chair. He kept his hand on it as he walked around it before sitting down, turning the display into something graceful.

He must be powerful. I've seen him awake at all hours of the day, and the sunlight weakens vampires—they must be pretty powerful to resist it.

Aristide continued, "I shall get used to calling her that, but I'm afraid it won't be until I finish processing the idea that *you* picked such a name out."

"Is there something *wrong* with the name?" Noctus asked, a hint of a growl to his voice.

"Not at all." Aristide swatted a hand through the air before he carefully set his stick down by his chair. "It's merely that 'Sweet' strikes me as a shocking name choice coming from the King of Mors."

The what? I turned away from the window, pausing my inspection of the frame. *Is the Mors a place or something? I thought as an elf, his title would be "king of the elves."*

It's not like there were more of them...right?

"I think it's a good thing you now have a cat," Ker said. "Magic knows you've probably never had anything as wholesome as a pet."

"Animals can be weak points that are easily exploited and serve no use," Noctus said.

Ker openly shivered. "Yes, that sounds exactly like something your tyrant father would have said. Pets are awesome. There's nothing else in the world that is quite like the love of a pet."

Noctus turned in his chair to look back at me. "Maybe," he said. "But she is slow to be won over."

I uneasily curled the end of my tail. *I've been warming up to you way faster than any normal cat would. What are your expectations? If you wanted me to come running to you every time I see you, you should have gotten a dog.*

It was very well to be sarcastic in my own mind, but the truth was if Noctus wasn't satisfied, I was going to have to dial it up, no matter how I felt about it.

"She's a cat," Aristide said. "Give her time."

Noctus rubbed at his cuff-like bracelets.

Ker frowned as she studied the bracelets. "Are they hurting you?"

Noctus glanced down at them. "No. They're nothing but a mild irritation. I don't enjoy that they dull my sense of magic, but it's possible to still maintain the barrier around the villa, so it's inconsequential."

Villa? He thinks this place is on par with a mere villa? What does he think Buckingham Palace is—a summer cottage?

I'd never thought that the most dangerous situation I'd ever face in my entire life would inspire so much scoffing, but it would appear my malfunctioning danger meter had inspired a twisted sense of humor in me.

Though I hadn't missed Ker's question. Apparently the shackles blocked some of his magic? That was interesting—though it didn't matter much. As I had witnessed in his bedroom, Noctus was perfectly lethal even without his full magic.

"I think it's ridiculous that upstart of a Paragon thinks he can attempt to shackle *you*." Aristide rubbed the side of his aquiline nose. "Though it's perhaps even more ridiculous that he believes it's working! As if there is anything that could be forged by wizards or fae that is capable of completely blocking your magic."

I yawned, because I knew the gesture would keep me from puffing up in surprise.

The Paragon was the top fae representative—not for the region, but for *all* of America.

He'd been hanging out in Magiford for a few years, and no one really knew why—until now, that is.

I feel both better and worse. If the Paragon knows Noctus is kicking up his heels in the area, there's a small chance I'm safer than I thought. But why hasn't the Paragon told the supernatural world that he exists?

Obviously the Seelie fae had figured out Noctus was here, but it didn't seem like they were certain he was an elf, much less that he was a king.

No matter how desperate King Harel is, he'd never willingly engage with an elf king. That'd be like trying to pet a hydra.

"How much longer do we have to stick around here?" Aristide asked. "Magiford is a charming city, but I still like Europe more—or Alaska, if you want to make Ker happy."

Noctus glanced at me—or at the window I was sitting in, more correctly. "We'll be here for the foreseeable future."

Aristide sighed and slumped in his chair. "Wonderful."

Ker tilted her head back and forth like a curious dog, making the braids of her dark hair slip over her shoulders. "And you still can't tell us why?"

Noctus let one hand drape over the side of his computer chair, giving him a casual charisma that was unfair because he was an *elf*! "I cannot."

Ker nodded, accepting the reason.

I licked my paw pad just to give myself something to do, because Noctus glanced at me again, and I was pretty sure every time he looked at me I lost a day of my life.

They're here in Magiford by Noctus's choice, and no one knows why they need to be here besides him? Maybe Charon knows and Noctus hasn't told Ker and Aristide because they're not elves. It is a little weird that a vamp and a wolf are hanging out with him like they're BFFs when vampires and werewolves sided with the rest of supernaturals against elves.

The whole situation had just become way more cloak-and-dagger than me stumbling on an elf king—which was saying something, because that alone was enough to shake the foundations of Magiford.

And I'd learned all of this, just because I acted like a cat.

If I had better nerves, I could apply to the Curia Cloisters for a special task force position. Apparently I would make an excellent spy...if I stopped losing my hair as a cat and my pulse ever returns to normal after my little visit to the "Mors Villa."

Once I got out of here, I was going to buy myself an entire box of donuts—chocolate and vanilla, swimming in frosting—and a gallon of milk. I needed both to recover.

Ker sat on the bookshelf by the windows and leaned up against the wall. She pet me with a gentle smile in her eyes, and I purred a little.

"At least you've found something to amuse you," Ker said.

Could you please not phrase it like that?

Noctus glanced at me one last time. "Yes."

Ker and Aristide left after a few more minutes, leaving me alone to ponder their existence in the elf city.

Hours passed. Noctus stopped occasionally to come pet me and look out the window, but by mid to late afternoon I gave up my perch and switched to the cat bed, trying to catch a snooze in case the chance for an escape presented itself later.

I was mostly out of it when the door creaked. I opened my eyes, then automatically puffed up the hair on my back when I realized Charon had somehow soundlessly appeared.

Noctus didn't even look up; he was flipping through some documents. "What."

Charon flipped his hood down. "There have been a few problems."

Noctus set his documents aside. "Something that requires I visit the village?" His gaze skated past Charon, deeper into the villa. I had a feeling he was referring to the tiered city outside, in which case Noctus had a serious problem with estimating the size of things.

"No," Charon said. "Nothing like that. There have been three incidents in the past five weeks where one of our people has had a recently purchased magical tool or artifact malfunction and result in injury."

"It's not a side effect of magic dying?" Noctus asked.

"I wondered, so I pulled a few reports and discovered that in the past three to four months, it seems like bad artifacts are flooding Magiford. Close cities—like Chicago and Milwaukee—are experiencing some troubles, but not on the scale of Magiford."

"And beyond the Midwest?"

"Only a few instances."

"Then it must be something deliberate." Noctus leaned back in his chair. "Magiford is the strongest magical spot in the USA at the moment. If other cities aren't experiencing this, Magiford shouldn't, either."

Really? I burrowed deeper into my expensive cat bed. *That's a little odd considering how desperate the lower leveled supernaturals are getting. Unless...is it worse outside Magiford?*

I tucked my paws under me so I resembled a blackened loaf of bread. *I wonder if that's why he's set up his kingdom here—because he thinks it has stronger magic.*

Charon was watching me, his expression contemplative. "It's possible it could be shoddy workmanship." He changed his grip on his papers and walked in my direction. "All three instances pertained to newly purchased artifacts. It seems to me this is the result of our people purchasing magical goods of lower quality."

Why do the elves have to purchase magical goods of any sort? They're elves. They made *the enchanted armor sets and artifacts that the fae treasure and use. Hey!*

Charon scooped me up, carried me the short distance to Noctus's desk, then set me down on top of it.

I stiffly stood there, my paws on what were—I was assuming—important documents. *What am I supposed to do now?*

Noctus petted me for a moment, and Charon nodded in satisfaction.

"You have the reports on the incidents?" Noctus asked. He held his hand out to me with his palm facing me.

This again? Does he expect me to do something? Is this why he's convinced I don't like him enough? I gathered my courage and butted my head against his hand and rubbed my cheek against the base of his palm.

My reaction must not have been what Noctus wanted, because he pulled his hand away.

"Yes. Here they are." Charon tapped his papers on the table, gathering the already neat bundle into an obsessively lined up stack, then passed them over to his king.

Before Noctus could even start paging through them, Charon dug into a pocket of his suit coat. "Might I suggest—? She may be interested in it." He passed Noctus a toy mouse made of blue velvet cloth with silver embroidery that was stuffed with catnip.

Yuck. Catnip was the worst. It didn't affect me like a cat, but the taste always leaked through the fabric, and I didn't enjoy the herbal flavor.

But as Noctus set the toy mouse in front of me, I knew I was going to have to do *something*, so I batted at it with my paws, making the bell attached to the toy mouse's tail jingle.

Noctus observed for a moment, then picked up the papers from Charon and started reading.

Charon stood still—not moving a single muscle, though he watched me, which I wasn't a fan of.

I played with my mouse some more, chasing it across some papers in the hope that if I got annoying, they'd boot me off the desk.

Instead Noctus smoothed down the hair on the top of my head before flipping a page.

The wrinkles on Charon's forehead cleared, and at that moment I realized that—to him—I was a form of stress relief for his king.

That means he's going to be the most dangerous one, because he'll get invested in me.

I batted my mouse off the desk, but Charon caught it—lurching so suddenly into motion he set off my cat reactions, and I arched my back and puffed up the fur on my spine.

Charon placed the mouse back on the desk, then attempted to give me a kibble treat.

Yep. He's dangerous alright.

Noctus turned another page. "All of the issues happened outside our realm, inside Magiford?"

Charon straightened his shoulders. "Yes, Your Majesty."

Hoping I'd played with the mouse enough to satisfy them, I padded to the edge of the desk, intending to jump down and return to my bed.

Noctus stood and picked me up before I had the chance to escape. "And the latest incident resulted in injury."

"Yes. It happened two days ago. Valaria—mid-twenties, lives with her sister—was exploring downtown Magiford and was only using the item—a golden pocket watch—as a glamour to hide her eyes and ears. The watch exploded, leaving her with an injury on her thigh as she'd been keeping the watch in a pocket."

Noctus turned his back to Charon and stared at the windows —the fancy ones that overlooked his city.

As had become my custom, I clung to the neckline of his shirt, meowing a little when he unexpectedly pushed me higher up his chest.

I wasn't about to stop clinging, so I just moved my paws up higher, turning my half hug into a full on cat embrace.

Noctus didn't seem to mind, he stroked my shoulders as he stared down at the bustling streets.

I rested my chin on one of my paws and peered over his shoulder at Charon.

He was watching with a slightly tilted head, his eyes flicking from me to Noctus as he discreetly pulled out another cat toy from his coat pocket and set it on the desk. This toy was a ball of sparkly, crinkled, foil-like paper, and it made me suspect that Charon had to have some kind of noise-canceling spell cast on himself as those kinds of cat toys normally crinkled like a chip bag opening at 2 am after everyone else in your family has gone to sleep.

"It's suspicious enough to warrant an investigation." Noctus finally turned back to Charon.

Charon folded his hands behind his back. "Even though it doesn't appear to be only affecting us elves?"

"Whether it's affecting anyone else is not my issue." Noctus sat down, still holding me against his chest. "It is apparent my people are ignorant enough that they can't tell inferior goods from well-made ones. Teaching them that kind of discernment would take more planning and work than simply getting rid of the source of bad artifacts."

What a thoughtful, benevolent monarch. Despite his harsh words, he's going to fix the problem for his people—and maybe help other supernaturals in the process.

The idea was so weird that it made me wriggle out of Noctus's grasp and jump onto the desk.

"Understood," Charon said. "I'll organize a party and look into the matter."

I stretched, then leaped off the desk.

"No," Noctus said.

I'd been padding my way back to my fancy bed, but at this proclamation I couldn't help but look back at Noctus.

He was rubbing one of his magic-blocking cuffs, his eyes thoughtfully narrowed. "I'll investigate the matter myself."

Charon stared at him. From the way the muscles on his face seemed to slacken by two degrees, I got the feeling he was surprised.

I sat down in my bed, curling up in a ball so I was positioned perfectly to see both of the elves.

"Do...do you want me to arrange a group to report to you?" Charon asked.

"No. Ker and Aristide will help me."

Wrinkles spread around the corners of Charon's eyes, but I couldn't tell if it was concern or another emotion since the rest of his face was expressionless. "That means going into Magiford, if you wish to investigate the scenes of the incidents."

"I'm aware," Noctus dryly said. "I'll manage. I want this matter taken care of immediately."

"Understood," Charon said—it seemed to be his catchphrase. "I will leave the matter in your capable hands, Your Majesty."

Noctus stood up again as I closed my eyes to feign sleeping.

"We'll visit the location of the latest incident—the one involving the gold pocket watch—and inquire with any of the nearby businesses to see if they noticed anything," he said.

"Ahh, yes. Valaria was standing in the parking lot of a human-owned business. I believe there may be camera footage of the event."

"Then we'll start there." Noctus strode across the office, hesitating by my bed.

I did my best performance of "sleeping" ever, and managed to keep my breathing slow even though I felt his eyes on me.

"I need to feed Ama again before we leave," Noctus said.

"That won't be a problem—I believe the business is already closed for the day," Charon said. "It is a coffee shop. Those tend to close early in the day as humans are not very nocturnal."

Noctus nodded. "Then we will go there tomorrow morning, and tonight I will show Ker and Aristide the files." He strode toward the door, my heart beating faster with my glee.

He's going to leave me here!

"As you say, Your Majesty." Charon peered at me before following after his king. "You said you need to feed Ama again? Might I assume, then, that you got her to partake in some kind of food?"

"Yes—roasted chicken."

"I'll make a note." Charon closed the door to the study.

Yes! This is it—my chance for escape!

Although I was so excited I could barely feel my paws, I made myself pretend to sleep for three more minutes. Then, I got up with a big stretch and a wide yawn.

I meowed, then made my way over to the windows.

When I peered through the stained glass windows the sun was

hovering over the horizon, just as it was in Magiford. It was almost nighttime.

I guess that answers the question if the city's time is linked up with earth.

I jumped up onto the small windowsill and peered outside.

No one was out on the front lawn of Noctus's place. But the blond girl—who looked like she was maybe in college—was still outside her house, attacking an overgrown lilac bush while the elderly men on the crowded porch of the house next to her appeared to be shouting encouragement at her.

Now is my chance to run. I just hope this window doesn't need a lot of strength to open.

I still didn't want to risk turning into a human in the "villa", particularly given the various displays of magic power that I'd witnessed.

A cat opening a window was weird enough, but I didn't need anyone seeing my face and figuring out how to identify me, and I wasn't sure this was going to work.

It took about five minutes of straining—I alternated between using my head and my paws—to flick the window lock up.

There wasn't any mechanism that I could see that would open the window, so I braced myself on the sill and leaned hard into the glass. It wobbled a tiny bit, breathing hope into my feline heart. I slammed my shoulder against the pane, praying that the thumping noise wouldn't draw anyone back to the study.

In the end, I was able to push it open just enough to let a small cat through. It only worked because the little Cape Cod house was old, so the seal on the window wasn't very strong.

No wonder they have all the fireplaces—this place would cost a fortune to heat in the winter!

For a fleeting moment, I felt bad about leaving the window open before I remembered that I was fleeing an *elf king*.

I hopped through, feeling a brief buzz of magic. There was a disorientating swirl from the magical gate enchanted into the window, and then I landed on the front lawn of the Cape Cod styled home.

My heart pounded in my throat as I ran across the lawn. Cautiously, I stuck my nose through the spokes of the wrought iron fence. Feeling no resistance—and no pull back toward the house—I pushed my head through, then wriggled my shoulders and the rest of my body after.

CHAPTER NINE

Chloe

With all four paws planted on the sidewalk, I was officially out.

It worked!

Either Noctus didn't have any spells up—unlikely—or in addition to being immune to most forms of magic, I was also immune to elven spells—more likely.

I could hardly believe my luck as I ran up the sidewalk, heading out of the cul-de-sac as fast as I could.

As soon as it opened into a new street, I started crossing through backyards, heading up toward the east side of the city, where my studio apartment was.

I made it into the downtown area, and found a back alleyway between a coffee shop called Dream Bean, and the building of a defunct newspaper which was getting remodeled into a restaurant or store based on all the equipment in the front windows.

Regardless, all the construction people coming and going made it easy for me to slip into the back alley and crouch next to the dumpster.

I drew on my magic, and before I could blink I was human.

I stood up, taking careful inventory. I had my purse, complete with my wallet, keys, and cell phone, and I was still wearing the clothes and my white flower-patterned scarf from my last shift at the Book Nookery. It was a shame, but I'd dropped my donuts when running from whatever had been chasing me two days ago.

I tucked my brown hair behind my ear, trying to get it out of my face as I dug through my purse, unearthing my cell phone.

I swiped it open and hurriedly opened my text conversation with my brother and sister.

They'd each sent a few inquisitive texts that I hadn't responded to. In fact, Joy's latest text—which was the daily cute cat picture—included a rather ominous line.

If you don't respond soon, Chloe Grace, I'm going to drive down to Magiford to check on you.

She'd used my middle name, which meant it wasn't an idle threat. She lived in a suburb north of Milwaukee, and was roughly an hour and a half away given that Magiford straddled the Wisconsin/Illinois state line. Pat lived even closer, but he hadn't said anything. Yet.

I glanced up and down the alleyway and rubbed my nose, trying to ignore the scent of coffee grounds and rotting fruit, before I headed out of the far end of the alley, popping into a tiny parking lot that backed into the city boardwalk—the massive wooden walkway the city had built around the two lakes that squatted at the center of Magiford.

By the time I'd reached the boardwalk, I'd composed my response.

Hey, sorry, I couldn't get to my phone—which was true, if I didn't think about it too long. *I didn't mean to worry you guys! Any updates from Mom and Dad?*

Only a few seconds passed before Pat, my older brother, responded.

Glad ur OK. Next time call us from ur work line.

Joy was only a moment behind our brother. *Mom and Dad are in Arizona now, but they plan to head to Colorado soon. Arizona is getting too hot for them and the motorhome's air conditioning isn't working that well. Mom asked about you—you should call them.*

Our parents—or rather my adopted parents, but they'd be crushed if they heard me call them that, and I'd never thought of them as anything besides my real parents—had retired recently and were living out their lifelong dream of driving a motorhome across the USA.

They'd left about a month ago, and didn't plan to return to Wisconsin until Christmas time.

I tapped away on my phone.

I'll call them. Thanks for checking in!

I got a flood of emojis in response from my sister. Pat said nothing—not surprising, he was the strong silent type.

Smiling, I put my phone back in my purse and picked up my pace. I'd been heading in the general direction of my apartment.

I have a shift at Book Nookery tonight, but maybe it would be better if I called in sick?

I didn't want to loaf around my apartment after being cooped up for so long. But I couldn't deny I burned with the desire to shower and check my fridge; I was pretty sure I had a carton of coconut milk and some cow milk that was going to expire soon. But I needed to figure out what to do about...everything.

I fussed with my scarf, pulling it off so I could scratch my neck, only to feel a soft fabric. I almost leaped out of my skin in surprise, then tossed my scarf into my purse before I grasped at my own neck, my fingers scraping against something that felt suspiciously like lace, and my nails nicking something hard and rock like.

No, that's not possible.

I dug my phone back out and turned on the selfie camera, pointing it at my neck.

Fitting snugly around my neck was the collar Noctus had

stuck on me. The three red gems gleamed in the light of the setting sun.

I need to get this off of me, now!

I slipped a finger under the soft material—it was a comfortable fit despite the fact that I'd been wearing it as a cat—but when I tried to pull it up over my head, it wouldn't budge.

I even put my phone away so I could yank at it with both hands, but while I could get my fingers under the collar, the fabric would pull away but not move up or down.

This can't be happening. If anything, it should have stayed with my cat form, not switched to my human form!

With the pads of my fingers gliding across the gems, I felt the faint buzz of magic within it. Dazed, I leaned against the wooden railing of the boardwalk.

Maybe the collar is spelled to stay on me no matter what. I mean, why would you bother to put anything else on a cat collar? I doubt he'd use a listening spell—what would be the point?

Regardless, this was a worst-case scenario. I needed to get it off, immediately.

The Curia Cloisters were my best bet, but I wasn't sure if it was the safest.

The Paragon knew about Noctus but hadn't told anyone—or, more likely, the Paragon had only told the top level players in the supernatural world, and possibly the members of the Regional Committee of Magic.

If I strutted into the Curia Cloisters and blew the secret, I'd be opening a can of worms I'd never be able to close again. Given that my current method of survival was to avoid all attention, that might not end well for me, particularly if the Curia Cloisters were even more reluctant to hire me now that I had an elven collar on my throat. Being taken in as a stray pet by the elven King of the Mors probably wasn't going to do much for my bid to be hired on as a secretary, and for all my jokes about spying, I wasn't suited—much less trained—for that kind of work.

Still, the Curia Cloisters were the best choice.

Do I even want to stay in this city now that elves are around? But where else could I go? Unless I want to move to another supernatural epicenter, less supernatural populated cities are even more dangerous as there are fewer laws.

I worriedly rubbed at the gems on my collar and tried to collect myself.

I just need a little time to review my options. Impulsive decisions are rarely the best, and I should see if I can find out anything about the magic in this collar. I spun in a circle so I pointed in the opposite direction, and started walking for Book Nookery.

It seemed I would be going in to work today—and I'd be begging Ms. Booker for a chance to read her elven tomes.

"YOU WANT TO READ *WHAT*?" Ms. Booker's voice was as sharp as my cat claws.

I winced—I hadn't heard my boss lose her genteel tone very often. Only twice, in fact, and each time it had been to throw out a mouthy customer.

I clasped my hands behind my back and tried not to cower before my petite boss. "I know your books about elves are part of your personal collection, but I've encountered some elven lore that I'd like to research more."

Ms. Booker set down her teacup and frowned at me. "The elves aren't something you want to approach lightly, Chloe dear." She narrowed her eyes as she traced over my slightly rumpled clothes—the same ones I'd worn at my last shift. "They're a dangerous topic that's best left alone, for those older and wiser."

Based on the way she was staring at my clothes, I think she meant to imply I was too silly and young to handle it if I couldn't wear fresh clothes to my job. I, however, was sweating buckets, hoping she wouldn't notice my new accessory, which I'd done my best to hide by winding my neck scarf over it.

"It would mean a lot to me," I tried.

"No." Ms. Booker turned away and started to mince off to the stairs. "I'm afraid you're still too immature to handle it."

"It has to do with my abilities," I blurted out—truthfully too. I was worried because they *hadn't* worked against the collar.

Ms. Booker paused and looked back at me.

She knew about my magic—and the battle I'd been enmeshed in as I tried to find where I fit in. I had told her during my interview, in case she didn't want to hire me as a result. (Some supernaturals could get snobby about pedigrees and abilities.)

Ms. Booker glided back to me. She peered up into my face, her eyes narrowing to small slits behind the delicate frames of her glasses. "Come with me." She turned back to her staircase and started up it, gripping the banister as she climbed.

My shoulders must have dropped three inches in my relief. I let out the breath I'd been holding and followed her.

The landing at the top of the staircase only held plants and a few wooden chairs.

Ms. Booker led me to her private office—which was the first door off the landing.

It was fairly standard—she had a desk, a computer, a filing cabinet, and a lockbox. The typewriter sitting on an end table was a little unusual, but it had been there since the day I'd started at Book Nookery, and it was kept spotlessly clean—like the wall-to-wall bookshelves that lined the room and were crowded with stacks of books, old and new alike.

The only sunlight in the room came from a skylight, and Ms. Booker had a special shade for it because sunlight could damage her books.

Ms. Booker pulled a key out of her pocket as she approached the only locked bookshelf in the house, which was housed in an iron cage that glowed with magic.

The seal on the cage created a burning sensation I felt in my toes—dragon shifter magic.

Whatever tomes Ms. Booker had under lock and key, she had paid some serious money to protect them. Dragon shifters rarely performed magic for anyone besides themselves, and when they did it was *expensive*.

The lock clanked open, and Ms. Booker stepped aside, tugging the iron door to the cage open. "This shelf contains all the books I have on elves. I would advise you to *not* look at the other shelves—it wouldn't be wise for your health."

With that dire warning, I knelt down and made sure I kept my gaze on the shelf she'd pointed out.

About half the books were in languages I didn't recognize. But there was an old leather-bound book with tattered yellowed pages that was written in something that looked like Shakespearian English, and a book that appeared both modern and ancient.

It was simply titled "Elves", and inside it used modern English, but everything was written by hand, and the book itself appeared to be handmade and covered in dyed cheesecloth.

I reached for the books but hesitated at the last moment, my fingers hovering over their spines. Magic radiated off of them, and I was focusing really hard so I didn't feel the magic from any of the other locked books, but this was pretty intense.

I hope I'm not biting off more than I can chew.

I rolled my shoulders back, then slid the books off the shelf. "Thank you, Ms. Booker."

Ms. Booker swung the door shut with a dainty push of her gloved hands, then locked the cage. "You are free to take the books downstairs, but whenever a customer comes in you must place them down by the cash drawer."

"I understand. Thank you." I bowed, then curtsied because I wasn't sure which she would prefer, and backed out of the room.

I hurried down the stairs and practically threw myself at the desk. I moved the keyboard from its sliding drawer and placed the books there, so I could read them without showing their covers and move them without letting anyone see what I was looking at.

I started to reach for one of the books, when I noticed a pair of scissors on one of the desk's shelves.

Thinking of my collar, I snatched the scissors up and very carefully arranged my phone so I could see myself on my screen. I slid one of the scissors' blades under the collar and tried cutting the fabric, but it didn't work. The scissors closed down on the material, but it didn't cut through it.

I didn't think it would be that easy. But it's better to try than to be an idiot and assume.

Disappointed, I put the scissors back and dug out the carton of milk I'd bought on my way over. I took a swig for fortification, then stored it on a shelf by itself so it couldn't harm any books even if I accidentally tipped it over, then started with the leather-bound elf book, which seemed to be a history of the elves and contained a lot of beautiful illustrations.

As the sky turned a velvety black I settled in, hoping I might be able to find something that would help me with the collar.

BY FIVE THIRTY in the morning, I was physically exhausted from going so many days without any kind of deep sleep, and my brain had reached the intelligence level of a gelatinous jellyfish washed up on a beach.

The Shakespearian book was a chronicle of the elven history, but I hadn't set it aside because it answered a very important question I'd had about Noctus's kingship.

It turned out the elves—similar to the fae—had multiple royal families, each with their own specialization. One royal family was said to be particularly gifted with creating and filtering magic, while another was skilled at summoning and could call out creatures from the fae realm.

Noctus was apparently from the Mors royal family, which—based on the book—specialized in *war*. Specifically, their magic was most useful for death and killing, which they used to wage war whenever they felt like it.

The book claimed the entire family had been wiped out in a massive bloodbath, and their downfall was the tipping point in the war against the elves. Without their death dealers, the elves had lost their major fighting force.

There weren't any details about the way the Mors had been defeated—not even an illustration. It only said that one incident had taken out the entire Mors royal family.

I guess it's an extra good thing I got out of the villa when I did.

I shivered and put the history book on top of the cash drawer.

Ms. Booker would be down any minute to relieve me, but I was torn on whether I should head home, or try to muster through reading the second book—which still weirded me out, even though I couldn't really point to a reason why.

I was studying its cover when I heard the chime of the bell on the front door. I seamlessly set the book on the cash drawer, then put on my customer-service smile. "Good morning, and welcome to Book Nookery..."

I trailed off when I saw who'd entered the shop.

Noctus sauntered in, wearing sunglasses, charcoal black slacks with a matching vest, and a dark blue dress shirt with the sleeves rolled up to his elbows. "Good morning."

CHAPTER TEN

Chloe

Behind him, Aristide entered—he was wearing a dove gray suit, but was holding the handle of a neon yellow harness strapped to an enormous wolf.

There was no mistaking it, the wolf—who had an undercoat of dark brown and black with an overcoat of red, so she almost looked like she was on fire—had to be Ker. She gazed around the shop with curiosity and raised her nose to the air, scenting out the place.

Oh boy, this is one heck of a coincidence...

Aristide fidgeted at the entrance, kickstarting my brain.

"Can I help you?" I cleared my throat and set my hands on my desk, concentrating on trying to stay calm so my heart didn't leap out of my chest.

I knew from experience that I smelled different as a cat versus a human—there was no way Ker would be able to scent me.

Noctus smiled—or rather, the muscles around his mouth softened—but he didn't remove his sunglasses as he approached the desk. "Yes, if I could bother you for a moment."

"You're looking for a book?" I asked. I was going to have to wash this shirt twice with the amount of sweat I was producing.

"No," Noctus said. "I'm looking for a cat."

The last three years of stress and anxiety had beaten the dramatics out of me, but at that moment I swear I felt my heart depart from my body, off to greener pastures and less stressful situations.

"Oh?" I said, garbled and barely understandable. "I'm afraid we only sell books here, not cats."

"I understand," Noctus said. "But I have a tracking spell on my cat, and I've tracked her to this area."

The collar. I knew it was too fancy to be ornamental, especially if it managed to stick with me!

That killed my so-called breakout. If Noctus could use the spell, I'd never be able to escape him.

"Might I search your front and back yard?" The way Noctus said it, it didn't really come out as a question, but more of a requirement. "The spell doesn't give me a lock on her exact position, but it is fairly precise, so I know she must be close by."

I glanced from him to Ker—who was still sniffing the air, but didn't seem inclined to come in any deeper.

If they go outside, maybe I can slip out. I have one last chance to evade him: the Curia Cloisters. But if he catches me before then, I'll have to live as a pet until I get this collar off.

"You can search the yards," I said. "But you can only come in and out of Book Nookery through the front door."

"Understood." Noctus sauntered back to his friends, slipping his hands into the pockets of his slacks.

As soon as the door closed, I grabbed the elven books and bolted.

Time to run!

I ran up the stairs, taking them two at a time. When I leaped to the top stair I almost bowled over Ms. Booker. "Thank you for letting me read the books, Ms. Booker." I spoke so fast, the words were a jumbled mess as I pressed her books into her arms. "I'm sorry, but there's an emergency. I won't be able to come in for the next week, maybe two. If you have to fire me, I understand."

I started backing up, and almost fell down the first stair. *Go, go, go!*

I needed to get out of here before Noctus figured out what was going on—particularly because I couldn't involve Ms. Booker in this. She'd done so much for me. I couldn't repay her by setting the last King of the Mors loose on her and her store.

Ms. Booker shifted her grasp on the books. "I'll get your shifts covered, Chloe dear—but is everything all right?"

"No." I skidded down the last few stairs in my hurry, landing on the bottom with a jolt. "But I don't know what to do. Thank you!"

I peered through one of the giant windows in the entryway—I could see Noctus standing on the sidewalk with his hands still in his pockets while Ker sniffed at some of the purple petunia flowers Ms. Booker had planted in pots.

If they're up front, I can go out the back.

I ran back into the kitchen and grabbed my purse, barely noticing that Ms. Booker had arrived at the bottom of the staircase.

I zipped out onto the back porch and changed into a cat, then crossed through the backyard of the shop's neighbor, heading toward the Curia Cloisters.

It was unfortunately a long way off, but I couldn't risk changing into a human to get on a bus or anything.

If Noctus sees me while he's tracking "Amalourne", he might put two and two together. The chances that I make it to the Curia Cloisters aren't good, so I need to be prepared in case I don't make it.

I had messed up by not going to the Curia Cloisters. Maybe. Or maybe the Paragon would have intercepted me for the sake of keeping Noctus a secret? I didn't know enough information to make a truly good decision, but one thing was for sure: I hadn't thought Noctus was an obsessive enough owner to give the collar a *tracking spell*.

I stayed off the streets and sidewalks as much as possible. I thought it was safer that way, but I was in the middle of someone's tiny garden when fear slammed into me—the same icy, all consuming kind I'd felt that had forced me to throw myself at the Seelie fae.

I turned, able to peer over my back thanks to my cat flexibility. Horrifyingly, there was something there: a darkened shadow lurking at the corner of the next-door house.

It was thick and too substantial to be a mere shadow, and with it this close I could feel its magic with my whiskers, but my fear was too overwhelming to identify it.

I was wrong, I realized. *Between the elf king who hand feeds me chicken and has a quite possibly offensive nickname for me and this thing, the elf king is a lot safer. Even if he is the king of death.*

I ran, streaking under bushes and fences—anything that would make me a difficult target as I sprinted downtown.

The shadow trailed me, slowly gaining inch by inch. When I ran around the corner of a house, I caught the shadow at just the right angle that I could see into it—as if it was a hazy cloud.

The tracker was a man—leanly built with red hair that looked as if it had been dyed in blood. Most alarmingly, he was carrying some kind of crossbow, and his eyes were tracing my path. My heart felt like it might burst in my chest from the fear, but I refused to give up.

Now more than ever I needed to get to the Curia Cloisters. Whoever was tracking me...I had a feeling he wasn't going to stop again for some low leveled Seelie fae.

Cats can run really fast...for very short distances. But the burst of speed I put on got me far enough ahead of him that I was able to make it to the edges of downtown Magiford—which was both welcome and increasingly tricky as there weren't as many things to hide under.

I zigzagged, my ears full with the sound of the tracker's sprinting footsteps behind me.

I was almost to main street, but the tracker was catching up on me. A few more blocks and he'd be able to catch—

"There you are, Amalourne." Noctus appeared in front of me, seemingly out of nowhere. He picked me up before I could dart past him. I wiggled in his one-armed grasp, still panicked from the tracker.

I struggled, twisting until I could peer back in the direction I'd come from.

I saw the shadow covering the tracker. It was stationary about one block down. A few heartbeats, and the shadow—and the tracker—retreated. He moved back a block, then turned off, lessening the fear pumping in my small body.

Whoever he is...he's scared of Noctus.

Speaking of the elf king, he was oblivious to the fear he inspired. He flicked his sunglasses up and stared at me, his hypnotic eyes tracing over me from my whiskers to my tail.

Relief and disappointment warred within me. I was safe—sort of—but I was back to square one. Except it was worse. Now I knew I'd never be able to escape Noctus unless I figured out how to ditch the collar.

Telling him what I was still wasn't an option—Charon or one of the others would end me before I got a full explanation for the sin of learning about Noctus and the elf city.

Noctus put a finger under my chin and tilted it up so he could inspect my neck. He tried to roll me onto my back, but I dug my claws into the sleeve of his dress shirt and held on, so he stopped trying.

"Peace, Amalourne," Noctus said. "I'm trying to get a look at you."

A look at me? Why?

Now that I had a few brain cells to rub together, it occurred to me that Noctus wasn't as bad a choice as the tracker, but he wasn't safe, either. *Has he realized I'm the girl from the bookshop?*

"You are, at least, unhurt." He narrowed his eyes. "Though I will have to ponder why you felt the need to *leave*. Later."

I started to tuck my neck into my shoulders, shrinking a little under his scrutiny. *At least I have a track record of surviving him. And as terrifying as Noctus is, he doesn't feel like...panic. He's too controlled for that.*

When it came down to it, I'd rather face off with Noctus, who I could potentially survive even if he was a living legend, rather than whatever was chasing me. Judging by the crossbow the guy had carried, I was pretty sure he intended to kill me. And I had no idea why.

Is he with one of the fae Courts? But why would he care about me, then? I'm not a fae.

Conversely, as long as I played the role of pet, Noctus wasn't going to do anything to me.

It's still terrifying, but at least staying with Noctus means a longer life expectancy. For now.

Noctus was still frowning at me—which was scary in a different way.

I forced a purr—the most sputtering, inconsistent purr ever done by cat kind—but Noctus straightened up, flicked his sunglasses back into place, and held me with a gentle but firm grasp as he headed back south.

Aristide was standing about a block ahead of us, still holding the handle of Ker's harness.

Ker howled for a note—a delighted, high-pitched yip.

"Ahh, you found her, Noctus?" Aristide asked, interpreting the noise.

"I did. She's fine—unharmed and seemingly in good spirits." Noctus let Ker sniff at me—as a werewolf she was larger than a typical wolf and had no problems reaching me and licking my face.

I crawled higher up Noctus's waist after that, getting into a more secure position with my paws anchored in the neckline of his shirt.

"Shall we head for home, then?" Aristide asked. His stance was very casual considering he was a vampire standing in the warm glow of dawn.

Just how old and powerful is he? He's not even carrying an umbrella or anything to shade himself from the rising sun.

Noctus paused when we reached the vampire and the werewolf. "No."

"Don't you want to drop her off?"

"Charon is waiting for us at the café."

"You can't just walk around carrying a cat. It's been a while since I've seen society, but I know that much, at least, is true."

"The café is pet friendly." Noctus ambled off, leaving Ker and Aristide behind.

Aristide sighed. "Fine, be *that* weirdo. I knew your long life was eventually going to make you crack. Ker, find Queen's Court Café."

Ker gave a happy "*Awoo!*" noise before she followed Noctus, her nails clicking on the sidewalk.

Queen's Court? That's where we're going?

Queen's Court Café was a popular coffee shop downtown that famously catered to the fae Night Court and their obsession with their queen and her king, and welcomed pets of all kinds.

Queen's Court was only a five minute walk away, taking us past some scenic areas, most notably the large clocktower—which looked like it was almost ready to open to the general public—and Magiford Donuts.

When we arrived at the café, Charon was waiting, standing by a black vehicle that I'm sure was a luxury brand, but I knew nothing about cars, so it was lost on me.

When he saw us he stepped away from the car and bowed. "Your Majesty."

Noctus nodded at the greeting as he scanned the parking lot. "Where was she at the time of the accident?"

"Valaria was standing in this area." Charon walked a three-foot section of sidewalk, which was perfectly in sight of Queen's Court.

There was no sign of the accident—the sidewalk was clean.

Ker sniffed around the cement, her black nose twitching as she sorted through scents.

Noctus shifted me in his arms. "There's latent wild magic here," he said. "But nothing that would set off an artifact."

He can sense wild magic? That's frightening.

"That would support the supposition that the problem does indeed lie with the artifact," Charon said.

"Did you look the watch over?" Aristide asked.

Charon shook his head. "The Curia Cloisters were involved and took the broken watch as part of their case. It would not be... wise to ask for it back considering how we are attempting to avoid their attention."

"But you said the owner of Queen's Court saw the incident?" Noctus turned so he faced Queen's Court Café.

The café had a paper sign that welcomed pets, and the logo that hung outside over the door had glittery stars.

"Indeed," Charon said.

"I suppose that's something," Aristide grumbled.

When Ker finished sniffing, she sat on the ground and wagged her tail.

"Ker's finished," Noctus said. "Let's go."

Noctus sauntered down the sidewalk, approaching the café. He shifted me to one arm so he could open the door, and stepped inside.

The café had the sharp smell of coffee, punctuated with a surprisingly strong smell of apples, which probably came from the enormous sack of apples that was set on a counter by the tiny drive through window.

There were pictures of the Night Queen and her king, strings of tiny lights crisscrossing across the ceiling, and walls colored deep blue and dotted with gold and white specks that represented the night sky.

Whoever decorated this place definitely knew their target customer base, I thought as I studied a moon shaped clock fastened to the wall.

"Welcome to Queen's Court Café." A young guy standing behind the counter indifferently sniffed as he jabbed a few buttons on the register tablet. "What do you want—oh. All animals are required to be secured with collars and leashes." He pointed to me.

"She has a collar," Noctus said.

"But no leash," the teenager pointed out. "Animals must be leashed for safety reasons—and *that* is *not* a dog. That is a werewolf! Is that even *legal*?" The barista leaned over the counter to gape at Ker.

"How dare you judge my service animal?" Aristide scoffed. "She is prized for her guidance abilities."

Are they seriously trying to pretend that Ker isn't a werewolf? Why?

The barista wasn't buying the act any more than I was. He screwed his freckled face up as he peered from Aristide to Ker. "Do you not *know* it's a werewolf? Because, dude, it totally is."

"Landon, don't pester the customers." A smiling woman emerged from the back area, fixing the ties of her black apron.

Landon pointed at me. "I'm not pestering, I'm enforcing rules. The cat doesn't have a leash. Also, do we allow transformed werewolves in the store?"

The woman glanced at Ker. "Well, the guide canine has a harness, which follows store policies. Would you like some chicken jerky?"

Ker whipped her tail back and forth, almost taking out a chair.

"Here you go." The woman opened a glass jar and passed a dog treat over to Ker, who sniffed it before eating it.

The woman turned to me, already reaching for another glass jar. "What about you?"

"Ama is a picky eater," Noctus said.

I mournfully gazed at the glass bakery stand that was built into the counter. *But she has donuts...I doubt she'd offer one to a cat. But donuts!*

"I see, I can respect a cat who knows what she likes." The woman winked at me, then smiled at Noctus. "Though I am afraid Landon is right. We require leashes on all animals—for their own safety."

"Sir." Charon stepped out of the shadows, scaring the fur off me—how did he do everything so silently? "If I may?" Charon offered out a leash.

Of course, it was made of a soft, luxurious light blue material I didn't recognize, with white jewels that looked suspiciously *real* for accent. Noctus took it and clipped it to my collar—which didn't have a metal loop or anything, so he clipped it over the fabric.

"Thank you." The woman rested her hands on the counter. "Now, how can we help you?"

"I suppose you don't happen to make *caffè marocchino*?" Aristide asked.

The barista tilted her head back. "It's not on the menu, but I can make it."

"Truly? Then I'll have that, please." Aristide brightened and almost dropped Ker's harness in his exuberance.

Noctus glanced at his friend. "Really?"

"If you won't go back to Europe, the least I will allow myself to do is eat and drink things that remind me of it." Aristide reached into a pocket and pulled out a wallet. He flipped it open, his fingers skimming the top seam before he reached an edge of the wallet and plucked out the credit card tucked in a slot there.

The barista picked an espresso sized disposable cup and wrote on it. "That's one caffè marocchino, coming right up—Landon?"

"On it!" Landon took the cup and strode off.

"Can I get you dears anything else?" the barista asked with a smile.

"We don't want anything to drink." Noctus stepped aside so Aristide could pay. "But I have a few questions for you."

"Whatcha got?" the barista asked, a friendly tone to her voice that made her easy to like.

"Last week a young woman had an accident out on your sidewalk, by your parking lot."

"Oh, yeah! I remember that," the teenager—or maybe he was a college student considering it was a weekday—Landon, shouted over the squeal of the espresso machine. "Her magical artifact broke, and there was this explosion—like sparklers going off."

"I am an acquaintance of her family," Noctus smoothly said, "and I am looking into the incident."

"I see. I'm afraid I can't tell you much." The barista processed Aristide's order, then—after glancing at Ker—set his card back in his hand. "She was walking on the sidewalk, and it went off. We didn't see anything that would have caused it."

"I was told there is security camera footage?" Noctus asked.

It is a little odd to think that an elf king is acting as a detective, I pondered as I watched the incident with abstract interest—though I was still mostly just relieved I'd avoided the creepy tracker guy. *Maybe it's because he's better at passing as a human? I mean, he's more convincing than Charon the Shadow Stalker, but not by much given his sculpture-like looks.*

"Our security cameras did pick it up, but the Curia Cloisters already took a copy of it—they said they didn't see anything, either. Wasn't it just a poorly made item?" the barista asked.

"Could I get a copy of the camera footage?" Noctus asked.

The barista started to shake her head.

"Please," Noctus added.

The nicety might have been shockingly polite given that he was a king, but I felt the magic threaded into the word, and my whiskers tingled with the knife-sharp sensation of his elven magic.

What is he doing?

I peered at the barista, and watched her stop her head mid shake. "Sure," she said. "Let me just go back to the office and get that for you."

Ah—he dazzled her.

That wasn't necessarily the proper term to describe what he'd done, but he'd essentially used magic to nudge the barista into doing what he wanted.

Fae were capable of such trickery on non magical humans, and powerful vampires could use pheromones for a similar effect, but it seemed like elves were capable of such magic, too.

How fun.

"Here, we have a USB drive." Charon passed a tiny jump drive over to the barista, who took it before she walked off.

Landon frowned at her back, then peered at Noctus and his entourage. "I guess it makes sense. You are even better looking than King Rigel," he said, naming the famous Night Queen's husband.

Noctus pushed one eyebrow up so it peeked over the frame of his sunglasses.

"That's probably why she did it." Landon waggled a finger at us. "I'm still not convinced a werewolf on a harness is legal, so you're on thin ice with me, Mr. I Look Like An Angel And A Fae Had A Baby!"

Even though I was brought up by humans, I'm never mentally fortified enough for just how brave their ignorance makes them.

"Here's your drink, I went a little heavy on the cocoa powder." Landon set the drink on the counter, positioning it in front of Aristide. "It's right in front of you—your twelve o'clock."

Aristide reached out and found the disposable cup. "Thank you." He took a sip. "It's not as good as a real Italian caffè marocchino from a bar, but this is far better than the swill most American cafés serve. My compliments."

Landon squinted at him. "Thanks?"

The barista returned a moment later. "Here you go. I hope the young lady is all recovered and isn't too hurt?"

"She's doing fine. Thank you for your concern." Noctus's voice was silky from the magic threading through it, but he took the USB drive and passed it off to Charon.

"Regardless, good luck with your search," the barista said.

"Thank you," Noctus said.

"Thank you for the not-swill," Aristide said as Ker started for the exit.

Charon got to the door first and held it open for Aristide and Ker, and stood at attention as Noctus passed through last.

"They were weird," Landon grumbled.

Charon released the door, and it started to slowly swing shut.

"*Landon*."

"They were! And why did they need the footage when everyone knows the problem was with that girl's artifact?"

Humans even know about the bad artifacts? That's interesting.

Against my better judgment, I was a tiny bit intrigued in the case. It was safer to not get involved and to take in as little information about Noctus and the elves as possible, but I hadn't slept deeply in days, and it made me more daring—or maybe stupid—than I'd normally ever be.

Landon—oblivious to my lunatic ideas—continued, "I bet she bought it off the sketchy dude selling artifacts around here."

CHAPTER ELEVEN

Chloe

Noctus whirled around so fast, it made my belly flop in my gut. He yanked the door back open. "What did you say?"

Landon sucked his neck into his shoulders. "Uhhh..."

"About an artifact seller." Noctus stalked back inside, Charon coming with him as Ker propped the door open with her hind end.

"Oh." Landon fidgeted behind the counter. "I bet she bought it off the sketchy dude?"

Charon pulled a notepad out of his coat. "Who is 'the sketchy dude'?" he asked, his inflection perfectly reflecting Landon's even though his voice was flat and emotionless.

Landon and the barista exchanged glances.

"About four months ago, there was a man who was attempting to sell magical artifacts in one of the human farmers' markets." The barista worriedly wiped her hands off on her apron. "It was unusual given that there's a separate market for supernaturals to sell their goods in."

The haze that the lack of sleep had over me evaporated as I realized exactly what she was saying.

By unusual, she means illegal. The supernatural markets and stores are organized meticulously to keep the humans safe and under the illusion that supernaturals are harmless. You can't sell anything magical in Magiford—or in any city—without a special permit.

I uneasily shifted in Noctus's hands, and for once was thankful that he had his arms wrapped around me.

"He disappeared all of a sudden," the barista continued. "We assumed the Curia Cloisters found out about it and put an end to it."

Charon stepped aside when Ker and Aristide re-entered the café, making room for them to join in.

"Was there anything besides the location he was selling in that made him suspicious?" Noctus asked.

"He was weird," Landon said. "Weirder than a werewolf on a harness."

"Landon, you need to let that go," the barista said in a sing-song voice.

"He didn't make a very convincing human," Landon added.

"How?" Aristide asked, his voice serious and compelling.

A thick, syrupy sensation rubbed my nose, which was how vampire powers felt to me. He must have been breaking out his vamp-y pheromones for the occasion.

Aristide is old enough to use pheromones? I would have guessed he'd been turned in the last century or two based on how well he's adapted to modern society. How old is he?

I sneezed twice, and Noctus adjusted my collar on me. Like most magic, pheromones didn't work on me, but the sensation on my nose was ticklish.

"He looked human—he dressed it, too." Landon scratched his elbow and mashed his eyes shut as he tried to remember. "But whenever me or my friends asked him about what he was selling, he copped that 'I'm-better-than-you' attitude that some supernaturals get. And he didn't seem to get how money worked."

"What did he look like?" Charon asked.

"Blond hair, taller than me?" Landon shrugged. "It's been four months, so I don't remember him very well."

Thinking, I leaned into Noctus and set my chin on his shoulder. *With a description that vague, there's no possible way to track the guy down.*

Noctus took a step closer, some of the intensity he'd been keeping locked up slipping through whatever glamour he was using. "What made you think the artifacts he sold were faulty?"

"There were a couple instances where they broke," Landon said. "One singed the eyebrows off a guy who came in here for some coffee. Took weeks for them to grow back in."

Noctus and Charon exchanged glances.

"Four months would line up with when the influx of broken artifacts began," Charon said, his voice quiet.

Noctus inclined his head.

Mathematically speaking, chances are that it's a coincidence, but broken artifacts weren't a problem before this. Still, if the guy disappeared, why are busted artifacts still entering the market? Is he still around? I twitched the tip of my tail as I considered the question.

"What kind of artifacts did this man sell?" Aristide asked.

"Small ones," Landon said. "It varied a lot—jewelry, coins that he claimed were ancient, that kind of thing. It seemed like a tourist trap."

"Do you know for certain the Curia Cloisters got involved?" Noctus asked.

"Well...no, we're just humans. They wouldn't tell us, and that's not the kind of thing they publish in their public newsletter," the barista said. "But the man just disappeared, and no one has seen him in months."

Noctus shifted me from one arm to the other. "I see. Thank you for your information."

Charon again held the door open for Noctus and me, and Ker and Aristide. Once we were all out, Charon headed across the parking lot, to the sidewalk.

Ker and Aristide took a slightly different route so Aristide walked down the incline to place him in the parking lot and then up another incline to get back on the sidewalk so he didn't have to traverse the potentially dangerous curb from the storefront.

Noctus took a more direct, jaywalking route, but once he reached Charon, he stopped and looked back at the café.

The sun had risen higher in the sky, so the sky was no longer the grayish-red of dawn, but a pale blue with some leftover pearly pink from the rising sun.

I was almost swaying with exhaustion, but my thoughts were still occupied with what Landon and the barista had told us.

Back in Noctus's office, Charon said this was affecting more than the elves. I guess this proves it. But why would anyone try this in Magiford? It should be the safest city for a supernatural in the Midwest, that's why I moved here!

The longer I stayed with Noctus, it seemed the more uneasy I felt about the city. But it wasn't truly dangerous, right? Or did I need to think about moving?

The idea reminded me of the tracker, and that he was after me for reasons I didn't know or understand. *He's found me twice now...is he hanging around, waiting for me to leave the scary-safety of Noctus's protection?*

I did a thorough scan of the street, and I didn't see him—or feel that horrible fear he inspired in me. He was gone—for now. At least whoever he was, he definitely was scared of Noctus.

Well, the enemy of my enemy hopefully won't kill me?

"Do you think we'll need to bust into the Curia Cloisters to look at the watch?" Aristide asked once he and Ker reached the sidewalk.

Noctus scratched me under the chin. "At this time, I think we have enough leads that it's unnecessary," Noctus said. "Though that may change in the future."

I sat pliantly in his arms, content to merely exist after having lived on sheer adrenaline for the past...however many days.

I must have been tilting a little dangerously because Noctus supported me with both arms, and I almost fell asleep...until I heard the coo of a pigeon.

No, it couldn't be.

I snapped my eyes open to see my silly trash griffin friend, French Fry, perched on the sign for Queen's Court Café.

"A heist, that will be something to look forward to," Aristide grumbled.

Charon flipped his tiny notebook shut. "Your orders, Your Majesty?"

Noctus adjusted his sunglasses as he considered the question.

Back in the impending accident that was my future, French Fry flung himself into the air and dropped about two feet like a dead weight before his pigeon wings got enough momentum going. He glided over to a nearby no parking sign—he had a thing for signs—and tried to perch on it.

He wobbled dangerously but clung to it with a stubborn determination that made the whole sign shake, before he managed to balance on his raccoon hind end.

His extra round skull seemed even bigger and emptier than normal as he turned his head sideways so he could peer at me, his orange-y-red eyes bulging.

Charon glanced at French Fry, but he must have written him off as not dangerous because he turned his back to the tiny griffin. Ker seemed more interested. Her eyes were bright, and she even wagged her tail a little as she studied him.

"Search for the man the barista described, and find out if he was a supernatural as they thought," Noctus said, drawing me back into their conversation. "I'll need to interview Valaria, but it does appear that our assumption was correct, and someone is selling faulty artifacts."

I cautiously watched French Fry and flicked my tail, trying to convey that he needed to stay away.

"But why sell faulty artifacts to begin with?" Aristide tapped his white cane on the ground for emphasis. "It's a risky business—especially if this supernatural was attempting to sell to humans *and* supernaturals alike. The Curia Cloisters will come down hard on him."

"I don't care why he did it," Noctus said. "I only care about stopping him."

As Noctus had been talking I realized that French Fry was balancing on his raccoon hind end, because—true to his name—he had two french fries clenched in his bird front feet.

No, no, no—French Fry, don't do it!

I meowed at French Fry, a loud, angry sound that made Noctus look up, just as French Fry tossed one of his fries at me.

It hit Noctus in the chest and bounced off him, falling on my front leg that I still had latched on to Noctus's shirt.

French Fry was stupid, but at least he was a crack shot.

Ker gave a little howl of what was clearly laughter, and Noctus seemed to be staring at the french fry nestled into my fur—I couldn't tell for sure since he was wearing his sunglasses.

French Fry cooed his delight that he'd made his shot, then stuffed his remaining fry in his beak and promptly choked.

Aristide tilted his head back, his eyes narrowing as he pointed his face in French Fry's direction, but not quite able to track where the griffin's body was.

"One of the vermin hybrid griffins from the fae Night Court is sitting on a nearby sign and has tossed human...'food' at His Majesty," Charon explained.

"It sounds like it's dying," Aristide said.

"It might be, from its own stupidity." Noctus picked the fry off me and flicked it onto the ground. "It appears to be choking on something."

"Sounds intelligent," Aristide said.

"Very," Noctus said. "Charon, where is the car?"

"I'll pull it around." Charon bowed slightly, then stalked down the sidewalk, disappearing around a corner.

It was quiet for a moment, until French Fry got his airway cleared and started cooing at me again.

"I'm glad you're looking into this yourself," Aristide abruptly said.

Noctus supported me with one arm so he could comb his hand through his hair. "You think I don't work enough?"

"No," Aristide said. "You work too much. It's why everyone has welcomed your cat with a scary amount of enthusiasm. But you're so intent on *repenting* for what you've done, you stay locked up in your home."

Repenting? For what? Isn't he angry about how the elves were wiped out—especially the Mors?

"I'm not repenting," Noctus said. "I did what was necessary."

"I am all too aware of that, my friend," Aristide said.

Ker stretched her head across the gap between the two men, nudging Noctus's side with her nose.

"But doing the right thing doesn't mean you don't carry wounds from it," Aristide continued.

Noctus snorted. "After all our years together, I would think any noble thoughts you had about me would have shattered long ago."

"Oh, don't worry yourself," Aristide said. "I never had any noble thoughts about you to begin with."

"How reassuring."

Aristide grinned, and what maybe could have passed as a half-smile briefly curved on Noctus's lips.

I feel like the more I learn about Noctus, the more confused I am. He's an elf—there's an endless number of things he could and should be repenting for. And yet Aristide—a vampire, *who, by all rights shouldn't be living with an elf—is concerned for him? Bizarre.*

Aristide, Ker, and Noctus turned when a black SUV pulled up to the side of the street—Charon had arrived.

Noctus opened the side door, but before anyone got in, Aristide wrinkled his aquiline nose. "*What* is that retching noise?"

"The trash griffin just puked."

"Charming."

BY THE TIME we got back to Noctus's house, I knew there was no point in trying to escape—for now, anyway.

The collar was a problem—one I didn't know if the Curia Cloisters would be able to help me with depending on the Paragon's angle—the tracker guy was still roaming around with a crossbow, and I was so tired I didn't even mind that Noctus was carrying me around.

Yep, this is as safe as I can get right now. And to think my biggest disappointment used to be that the Curia Cloisters wouldn't hire me.

Charon parked the car in the Cape Cod's garage—which didn't seem to be connected to the villa.

Noctus, Charon, Aristide, and Ker trooped out to the front yard and entered the house through the front door and the mind-bending magical gate. After a brief sensation of darkness and being swung upside down in the void of the gate, we emerged, stepping into the familiar and luxurious hallway.

Aristide undid the buckles of Ker's harness. "Thank you, Kerberos."

Kerberos? Like...the three-headed dog from Greek mythology? Is that her full name, or a nickname?

Ker woofed at him—or at least I suspected it was supposed to be a woof, but it was too musical and throaty to pass as one.

"Charon, send roasted chicken to my room," Noctus ordered as he strode down the hallway, carrying me.

"As you wish, Your Majesty."

"Thanks," Noctus said as the two split off.

Noctus reached the staircase and started climbing it. I hunkered into a mound of fuzz in his arms.

Here we go, back to his room. Who knows how long I'll be stuck in there this time? I guess it doesn't matter right now, though. I'm planning on sleeping.

I sighed as Noctus reached the second floor, then slipped into his room.

He set me down on the ground.

I tottered off to where my bed had been the last time I'd been in his rooms, belatedly realized it wasn't there, then turned in a confused circle.

"You should drink." Noctus nudged my pricey water dish with his toe, then strode across the room, entering his bathroom.

Noctus opened the door and flicked on a light switch, giving me a glance of what I used as my temporary bedroom on the rare occasion that he slept, before he shut the door.

Water, I agreed with him. *Then sleep. Since I can't find my bed, I'll use the chaise lounge.*

By the time I finished drinking, Noctus emerged from the bathroom, this time wearing what looked like some kind of modern fighting gear of black pants and a black vest with pockets that looked handy for storing weapons in.

He saw me aiming for the chaise lounge. "Not there, Amalourne. Come."

Not there? Why not?

I was so tired my paws were dragging, but I followed Noctus, up until he climbed the stairs to his bed and plopped down, then showed me my cat bed that was now positioned by his pillow.

No. No way.

I turned around and tried to run off, but I was clumsy in my exhaustion and tripped over my own paws, giving Noctus the chance to swoop in and pick me up.

"I will give you free rein of the house, Amalourne, since keeping you in one room apparently irritates you, but you are eating and sleeping first." His voice was hypnotically soothing as he carried me back to his mattress.

He settled me down in my bed as if I was made of glass, when someone knocked at the door.

Charon poked his head into the room. "I have the chicken, Your Majesty."

Noctus beckoned for Charon to approach us.

Charon offered out a porcelain dish filled with chicken cut into cat sized pieces, settled on a silver tray.

Noctus took the plate and settled it by my pillow. "Thank you, Charon. That will be all."

He's letting me eat in bed? That seems unsanitary, but I'm too tired to refuse.

I managed a few bites before the overwhelming siren song of sleep—a deep sleep—tugged at me so badly I actually sagged forward and fell face first into my meal.

"Amalourne," Noctus said in what could almost be mistaken as a laugh. He picked me up and leaned back on a pile of pillows, propping me up on his chest, then proceeded to give me tiny bits of chicken.

I'm practically living Joy's dream. She always said her ideal life was to lounge around on an enormous bed and eat delicious food—though she never said anything about handsome supernaturals. Still, even with Noctus, this is pretty fun. Probably because I'm a cat, though, and I'm too tired to be scared. If I was a human this would be...awkward squared.

When I was so exhausted I couldn't even open my mouth anymore, and my belly was bulging, Noctus shifted me back onto my bed.

I was vaguely aware that he slipped from the room before I

passed out, dead to the world, as I finally slept deeply for the first time in days.

I WASN'T sure how long I slept, but it must have been until lunchtime, because when I did wake up it was to Ker carrying a tray of chicken.

"Ama? Are you awake?"

Huh? I pulled my head out from the seam I'd stuffed it in, my hair sticking in different directions. *I'm awake—food!*

I shook my head, then trotted down the stairs, feeling a lot better since I'd eaten and slept.

I had a drink of water and a bite of chicken after Ker put some in my cleaned bowl—I had a feeling I was probably going to be sick of roasted chicken by the time this was over.

For now, though, the food restored my good spirits and ability to think.

Maybe instead of relying on the Curia Cloisters, I'd be able to figure out how to ditch the collar during my sojourn here, but I'd always been conservative when it came to hope, plus, I also had my unwanted stalker to deal with. But if I was hanging out in Noctus's villa, maybe he'd give up?

As long as I can get back to Book Nookery within two weeks, since that's the time frame I pitched to Ms. Booker. It was doable. It had to be.

Ker watched, confirming I'd eaten a little, then stepped up onto the edge of Noctus's reflective pool and stared down into it.

Curious, I joined her, putting my front feet on the ledge and peering over the side.

"Wondering what I'm doing, Ama?" Ker crouched down, easily balancing with her werewolf athleticism. "I'll tell you! I'm doing self-affirmations."

She pointed to her reflection in the pond. "Do you see that

wolf? She's a strong, kind wolf. She is confident, motivated, and smart, and has wonderful fur and a good nose. And she's me!"

I stared up at Ker.

Does a werewolf really need confidence building exercises? They're apex predators.

Apparently, they did.

Ker jabbed her finger at the water again. "We're going to kick some butt and have a great day! The magic pool wills it!" Ker whispered to me. "The pool isn't really magic. Aristide just says that to rib Noctus about the questionable architecture that goes into having a pool in one's room. Aristide hates the pool because when we first moved into the villa, he fell in twice before he learned the layout of the room."

I licked my chops, thankful for the information, but also a little confused why everyone in this house was so okay with talking to a housecat, when most likely none of them had any experience with domesticated animals.

The door opened, and Noctus stepped in. Taking Ker's pose, he asked, "Already trying to recruit my cat for your Dale Carnegie cult?"

"*How to Win Friends and Influence People* is a classic!" Ker said.

"I'm not convinced. Did she eat anything?"

"Just a little chicken. I think she's full." Ker hopped off the edge of the pool and inspected my bowl.

I meowed and sauntered up to Noctus, continuing my "Win His Trust" campaign now that I was stuck here. I rubbed my face on his black pants and purred.

Noctus unfortunately took that as an invitation to pick me up—something I wasn't overly fond of now that I was fully functioning again.

"How was the release?" Ker asked.

Release? Release of what? A book?

Noctus shrugged, not even wincing when I accidentally

clawed him while I tried to climb higher up his torso. "It was fine."

I made it all the way up to his shoulders, crouching low on them—though I was careful to keep my tail out of his face.

When my siblings walked around with me on their shoulders, they complained a lot that I'd get cat hair up their noses, and I did *not* want to insult the elf king in a similar manner, particularly when I was hopeful he'd let me stay in this position. I was a lot more comfortable on his shoulders—where I could control my movement and spring off him—than in his arms, where I depended on him not to drop me.

Noctus reached up and tickled me under my chin, then turned to the door, heading for the hallway. "Charon has located the elf, Valaria, who had the exploding pocket watch and is taking her to a parlor."

Ker trotted after us, closing the door to Noctus's bedroom when we stepped into the hallway. "Do you want me to come with you? I assume you'll talk to her now?"

"Yes—your lie detection skills would be a boon, though I don't expect she has anything to lie about."

Werewolves had such strong senses, they could literally sniff out biological/chemical changes in a body, and they could hear things like increased heartbeat, rapid breathing, stuff like that.

It was hard to lie to a wolf as a result. It could be done, but only if you could keep your cool.

"Very well, then," Ker said. "I'd be happy to sniff her out for you."

"Thank you." Noctus descended the stairs, going more slowly than usual—I think for my sake.

I purred when we reached the bottom of the stairs, and Noctus held his hand up—palm to me.

I blinked as I stared at his palm, noticing the callouses. *I wish he'd just say whatever he wants me to do. He seems pretty fixated with this.*

"What are you doing?" Ker asked, sharing in my confusion.

"I'm trying to teach Ama a trick," Noctus said.

You want to teach a cat *a trick?* It was only because of my abilities/magical balance that I didn't fall off his shoulder in surprise.

"I read that cats are capable of learning such things, and that it can be good for mental stimulation," Noctus continued.

"Cool. What are you trying to teach her?"

"High five."

High five? That's what you've been trying to get me to do? Wow. For a superiorly intelligent race, five minutes of watching a YouTube video on teaching tricks to cats would have made this so much easier for both of us.

"Aww, that will be adorable!"

"Perhaps, except she doesn't seem to understand it," Noctus said.

Ker tapped her chin in thought. "Did you ever explain it to her?"

"I have not. That is my mistake." Noctus tilted his head, moving his shoulders and forcing me forward so he could see my furry face. "Ama, when I hold out my hand, I want you to tap your paw against it—in a high five."

If Aristide had been around, he would have surely had something to say, but Ker and Noctus were so convinced of my genius as a cat, all they did was watch me with great expectation.

I should probably just go for it. I think he'd be more suspicious if I didn't react...

I crouched even lower on his shoulder and, reluctantly, stretched my paw out. I didn't try to tap his palm—I figured even proud pet parent Noctus might get suspicious if I caught on that fast.

But it didn't matter, Noctus moved his hand so his palm pressed mine. "High five," he repeated, then he scratched my chest.

"See?" Ker said. "She's smart, she just needs a little help."

Before Noctus could agree, Charon emerged from an inlet in

the hallway, wearing his usual hood and linen clothes—maybe it was the clothes he had enchanted for silence?

"Your Majesty," Charon began. "The Paragon is here to see you."

Noctus sighed. "Ker, could you go ahead to Valaria?"

"Thanks for taking one for the team. Good luck." Ker's forehead wrinkled in a rare sign of concern. She nodded to Charon, then trotted off, heading up the hallway.

Noctus turned toward the front of the house—although with all the magical windows and things I couldn't be sure it was the front, but it was in the direction of the front door of the Cape Cod home—and stalked down the hallway with enough irritation to make a cat proud.

Wait, are you seriously taking me to go see the Paragon? Have you thought this through?

My fur started to puff up with my nerves.

It wasn't that I thought he'd recognize me. While the Seelie and Unseelie Courts knew all about me, there was no way someone as powerful as the Paragon had been informed of the random, unidentifiable human supernatural who could turn into a cat.

But! I don't like meeting powerful people! They're playing in a game division I want to stay leagues away from!

"Did the Paragon just arrive?" Noctus asked.

"He's been here for several minutes—I had time to serve him refreshments," Charon said.

"And you didn't think to inform me until now?"

Charon ducked his head. "I apologize. I sent a message to your cell phone, but I believe you left it in your study."

Cell phones work in the fae realm? But mine only has one bar in my apartment.

From the way Noctus eyed Charon, I was guessing it was a lame excuse, but he didn't say anything when he stopped outside an ornate door.

This is my stop, thank you.

I tried to abandon ship, but Noctus reached up and put a firm hand on my shoulder blades—pinning me in place—before he flung the door open.

I recognized the room from my late-night non-fiction reading adventures at Book Nookery as a "drawing room", because family rooms were for peasants.

Gold curtains pulled away from enormous windows that were more than twice as tall as I was in my human body. Outside there was a view of part of the city, and the mountains extending past, which confused me even more about the physics of the villa.

The walls were plain white, though I was pretty sure that was only because the place would have been unbelievably gaudy otherwise.

Four chandeliers hung from the cathedral ceiling, which was decorated with fleurs-de-lis that I was fairly certain were leafed in pure gold. There was not one, but *three* of the ever-present marble fireplaces, and the floor was covered with a dark aqua rug ornamented with budding gold flowers.

All the furniture was gold with golden tasseled pillows, and gold leafed carvings in the arms and legs of the chairs and tables.

Perched on one of the gold chairs, sipping from a delicate cup of tea, was a wizened old man: the Paragon.

I saw what the rest of the world saw for about two seconds: long, silky white hair and a well-groomed mustache that drooped past his chin, eyes magnified by the wire rimmed glasses that were perilously perched on the end of his sharp nose, and a stooped posture.

And then the overwhelming sensation of magic swamped my senses like a bad allergy attack, making my eyes water and tickling my nose until I sneezed.

Hold the payroll—the Paragon is wearing a glamour?! And a glamour so strong I didn't immediately see through it?

My magic surged in me, working to disassemble the glamour

to my eyes. Thankfully, I was still sneezing, so I didn't see through it.

I didn't *want* to see through it. The Paragon was using such strong magic, I couldn't even tell what kind it was. If he was that desperate to keep whatever he was hiding a secret, I was going to be doubly desperate *not* to see it.

Elf king with a city sized secret, or the national fae rep with a personal mystery, I didn't want to get involved in either. Most people assume that with the right knowledge, they can pressure someone in power and maybe blackmail them.

I knew better.

Stop, stop, stop! I grappled with my magic, trying to stop it. *This could get me killed!*

Between the sheer strength of the glamour and me managing to suppress my magic enough, when I opened my bleary eyes I saw what the Paragon wanted everyone to see: an old fae in dark blue robes with a spell woven into the fabric that made the cloth glitter.

My magic shivered, and I could sense it was going to peel back the glamour if I gave it a chance, so I squinted hard and tried not to acknowledge the overwhelming magic.

It was then that Noctus stepped into the room, and the Paragon naturally turned his gaze to the elf king. When he caught sight of me—still perched on Noctus's shoulders—his eyes bulged, and he spat out his tea, spraying it across the gold and white table positioned in front of him.

CHAPTER TWELVE

Chloe

For a second, I was terrified he'd realized what I was.

"You have a *cat?*" the Paragon blurted.

Good, good, good. I am so glad I'm such a non-happening in the supernatural scene he couldn't possibly know I exist. I can do this—as long as I can beat off my magic!

Noctus raised an eyebrow.

Charon did not take the Paragon's display as serenely. He didn't make a noise, but two wrinkles appeared around his eyes, signaling his severe displeasure. "Please. Allow me." He walked twice as fast as Noctus and pulled some kind of white kerchief from his cloak, which he used to mop at the mess the Paragon had made.

Noctus sat down on a settee, which I took advantage of and hopped from his shoulders to a cushion.

Okay. I've got certain death next to me, and probable death across from me. If I don't die from making a mistake, my anxiety might make my heart explode.

I wanted to run, but I knew Noctus expected me to be

besotted by whatever his mysterious powers were—I would have looked that magic up if I'd known I was going to play pet cat for the foreseeable future.

I risked glancing at the Paragon again. My powers had settled down enough that if I squinted, I could hold on to the glamour the fae put on display. *I guess I better stick around for a few minutes.* Reluctantly, I sat down on the cushion and curled my tail around my paws.

Noctus, seemingly satisfied I hadn't fled, placed a hand on my back. "What do you want, Paragon?"

"No, no, no, no. We are going to discuss this beautiful creature." The Paragon gestured to me.

"She's mine," Noctus said.

The Paragon slapped his palms on the most likely priceless and half cleaned/slightly tea spattered table. "Obviously—a feline this friendly is not likely to belong to Sir Grumps A Lot over there." He nodded his head at Charon, who was folding his kerchief with obvious disgust.

Friendly? How am I friendly? I tilted my head a little, then meowed for the effect.

"My lady." The Paragon held his hand out for me to smell, then bowed, except he was already stretching so far to reach me he almost had to press his face into the table to perform the bow.

I did *not* want to get anywhere near him when he was packing such a powerful glamour, but I didn't have much of a choice, so I reluctantly sniffed his fingers, feeling the silky fae magic that wrapped tight around him like a robe that was present under whatever overpowering glamour spell he was using.

Noctus didn't frown—his expression didn't even change—but I could feel the quiet intensity of his elf magic despite the magic shackles on him, so when I finished sniffing the Paragon, I scooted a little closer to Noctus.

Noctus took this as an invitation to pick me up, but he didn't seem to mind when I dug my claws into the fabric of his black utility vest as he set me against his chest, angling me so I could put a paw on either side of his neckline as I liked to do.

It's weird how thoughtful he is about a cat when—

"You get cat hugs? That's not fair! Aphrodite won't even hug me like that—how did you get her to do it?" the Paragon demanded.

I was assuming, based on the context, that Aphrodite had to be a cat—but the thought barely flickered through my mind before the Paragon's large nose filled my vision. He had seemingly teleported from his chair to behind the settee so he could poke his head up over Noctus's shoulder and peer down at me, startling me so badly my fur puffed up.

Noctus tried scratching my chin, but I was too weirded out by the Paragon—who was now jutting out his lower lip in a pout, which was pretty weird looking for someone who appeared to be older than my grandparents—to even pretend to purr.

I shrank back a little from the Paragon's scrutiny, pressing my furry face into Noctus's neck. *Why me? I just wanted to live a safe life!*

"Wait—you don't even know why she does it, do you?" the Paragon guessed. "You're a first-time pet owner if I ever saw one—you're too stunted with your actions and haven't gotten used to her yet. Not to mention you are quite obviously jealous and proud."

"You are obscenely covetous and proud of your bald cat," Noctus said.

"Yes, because Aphrodite is a beautiful feline and deserves all the admiration in the world!"

"She is also overweight, which I've read is highly detrimental to felines."

"You take that back!" the Paragon shrilly shouted.

This is swerving off my worst nightmares and turning into something just...weird.

Noctus was still trying to get a purr out of me, but I was not having it—this whole situation was too bizarre.

Noctus sighed—a dangerous sound that made me freeze where I was. "Sit down, Paragon, and ask what you came here for."

"Fine, fine, fine. You're no fun." The Paragon sulked all the way back to his seat and flopped down with none of the grace that usually adorned the movements of fae-kind.

The Paragon picked up his mostly empty teacup and peered into it for a moment. His eyes strayed to Charon, who was standing by the door, then he jerked them back to Noctus.

There was something about his eyes. They were wise and intelligent with the typical twinkling of fae cunning, but there was also something *youthful* to them, which was more apparent as my magic started to burn away at the glamour again.

Nope—no. I'm not looking—I'm not going to notice anything!

I pointed my head away from the fae and sneezed again from the ticklish sensation of the overwhelming magic.

"I'm here for my monthly request—no, my monthly begging session." The Paragon's voice hardened into a serious timbre, and his smile morphed into something painful. "Please, King Noctus. Tell me where she is."

She? Wait—I don't want to know this either! I peeled myself off Noctus and jumped back down to the spot next to him.

"As I have told you every time you've come here, I don't know," Noctus said.

"Hogwash. You know perfectly well where she is." The Paragon scoffed and looked away. He took a moment to massage his wrinkled forehead, then turned back to Noctus. "*Why* can't you tell me where she is, elf king?"

Noctus mutely watched the Paragon.

I, considering an escape plan, peered past Noctus to the door where Charon stood.

Charon was looking curious—or at least as curious as Charon

would let himself be—with his eyebrows set maybe a fraction higher than usual, and the set of his mouth not so sharp. He didn't even pull up the hood of his cloak though it had drooped down over his shoulders.

"We *need* her. Desperately," the Paragon said. "She might be the key to saving us all."

I don't want to hear this. I'm not hearing this.

"Perhaps, but that doesn't mean I know where she is," Noctus dryly said. "I'm not only from the line of Mors, but I am *the* Kingslayer. If I were to meet another elf—an unlikely thing considering not many survived the war—they would hate and fear me as much as any other supernatural would."

Wait, does that mean the Paragon doesn't know about the elf city? Because the way Noctus phrased that is pretty misleading. Also, Kingslayer?

That sounded ominous, but the whole meeting had me sky-high on anxiety, so even that kind of title couldn't do much more to bother me.

Regardless, it's time to leave.

I stood up and stretched. Neither supernatural looked at me —an excellent start!

A long-suffering sigh that lasted a good ten seconds leaked out of the Paragon, and he slumped in his chair. "Fine. Keep your secrets. I know better than to hope for a true answer anyway."

I'd made it to the far side of the settee, when the Paragon abruptly tilted to the side and fell to the floor, then crawled around the table and poked his head up over the arm of the settee so he could peer down at me.

"But you'll have to share at some point," the Paragon continued. "The speed at which wild magic is dying has rapidly increased over the past decade. Magic is failing."

I casually studied my paws like I was contemplating licking them. The slow death of magic didn't affect me much. With no magical support besides Ms. Booker and maybe French Fry, I didn't have the opportunity to witness the effects. Besides, I was too concerned with surviving and not getting my human family involved.

"If it gets much worse, even *you* won't be able to survive, Noctus." The Paragon dug into a pocket of his robe and pulled out a tuft of feathers tied to a string—a cat toy.

He dangled the feathers in front of me.

Maybe I should bat at it—to be obliging. Woah!

The Paragon abruptly flopped to the floor, disappearing from sight.

I peered over the edge of the settee as he shuffled around so he was on his back. He beamed up at me and thrust his fist up into the air, shaking the feathers in front of me.

Baffled by this bizarre behavior, I turned to Noctus, relieved to see he was also staring at the Paragon, though his look held as much regard as I'd hold for a bug.

"*What* are you doing?" Noctus's words burned with incredulity.

"I'm putting myself lower so your companion—whose name you have neglected to share with me—can be put at ease seeing that she is in a superior position above me."

Things are looking up—maybe he's insane!

I turned away from the Paragon and the edge of the settee, intending to jump over the backrest of the settee and walk myself away.

Whatever they were talking about—some elf lady, wait, no, I didn't even want to know that much—I didn't want to hear it. All I needed to figure out was how to get the collar off and who the tracker was, and they weren't very likely to talk about that.

I crouched, but before I could jump, Noctus picked me up, stood, then placed me on his shoulders.

I balanced there, tempted to wail my disappointment at my foiled exit. *Drat your intense pet-ownership!*

"Leave my cat alone," Noctus told the Paragon. "I don't want you traumatizing her with your weirdness." He strode over to the sideboard, where a porcelain tea set was arranged.

The Paragon popped into a kneeling position, his glasses askew. "How dare you!" He made a show of dusting his robes off, but his outrage faded as his posture grew taller. "It is getting bad out there, Your Majesty." He adjusted his glasses, and I could again see just how *dangerous* the Paragon was despite his loony act. "Soon, it will touch even you in your gilded halls once things get bad enough."

He didn't mention the city. I'd say that means my guess that he doesn't know is right. I braced myself on Noctus's shoulders as he poured himself a cup of tea.

"Things are not nearly as bad in Magiford," Noctus said. "Magic seems to have rebounded a little, even. Why else do you think I'm here?"

The Paragon narrowed his eyes. "I don't know, but I wish I did."

Noctus's lips shaped into a smile that didn't reach his eyes as he picked up his tea and returned to the settee.

"Things have gotten marginally better," the Paragon said. "I have my own theories as to why that is."

"But you are not going to share them?"

"Not as long as you refuse to tell me where *she* is."

Noctus elegantly sat down on the settee despite balancing me, his tea, and the untold number of weapons he carried on his person during the process. "I cannot tell you what I don't know. But if you choose to be stubborn in this way, that is your own burden to bear. I am content to live where wild magic is starting to regrow."

The Paragon flopped back into his seat, this time with a grunt. "Wild magic might be doing better, but the city itself has become increasingly more and more on edge as supernaturals do stupid things in their fears over the end of magic and their greed for power."

I'm becoming more on edge, I gloomily thought. *I thought Magiford was safe. Now I know there are elves running around and the top fae rep is wearing a glamour thick enough to choke a dragon shifter with. Safety is an illusion.*

"Is there something in particular you are referring to?"

"Not specifically—though the Seelie and Unseelie Courts and their endless posturing is enough to make me pack my bags." The Paragon scowled.

Oh, they are the least of the problems, please let me assure you.

"Isn't there a candidate for fae emperor for the first time in decades?" Noctus asked. "Tell the candidate about it and save yourself—and the city—the extra trouble they're causing."

For the past few decades it had been assumed that the idea of a fae emperor was going to die out—one of the first signs of magic's slow death.

The fae emperor was a fae king or queen who managed to unite all the Courts in every region beneath them—a very different position from the Paragon who merely represented fae interests on a national scale and didn't belong to any specific Court.

The idea of a fae emperor had been especially contentious as the fae Courts grew more selfish and unable to work together... until a half-human-half-fae named Leila was crowned Queen of the Night Court and changed everything.

The Paragon frowned. "You seem to be personally affronted by the Seelie and Unseelie Courts."

"They make for annoying neighbors." Noctus raised his hand to pet me.

The Paragon shrugged. "That's one way of putting it. And yes, there is a possible fae emperor—or empress, as it is. But Queen Leila is occupied with rapidly solidifying her power base. Half of the United States is under her control, and she's barely able to keep up with it. As it stands, securing her title is more important than the spats between the local Seelie and Unseelie.

The smaller Courts will have to last a little longer without her attention."

Noctus started to shrug, then seemingly remembered I was still on his shoulders, so he settled into place. "If they bother me too much, I will have to correct them."

I stepped down from Noctus's shoulders onto the back of the settee, my tail twitching as I balanced there.

This time, when Noctus tried to pet me, I rubbed my cheek against his finger and purred. He seemed satisfied with this, so he didn't try to grab me when I jumped off the back of the furniture piece.

"They're scared—the supernaturals who haven't had strong leaders step in, that is. It's the small things—like the breaking artifacts—that rattle them most because those are things they're forced to face," the Paragon said.

"You've heard of the breaking artifacts?" Noctus asked in a voice that was so casual it was almost bored.

Wow, yeah, Noctus is deadly not just with weapons, but acting, too.

I padded up to Charon, who was standing in front of the closed drawing room door and staring at the opposite wall like a statue.

"Of course," the Paragon said. "Since I'm playing parley for the Seelie and Unseelie while Queen Leila is otherwise occupied."

That got my attention, before I realized, no, I didn't have to worry. The Unseelie and Seelie fae saw me as a plaything. If the Paragon was parleying between the Courts, I wasn't going to come up in the discussion. He didn't know about me or my abilities...I hoped.

"I've heard of *every single* broken artifact the two Courts have had the past few months." The Paragon rubbed his forehead and frowned. "Of course, each Court is accusing the other of sabotaging them. But I suspect there's more to the matter given how badly it is affecting both sides."

That means the Courts, at least, aren't involved in this bad artifact business. I sat down in front of Charon, but he still didn't seem to notice me.

"I heard rumor of a supernatural dressing as a human who attempted to sell faulty magical goods—though he disappeared some time ago," Noctus said.

"If there was, I haven't heard anything of it—though there must be a seller who is behind all of this," the Paragon said.

That kills the theory that the Curia Cloisters took care of the seller. The Paragon would have known about him if that was the case.

"I see. Good to know the leadership in the Curia Cloisters is being proactive," Noctus said.

"Nothing has hurt the vampires or wizards yet. As soon as that happens, they'll move. I promise it!"

With my nerves fraying and my eyes still burning from the Paragon's glamour, I was overplaying the role of cherished pet. I peered up at Charon and meowed as loudly as I could.

Charon gazed down at me, but instead of letting me outside like I wanted, he picked me up, carried me back to the settee, then set me down next to Noctus.

I placed my paws on the back of the settee so I could peer over it and watched as Charon returned to his place by the door as I twitched my tail back and forth.

Before I could come up with a new plan, Noctus picked me up and again placed me in his lap, seemingly determined to keep me with him.

My magic is about to poke through the Paragon's glamour any moment, and they're talking about stuff I shouldn't know for the sake of survival. If I can't leave...I suppose I could pretend to sleep?

I tucked my paws under my body, then wrapped my tail up tight so nothing was sticking out before I closed my eyes so I wouldn't see the Paragon.

Noctus and the Paragon's conversation continued. I didn't know whether it was my determination not to hear anything, or the exhaustion from what I'd been living through, but the deep rumbles of Noctus's voice slowly soothed me into a doze, and I fell asleep.

A DAY PASSED, and I knew I needed to slip out and change into a human—even just for a moment.

It wasn't that I was going to try to run away—nope, the collar was still stuck firmly on my neck, so that was useless—but because I needed to text message my siblings back.

After everything I'd learned about what was going down in Magiford, I didn't want them anywhere near here. But if I didn't work out a system that let me frequently text them, I was going to be in trouble.

Thankfully, it would be easier this time as Noctus had started giving me free range of the house—though whenever Charon or Ker found me, they always carried me off to Noctus for some reason I hadn't been able to discern yet.

I sat outside of Noctus's study, having just slipped out after spending the last hour being a "good cat" since Ker had dumped me on Noctus's desk.

I'd also taken the opportunity to snoop around his bookshelves and see if there was anything that could help me with my collar—because whatever spell Noctus had used was almost *certainly* recorded in one of the books—but unfortunately the two shelves of books I'd gotten to explore were all written in *Elvish!* At least I assumed it was Elvish. Whatever language it was, I couldn't read it.

Since the books were proving fruitless, I'd taken the opportunity to slip out. Now, I had an estimated thirty minutes before anyone would think to look for me again, and I needed to use them wisely.

I can't open the windows of Noctus's office while he's in there, obviously, but I'm not sure I can get through the magic gate.

Still, it would be the easiest option, so I trotted down the hallway to investigate.

The golden gate radiated magic, but when I cautiously pawed at it, nothing happened besides my paw tingling.

It had a bunch of convenient, cat sized holes in the design, so I took a risk and pushed my head through. I felt the weird swirl of magic that physically moved me as I stepped through the gate, then slammed into the closed front door of the Cape Cod house.

Well. This certainly complicates things.

Sitting in the doorframe—sandwiched between the door and the gate—I could see that the Cape Cod house thankfully had a lever style doorknob, which was the easiest kind to open as a cat.

It took some ungainly hopping, but I was able to grab the tip of the lever and pull it down. As soon as the door clicked—apparently elves didn't worry about strangers walking into the house, but given what I'd seen Noctus, Charon, Ker, and Aristide do, I wouldn't be worried about it either—I stuck my nose in the narrow gap and pushed the front door open, just wide enough to let myself out.

I bumped the door so it was mostly shut, then trotted down the sidewalk and hopped through the spokes of the wrought iron fence. I hotfooted it down the street, heading deeper into the cul-de-sac as I searched for a safe place to transform.

I found it four houses down, where someone had let a lilac bush swallow up their mailbox, providing lots of thick, leafy coverage.

I crouched down and triple checked no one was around.

The only people outside were the cute blond across the street from Noctus and the porch full of elderly gawkers, but I was well hidden from them in the bush.

So I tapped my powers and changed, becoming a human—again, *still* in the same clothes I'd worked two shifts in.

I slipped out of the bush, fixed my white, flower patterned scarf around my throat to hide the still present collar, and then casually walked up the sidewalk, fumbling to find my phone so I could start replying to my siblings.

As usual Joy had sent me a cat picture of the day—this one of a black kitten that had a faceful of yogurt.

Hah, look. It's 1 of ur baby pictures, Pat had texted.

Very funny, I said. *Almost as funny as that time Mom and Dad grounded you both for a month after you showed me off to your friends as your new pet kitten*, I typed back.

You were so cute as a baby, Joy wrote.

Truth. what happened? Pat texted. *Kidding!* he added before our sister could swoop to my rescue.

Since my siblings were older, we'd gotten into all kind of cat-related shenanigans—not just shelter-related ones, either. Once, one of Joy's exes stole me, thinking I was her beloved pet cat since her phone had tons of photos of my cat form—mostly so if I got taken they could easily put up missing cat posters within hours. Pat broke into the guy's place that afternoon to try to free me, but I'd already broken myself out and was trotting home.

Fun times.

I shot off a quick text to my parents before I realized I was about a house away from Noctus's Cape Cod. So I crossed the street to avoid it. I was going to make a loop to the front of the cul-de-sac, change back into a cat there, then come back, but in the meantime I didn't want to tempt fate.

I made another attempt to straighten my clothes, then adjusted my scarf as I peered up at the sun. It was good to be outside and to stretch for a bit. As giant as Noctus's villa was, I missed the sunshine.

"Good morning!"

Surprised by the greeting, I paused on the sidewalk. "Good morning."

It was the neighbor across the street—the pretty blond who was very diligent with her lawn, even though she looked a tad young to be a homeowner.

Probably her parents' place. She looks a couple years younger than I am.

She was holding an old weedwacker and was wearing grass-stained jeans and a faded t-shirt, but her smile was bright and the warmth of her personality leaked through her eyes. "I don't think I've seen you before—are you new to the area?" Her voice hitched hopefully as she set her weedwacker down and approached her hip high, white picket fence.

"No." I smiled—the gesture much more anemic and wan than the neighbor's bright grin—as I tried to come up with a believable reason. "I'm just visiting friends in the area, and I wanted to take a quick walk."

"That's a shame—we could use some younger people in the cul-de-sac." She snapped her fingers.

"Speak for yourself, you whippersnapper!" The shout came from one of the elderly neighbors crowded onto the porch of the house next door.

The three older men—all of them wearing suspenders and baseball caps—perched in wicker furniture on the porch cackled to each other, then toasted themselves with sweating glasses of iced tea.

"Aww, you know I love you, Uncle!" the blond neighbor laughed.

"You love me like a toothache!"

"Or like the sweets that give you a toothache?" The young lady wiggled her eyebrows at him, then turned back to me. "I'm Shiloh, by the way." Shiloh wiped her hand off on her shirt, then held it out.

She was so nice and inviting, I was reaching to shake her hand before I was even aware of it. "I'm Chloe," I said.

"Chloe—that's a cute name." Shiloh leaned back, her smile turning playful as she shook a finger at me. "And you're a supernatural, aren't you?"

My mouth dropped, and I gaped at her, shocked.

H-how? Did she see me transform?

"You are!" Shiloh laughed in delight. "I didn't know for sure, but I had a hunch! Don't worry—I know better than to ask you what you are. It wouldn't be polite!"

"How did you know?" I asked.

Shiloh tilted her head. "It wasn't anything in particular. I've always been good at picking out supernaturals. There's some kind of...aura? Or feeling? I can just tell—it's the magic, I think. You were the hardest supernatural I've ever picked out. It didn't even occur to me you were one until we shook hands."

She must have wizard blood in her—or something else. Supernaturals aren't supposed to be able to feel me.

"If you're a supernatural, I assume you live here in Magiford? Or are you just visiting?" Shiloh tucked a strand of her blond hair that had fallen out of its ponytail behind her ear.

"I live in Magiford," I said. "I moved here a few years ago. Though I don't live in this area—I've got an apartment that's more north." I peered up and down the road. I swear I could feel Noctus and his simmering power, but I didn't see him at all.

"Another local—how fun! I grew up here—even though my family was just normal humans." Shiloh scrunched up her nose. "It's a little boring. But I love my neighborhood—don't I, uncles?"

The elderly men on the porch rattled their iced teas at her.

"You love it a little too much," one of the men shouted. "You should be out dating, or bettering your mind or—" He turned to his friends. "What was that other poetic nonsense we got in our fortune cookies last night?"

I laughed and rubbed my arms, which were pebbling with goosebumps as I swore I could feel Noctus's knife-like magic in my ribs. *Yeah, Noctus is close by. I better get out of here as soon as I get the chance.*

Another one of the men pointed with a thin, knobby finger at Shiloh's lawn. "You missed a spot!"

"I still love you, uncles!" Shiloh shook her head a little, but the set of her lips was fond as she turned back to me.

"It was nice to meet you and...your neighbors?" I guessed.

"Oh, just call them uncles. They're a little gruff, but they mean well! Our whole neighborhood is friendly. Isn't that right, Mr. Shade?"

"Shiloh."

I jumped at the sound of Noctus's deep voice coming from directly behind me.

CHAPTER THIRTEEN

Chloe

"I've told you before to call me Noctus. Who is your friend?" Noctus's eyes flicked to me, and he cocked his head. "The clerk from Book Nookery?"

"Book Nookery?" Shiloh asked. "Why bring up a bookshop?"

Noctus's presence still had me frozen, but my loyalty—and training—to Book Nookery kicked my mouth into gear without my brain's supervision. "Book Nookery is a twenty-four-hour bookstore open for your convenience—whether you finished binge reading a book in the middle of the night and need the next one in the series, or require a source for a research paper due the following morning, we're dedicated to all of your bookish needs," I recited, the speech engraved on my heart. "Although we specialize in books for the supernatural, Book Nookery is a human friendly business and was voted top bookstore in Magiford after a brutal battle with Cat Tails—a bookstore-café combo."

I shut my mouth so hard my teeth clicked, cutting off the spew of words Ms. Booker had made me memorize. (She'd been extremely competitive about the voting. I wasn't sure Cat Tails even knew the competition had happened, much less cared, given that they catered to a totally different clientele and were located near the Curia Cloisters.)

Deep breathing—that's the key. I inhaled deeply through my nose, trying to calm my frantically beating heart.

"You said we, so you work there? That's so fun!" Shiloh said.

"If you don't know that much about her, then you're not friends?" Noctus asked.

He wasn't wearing his sunglasses—he didn't have to, he'd cast a low-grade glamour on himself that covered up the eerie swirl to his eyes, and made his ears appear human. With my abilities that automatically canceled such magic, I had to squint to see it. But when he looked at me, I could feel the probe of his magic—as shackled as it was.

Don't be suspicious. Just. Be. Normal!

"No." My laugh was canned and hysterical sounding. "I just met Shiloh while out on a walk."

"I was hoping she was a new neighbor. It'd be a miracle to get someone my age in this area," Shiloh said.

"I'm your age," Noctus said in a voice that was even less convincing than my laugh.

Shiloh's smile was sympathetic, but I couldn't help letting my disbelief that he was *that* inept flicker across my face, making my mouth screw up and my forehead wrinkle.

Noctus tilted his head as he studied me, his mouth curving slightly.

"Mr. Shade, you are *not* my age," Shiloh said. "I don't know how old you are, but you've looked the same since you moved into the neighborhood—and I wasn't even a teenager then!" She peered over her shoulder at the uncles, then leaned over the fence. "Besides, I know you're a supernatural, even if I can't figure out what kind you are. Back me up, Chloe!"

Shiloh—as frightening as a bunny—turned to me, along with

Noctus, who raised both of his eyebrows and had probably committed my name to his memory banks with my luck.

"Uhh." I looked back and forth between the two. "Maybe he just has a good skincare routine?"

Interested, Shiloh swung her gaze back to Noctus. "Actually, that is a pretty good point. Do you moisturize, or is this just a side effect of your magic?"

Noctus stared at me for a moment longer. I could feel him measuring me, so I almost collapsed with relief when he looked back at Shiloh. "I'm sure I have no idea what you're talking about."

I wiped sweat from my forehead and tried to plan an exit. Unfortunately, Noctus was blocking my pathway out of the cul-de-sac, and retreating back to the bush wasn't an option with so many people watching.

I needed to bide my time, or try to move around him if my heart could handle it.

If I don't do anything that raises his suspicions, I'll be okay. Besides, I know personally that he's kind—no, that's taking it too far—gentle—nope, not that either. Uhh...reasonable enough to hand feed a cat and hold it like a baby. Surely, that means he's not—

Noctus happened to meet my eyes, and I could see his intense, spiral eyes through his glamour.

Nope! Nope, he is the King of the Mors Elves—the king of death!

"What brings you outside today, Mr. Shade?" Shiloh asked.

"I'm looking for my cat," Noctus said.

"Oh—I think I saw her! You said she was black when you told me all about her, right? She went down the cul-de-sac," Shiloh said.

Noctus looked, but unfortunately didn't move. "Thank you. I'm sure she's fine, but I don't want her wandering too far, as she had when I met you, Chloe, at Book Nookery."

"She made it that far? Wow—she can cover distance!" Shiloh said.

"She does seem to be a cat graced with an abnormal amount of stamina," Noctus said.

The conversation was making me uncomfortable enough to step off the curb and walk in the street for a few paces. "I hope you find your cat, but I should be getting back to my friends," I said.

"Oh, of course! You have a great day, Chloe." Shiloh waved before she picked up her weedwacker again.

"Thank you, it was nice to meet you." I smiled at Shiloh, then scooted a few steps up the sidewalk.

The elation of freedom beckoned me on, and I felt my steps grow lighter—

"Chloe. Allow me to walk with you."

Only to come crashing down when Noctus caught up with me with one step of his longer legs.

"Oh, um, what about your cat?" I nervously asked. "Don't you want to find her?"

"It doesn't seem she's interested in leaving the area," Noctus said.

"What?" I said, lost, until I remembered his unfortunate tracking spell.

Even if he's not able to pinpoint my location, he can at least tell that I'm staying in the same area, darn it. I can't go very far, or then the spell might *tell him the cat is moving!*

I slowed my walk to a crawl and even paused to wave to the uncles on the porch.

"Finally, a love life!" one of the uncles cackled.

"Maybe." Another one who had a perfectly trimmed mustache swirled his iced tea. "Looks a tad too scared for love."

"Don't worry, Noctus," the first uncle shouted. "We'll be there for you if this fails!"

"I was actually referring to the young lady."

"Oh, in that case: chin up, lady!" the last uncle hooted. "You can take him!"

I laughed nervously and weakly waved to the trio.

"So...you're a supernatural," Noctus said.

I was very proud of myself that I didn't wheeze at Noctus's calm observation. "What makes you say that?"

"You work at Book Nookery, and Shiloh mentioned that I was a supernatural in front of you," Noctus said. "She'd never do that if you weren't a supernatural as well—she's very aware of when one of us is attempting to keep our true selves hidden behind a front." His voice was...different.

I couldn't put a finger on how it had changed, but there was something about his tone that was different from when he spoke to Ker, Aristide, Charon, or even Shiloh.

"Well, I am a supernatural," I admitted—it was impossible to say otherwise when I'd confirmed it to Shiloh.

Noctus narrowed his eyes. "Wizard?" he guessed.

"A subset, yes," I said.

There was a moment of silence. "You aren't going to ask what I am?"

"That would be rude," I said. "Particularly since I'm positive you aren't a wizard."

There—that's a good way to explain my nervousness. Wizards are considered the bottom of the supernatural food chain, so if I theoretically thought he was anything besides human, it would be enough to make me anxious.

"And what makes you think I'm not human?" Noctus asked.

"The glamour," I blandly replied, again hiding behind a screen of humanity.

As well as I could understand, wizards sensed magic like I did, so it wouldn't be too hard for a wizard to realize he was using a glamour.

"Ahhh yes." Noctus rubbed one of his metal shackles—which matched the vibe of the black utility vest and pants he was wearing again today.

The silence was uncomfortable, and Noctus didn't look at all inclined to leave, so I blurted out, "I'm glad you found your cat. It's good to be a diligent pet owner and care for your pet. They depend on you after all," I rambled.

Noctus had been inspecting me—from the way he was eyeing my pants I was pretty sure he was trying to figure out if I had a secret weapon cache on my body like he did—I did *not*. But at my nonsensical sentence, he tuned in. "Yes," he said. "Tell me, is it common practice among humans to *fix* their pets?"

"Yes," I said, then realized what he was thinking. "I mean, no! Sometimes. Maybe." Internally I was kicking myself.

As a cat I'd been forced to blend in a time or two with stray cats, which had made me a huge advocate for pet owners to get their pets spayed and neutered. *But!* The pet Noctus was considering getting fixed was *me*!

Internally, my panic was sounding off every figurative alarm I had. *Change the topic—change the topic!*

"I mean, humans frequently get cat doors installed, but that doesn't mean you need one," I said.

"What does a cat door do?"

"It lets the cat go in and out without you having to open the door for it."

"Hmm." Noctus's expression was thoughtful.

Perfect, time for an escape!

"It was great meeting you, Mr. Shade," I said.

"Noctus," he corrected.

"N-N-Noctus," I stammered.

Noctus studied me for a moment, and I could *feel* him weighing out my threat factor.

Is he doing this because he's that paranoid about someone discovering his city? Or is he just that neighborly? Shiloh and the uncles seem to know him pretty well.

"You're very jittery for a supernatural," he said.

"That's because I'm a wizard subset," I said with real feeling. "I know where I stand in our society—the bottom."

"I see." Noctus smiled—it wasn't a full on grin, but closer to subdued amusement.

At least it reached his eyes. His eyes seemed to almost swirl, and as I stared into them, I swear I could feel something deeper.

Noctus abruptly offered out his arm, breaking my fascination with his eyes.

"...Um?" I said.

"I'll walk you to the end of the cul-de-sac."

"Oh, that's not necessary," I protested, still not keen on moving much in case he made the connection between Ama's movements and, well, me.

"I insist," Noctus said. The flicker of amusement was gone, and his voice was heavy with power. I was officially speaking to the elf king, not the protective neighbor.

Woah. He really wants me to take his arm. Chances are, that means he's going to try to feel me out or something.

There was a risk he'd figure me out—from either the touch or from the movement. Did I dare?

Noctus started to narrow his eyes, and I could feel his thinly tethered power held in check by the shackles.

"Okay," I squeaked. I reached out and tucked my hand against his forearm, praying magic in general wouldn't let me down.

I held my breath as I felt Noctus's magic grow next to me, like flames flaring higher and higher.

The sensation faded, and Noctus's stance relaxed back into the posture he'd displayed as a friendly neighbor as he guided me down the sidewalk.

"You are very interesting, Chloe of Book Nookery," Noctus declared.

"No, I am not. I'm not interesting at all. I'm very boring," I said.

Noctus chuckled—a sound that was deep, even, and warm like a bonfire. "I must disagree. You actually remind me of someone."

"Really? Who?"

"My cat."

My heart stopped, my brain stopped, everything in my body stopped as I was frozen by ice cold fear.

"Noctus!" Aristide poked his head out the front door of the Cape Cod home and was scowling into the yard. "You said you were coming outside to grab Ama. Have you found her, or have you decided to give in to your baser instincts and live in the wild?"

"If you'll excuse me, Chloe, it seems I must attend to my howling friend, or he'll disturb the neighborhood," Noctus said.

"Of course." I let go of Noctus's arm as if he were made of fire and stepped to the side.

"*Noctus*." Aristide managed to make the shouted name sound like an insult.

"I'm coming," Noctus called as he crossed the street. "I haven't found her, yet. But I met someone new, and I've decided to get Ama a cat door."

"Congratulations to Ama. What the heck is a cat door?"

I didn't stick around to hear the conversation. I booked it down the sidewalk, and when I found a large evergreen tree encroaching on the sidewalk near the mouth of the cul-de-sac, I darted behind it, wrestling my way into it before I changed into my cat form.

I ran through backyards, shimmying my way over any inconvenient fences with ease. I had to hop onto the top of a tool shed and jump on a house to avoid a backyard with a dog outside, all to take me back to the bottom of the cul-de-sac so I could nonchalantly emerge from the opposite direction human me had headed.

That was close. I hope Noctus isn't so diligent that he comes to find me every time I run off to text my siblings, or I'm going to lose more hair than I already have!

CHAPTER FOURTEEN

Noctus

I climbed the last set of stairs, taking myself out of the dungeon and up to the main floor of the villa. The haze I felt from the activated shackles settled over me, dulling my sense of magic.

I didn't enjoy the sensation, but it was a minor irritation. Even with the shackles on, I could still harness enough magic to be useful—something I was attempting to keep the Paragon from learning, hence the need for the releases.

I rolled my shoulders back as I climbed the spiral staircase to my private floor. I glanced down the hallway, looking at the doors to Ker's and Aristide's rooms, but the duo was still downstairs in the dungeon. I was the only one on this floor.

I opened my bedroom door and started toward my weapons closet, when I felt a warmth that drove away some of the mental fog bloom behind me.

Amalourne meowed as she trotted into my room.

I turned on my heel, heading back to the door—and her.

"Amalourne, good afternoon." I scratched her cheeks, eliciting a deep purr, before I picked her up, making her purr sputter.

The touch made the magic in the collar react, and I felt it caress my fingers, sinking underneath my skin and producing a warmth and reassurance that had made me fonder of my cat than was reasonable.

The magic I'd cast on the collar was taboo, because it was dangerous for me. But Amalourne was a cat, and didn't understand what she could potentially do. Instead, I just felt her willingness to reach out, and it amplified the peaceful sensation she already inspired, making holding her one of the most relaxing experiences in my life.

Amalourne didn't like being carried or held—I could feel her entire body stiffen and her heart sputter in her chest when I held her. But she hadn't ever tried to warn me off, and she was starting to relax when I carried her these days, so I was hoping she was growing used to it.

I stood in the doorway and petted her until she started purring again—though at a much softer volume than she had before—and considered my options.

I had intended to swap out some of my weapons in my armament closet.

But Amalourne doesn't like weapons. She does, however, like books.

"Let's go somewhere you'll enjoy more," I said.

Amalourne meowed to me, and adjusted her paws so one was on either side of my neck and she could rest her chin on my shoulder, giving a warm little cat hug that I'd become stupidly fond of—though at least I wasn't alone in this, as Ker and even Aristide enjoyed Amalourne's hugs, too.

I left my room and headed for the stairs, planning to go to my study.

It had only taken me a day or two to realize I had a studious cat—or at least one that found the smells and sights of books interesting as she liked to inspect my shelves. She'd be far happier rubbing against the priceless spines of some of the rarest elven tomes in existence than seeing my weapon storage—which was likely to make her puff up and hiss if history was any indication.

How hilarious. The elven king of war *has a cat that dislikes weapons. Life does like to play its jokes.*

As ridiculous as it was, I'd bend for the sake of my new pet's happiness. Taking her from the fae, and then performing the forbidden magic on her collar, had both proven to be excellent decisions.

Aristide, Ker, and Charon had bled and fought with me. Ours was a blood deep friendship that I owed much to. But Amalourne...she brought into my life—into all our lives—a certain kind of brightness I hadn't realized was possible for me to possess.

So if weapons made my cat nervous, I'd make sure to avoid them when she was with me.

She seems intent on being independent and going outside. I am glad I had Charon order the electronic cat door kit the Book Nookery clerk recommended.

Ahh, yes. Chloe.

I'd been...*intense* when I met her. She was talking to Shiloh, and just happened to appear in my neighborhood when I was again looking for Amalourne?

Considering the first time Amalourne got out and went to the Book Nookery, I highly doubt it is a mere coincidence.

It was likely she was connected to Amalourne.

My cat had a previous owner—she was too friendly and well-kept not to. Also, there was something about the way magic seemed to just...cluster around her that made it obvious she wasn't a normal cat.

But the human hadn't said anything when I'd mentioned my cat on both occasions when I met her. She'd seemed particularly intent on getting away from me.

Ironically, she didn't reek of the all-consuming fear that overtook most people who realized what I really was. Her fear was less personal. It almost reminded me of Amalourne when she was trying to squirm out of something she didn't want.

Maybe she really was Amalourne's previous owner, but has chosen not to say anything. It could explain why she's suddenly appeared—although I was almost certain Amalourne's previous owner had to be fae to keep a cat that seems to attract magic.

I paused outside the door to the study, considering the matter.

Does it even matter? She isn't a threat—not to Shiloh, the neighborhood, or the remaining elves.

It had taken touching her for me to feel wild magic around her, and even then her magic was subtle, but pleasant enough.

Amalourne meowed, drawing my attention back to her.

I petted her, then opened the door to my study.

It doesn't matter at this point. If she keeps showing up, I will investigate.

CHAPTER FIFTEEN

Chloe

I was sleeping in my bed in Noctus's office, having been carried there *again* after dinner—more roasted chicken.

As tasty as the roasted chicken is, I'm starting to get sick of it.

I rolled around, hanging one of my paws off the side of my bed so it dangled over the edge of Noctus's desk—where my bed had been relocated to, despite there being a general lack of workspace.

It'd been a week since I'd run from the Book Nookery and was forced to accept my new life as pet to the King of the Mors Elves.

I'd finally caught up on sleep, but my sleeping patterns were weirder than usual, mostly because whenever Noctus slept he carried me off to his bedroom, but I *wasn't* going to sleep when he slept. That would have been so foolish it would serve me right if I got killed in my sleep. So those nights I spent sitting in one of his bathroom sinks to doze, and thanked my lucky stars that he only seemed to need sleep every two to three days, and rarely slept for more than five hours.

Noctus petted my side, and I purred as was expected.

There was something very soothing about being petted. I closed my eyes and set my chin on the edge of the bed, but when I felt him try to pet my belly I batted at him with my claws, growling deep in my chest.

Aristide popped out his earbuds—it turned out he was a podcast junkie, and this week was binge listening to true crime podcasts. "Still trying to pet her stomach?"

Noctus turned his frown from me to Aristide. "You recognized her growl?"

"She only makes that sound when you press her personal boundaries and try to pet her stomach," Aristide said. "Which I quite applaud her for. Keep your personal boundaries against him, Ama. Someone needs to!"

"I don't understand." Noctus seemingly ignored his friend as he scratched under my chin and I purred again. "She's perfectly happy in all other areas. I'm an elf, she trusts me. She should be willing to trust me to touch her stomach."

Not that area. Not ever! It's too weird, even for the sake of keeping my cover.

I casually licked a paw and scrubbed at my face.

Aristide set his earbuds on an end table next to his embroidered chair. "Even though you're an elf, I don't expect your natural magic would be able to overwhelm an animal's nature so entirely that they'd go against their personality. She's a cat. They're finicky by nature."

I don't believe that you're old, Aristide. You're too modern and smart! I hopped out of my bed and ambled over to the nearest bookshelf, studying the books.

I had yet to find anything helpful—or written in English—but I was going to keep looking.

I suspected the magic books were on that top shelf that lined the ceiling of the room, but whenever I went more than four shelves high on a bookshelf, Noctus pulled me down. Not out of concern for his books—like any proper book lover would be—no, no. He was convinced I'd hurt myself getting down.

Me.

A *cat*!

"Perhaps she is finicky," Noctus said. "But I've never before encountered anything—supernatural, human, creature, or otherwise—that was able to resist."

"Then it's *high time* you do," Aristide said. "It'll do you some good to experience limitations like the rest of us."

"She's not eating as happily as she used to," Noctus said.

I was so startled by his observation I almost stopped sniffing the green, leather-bound book—Elvish, of course—I'd been inspecting. *How did he know?*

"Maybe she's getting sick of chicken?" Aristide set his hands on the arms of his chair and ran his fingers across the textured fabric, which I noticed he had a preference for. "I would be by now."

Noctus pushed his keyboard away, then stood up and walked around his desk. He picked me up, cradling me against his chest as he perched on the edge of his desk.

I was getting used to the roller coaster ride of being carried around—by Noctus, anyway. He'd gotten much better at holding me in ways that felt more secure, and he didn't seem to mind my cat hugs.

He maneuvered me so I half sat on his legs and was still cradled by his right arm, then he held out his left hand. "High five."

I waited a moment—no matter how smart Noctus was convinced I was, he'd notice if I suddenly perfected the trick after he explained it to me once—and slowly stretched my paw out. I stayed still for a moment as Noctus watched with interest, then gently pressed my paw into the palm of his hand.

Noctus's lips curved, and he rubbed under my chin. "Such an intelligent beauty."

His voice was so genuine and warm, for a moment I actually felt *proud*.

I can't believe it. I'm going to blush. As a cat!

I was saved from any further personal embarrassment when I heard something in the hallway. Noctus and Aristide both looked up and watched the door.

It clicked open, with both Charon and Ker standing in the hallway.

"Excuse me, Your Majesty," Charon said. "But there's been another incident with failed artifacts."

Noctus's arms were gentle as he held me, but his voice was as hard as ice. "Where?"

Why am I here? I sat on Noctus's lap, trying to process what happened as the SUV made a turn and went over a pothole that rocked the vehicle.

After Charon's announcement about the faulty artifact, Noctus decided they needed to go on a field trip to see it.

But who would bring their cat on an important investigation like this? Aristide needs to get him a book about pet ownership.

I wasn't thrilled to be coming with. Although I needed to stay in Noctus's good graces, I wanted to be as uninvolved with his kingdom as possible for the sake of my own life.

It had occurred to me, however, that there was perhaps one possible upside to the field trip.

It might give me a chance to see if the man tracking me can find me whenever I venture out. He hadn't popped up when I'd turned human to text my siblings, but I hadn't left sight of the Cape Cod house, so maybe all I could conclude was that he hadn't figured out where Noctus lived. Yet.

Or maybe Noctus had some powerful magic on the house—which was more likely.

Charon flicked on the vehicle's blinker, then made a turn.

Noctus narrowed his eyes as he stared through the windshield—he was sitting up front, with Aristide and Ker on the back bench seat. "The Seelie and Unseelie territory lines have shifted, again."

Charon checked his mirrors—he was such a proper driver he'd even removed his usual hood for this excursion. "Is that something to be concerned about, Your Majesty?"

"No." Noctus glanced down at me. "I doubt it has any bearing on the incident—it's just more proof of the rapid deterioration of supernaturals."

It was oppressively silent for several long moments after that cheerful observation.

Eventually, Aristide yawned, flashing his pronounced fang teeth, then rested his head against a headrest. "How much farther?"

Ker—who, in her wolf form, took up the rest of the bench seat of the SUV and still looked cramped—woofed.

Based on the way they'd acted back at the villa, I concluded Ker only entered Magiford as a wolf. They hadn't conveniently explained why, the transformation just seemed...routine. From the way Charon knew to open the side door for Ker, to Aristide gathering up her harness, it was a practiced routine.

"This is the area," Charon announced. He tapped on the driver-side window, pointing to a nearly finished apartment building. The roof was on and the windows were in, but it looked like they were working on water and electric installations based on the not-yet finished walls and general lack of working lights.

"The Curia Cloisters have not yet been informed?" Noctus asked.

"Correct, Your Majesty," Charon said. "The incident happened less than twenty minutes ago to an elf named Prydwen—though he goes by the human name of Paul inside Magiford. He sustained minor wounds, but said he was fine to wait for our arrival before notifying Cloisters representatives."

"Were there any humans present during the incident?" Aristide asked.

"None were directly near him," Charon said. "I believe there were several nearby, however, which is why I estimate we have only twenty minutes before we need to call the Cloisters."

"Twenty minutes should be plenty of time. Right, Ker?" Aristide held his hand up.

Ker placed her chin on his palm and woofed her agreement.

Charon found street parking and—as proof of his magic—managed to do a perfect parallel park with the boat-like SUV.

I swear, some supernaturals get all the best skills.

Noctus slipped out of the car and shifted to holding me with one arm so he could open the side door of the SUV for Ker.

Ker hopped out and waited for Aristide to get out of the car before she slipped into place at his side and he grabbed onto her harness.

Aristide and Ker headed to the crosswalk so they could get onto the sidewalk without needing to take a step up onto the curb. Noctus, carrying me, followed behind them.

Somehow Charon had already crossed the street. He was standing with an elf whose glamour was so thin I could barely feel it, but I could see it was straining to cover his long, tapered elf ears and his oddly swirled eyes—which were a beautiful green color, but were hazed with worry.

"Prydwen," Noctus said as he approached the elf.

The elf immediately started to go down on one knee. "Your Majesty," he murmured. His eyes didn't stray from the ground, and he'd given no visible reaction to the sight of his sovereign carrying a cat around.

"Stand," Noctus said, his voice empty of inflection. "We don't want to attract attention."

"Yes, Your Majesty." The elf stood, wincing when his bandaged hand brushed his pants. He still wouldn't look at Noctus but kept his eyes on the ground and his voice quiet.

Elvish custom, maybe?

Noctus shifted, looking away from Prydwen to two other elves who were standing further down the sidewalk on either side of a small pile of twisted metal dropped on a chunk of blackened sidewalk.

Farther down—at the end of the block—were a man and woman, both human, watching uneasily.

They must have been the "nearby" humans Charon mentioned.

Noctus looked from the hunk of metal to Prydwen. "What happened here?"

"The tool I use for my daily glamour broke when I was coming home from work. It caught on fire—magic flames, so it took me a moment to yank it off my belt and put it out." Prydwen tugged the long sleeve of his shirt over his bandage. I was wondering why he was wearing a long sleeved shirt on such a warm day, but I saw a flash of his wrist on his undamaged arm, and it had a sparkle of magic to it—I was pretty sure it was some kind of tattoo.

"Did it give any kind of warning?" Noctus asked. "Could you feel the metal start to heat up, or the magic on your glamour start to fail?"

Prydwen shook his head. "No, Your Majesty. There was no indication before it suddenly blazed with magic. After I got it off, I called your offices."

"Do you remember where you purchased this particular artifact?" Noctus asked, shifting to accommodate when I latched my paws on either side of his neck and scooted up his chest so I could peer behind him.

Aristide and Ker stood behind him, Aristide looking bored and Ker sitting like a model dog, but I wasn't fooled. Ker's nose was twitching, and based on the way Aristide had his head tilted, he was listening not just to Prydwen's explanation, but the blood rushing through his veins, too.

"Yes, I remember, Your Majesty." Prydwen dropped his chin for a head-bobbing version of a bow. "I purchased it two months ago, from a female fae. I don't know what Court she was with, but she was roughly five foot six, brown eyes, shoulder length blond hair that was real and not a fae glamour. No facial marks or tattoos, though she did have a piercing at the top of her ear I haven't seen on many fae. Her clothes were human—and trendy—but they looked stiff and unworn. Her magic was strong, so she'd been to the fae realm recently to reconnect with magic."

Prydwen tucked his hands behind his back and casually rattled off the detailed description as Charon scribbled his words down in his small notepad.

I guess this shows how the Mors elves are suited for war—he was able to remember that much after two months.

I shivered, once again thankful for the knowledge that elves had specialties—it made it a tiny bit more fair that such a superior powered elf was an "average" specimen among elves when I knew he couldn't make artifacts by himself, or do any of the other elven specialties I'd learned about from Ms. Booker's records.

"Where did you meet this fae and purchase the artifact?" Noctus asked.

Prydwen turned slightly to look in the direction of the downtown area. "She was on the list of official Curia Cloisters reputable business listings as Bright Light Artifacts. There was no location listed; she requested I meet her in the downtown area, on Liberty Lane, and showed me a number of artifacts to choose from."

It took me a moment to place Liberty Lane—it was off main street and mostly had clothing stores and a few real estate offices, but the new donut shop that I loved was two streets over, so I'd become familiar with the street.

Charon turned a page in his notepad. "Did you feel any magic in the area when the artifact failed?"

"No," Prydwen said. "None at all."

Noctus nodded, then turned to Aristide. "Anything to add?"

Even with Noctus turned away, Prydwen didn't look up.

I meowed at him, just to see if he'd react. His eyes shot up to see me peering over Noctus's shoulder at him, but he slammed his gaze back down to the ground immediately after.

Yep, in today's episode of "I'm Being Cuddled By A Killer", it's scary that such an obviously competent elf is so terrified of Noctus he won't look at him.

"Do you have any suspicions why your artifact failed?" Aristide drawled.

Prydwen blinked. "No," he said. "I paid a reasonable price for the artifact, and it appeared to be made well enough—though nowhere near elven caliber of course. While I didn't know the artist behind it, I trusted they were reputable to be listed on the Curia Cloisters' website."

I mentally applauded Aristide for the out-of-the-box question—which was just as revealing as some of Noctus's earlier questions, if not more.

What this means is that this wasn't some sketchy, back corner deal—and obviously not the guy who was scamming humans several months ago.

"Is that all, Your Majesty?" Prydwen timidly asked.

"Yes." Noctus gestured at one of the two elves standing over the ruined buckle. "Take a potion to help your injury, then call the matter in to the Curia Cloisters." His eyes briefly went to the humans, who were still watching. "When they arrive to take your statement, tell them you called a friend for help first, who recognized the artifact failing and told you to call it in."

"Understood. Thank you, Your Majesty." Prydwen dropped his chin again, and took the vial from the security elf who offered it to him.

Noctus moved on to the buckle, giving me a push up when I pulled myself onto his shoulders.

He crouched down next to it and held his hand over the buckle. I could feel his sharp magic, but he must not have felt it was enough, because he frowned at his bracelet-shackle that glittered in the sunshine. "Charon?" he asked. "Can you confirm a few things for me?"

"Of course, sir." Charon knelt next to him and extended his hand, his fingers glowing with magic.

"I don't sense any lingering magic," Noctus said. "Can you?"

"I'm afraid not, sir." Charon tapped the buckle—which was styled into a stag's head that was misshapen from the incident.

"It seems it was made by a fae—do you agree?"

Charon narrowed his eyes. "Yes. It has their tricky, unnecessarily ornamental magical print all over it. Unfortunately, I can't tell if there was a spell that made it collapse, or if it was simply shoddy workmanship."

Noctus can tell all of that with his magic shackled? Sheesh, maybe I haven't given my "don't notice me" magic enough credit.

Noctus ran a finger over the blackened sidewalk. "The seller was obviously not the man we learned about from Queen's Court Café."

"Does that matter?" Aristide edged closer with Ker, giving the werewolf a chance to smell the area. "Even if the seller was different, it could be the same fae making the artifacts."

"A valid point," Charon said.

"Yes." Noctus rubbed a tiny piece of grit between his fingers. "That will be something we may have to investigate." He glanced from Charon, to Aristide, then Ker. "Does everyone have a read on it?"

They nodded.

"Then we'd better leave. I imagine the Curia Cloisters will act swiftly." Noctus stood—I had to dig my claws into his shirt to stay on his shoulders—then headed for the car.

"What do we do next, Your Majesty?" Charon asked.

"We look into Bright Light Artifacts," Noctus said. "And see if they're still in existence."

"You sound like you don't think they are," Aristide said.

"I don't," Noctus said. "All signs point to this being done on purpose—an act of sabotage or subterfuge."

On purpose? I crouched low on Noctus's shoulders as he crossed the street. *But* why? *Who would want to hurt other supernaturals like this? Particularly in public places where humans can see?*

THE FOLLOWING MORNING I LAY—UNSUSPECTING and bored—on the floor of Noctus's bedroom, trying to figure out how I could text my siblings without getting caught.

I need an easier system than slipping out the front door. I was hoping Noctus would get a cat door after the conversation I had with him as Chloe, but so far...nothing.

I lay on my side and thoughtlessly batted at one of the new "mentally enriching" cat toys Charon had gotten me. It was a plastic, tube-like ring with a ball inside. I could fit my paw through the slot in the side of the ring-tube, but the ball would never pop out.

I wasn't insulted by the toy—I was actually touched that Charon had continued buying toys for me and was very intent on trying to lure me into playing.

Maybe that was what made me lax—I was so certain in the security of my cover, I only half listened as I heard footsteps approaching the open bedroom door.

Maybe I could find an abandoned bedroom with a walk-in closet, close the door, turn into a human and text my siblings, then turn back into a cat?

Although I now had free rein of the house, I hadn't done much exploring. I didn't want to see *any* of the skeletons in Noctus's many closets.

But if I transform inside the house, I run the risk of Noctus—or Charon, for that matter—having some kind of spell in place to catch that sort of thing. Although...Ker transforms whenever she wants without a problem. And no one knows what I am. Is it even possible to set up a spell that would notify them about me when I have the magical presence of a paperclip?

The truth was, figuring out how to text my siblings was the smallest issue. I still needed to figure out what to do about the collar—and the tracker.

The collar is still first on my list, but I haven't found any books written in English, much less about elven enchantments. I'd swear in a villa this big Noctus would have a bigger library. Or maybe he does, and I should risk looking for it. Regardless, I have got to get this collar off, or the second I get out Noctus will come find me and drag me back to the villa.

That wasn't a guess, but proven. It had happened twice since I started slipping outside to text my siblings, and I didn't want Noctus getting suspicious about "Chloe from Book Nookery's" sudden presence in his neighborhood.

In conclusion, I couldn't leave to get help, and I couldn't find any research materials in a language I could read.

I still haven't gotten to the top shelf of books in Noctus's study. He won't let me up there...

I batted at the ball some more and lay flat on my side, barely noticing when Noctus and Aristide entered the room, Ker padding behind them in her wolf form.

"—still need to complete the quarterly barrier inspection," Noctus said.

"Is that really necessary?" Aristide asked. "The barriers have been solid for centuries—and with those shackles on would you even be able to reinforce them?"

"I am aware that in most ways I am a terrible king," Noctus said. "This is one of my few actions that reassures the town. I do it for their sake, not the sake of the barrier."

Following my plan of clinging to ignorance in the hopes of pleading innocence if Noctus ever found out what I was, I didn't pay much attention to their conversation.

So I haven't made any progress at all on anything important. How many days has it been? I need to contact Ms. Booker. I've obviously lost my job by now—which is fair, considering.

"You're not a terrible king." Aristide reached out, setting his hand on the back of a chair. I vaguely noted he didn't sit down like he usually did. "You have protected your people for decades. That they've survived this long is astounding. You just don't care about all the showmanship your family loved. And thank goodness—the number of war parades your brothers threw was *exhausting*. It made it impossible to get any work done."

I should try going into the study when Noctus isn't there to get to that top shelf. Last time I tried it Charon found me and carried me off, but if I try it enough times surely there will be a moment where even Charon won't notice. Or maybe I should try using an elven blade to cut the collar? I'm getting desperate enough I could try it—wait, Aristide knew Noctus's brothers?

Noctus didn't say anything. He crouched at my side to pet my head. I was so careless in my boredom, I didn't even realize his objective until he rubbed my belly.

I shot upright, puffing up so I was about twice my usual size, and crab walked away, hissing and shedding hair as I went.

"You just won't give up on rubbing her belly, will you?" Aristide asked.

"I googled it. It's a sign of trust."

Aristide snorted. "Maybe, but you have no idea what her background is. Maybe the fae abused her and hurt her there."

"*What?*" Noctus's voice was deep and rolled like thunder.

CHAPTER SIXTEEN

Chloe

I skittered into the bathroom, then stuck my head out to peer back at him.

For the first time ever I saw a hint of anger in Noctus. His lips were set like marble, and there was something within him that seemed to glow—like a star preparing to explode.

"It's a conjecture!" Aristide said. "Who knows, maybe they also hand fed her chicken. The point is, you need to respect her boundaries!"

Noctus was unnaturally still for a moment. When he straightened, the pressure in the room evaporated, and he was his usual self. "I see. Fine, I'll do that." He switched his gaze to me. "I won't attempt to rub your stomach until you're ready, Ama."

I don't believe you.

I flattened my ears and gave him the eye—or as best I could while being a furry cat—then sat down on the cool bathroom tile.

Noctus watched me, a hint of a smile playing at his lips.

Aristide made a show of flicking his silvery brown hair off his forehead. "I'm glad for all our sakes you'll adjust. You know, considering you are an apathetic king, you are a downright tyrannical pet owner."

Ker gave an "*Awoo!*" in agreement as she padded past Aristide and skirted the reflection pool.

"Ama is mine," Noctus said. "I should be her everything."

"She's a cat. That's never going to happen," Aristide said, his tone placid considering we'd just witnessed Noctus's terrifying displeasure moments ago. "Also, let me rephrase my previous judgment—you are a tyrannical, *jealous* pet owner. Now, back to more important matters than your well-groomed feline: did you find out anything more about the breaking artifacts?"

Ker joined me in the bathroom, her nails clicking on the tile. She licked the top of my head. It took what little guts I had left in me to stay sitting while she messed up my fur, but this was better than the last time she'd tried to lick me and wrapped her tongue around my entire head.

"Not much beyond confirming Bright Light Artifacts no longer exists. Not even Charon could find any records about them," Noctus said.

"That's pretty troubling since they must have been registered with the Curia Cloisters in order for Prydwen to find them on their website."

"You have far more confidence in the Curia Cloisters than I do, for I don't find it surprising at all," Noctus dryly said.

Ker playfully nudged me, bumped the door so it was almost completely shut, then started the transformation from wolf back to human.

For shifters—werewolf or otherwise—shifting was a painful process that took typically forty seconds to a minute as their bodies literally rebuilt their bone structures and muscle. They also always shifted in the nude—because it was impossible to wear clothes during the process.

Since getting a face full of werewolf butt was not something I wanted to experience, I ran.

I tucked my tail and shot out of the bathroom even faster than I'd entered it, aiming for the throne-bed, which I could hide under. I almost made it to the stairs when Noctus intercepted me and picked me up.

"Ker." Noctus arranged me in my cat-hug position. "You scared Ama."

Yeah? Well, you don't sound upset about that, I mutinously thought as I clung to him.

In a tiny show of vengeance combined with keeping my cover, I rubbed my slobber-wet head against his neck.

Noctus didn't even notice.

"Maybe Ama has a thing against nudity?" Aristide laughed at his "joke," which was closer to the truth than he knew.

"Sorry," Ker shouted from within the bathroom. She emerged a moment later, wearing pants and a shirt that fit her too well to be anything that belonged to Noctus.

Apparently she had clothing stashes placed strategically around the house?

"Are we ready, then? We should go," Aristide said.

Go? Go where?

"Yes." Noctus carried me across his bedroom and slipped into the hallway, heading for the spiral staircase.

Aristide and Ker followed behind, the werewolf and vampire bumping shoulders in a friendly way.

"I heard you say you can't find Bright Light Artifacts—does that mean we can assume someone is selling dud artifacts on purpose?" Ker asked.

"It's the likeliest situation, though we lack absolute proof, so it would be wise to keep an open mind," Noctus said. "However, there was no trace of Bright Light Artifacts in any of the Curia Cloisters online listings. Charon even went to the Cloisters and looked up their business licenses—nothing."

"But the question is, are they purposely selling cheaply made artifacts for a profit, or are they purposely selling artifacts that they *know* will degrade and damage their users?" Aristide asked.

"It's most likely the latter," Noctus said.

"How can you know? Stairs, Aristide," Ker warned him as Noctus started down the staircase.

"Yes, I have the villa memorized, *thank you*, after the centuries we've spent in this place," Aristide said. He didn't even slow down as he shifted from walking to trotting down the stairs.

After the centuries we've spent? Is he referring to himself and Noctus, or is Ker included, too? But that would be impossible! If they make it to old age, werewolves can be longer lived than humans, but only by a decade or two. Ker can't be hundreds of years old.

"I am betting they're selling artifacts designed to harm their users because a dud artifact would simply stop working. At most, it would crack and crumble into nothing. That the artifacts are hurting supernaturals as they break...it cannot be accidental." Noctus stepped off the last stair and started walking, splitting off from the main hallway and going down a side corridor I hadn't been carried through before.

"So what next?" Ker asked. "Because there's no way you'll be satisfied to wait for the next victim."

"We go to the Curia Cloisters."

I perked up. *Wait, you're going to the Cloisters?*

Noctus pushed a door, which opened into a very impressive chamber that was gorgeous enough to pause my thoughts.

It was at least two stories tall, with dragon-like gargoyles guarding the base of two vaulted ribs/support pillars and a red carpet stretched all the way to a set of giant double doors a troll could have comfortably walked through.

"Are we going to the Curia Cloisters legally, or illegally?" Aristide asked.

"Both," Noctus said.

"That means mostly illegally," Ker confidently said.

I whipped my attention back to their conversation. *Wait, if you're going to the Cloisters, could I tag along? That would be convenient!*

The question would be...what would I do there? I'd already decided that since the Paragon knew about Noctus—not to mention that he wore a majorly overpowered glamour—it wouldn't be wise to ask him anything.

He wanted information from Noctus, and if he learned I could potentially see through the glamour, he'd be highly motivated to toss me back to the elf king, if not eliminate me himself.

Maybe there's a resource I could check at the Curia Cloisters? Surely they must have some information about elven magic that I could use for my collar. Or maybe I could see if the tracker guy is a wanted supernatural criminal?

"I need to see the pocket watch that the Cloisters took," Noctus said.

"Why?" Aristide asked.

"To confirm if the maker of the pocket watch also made Prydwen's belt buckle," Noctus said. "If they did, then we can be certain these events are malicious."

"Ahh, that's true, since Prydwen and Valaria both described different sellers—and from different times and places," Ker said.

"Why *else* are we going?" Aristide asked. "I know you. If you just needed to see the pocket watch, you would have gone by yourself without telling us."

"Because I want the records of all other similar incidents." Noctus shifted me to one arm, then held his hand up—palm out—at the two giant doors.

"Even though it doesn't involve elves?" Ker asked.

Noctus briefly glanced back at her. "As I said before, I will act in the interest of supernaturals if it means we benefit. In this case, stamping out this artifact dealer will give me back hours of my life that I won't spend listening to my people complain about their terrible artifacts."

Aristide laughed. "You can't deceive Ker and me, Noctus.

You'll stamp the dealer out because you're concerned for your people."

That's probably true. Based on what I've seen, Noctus is a very dutiful king—if not very affectionate.

Noctus made a noise in the back of his throat, and the doors swung open, blinding me with sunshine.

City sounds hit me—laughter, the hum of engines, the harsh cry of seagulls.

My eyes adjusted to the light, and I realized we were on a large platform made of a stone so white it reflected the sun, making the area even brighter than usual.

The tiered city was spread out before us with an impossibly long, staired walkway cutting between each layer. Behind us, I could finally get a good look at Noctus's villa.

Like the city, its walls were white, and its red, clay tiled roof was steeply pitched and went straight into the side of the mountain. Giant sculptures of winged warriors crouched on the edge of the roof, looking like stony guardians, and green ivy crawled up one side of the castle. I'd say it ruined the perfect image of the house, except it had tiny golden flowers that glittered in the sunlight, adding to the beauty.

Wait—I don't want to go into the city. I don't want to see anything that would make Noctus think he needs to kill me to keep his secrets safe, plus that first night I got here Aristide said elves are superstitious about cats!

I tried to struggle out of Noctus's arms, but he kept his arms gently locked around me, even when I dug my claws into his forearm.

"Peace, Ama," he murmured to me. "I'll keep you safe."

Okay, except who is going to keep me safe from you *when you find out what I am?* I tried one last desperate wiggle, but I couldn't get free. I was seeing the elf city, whether I wanted to or not.

Noctus started down the stairs, getting off when we reached the top tier of the city.

Trumpets sounded from the villa, but even as I peered over Noctus's shoulder I couldn't see any instruments—or anyone at all—back by the doors we'd come out of.

Does Charon have trumpeters on standby all day long, just in case Noctus goes outside?

Now that we were finally in the city, I looked around with cautious interest—this was, after all, the first elven city I'd ever seen.

It was remarkably beautiful, and somehow both foreign and so familiar.

Outside a hair salon, a scooter was locked to a lamp post that had an unlit lantern on top of it. Next to the scooter was an actual *horse* tied to a hitching post.

A vegetable and fruit stand constructed of wood that was probably older than me was built into the sides of a white building. After staring at the puppy and kitten spattered posters hanging in the front window of the building, I recognized it as a *pet store*.

The road was brick and stone, and there were tall aqueducts that zigzagged over the buildings, skimming water off the immense waterfalls that roared over the side of the mountain, falling on either side of the city. But I saw more than a few elves talking on cell phones, riding scooters, and cruising around on skateboards.

It's weirdly historic and modern at the same time.

A truck rumbled down the street, its bed filled with armor and axes that clanked as it drove toward what looked like some kind of practice area at the far end of the street.

It seems the Mors haven't entirely lost their hobbies...

An elf carrying a sack of what looked like purple-colored apples glanced at Noctus as she passed us. She did a double take, then dropped her fruit and fell to a knee. "Your Majesty!"

Within the blink of an eye, traffic had come to a halt, and everyone was kneeling, their heads bowed to Noctus. Even those who had been driving shut off their vehicles, piled out, and kneeled on the road.

Noctus studied the street, scanning people and buildings alike. "Stand," he said.

No one stirred.

Are they that scared of him? But he told them to stand...

I meowed in my curiosity, and up came the heads. I found myself the center of attention as the elves peered at me, shock flitting across their faces.

I thought Charon said he was going to tell everyone, "so there would be no accidents"?

The longer I watched, I realized they weren't afraid of me. Despite what Aristide had said, none of them looked angry or upset with my presence. It was Noctus they looked to with skittish expressions like stray cats that were afraid of humans but still wanted to be petted.

Self-conscious, I tucked myself closer to Noctus, thankful for his broad chest.

"Is that the cat?" It was whispered so quietly I almost didn't hear it, but Noctus turned to face the child who'd said it—a young boy with big eyes that were even larger than usual when he realized Noctus was looking at him. He immediately lowered his gaze, trembling a little as he leaned into an older woman kneeling with him.

Noctus watched him for a moment, then looked at me.

There was something in his face that held...regret. Maybe it was the way faint lines creased his eyebrows, or the way he clenched his jaw, but I could feel it on him.

He's an elf. He probably deserves to be feared. But...he has a kind side to him, which I have experienced firsthand.

I wriggled in his arms so I could brace my paws on his shoulder, then I peered into his face. Holding my breath—and using every ounce of courage that I had—I bumped my nose against his, then meowed again.

Noctus rewarded me with a slanted smile, and I could feel some of the tension slip away as everyone watched with interest.

"This is Ama." Noctus's voice was loud in the unnatural silence of the street. "She is, indeed, my cat. You can identify her by her collar." Noctus tapped the three red gems on my collar, which glowed at his touch.

Hmmm, I'm not sure I like that. How much magic has he packed into my collar?

I meowed at Noctus, but he continued to address the crowd. "She is friendly, and she has free run of the villa. If you see her, it's fine. I know where she is."

Oh, this thing definitely *has more magic than I picked up on. Does that mean if I ever want to get it off, I'm going to have to start learning the Elvish written language? But that will take months!*

I should have just come clean when he first brought me into the house—but I had no way of knowing he wasn't malicious. And besides, I still didn't know how he survived the family massacre that was so bad history books wouldn't talk about it.

"I will be conducting a barrier patrol today," Noctus continued. "Nothing more. Stand, and go about your business."

This time, everyone slowly rose to their feet, glancing at each other as they reluctantly returned to their work.

It took a minute for the noise level to grow again, and everyone was still peering in our direction every so often, but the truck with the armor and weapons started up again, and people started entering and exiting stores.

I, meanwhile, went back to clinging to the neck of Noctus's shirt. *Barrier patrol? That's what he and Aristide were talking about when they arrived, walking the barrier to make certain it was holding.*

"It seems Ama has done more for you than all the detailed instructions I've given you about '*How to Win Friends and Influence People*'," Ker said.

"Did everyone relax when they saw Ama?" Aristide asked. "I heard their heartbeats slow down."

Noctus tickled me under my chin. "Her presence did seem to ease their usual anxiety."

Cuteness is a valuable weapon to wield as a cat. I've practiced in front of a mirror so I know how to look as charming as possible. It works great on humans.

Ker rocked forward and backward on her heels. "I'm glad you finally found something to soften your image—although, I still think Dale Carnegie's teachings would have helped if you'd actually put them into practice."

Noctus frowned. "Do I look like I need to make friends?"

"Noctus," Aristide said. "I can't *see*, and I think you look like you need friends."

Noctus stared at Aristide for a moment, then smirked. "If I need friends, *you* need friends."

"What kind of logic is that?" Aristide tapped his walking stick on the ground. "Or are you just devolving to insults? Why not go for Shakespearian ones—those were more fun."

"Ahhh yes, there is your vampire nostalgia for long gone history," Noctus said. "Shall I begin preparations for a coffin so you can take long slumbers?"

"Appreciating Shakespearian insults is *not* a sign of nostalgia! You take that back!"

Ker yawned, then shook her body like a dog as she ignored the argument. "How much of the city would you like to inspect before we ride the trail around the barrier?"

Ride? Ride what?

Noctus shrugged. "I was thinking this tier, and the highest." He opened his mouth to say more, but Ker tilted her head to the side, then glanced that way as well.

I only saw it was an elf Ker was gesturing to—I was too occupied with digging my claws through Noctus's shirt without nicking his skin to pay more attention than that. But Noctus studied the elf who had dared to approach him.

"Excuse me, Your Majesty, but...would Ama like a treat?"

Treat? As in food? Please don't be cat food...

I whipped around to face the blessed elf and his offering. I recognized Prydwen, the elf whose belt buckle artifact had exploded. He was holding what appeared to be a piece of bacon.

I immediately purred at the thought of consuming food that wasn't roasted chicken.

Noctus nodded, and Prydwen slowly held out the bacon.

My first bite made the volume of my purr double—it was some sort of candied bacon with a sweet and tangy taste to it.

I'm in heaven. Now if I could just eat something that wasn't meat, I could die happy!

Noctus caught me when I loosened my claws in my exuberance and almost fell off him. "Thank you," he said. "It appears she enjoys it."

"Does she like strawberries?" A girl who appeared to be maybe five or six stood next to Prydwen. She had his tawny colored hair, and she held out a ripe strawberry with much more confidence and far less hesitation than Prydwen.

"Oh—wait," Prydwen started, but it was too late.

With Noctus holding my weight, I could reach out, latch one paw around the red strawberry and mash it to my mouth.

Eating fruit as a cat was a little awkward—cats had teeth that were made for ripping. But having been on a meat-only diet, I was desperate, and I didn't care how inelegant it was, I wanted that strawberry.

The little girl giggled, but held on to the fruit so I could gnaw on it.

Noctus waited until I finished the strawberry before he adjusted his hold on me. Once I was no longer in danger of tipping out of his arms, he glanced at the girl. "Thank you."

Beaming, she curtsied to him. "You have a nice kitty."

"...Thank you?" Noctus said, with a hint of awkwardness that was almost cute.

He's clearly not used to kids.

Prydwen bowed. "Excuse us, Your Majesty." Prydwen took his daughter's hand and tugged her backwards with him. He peered once more at Noctus, this time with a hesitant smile—the slightly stiff kind that you exchange with someone you don't know when you walk past them.

Still better than shivering in fear.

Noctus watched the elf and his daughter leave and rubbed the top of my head as I licked my chops. "It seems Ama is an omnivore."

Ker clapped for me. "How very forward thinking of her!"

"Would you two stop it?" Aristide complained. "She's a cat—not Noctus's child."

Noctus adjusted his hold on me. "There's no need to be jealous, Aristide. If you wanted strawberries all you have to do is ask."

"Yeah, Aristide," Ker said. "Do you want me to call the little girl back? She had a whole basket of fruit."

Aristide groaned. "Sometimes I question my own intelligence for choosing to spend my days with the two of you. Come on."

Aristide started walking—tapping his walking stick on the ground. It took me a moment to realize he was listening to the echoes of the tap to guide him.

Ker and Noctus followed him, and we made it past two stores before we were stopped again, this time by a beautiful woman elf.

"Valaria," Noctus said.

I hadn't heard many elf names, so I recognized it as belonging to the woman who had lost the pocket watch outside Queen's Court Café, even though I had never seen her and only heard Charon and Noctus talking about her.

"Your Majesty." Valaria bowed—her nerves obvious through her audible gulp and the slight pallor. "I thought—that is..."

I meowed when I noticed Valaria was holding what appeared to be a pink ribbon embroidered with tiny black cats.

"That is beautiful embroidery," Noctus said.

"Y-yes. Thank you." Valaria bowed her head, making the intricate braid her hair was folded into cascade over her shoulder, then held out the ribbon. "I made it for Ama."

"She made what?" Aristide asked.

"A pink ribbon," Noctus answered, then shifted his gaze back to Valaria. "Your thoughtfulness does you credit. Ker?"

"I'm on it—I'm an expert bow-tier!" Ker winked as she took the ribbon from Valaria. She slid the fabric under my collar, tying it in a large bow on the back of my neck. "She looks so adorable with it!"

Noctus stared at me for a moment, before a subtle smile twitched across his lips. "She does." He was still smiling when he shifted his gaze to Valaria. "Thank you."

Valaria rapidly blinked, then looked back and forth from Noctus to me, as if she was puzzling through an interesting mathematical equation.

Do I need to thank her or something?

I tried out one of my quieter meows that I liked to think was sweeter, but it didn't brush away the wrinkles of her furrowed forehead.

Instead, she looked almost more surprised. "I am glad you have a new companion to bring you additional joy, Your Majesty," Valaria finally said. "She is very charming."

One last bow, and she was gone.

"Just like you, it seems none of your people hold with elven tradition of a dislike for cats," Ker said as the elf maiden scuttled off. "In fact, I think you should have gotten a cat ages ago. Or maybe we should have done city inspections with me in my wolf form to soften your image?"

"I don't think your wolf form would help," Noctus said. "It would probably worsen the issue. Aristide," he called.

Aristide reached out, and Noctus set my head under the vampire's palm. The vampire petted me, then caressed my new bow, his fingers tracing the embroidery stitches. "Beautiful," he said.

When he let go, the pair wordlessly started forward, Aristide again using the sounds of his cane to guide himself.

"How dare you say I'd make things worse for your image, Noctus? I'll have you know I'm an adorable wolf!" Ker said.

"You're the size of a pony," Noctus said. "Adorable is not a word used to describe a predator that large."

"It is when you're fluffy," Ker said.

I purred my laughter as I arranged my paws against Noctus's neck for a proper death hold. *I'm with Noctus on this one. Your fur coloring is too...intense to be cute.*

"Aristide, there's a horse a few yards up," Noctus called.

"I smell it," Aristide said.

In a move that seemed so practiced it was automatic, Ker ambled up to Aristide, walking ever so slightly in front of him. He kept using his cane and tapped the end on the ground, but he also held on to the back of her right arm—which she kept long and relaxed—with his free left hand.

"The stitches on the ribbon felt tight; it was very well made. And it's in a cat shape, right?" Aristide asked.

"Yes—black cats, like Ama," Noctus said. "We're going around the horse."

Ker stepped away from Aristide's path, making a wide arc around the black horse.

"That is thoughtful, particularly because no one had seen Ama until now, correct?" Aristide asked.

"I frequently find her with her nose pressed against the glass windows of my bedroom looking out at the city," Noctus said. "But unless my citizens have telescopes and a newfound sense of voyeurism, no."

"Everyone's been talking about her," Ker said as we drifted back into place on the raised part of the road. "She is your first pet, after all. We're back on the path, Aristide."

"Even if she's Noctus's first pet, and is particularly well mannered for a cat—which even I have to admit—it seems unfair that she gets gifts!" Aristide released Ker and went back to tapping his cane on the ground in front of him, listening to the noises it made. "I've been your friend for centuries, and I've never gotten a gift."

"You also don't purr for people," Ker said. "That's a pretty charming trait."

"I could purr," Aristide sniffed. "I'm sure I'd be great at it."

Although Aristide and Ker were always fun, I paid less attention to their conversation as I watched the elf city.

Three peacocks roosted on one of the hitching posts meant for horses, their bright plumage glowing in the white city. One of them wailed at a kid on a bike who got too close to them.

Trees and plant life seemed to sprout out of every nook and cranny, their thick branches enclosing entire buildings. The white city was lush with flowers of every kind and color, giving the air a flowery smell that paired nicely with the crisp scent the roaring waterfalls provided.

"Are you seriously bringing Ama with us to check the barrier?" Aristide asked.

"No," Noctus said. "I'll take her back to the villa before we patrol the bottom layer of the town."

The line of buildings broke for a frothy river that churned through a chasm carved through the city.

Noctus and the others walked over the bridge—which had a barely discernible arch to it—but the sides of the bridge were reinforced with an elaborate wood railing that had gems affixed into it. When the sunlight shone, the gems cast rainbows across the city street.

"Taking her back is the sensible thing to do," Ker said. "I'm not sure how she'd like riding a horse."

"Given the near constant, frantic beat of her heart, I'd say not well," Aristide said.

Yes, thank you, Aristide! You must have had a cat at some point—you're very knowledgeable.

We turned, crossing through a white gazebo placed in the center of a green space.

"I just wanted to let her see the city since she seems interested in it," Noctus said. "Perhaps she'll be more inclined to come out here instead of the human neighborhood."

"Cats do what they want," Aristide said.

"So you've said." Noctus glanced down at me.

I'd been gawking at two elf girls who were fishing in a pond inside the green space—*What are they hoping to catch?*—but when I felt his eyes I peered up at him.

When he didn't look away from me, I meowed—slightly confused by the attention.

Noctus held his hand up—palm facing me.

I didn't even wait for the verbal cue, I shifted my weight so I could tap my paw against his palm, giving him a high five.

Something in his hazel brown eyes warmed, which made his eyes look less steely and more golden. He leaned forward, briefly pressing his forehead against mine.

I felt magic—a warm, reassuring kind of magic that wrapped around Noctus's sharp elven magic. I hadn't felt anything like it before; it was almost...a connection.

CHAPTER SEVENTEEN

Chloe

Before I could think through the magic, Noctus pulled back, and adjusted the way I leaned against him. "Are there any places you two would like to visit?"

"I'm thinking we should hit up every food vendor," Aristide said. "To see if Ama can snag us some free food."

"You're a vampire," Ker said. "You don't even *like* food."

"No, but you do," Aristide said. "Besides, what's the point of—what are you always saying?—meeting companions and dictating to people, if you can't use your skills to get things?"

"First of all, it's *Win Friends and Influence People*. And you do it because it's nice to be confident and liked," Ker said.

Noctus's exhale sounded similar to a dragon breathing fire. "You have *not* heard Ker talk about Dale Carnegie's principles since the day she got that wretched book all the way until now to bait her like that."

As we started down a new row of stores I rested my chin against Noctus's shoulder, content to peer over his back, getting a good look at the elf city that extended around me.

I want to get this collar off, but there are things I enjoy about this...

AFTER HEARING NOCTUS, Aristide, and Ker's plans for their Curia Cloisters field trip, I decided the best course of action would be to sneak into the SUV before they left—not so I could go to the actual Curia Cloisters, but because I needed to go to the Book Nookery.

Book Nookery was a better resource than the Curia Cloisters—whatever I learned there couldn't be traced back to me, so if Noctus or the Paragon came knocking, no one could follow my trail.

Besides, I needed to check in with Ms. Booker to see if I had a job. Hopefully she was feeling kind enough to let me look at her books again. The biggest question, however, was whether she was fluent in Elvish. After seeing her private bookshelf, I was pretty sure she was. Which meant even if she had no idea what spell Noctus had used, she could at least give me an Elvish alphabet or something so I could start trying to learn it for myself and—in *months*, I could take another crack at Noctus's books.

Going to Book Nookery was a risk—I still didn't know what was up with the tracker. But he hadn't found me at Noctus's home, and last time he'd found me I'd been on the loose for the whole night. Hopefully that meant I could get to Book Nookery, talk to Ms. Booker, and then make it back to Noctus's home before the elf king got back or the tracker found me.

I didn't want to go to the Book Nookery from the Cape Cod house, because the tracker hadn't yet found Noctus's home, and I wanted to keep it that way. Plus, I wasn't entirely certain Noctus would let his pet wander that far from home.

The trick would be, how would I keep him from realizing I was in the car when he had that darn tracking spell?

With all of that weighing on my mind, it was remarkably easy to smuggle myself into the car.

It was somewhat early in the morning—maybe seven o'clock, when I trotted up to the cat door cut into the front door.

After my little trip to the elven city, Noctus had installed a cat door that only opened for me—or more correctly my magical collar—on the front door of the Cape Cod house, and in the door that opened to the elven city.

I didn't intend to ever use the latter cat door, but the one to the human neighborhood had made my morning texting sessions to my siblings a lot easier to pull off!

The new cat door chirped and opened, letting me pass through.

Happy, I flicked my tail as I hurried over to the garage. The garage door was open—since Noctus was leaving for the Curia Cloisters soon, Charon had begun his preparations, starting with a safety inspection of the SUV.

I sat on the driveway and licked one of my front paws as I watched Charon go down his checklist.

Once satisfied he stopped a foot away from me and bowed. "Ama," he said with a politeness not usually afforded to pets.

I meowed at him.

Charon nodded—as if I was a respected coworker—then walked to the front door.

As soon as he stepped inside I ran into the garage. The window on the driver's side was rolled down. I hopped in with ease given the agility of my cat body, then nosed my way through the SUV, trying to find a suitable hiding place.

I settled on the trunk.

Since it was an SUV, the trunk was part of the vehicle, not a separate compartment, which would make it easy to get in and out of, and I wouldn't suffocate from lack of air.

But there wasn't much of anything to hide under, either. There was an ice scraper, a mini snow shovel, a first aid kit that was stocked with bandages and potions and was strapped to the side of the SUV, and a folded winter blanket.

Thank goodness Charon hasn't removed the winter weather gear yet.

I bit a corner of the blanket and dragged it over to a small space between the back seat and the raised wheel well. I backed into the space and tried to drape the now half-folded blanket over me as best I could.

I had just enough time to wedge myself into place and hope Charon didn't take corners too tightly before the door opened.

"You first, Ker," Aristide said.

Hidden under the blanket, I almost panicked. I'd forgotten, *Aristide could hear my heartbeat!*

They were going to find me, and it was going to be a suspicion inducing moment, I already knew it.

I huddled lower under the blanket and held my breath as the SUV rocked when Ker hopped in.

Three car doors closed in quick succession, and the SUV rumbled to life.

Aristide didn't say anything, even as I heard seatbelt buckles click.

The leather on one of the chairs creaked. "Is Ama in here?" Noctus asked.

The hair on my spine puffed up in my shock. *I thought maybe he'd figure something out once we were on the road, but how could he feel me already? I didn't think the spell was that precise!*

"She was out on the driveway a moment ago," Charon said. "I imagine she's sitting in her favorite bush. Would you like us to stop and search for her?"

"What?" Aristide shouted.

"He's listening to a podcast," Charon said.

That was promising. If he was blasting a podcast, maybe he wouldn't hear my heart.

"Ignore him," Noctus advised. "Ker?"

Ker woofed, and the bench seat buckled as she turned. I could hear panting, but I couldn't see anything through the blanket's thick fabric.

My tail puffed up, and I didn't dare breathe as Ker sniffed the air.

I should be able to avoid detection due to my magic. But I've never made friends as a cat, so could she pick up my scent?

Ker sneezed, then barked again.

"I believe that's the 'All is clear, Your Majesty'," Charon said.

"Fine." The leather of his seat creaked as Noctus shifted. "We can go."

Charon finished backing up. Unsecured as I was, the swerve he made to pull onto the road almost knocked me out of my spot —which wasn't a good sign for the rest of this trip.

Even so, I relaxed a little, depuffing some of my hair when I realized I hadn't gotten caught. *Magic is on my side—in this instance.*

When I was a kid I used to get mad that I had the deadliness of a kitten—or maybe a cotton ball—if you pitted me against the likes of a werewolf. But although I couldn't fight, at least I could slip around undetected!

If I had no morals, I could have been a cat burglar—haha!

I was so amused by my own joke, I licked my chops.

Ker leaned into Aristide and woofed again. I heard the vampire tap his cell phone screen, likely turning his volume down a little.

"So, what are we going to do first?" Aristide asked. "The legal stuff, or illegal?"

"Legal, first," Noctus said. "If things go south for the second half of our investigation, we'll at least have something to show for the trip."

"Sounds intelligent—I like it," Aristide said.

"We'll be visiting the archives first," Noctus said. "The Curia Cloisters is legally obligated to release records of every instance they are called out to investigate something. The details will be limited—all they must release is the location and reason for the visit, so it won't have any of the details their investigative reports would. But recording the locations alone might be enough to help us discern a pattern."

"And then we track down and check out the watch?" Aristide asked.

"Yes."

"Excellent. Nothing like a little breaking and entering to add excitement to a morning. That's why I prefer true crime podcasts at dawn."

"You've *only* been listening to true crime podcasts," Noctus said. "I'm surprised you haven't switched topics yet."

"Maybe I would if you hadn't made fun of me for listening to history podcasts."

"Why would you listen to history podcasts when we *lived* through it?"

"I have confirmed the wing in which the Curia Cloisters is keeping the watch," Charon said, breaking up the good natured ribbing. "His Majesty will have to be the one to check it, given that, besides myself, he has the greatest chance at recognizing the magic used."

"As long as magic cooperates," Noctus sighed.

"So Ker and I will be the distraction and you're the lookout, Charon?" Aristide guessed.

"Correct."

That makes sense. Charon keeps wearing that gray hood of his in public, which isn't exactly inconspicuous.

Aristide chuckled—a rich, throaty sound that almost made me puff my tail up again. "I'm thinking we dust off 'fighting friends' for this occasion, Ker. What do you think?"

Ker woofed.

"No, rejected," Aristide said. "I hate that one."

He can't possibly understand her, can he? Wolves can only communicate with members of their Pack in their wolf form.

I braced myself on the wheel well as Charon made another

turn. The blanket slid off me, and from my angle I could see the side of Ker's massive head. Thankfully, she didn't notice and was too busy shoving her nose in Aristide's face as she whined.

"I don't care if it's less dangerous. I'm not doing 'Nostalgia Vamp.' It's stupid, and only promotes hurtful stereotypes," Aristide said.

My heart pounded frantically—I had no idea how Aristide hadn't heard it. I bit the blanket again and frantically tried to pull it back over me. The blanket was made of fleece and was weirdly stretchy and had a slight dog flavor to it—probably from Ker.

"Nostalgia Vamp is not a stereotype so much as a scientific fact," Noctus dryly said.

I shivered under the blanket—from anxiety, not cold. It was a little stuffy.

Is it that they can't sense me...or have they just not noticed me?

I'd always been able to make a getaway in my cat form from other supernaturals. Humans were typically the bigger danger as they actually noticed me and would sometimes try to capture me if they thought I was a stray.

But I never thought the distraction magic would cover me so well. Though that does say something about Noctus. He's blocked from his magic, and he still must have felt at least a twinge of the tracking spell. Meanwhile, I'm sitting directly behind Aristide, and he hasn't sensed me.

Oblivious to my thoughts, Aristide made a strangled hiccupping noise. "If that's so, then what does that make me since I don't complain about modern living, I'm not nostalgic for less enjoyable times, and I don't waste my days sleeping?"

"Bizarre," Noctus suggested. "Or perhaps in denial?"

"*You*!" Aristide snarled. "As if you have room to talk! You're an elf king who's prouder that his pet cat learned how to give high fives than anything else you've accomplished in the last two centuries!"

"Ama is very smart," Noctus said. "She deserves to be admired.

Whereas you persist in listening to history podcasts when you think we can't hear."

"*What?*"

The rest of the car ride was spent with Aristide giving a sermon about his many modern ways. The blanket slipped off me once more, but it wasn't until the car slowed and rolled to a stop outside the Curia Cloisters that I realized my exit was going to be much more complicated than my entrance.

I need to get out now—with Ker and Aristide. If I wait and turn human and try to make my exit after Charon has parked, I'll set off the car alarm.

"Which entrance are we at?" Aristide asked as he opened his door.

"The main entrance," Noctus said. "Are we certain Ama did not mistakenly come with us?"

"Tracking spells aren't very precise. If it's telling you Ama is nearby, it probably needs to be renewed," Aristide said.

"This kind shouldn't need renewing," Noctus grimly said.

Huh? Why not?

Noctus continued, "Charon, we'll meet you at the public records."

"Yes, Your Majesty."

A car door slammed—Noctus's, because Ker rocked the car as she walked across the bench seat.

"What are you talking about? Unless you have some werewolf hunter blood in you, *Your Majesty*, all tracking spells need to be occasionally renewed." Aristide's voice was muffled as he stood outside the car. "What are you tracking her with?"

"Just get Ker's harness—and turn off your podcast," Noctus said. I could barely hear his deep voice—he must be walking away from the car.

"Touchy," Aristide grumbled.

When Ker started to jump out, I hastily jumped over the back of the bench seat, landing in the footwell area. From there it was easy to hop out and dart under the car, though I had to tuck my tail to keep it from getting slammed in the door when Aristide nudged it shut.

I crouched on the pavement, flattened as close to the ground as I could so when Charon drove off, the vehicle would clear me with plenty of room. I could only see Noctus, Aristide, and Ker from the shins down at this angle, but it was all the view I needed.

Noctus shifted his weight from foot to foot, turning so he was pointed at the Curia Cloisters. "Ready?"

Ker circled around Aristide, settling in at his left side.

"Yes," Aristide said. "Let's go have some fun." The three strode through the main entrance, disappearing inside.

It wasn't until the doors closed behind them that Charon finally pulled away.

I checked to make sure another car wasn't coming, then made my escape. I hopped on the sidewalk and ran, heading around the edge of the building, until I found a large bush I could safely change behind.

A blink of an eye, and I was human.

"Off to Book Nookery," I muttered to myself, grateful I could talk again.

After spending the majority of my hours as a cat, there was something gratifying about being able to open my mouth and speak.

I dug out my phone as I trotted off in the direction of Book Nookery.

Joy had sent the day's cat text, and Pat had added in a photo of a cupcake loaded with frosting that made my stomach growl.

Looks like a healthy, nutritious breakfast, I texted.

Ur just jealous, Pat replied.

I can top you, Joy wrote back.

Seconds later, a picture of a chocolate crepe filled my screen.

This time, my stomach growled so hard, I felt it in my throat.

"That's it—I need a pitstop," I decided. "And maybe a bribe."

I changed the direction I was heading in, so I would veer closer to downtown as I trekked my way across Magiford.

I was hustling, so it only took about fifteen minutes to make it to Magiford Donuts.

The storefront was small, with no chairs and only a few tables that were also stacked with napkins and plastic forks and knives. The actual store part of the bakery was barely more than a hole in the wall even though it occupied an entire building.

I opened the door—which had the highest pitched alarm on it that went on for what felt like forever—and the warm scent of dough beckoned me farther inside.

"Good morning," the clerk greeted—a wizard who had been boredly making little flames dance on his fingertips until I entered the store.

"Good morning." I barely remembered to respond to him as I gazed at the day's offerings.

The entire back wall of the storefront—from about knee high going all the way up to the ceiling—was covered with trays of donuts, some dripping in chocolate glazes that looked so silky they reflected light, others covered in strawberry frosting and then rolled in brightly colored sprinkles. The cream filled donuts —available in chocolate or vanilla and then rolled in powdered sugar—had the biggest section of the wall, but long johns dribbled with maple syrup, crullers, and apple fritters had the largest trays.

There was a pretty good chance they used magic to make them—I could feel the silky sensation of fae magic in my elbow, and the buzzy feeling of wizard magic in my fingers whenever I stepped inside the store—but I didn't care. The donuts smelled *divine*.

"I'll take a chocolate glazed donut and a buttermilk cruller, please." I scratched at my elbow, trying to ease the ticklish sensation of fae magic. "And then in a separate bag can I get a toasted coconut donut?"

The clerk rang my order up, and I paid—having to consciously make sure I swallowed often because I was drooling.

As the clerk stuffed my donuts in a wax paper bag, something banged, and the front windows rattled.

The wizard grimaced as he put the toasted coconut donut in its own bag. "That's one of our ovens. The industrial ones are loud sometimes."

"I can imagine." I took my purchases and ran outside, savagely ripping open my bag and snatching up my buttermilk cruller, biting a huge hunk of it.

It was heavenly—soft on the inside, and the crisp outer layer was softened by the rich frosting.

Oh, wow. The only thing that could make this better would be a tall glass of milk!

I hummed to myself as I slowly started plodding down the sidewalk, heading—once again—in the direction of Book Nookery.

By the time I passed by the giant clocktower—which still wasn't open—I'd devoured my cruller and started in on my chocolate glazed donut.

It wasn't until I was licking my fingers clean that I realized it was a little odd the wizard was working in the bakery, particularly since I hadn't seen any pins, buttons, patches—nothing that would identify what House he belonged to.

Wizards usually go for more scholarly jobs, unless the House has a business associated with it. That's kind of weird.

Maybe he was from a displaced family of a wizard House? It didn't happen often—or ever, really—except last year there'd been a huge scandal with wizards and their House, and it hadn't ended well.

Regardless, it didn't really matter to me. I just needed the sugar—and the bribe.

I heard a familiar cooing/squawking sound, and I looked up to see French Fry circling overhead, flicking his striped raccoon tail so it knocked him off balance as he flew.

"Hey, French Fry, it's been a while."

French Fry made a crash landing into a potted plant positioned outside an accountant's office, then skittered toward me, whipping his head from side to side so he could study me with one bulging orange eye, then the other.

I could see he was peering in the general direction of my donut, his tail puffed hopefully.

"Fine—but only because we're friends!" I broke off a tiny piece of my chocolate glazed donut and tossed it to him.

French Fry pecked at it, then swallowed it whole. To thank me, he flapped his wings and hopped around, frightening himself when he smacked into a trashcan with his furry raccoon rear.

I laughed, feeling stronger between my donuts and my little friend. "Glad to see you're still being you. Come on, walk with me. Just don't puke on my shoes."

French Fry cooed at me, then launched himself into the air and hovered nearby, shedding feathers like a dog blowing its coat.

By the time I finished my chocolate glazed donut, we were almost to the Book Nookery, which was a very good thing. The donuts were so good, I was tempted to eat the toasted coconut donut I'd gotten for Ms. Booker—she loved coconut.

I paced back and forth on the sidewalk for a little bit.

She's going to fire me. I've been gone too much, with no warning. I probably have enough money saved to cover two months of rent even if I get fired, but in order to keep my finances going I'll need a new job and to actually work. *That will be a problem if I'm still stuck living as a cat.*

But I'm getting ahead of myself. Even if she fires me, she might be willing to help me with this collar, and that's enough.

I glanced at French Fry, hoping for encouragement, but he was pecking at his reflection in the front window, completely ignoring me.

So much for encouragement.

I took a deep breath, then marched up the front porch, opening the front door to Book Nookery.

Ms. Booker was at the front desk, wearing a gray dress with a matching jacket that nicely complimented the streaks of gray in her hair, and reading a book. She set the book aside, folded her hands together, and leaned against the desk. "Ahh, Chloe dear. How good to see you again."

"Hi, Ms. Booker. I deeply apologize for my unprofessional behavior—it was never my intention to abandon my position." I scooted my way across the entrance and approached the desk, holding up the paper bag as an offering. "It's my mistake. I understand there will be consequences, but first please let me say thank you so much for the chance you gave me. I really enjoyed working at Book Nookery."

Ms. Booker looked from the donut bag to me. Her lower lip jutted out a little, but it seemed thoughtful. She abruptly disappeared behind the counter, and when she popped upright again she was holding the two elven books I'd borrowed.

"Stop your fretting, Chloe dear. Just tell me: what has happened to you?" She raised her eyebrow—which was penciled on with makeup—and held the books up.

I bit my lip and shook my head. "It's dangerous."

"You're standing in the Book Nookery, my dear. *Knowledge* is dangerous. After the library, we're likely the most dangerous place in Magiford. This house can protect us. Now, explain."

I swallowed as I stared at my kind boss, and debated just what I should say.

Can I tell her about the collar without getting into the elf part of the story? If Noctus realizes she knows, he'll probably kill her.

Noctus was more valiant than I'd ever thought an elf—much

less a king—could be, but I wasn't fooled. He'd put down any threat to his people, which would include my boss.

Ms. Booker set the books down on the counter and watched me for a moment. She cocked her head, shrugged a little, then tapped one fingernail—painted a shimmery pink color—on the desk.

I felt magic ripple through all of Book Nookery.

Something stirred. I couldn't tell if it was the books or the building itself, but I knew Ms. Booker was right. The house would protect us.

I sucked in a deep gulp of air. "I found the King of the Mors—probably the last elf king alive. I can't leave him because he's tracking me since he thinks I'm his pet cat, and I'm too scared to let him know I'm *not*. Also, some weird guy with the most fear-inducing magic I've ever seen is following me around. He only leaves me alone when I'm with the elf king. I'm stuck, because no matter what I do, I think I'll die. So I just keep living as a cat."

I panted when I finished blurting out my explanation, and for the first time since the tracker had chased me to Noctus, I felt marginally better.

It's a relief—to share all of this. Even if Ms. Booker can't help me.

When I finally met her gaze, I had to work hard not to hunch my shoulders.

Her expression hadn't changed—her lower lip was still jutting out, and her penciled eyebrows were high on her forehead. She did, however, shuffle out from behind the desk. "I see," she said. "This sounds like it requires a beverage. I'm afraid I only have cream—none of the milk you are so fond of. But would you care for some tea?"

"You believe me?" I asked, stunned.

"Chloe dear, the entire time you've worked at Book Nookery it has been your utmost goal to avoid any and all notice. You would never make up such a fantastical tale." Ms. Booker minced off into the kitchen. "Besides, I was almost positive one of the Mors survived the war."

"*How*? How did you know?"

Ms. Booker affectionally patted the wooden doorway to the kitchen as she passed through it, and I felt the magic that swirled in Book Nookery settle down once more. "Tea first. Tell me your story, and I'll tell you what I know."

CHAPTER EIGHTEEN

Chloe

"—Try not to listen to any of Noctus's business because that could come back to bite me, and I'm not sure if I can go to the Curia Cloisters because the Paragon seems to think they're pals, but I don't know what else to do. To leave Noctus I need to get this collar off. If I go to the Cloisters for help, they'll move on the information, Noctus will figure out I'm not a cat, and that might not end well for me. But if I don't go to the Cloisters, I'll have to learn Elvish or something to find whatever spell Noctus used, and that still doesn't solve the tracker that has been following me," I summarized.

I'd given my boss a vague picture of the situation—mostly just what she needed to know to explain the collar—because I didn't want Noctus feeling like he had to track her down if this all blew up.

I hadn't told her about Charon, Ker, Aristide, or the elven city. I didn't even mention that he was investigating the sudden influx of bad artifacts in Magiford, although I had told her about the tracker guy—in case he came skulking around Book Nookery.

Ms. Booker set her teacup down on the small kitchen table. "All of that is quite the conundrum."

"Yeah." I stared at my mug of tea, which had cooled to a lukewarm temperature since Ms. Booker had poured it for me. I didn't really like tea, but the peppermint aroma was soothing, and it was nice to hold something warm in my hands while I told her my story.

The coconut donut I'd gotten for Ms. Booker was on a plate, cut into fourths. Ms. Booker had eaten half, but after reciting everything that had happened to me, I'd lost my appetite, even for donuts.

"This collar that you can't get off, might I see it?" Ms. Booker asked.

"Oh, yeah. Of course." I hurriedly unwound the scarf from my neck, revealing the black lace collar with the three red gems.

When Ms. Booker leaned closer, I slipped out of my seat and walked around the table so I could crouch in front of her.

Ms. Booker gently slipped her fingers under the soft fabric and tugged.

Nothing happened.

She worked her way around the entire collar, attempting to pull on it. "It is indeed stuck on you," she said. "How very odd."

"Yeah, I think it's because the magic in the collar wasn't strictly cast on me, so my anti-magic abilities haven't kicked in," I said.

"I'm not so sure about that," Ms. Booker said. "Positive magic —things like fae potions—work for you, yes?"

"Yes," I said. "But they work on all wizards, too."

"But wizards are only immune to fae magic." Ms. Booker gently tapped the three gems at my throat. "Not elf magic, dragon shifter magic, or other equally powerful entities, as you seem immune to." She waved me back to my chair in a clear dismissal.

I wove around the table. "Do you think the Curia Cloisters might have the resources to help me get the collar off?" I jumped when I walked past the giant kitchen windows and something feathery thumped into them.

It was French Fry. He was slowly sliding down the glass, losing a feather or two in the process before he peeled himself free.

I shook my head at him as I sat down.

Ms. Booker smoothed the cloth napkin she had spread over her lap. "No. I don't believe the Curia Cloisters will be able to help you with the collar."

"No?" I repeated.

"No," Ms. Booker said. "I don't believe there is any being powerful enough in the Cloisters to remove it."

"Could someone like Queen Leila from the Night Court remove it? Or maybe a dragon shifter?"

Ms. Booker took a delicate sip of her tea. "I'm not sure if anyone besides Noctus himself can remove it."

If Noctus is the only one who can remove it, I'm doomed. I stared unseeingly at French Fry, watching him settle on the window sill.

Inspiration clicked into place as I watched the trash griffin precariously totter across the window frame. "Wait, if you think Noctus needs to remove the collar, then you know what magic is on the collar?"

"No. I can sense the strength of the magic on it, but not what it is. With magic that powerful, however, there is a very limited number of elven spells it could be. A few days' worth of research should uncover the answer."

I started to slump in my chair in relief before I remembered who I was with and sat up straight again.

"However," Ms. Booker continued, "you need to be careful, Chloe."

I stared at Ms. Booker for a moment, trying to figure out if she was being serious or not.

I *obviously* knew I needed to be careful—that was why I hadn't been keen on telling her!

"Yes," I slowly said.

Ms. Booker set her teacup down again. "I know you're concerned, and you're being quite levelheaded about this whole situation, but I'm not sure you understand the dangers."

"Noctus is essentially the elf king of *death*, and someone is trying to chase me down when I'm the supernatural equivalent of an ant. I understand exactly how bad the situation is," I said. "In fact, I feel pretty confident that it couldn't get worse!"

Ms. Booker shook her head. "I'm not referring to those parts of your issue, but your collar."

"What do you mean?" I warily glanced at French Fry. He had his head planted against the glass window and was peering with one eye in the direction of the trash bin.

"Despite the legends, elven magic is not infallible. The elves were feared because their magic had the least limitations and the widest variety of ways to apply it when compared to the likes of wizards and fae, *and* because they were physically superior. But elven spells themselves are like any other—they wear out, break, and slowly chip away as we've seen with the barrier spells in the fae realm. The spell placed on your collar is *not* like that, and there are only a handful of reasons why an elf would risk expending so much power on such a spell."

"So what you mean is, because the collar has such advanced magic, we can tell this isn't a small thing on Noctus's end?"

"Exactly."

"Oh." I gave in to the impulse to slump with this news. "That is a grim thought. But why would he invest such powerful magic in a *cat*?"

"I'm not sure, but once I figure out what type of magic it is, I'm sure that will reveal a few things. Sit up, Chloe dear. Slumping is for those who have lost, and you are not beaten."

I sat up again. "He named me Ama, if that helps. His friends said that's the Elvish word for 'sweet.'" I nervously tightened my neck scarf to the point where it was uncomfortably taut. "But he calls me Amalourne when it's just the two of us. Do you know what that means?"

"No," Ms. Booker said. "The elves were always secretive about their language and did not teach it to other supernaturals, so there weren't many records about it. I learned the written language, but even I have barely a child's grasp of the system—which is vastly different from their spoken word."

French Fry thumped his silly skull against the window, briefly drawing Ms. Booker's attention. She frowned at the trash griffin, and behind her back I made frantic shooing motions.

French Fry—blessed with maybe two thoughts in his empty skull—just whipped his head from side to side so he could peer at us with different eyes.

I wonder... I thought as I watched French Fry. *If Elvish was not taught to other supernaturals, how did Ker and Aristide know what it meant? On top of that, why have all the elves I've met spoken only English?*

Afraid to voice my thoughts, I shook my head as Ms. Booker daintily consumed another piece of the coconut donut.

"So what do I do?" I asked. "If you don't think anyone at the Curia Cloisters can take off the collar, who do I go to for help? Unless...do you think I should just tell Noctus?"

"*No,*" Ms. Booker sharply said. "As benevolent as he seems, you do not know how he would react to discovering you are human. It's possible you could survive the revelation, but..." she trailed off.

I watched her for a minute and traced the handle of my ceramic mug with my thumb. "You didn't seem surprised to hear he survived the war."

Ms. Booker nodded. "His body was never found at the incident that wiped out the Mors royal family."

"I read about that in one of the books you let me read," I said.

"You read a stilted version of it," Ms. Booker said. "In the days of my youth, I was curious about elves and did some research. I wanted to learn how we'd managed to win the war against them when the odds were overwhelmingly against supernaturals and vastly favored the elves." Ms. Booker frowned at her teacup and narrowed her eyes.

I shifted in my chair, afraid that if I said anything, she'd stop talking.

"I traced the turning point to the slaughter of the Mors royal family, as the history book said," she finally continued. "With the elves' best warriors gone in a violent act they'd never prepared for, it made the win for supernaturals at large possible. As a result, I researched the slaughter as meticulously as possible, and interviewed vampires and other supernaturals who had lived through the war. I spoke, once, to a vampire Elder who had seen the slaughter—or more correctly, what was left of it—with his own eyes. He told me the only thing capable of the destruction he saw was an elven weapon. And the only one capable of defeating the Mors king and his offspring..."

"Would be another Mors," I suddenly interjected, the answer to the riddle dawning on me. "Noctus killed them."

"Perhaps," Ms. Booker said.

I shot out of my chair, my heart beating frantically in my chest. "No, there is no perhaps. He once called himself a Kingslayer. He killed his *family*, and he was the eldest son. There was no reason for him to do it."

Ms. Booker picked up her teacup once again. "I wouldn't say that."

"What do you mean?"

"If he did indeed cause the massacre—which we don't know—out of greed, avarice, or what have you, why, then, did he not step in and lead the remaining elvish troops and vassals sworn to the Mors family to victory?" Ms. Booker asked.

But Noctus had stepped in...hadn't he? He was a king, after all—admittedly to a secret city, and he was doing everything possible to hide his identity and the existence of his people.

But even now he has a goal. He's in Magiford for a reason...and it certainly isn't because he's secretly planning to take over the supernatural world.

He—and his city—were too dependent on humans for that to work. From what I'd seen of the city, they didn't even have full grocery stores, just food stands. Based on the snatches of conversation I'd heard while being dragged around the investigation, I was pretty sure most of the elves worked regular jobs in Magiford.

Noctus, on the other hand, spent most of his time doing inspections and paperwork. He didn't even sleep all that much.

No one had known he survived the massacre because he'd disappeared. He played the role of king out of a sense of duty, not because he reveled in it. If his pet ownership was any indication, he probably would have been happier traveling around with Charon, Ker, Aristide, and a menagerie of pets.

Nervous about the line of my own thinking, I glanced at French Fry.

He'd settled onto the stair railing, preening his feathers. Sitting out in the morning sun like that, he almost looked pretty.

At least, he did until he puked.

How on earth did I end up with such a...weird sidekick? I'm not fae.

"One thing can be certain," Ms. Booker said, breaking the silence. "It's been generations since the elven war, and Noctus hasn't taken any actions against supernaturals."

"Yes," I agreed. "But what would drive the crown prince of the Mors to murder his family?"

"Something that isn't going to affect the outcome of this mess you've been dropped in," Ms. Booker primly told me.

"Right." With a lot of effort, I narrowed my focus back to my problem. "So since I can't tell Noctus because it's too dangerous, and if no one from the Curia Cloisters can get this collar off me... what do I do?"

"I shall conduct my own research on the magic used on your collar. When I learn of something, I will text you."

"Really?" I squeaked out, emotion making my voice thick.

"Truly," Ms. Booker said. "You are my employee. It is my duty to aid you in matters like this."

"Thank you. Thank you so much!" I barely managed to squeeze the words out, I was so overcome with relief.

Someone is on my side and is going to help me get through this. I'm not alone.

Ms. Booker patted my hand. "There, there, dear. I may not be able to find anything, but it's important you be armed with as much knowledge as possible before you decide on your next step."

"And what would be the next step?"

"My suggestion would be to attempt to alert the Paragon," Ms. Booker said.

I inhaled wrong and snorted a breath of air. *That's right, I didn't tell her about the Paragon and his glamour.*

If Ms. Booker knew about the glamour, that was another major risk. Based on the fact that I'd never heard before that the Paragon used a glamour, it had to be something he was hiding from the public.

As much as I wanted my freedom, I wasn't going to sacrifice my boss—who was kind enough to help me with all of this.

I cleared my throat and tried to speak as mildly as I could manage. "You don't think that's too much of a risk?"

Ms. Booker shook her head. "Since he knows about Noctus, he's in the best position to help you."

Doubt it. If he looked at all into my abilities recorded in my file at the Curia Cloisters, he'd probably act against me.

"But he's a fae. What if he tried to use me against Noctus?" I tried to reason without getting anywhere near the real danger I was concerned about.

"It's a possibility," Ms. Booker said. "But for all that he's a tricky fae, he is the Paragon—the representative of fae on a national level. You're better off trusting him than the average Seelie or Unseelie fae as he's tied down by responsibilities."

Except he wants something from Noctus. I had considered telling Ms. Booker why the Paragon visited Noctus, but she hadn't asked, and something in my gut told me this was something I should *not* share.

"You did say it sounded like the Paragon is a frequent visitor?" Ms. Booker asked, shaking me from my thoughts.

"Yes."

"Then I would begin with him. I'm not certain how you'll get him alone so you can tell him what you are, but he's a shrewd fae. He won't rat you out to Noctus—not when there's a possibility he could use you for his own gain."

I nodded vigorously enough to jostle my head, while planning to do no such thing. *I guess I should get started trying to learn Elvish after all.*

Ms. Booker pursed her lips. "Unfortunately, I don't believe I'll be able to help you with this man that is chasing you."

My eyes ached with tears I wanted to shed, but frankly didn't have the time for. "As long as I stick around Noctus I'll be safe. But I'd like to get a picture of the tracker—I'll need proof to take to the Curia Cloisters."

"Not the police?"

"No, not the police. He's definitely got magic—though I'm not sure what kind. He looks human, so maybe he's half human and half fae," I said. "If I can identify him, the supernatural authorities should be able to help me. Unless you have any other ideas?"

"I'm a bookshop owner, Chloe dear, not an elite fighter," Ms. Booker dryly said.

"Yeah. It's still just so confusing—why me?" I wondered. If I'd been with anyone else I'd let my head hit the table, but Ms. Booker wouldn't like that, so I settled for pressing the palms of my hands into my eyes.

"One thing at a time, dear," Ms. Booker advised.

"Yeah." I dropped my hands and glanced at French Fry again.

He was still on the railing, cooing to himself. "I should probably head out."

"You will head back to the elf king's home?" Ms. Booker asked.

"Not yet. I need to get a change of clothes from my apartment."

I was also so desperate for a shower I'd consider letting Noctus pet my belly to get one, but I didn't need to tell Ms. Booker *that*.

"Very well." Ms. Booker stood and brushed wrinkles out of the skirt of her dress. "In that case, be careful, and I wish you luck. I will have news to share with you about the collar soon."

"Hopefully good news," I said.

"Not likely," Ms. Booker flatly said. "But I suppose there is no harm in dreaming."

I winced, but only for a moment. "Thank you, Ms. Booker, for everything. I don't know how I would manage without your help."

Ms. Booker reached out and took my hand. "Of course, dear. We supernaturals must help one another."

AN HOUR later I'd made it across town, taken the fastest shower of my life, gotten new clothes, stuffed a spare set in the tiniest backpack I owned, and was heading back to Noctus's villa.

French Fry flew overhead, gliding from lamppost to lamppost. He wasn't a very good flyer on the best of days, so this involved smacking into a lot of lights, shedding a few feathers, and lots of fumbling.

I flicked one of his feathers off my shoulder as I passed under his latest perch.

I wonder how he has enough feathers to fly?

I started to chuckle to myself, when I felt my magic shift

inside of me. Something foreign tugged at my senses, and I felt an overwhelming, throat-closing sense of fear.

Oh no...

I turned around and saw the blackened cloud one block behind me. I could make out the now familiar, lanky shape through the smoke-like shadows. This time the cloud was thin enough I could see he'd dyed his hair an electric shade of blue, and he had a tattoo on his neck.

I would say it was a wizard's tattoo, but those start on the face and travel down, and his tattoo was only on his neck.

I bolted, changing course so I was no longer headed toward Noctus's place, but downtown.

I can't risk him figuring out where Noctus's home is, and if I'm by people it should be safer. He can't do much in public.

I was dressed for running—with the right shoes and everything—so I didn't look too out of place as I sprinted down a residential street.

The tracker chased after me, his footsteps pounding in my eardrums in tune with my heartbeat.

He didn't even try to call out to me as he chased, but I could sense his irritation that he wasn't closing the gap between us.

Don't try to chase someone used to running for their life—you'll never catch up!

I saw the high-rise apartment—the one Prydwen had been by when his belt buckle exploded—and kicked my running up another notch.

Almost there!

When I slowed down to take a corner, I risked peering back at him. He was still a block back, but he'd released a spell that was on my heels.

It was an electric green color, and it crackled like lightning, spitting sparks and hissing.

I braced myself, but the spell harmlessly brushed my skin,

passing me as it was unable to attach to me with my resistance to magic.

I expected the tracker to snarl, but the hardened planes of his face morphed into a toothy smile.

Why would that make him happy?

I kicked my pace back up into a sprint, extra motivated now that I was only a block or two from downtown.

I considered calling for help—the Curia Cloisters had a hotline for this kind of situation, but to call them, I needed to be able to *make* the call, which wasn't happening as long as I was sprinting for my life.

He didn't try to throw any more spells at me, but I heard the distinct click of a small blade being pulled free from a scabbard—he had a dagger.

I turned left and hustled across the street, running into the downtown crowd.

By this time, main street was hopping. People were out and about, stopping at cafés and the newly opened stores.

Moms held the hands of their kids, who toddled along next to them. A man walked past me with a pitbull carrying a nerf football in its mouth and wildly wagging its tail, and two elderly ladies laughed across the street as they entered a boutique clothing store.

I slowed my pace to something more socially acceptable so I could be mistaken for a jogger.

Okay, this is better. He's not going to throw a weapon in the morning rush with humans around.

As if to spite me, I heard a metallic whine.

I turned in time to see the knife he'd chucked at me.

I started to duck, but just before it reached me I realized that without me in the way, it was going to hit the mom walking about five paces in front of me and pushing her baby in a stroller.

Catch it! I must catch it!

Every nerve in my body lit up, and as the knife flew over my head I grabbed it out of the air, pure instinct and adrenaline combining to make my reflexes lightning fast.

I almost dropped the knife immediately—my hand was slick with sweat—but I clutched it as I tried to figure out what to do next.

The boardwalk is behind the buildings on the right, it will be even crazier there, so that means left. If I go a block or two off main street—closer to where Magiford Donuts is—it will be more abandoned as long as I avoid the bakery. I can try ditching him there and head to the Curia Cloisters.

I wasn't entirely sure if I wanted to head to the Curia Cloisters because they were safer, or if it was because Noctus was there and I *knew* he was safe, but I didn't have the time to ponder it.

I checked the road, then bolted across the street.

I tossed the knife into the first public trashcan I passed. I would have liked to hold on to it to see if it had any identifying marks on it, but it was only going to be a liability with what I was going to have to do next, and survival was more important.

I slipped down a narrow alleyway. Halfway down it was blocked off with a chain link fence that was taller than me, but there was a tiny parking lot beyond it, which I needed to get to.

Tapping into my cat-given agility that was my trade-off for more substantial magic, I shimmied up the fence. When the top of the fence hit my waist, I folded over it, used my arms to brace myself, kicked my legs up over the fence and then lowered them to the side so I was almost horizontal. Keeping control of my body, I landed lightly, then sprinted down the rest of the alleyway.

It spat me out into a tiny parking lot behind the buildings. I ran to the nearest dumpster and changed, sliding behind the green dumpster in my cat body.

The smell of garbage was overwhelming, but I barely noticed it as my body tingled from nerves and magic.

The tracker burst out of the alleyway. He looked in both directions and scowled, not able to see me. He ran past the dumpster, heading west.

I also needed to head west—northwest to be precise—to get to the Cloisters, but since he was throwing knives around humans, I could safely call the Cloisters and they'd immediately send a team out to nab him, no questions asked.

I waited until I couldn't hear him anymore before I left the safety of the dumpster and padded across the parking lot, going under parked cars whenever I could.

I didn't see French Fry in the sky—which was just as well; he'd be a clear mark of where I was. Once I made it to the edge of the parking lot I headed south down another street. It technically took me further away from the Cloisters—which were northwest —but I wanted to put some distance between me and the maniac.

I waited until I was pointed west again before I shifted from cat to human. I stopped long enough to slide my backpack off and dig out my cell phone, then threw it back over my shoulders before I started jogging again.

I kept my steps as quiet as possible as I unlocked my phone and brought up my contacts, finding the Curia Cloisters' emergency phone number.

I was just about to tap the call button when I felt lightning fizzle in my body. I looked up just in time to see the tracker lunge out from behind a parked car, brandishing a sword at me.

My reflexes kicked in, and I hastily turned into a cat, safely skittering under the sword and running up the street.

He chased after me, but I could run even faster as a cat. Unfortunately, my cat stamina was way lower, so I'd only be able to keep up this pace for a short distance, but I was able to put some space between us as I scrambled away from him.

How does he keep finding me? He can't have dialed into Noctus's collar —he found me before I ever met Noctus!

Just as I felt my cat body start to tire, the tracker threw an ax —a legitimate *ax* that was twice the size of me.

It hit the sidewalk right in front of me, biting into the cement and cracking it.

I skidded to a stop, and he was on me in a moment. I dodged when he tried to stab down on me with a sword.

Still moving by reflex, I tapped my magic and shifted to a human and slammed my elbow into the tracker's left eye.

He cried out and staggered back a step.

Clutching my cell phone—since I held it when I changed, it came back with my human body, I tried to dial, but the tracker recovered faster than I expected and tried to wrap me in a bearhug.

I slammed my head backwards into his nose—thank you, Pat, for insisting I learn basic self-defense—then switched to a cat so I fell through his arms as he cursed.

I jumped his ax and ran, turning at the first alleyway so I was heading north.

I skirted up an alleyway that had a car parked in it—but was easy for me to run under—and popped out into a street. I joined a sidewalk, trotting to a crosswalk that I could use to head north.

There were more people on the sidewalks now, but I needed to go north if I wanted to hook up with the Curia Cloisters.

My heart pounded in my little cat chest as I ran.

I'm not going to make it. He's going to catch up with me. I'm too far from help!

"Amalourne."

CHAPTER NINETEEN

Chloe

I locked my legs and skidded to a stop, frantically looking for my ray of hope—of safety.

I spotted him—Noctus—across the street, standing at a crosswalk with a frown.

I was so happy to see him, I vowed to let him rub my belly once that night—never mind what he was doing here instead of Curia Cloisters.

Frantically, I looked both ways before I zipped across the street. There was one car coming, but it was a block down, so I knew I'd make it.

"*Amalourne!*" Noctus apparently didn't share my estimation. He stepped off the curb and met me halfway across the street, picking me up before he moved back to his side of the street.

He muttered in Elvish under his breath as he carried me down the sidewalk. I was pretty sure he was swearing at me based on the rough sound of it, but his arms were secure, and he didn't complain when I frantically sank my claws into his shirt for my cat hug, even though I was pretty sure I nailed him with a few of my claws in my fear.

I peered over his shoulder, crouching as close to him as possible.

The tracker stood across the street, watching with a scowl etched into his stretched cheeks. He made no move to follow us —did he know what Noctus was?—and instead he fell back into the shadows of the buildings, blending in with everyone walking on the sidewalk before he faded away.

After a few blocks, my heart started slowing down, and I slowly felt the adrenaline drain from my body. I was relieved, and so thankful that I started purring, and even rubbed my head against Noctus's jaw.

"You are *still* an idiot," Noctus warned me. "Why do you keep running around downtown where you could get hurt? It frightens you—you cannot lie to me, Amalourne. I can sense your fear each time I come looking for you."

I was so happy I couldn't stop purring, but I did pause with my head jammed under his chin. *He can sense my fear while he looks for me? What the heck is that supposed to mean?*

It seemed Ms. Booker was right, and Noctus had some highly sophisticated magic on me.

I purred the whole walk back to the Curia Cloisters, and didn't stop until we saw Aristide sitting on a bench with Ker dutifully lying down in front of him.

Ker raised her nose, turned in our direction, then gave a happy "*Awoo*!"

"Welcome back," Aristide said, his tone as sour as a lemon.

Charon stood a few feet away from them, his arms clasped behind his back. His hood was down over his shoulders for the occasion, and when he saw us he straightened up even more, if that was possible. "Your—sir," he said.

Aristide—holding Ker's harness in his left hand—stood up.

"Tell me, I'm *dying* to know, are you turning paranoid in your old age, or did you indeed scent out your pet cat in downtown Magiford like a bloodhound?"

Noctus shifted me to one arm. "I found her, running as if the hounds of hell were chasing her. She was clearly terrified."

Aristide frowned, wrinkling the flawless skin of his forehead. "How did you even know?"

"She's my cat," Noctus said.

"That doesn't give you some weird bond with her that surpasses the abilities of magic," Aristide said. "Tell him, Charon."

"Sir is very capable and skilled," Charon said. "I can imagine with as much power as he has, even if it is restrained, it would be possible for him to form a bond with Ama."

"Charon, that was the opposite of helpful," Aristide said. "You're fired from being the secondary voice of reason for our rag-tag band."

Ker barked and wagged her tail.

"No, you aren't any better," Aristide said.

"I knew something was wrong," Noctus said. "I will always know when something is wrong with Ama. Now, let's go in. We need to finish and look at it."

It was almost certainly the pocket watch, which shocked me.

I didn't think he'd stop his investigation to track me down in Magiford—then again, he sounded pretty certain about knowing how I'm feeling at the moment. What on earth did he do to me?

"Very good," Charon said. "As you may recall, I have confirmed that the case file involving the pocket watch was listed as of interest, but not lethal, so it is in the evidence room directly next to the department entrance."

"Yes, I remember," Noctus said.

"I knew you would, sir, I was more concerned about Aristide."

"I have an excellent memory! And I'm obviously the most logical because—and I can't believe I have to ask this—but you're not seriously planning to take Ama in with us, are you?" Aristide asked as Ker guided him forward, heading toward the front entrance of the Curia Cloisters.

"Yes," Noctus said.

"Noctus, you can't just take a *cat* inside the Curia Cloisters."

"Why not? All kinds of shifters are allowed in," Noctus said. "I'm certain the bald feline the Paragon claims as a pet has been inside the Curia Cloisters before, too."

"Except your entire role is to avoid being noticed," Aristide said.

"I'm not putting her in the car—it's too hot," Noctus said.

"Fine, then at least have Charon take her."

"No."

"*No*? You insufferable, arrogant—gah!" Aristide growled. "Fine! But when this all goes south, you'll only have yourself to blame."

"It won't go south," Noctus said with absolute certainty as we stepped into the air-conditioned building. "It's my plan. It will work."

Aristide made a gurgling noise that made me suspect he was choking on his irritation as he and Ker slowed down—separating themselves from us.

I peered over Noctus's shoulders to watch Charon. I was trying to judge if he was upset, but the light-haired elf seemed content to walk along behind us.

Aristide is the only sane one of the bunch.

The Curia Cloisters—as always—was a whirl of activity.

A group of vampires dressed in what I thought were British regency clothes—men in silk top hats, fancy cravats, and fitted tailcoats, women in evening gowns with shawls—strutted past, walking in front of two werewolves wearing flannel shirts and holding their registration dog tags.

Wizards, all wearing shirts embroidered with their House emblem, trooped past, and behind them were two fauns, their goat feet tapping nervously on the marble floor.

The Curia Cloisters building was several stories tall with

multiple giant, theater-like rooms that supernaturals used to conduct regional business. There were also offices for the main supernaturals—vampires, fae, wizards, and werewolves/shifters—as well as classrooms used for education purposes, several rooms that were essentially used as courtrooms to decide legal issues between supernaturals, and—the newest addition—what was basically a small police station.

In the past few years, the Curia Cloisters had started a new task force program that was something of a joint police force made up of all types of supernaturals.

The task force investigated supernatural issues and responded to any public safety concerns—like artifacts that were self-destructing and causing damage instead of merely breaking down.

Noctus passed one of the main staircases and kept walking, staying on the ground floor and heading toward the back of the building.

Even though we walked through crowds of people, I only received a few curious glances. I wasn't sure if my magic was making me less noticeable, or people were used to seeing all kinds of weird things at the Cloisters. But even those who did see me shrugged it off, including the various secretarial and security staff we passed.

Ker posing as the seeing eye dog actually got more looks—not surprising. Most supernaturals would wonder what a werewolf was doing as a guide dog.

"Almost there," Noctus told me as we turned down a different hallway.

I repositioned my claws—and paws—so I'd be ready to leap off Noctus and sprint if things got messy.

I thought for a minute about leaving to find help for me, but I needed to give Ms. Booker time to research my collar, and I couldn't even file a complaint about the tracker because we were going to the task force where I'd have to make the complaint!

The entrance to the task force area—it had an official name, but I hadn't yet familiarized myself with the department as they hadn't had any staff openings I could fill—was marked off with some potent seals and spells.

As we passed through them, I felt them ghost over my fur, completely ignoring my presence. Pressed up against Noctus as I was, I could feel the magic sift through his body, searching for weapons or anything potentially harmful.

The hallway stretched on in front of us—it was lined with doors, although there was one massive opening that was tinted with a fae barrier so you could see the secretary seated at the desk by the empty picture window, but nothing beyond her. Double doors next to the desk led to the area beyond the window—presumably where most of the task force offices were.

The area had been retrofitted for the new department, so it didn't resemble a police station, although it was attempting to and having roughly the same success as a wild wolf would have pretending to be a pet dog.

Actually, based on the sign posted by the double doors, which stated *everything beyond the doors*, including "EVIDENCE ROOM A" and "EVIDENCE ROOM B", I was pretty sure the department would give most police officers ulcers. But human police officers also didn't have spells capable of igniting a fire. (Though even I had to question the intelligence of labeling the doors.)

Noctus stroked the top of my head. "That should work."

Confused, I glanced up at him, and realized he was gazing farther down the hallway.

It looked like the department wasn't quite done with remodeling their new area yet. Off on one side, velvet ropes attached to golden posts marked off a spot where the flooring and wall was torn up—it looked like they were attempting to install a fountain, but hadn't finished the plumbing.

Noctus slowed his walk and slipped his phone free from his pocket.

Charon casually strolled up to the water fountain—or as an

Eastern Wisconsinite like myself would call it, the bubbler—built into the wall and pretended to take a sip.

Noctus kept one arm under my back feet to keep me secure as he swiped his phone open and then opened a few different screens, which I was pretty sure was just a cover to look busy.

Aristide and Ker walked behind him, following the wall.

"There's a velvet rope barrier around an area they're remodeling farther down the hallway," Noctus said, his voice a quiet whisper. "It zig-zags, marking it off—starting at the wall and jutting out into the middle of the hallway."

Aristide paused, seemingly to check Ker's harness, but it was actually to laugh into her fur. "Excellent. This will be a breeze, then. Ker—if you would?"

Ker and Aristide walked on, going further down the hallway.

Charon finished pretending to drink, then slowly strolled up to the front window area and smiled at the secretary seated there. "I beg your pardon," he politely said. "I have a few questions, could you help me?"

Noctus looked from his phone to the surrounding area—as if he were studying a map and was unsure he was in the right spot. He paused in the middle of the hallway, just across from the double doors.

"I will do my best," the secretary smiled at Charon. "Are you here to report a crime?"

"Good heavens, no," Charon said. "I have a few questions about supernatural laws in Magiford."

Down the hallway, Aristide and Ker had turned around and were now walking back in our direction, sticking to the opposite wall.

Ker led Aristide straight into the rope barrier, knocking over one of the metal posts.

"Excuse me—goodness!" Aristide slipped when he stepped onto the ripped up flooring.

Aristide with his vampire reflexes and abilities was capable of righting himself, but instead he let himself fall, knocking over another post in the process and creating a lot of noise.

Ker howled in distress, raising a ruckus.

"One moment, please, it appears that vampire needs help," Charon said to the secretary before stepping away.

The secretary stuck her head through the window—which was exactly when Ker left Aristide and padded up to Charon, howling.

"Spot?" Aristide called. "Spot, where did you go?"

Spot? Really? That's the name he's going with?

"Oh dear." The secretary scooted out from behind her desk and pushed her way through one of the double doors, hurrying after Charon, who was following Ker—or "Spot" back to Aristide.

Noctus stayed motionless—I think he was making sure Aristide managed to snag her attention.

"Are you hurt, sir?" the secretary asked.

"A little bruised, but where is my dog? What happened?"

"You walked into a rope barrier around a construction area." Charon made a show of trying to catch Ker, as she anxiously circled Aristide.

"A rope barrier? Why would you use something so flimsy to mark off a dangerous area? Anyone with visual impairment wouldn't see it, and it's not like Spot understands what they are!" Aristide said.

"I'm so sorry. I will make sure to bring that up to the construction crew," the secretary babbled. "Um...is this really a dog? Or...?"

"How dare you?" Aristide gasped, his voice getting loud. "Of course Spot is a dog! What are you implying?"

This inspired more hasty apologies from the secretary, but I didn't get a chance to hear them as Noctus strode toward the double doors.

He easily pulled one open—they weren't even locked. The

problem was the opalescent barrier that stretched across the door.

I'll get through that fine, but how is Noctus going to make it happen?

Noctus pulled out what looked like a letter opener fashioned in the shape of a miniature sword. The edge was dull—which was probably how he'd managed to smuggle it past the scanning spells.

The mini-sword glowed with a foreign script—I couldn't tell if it was Elvish or fae—and when Noctus stabbed through the layer, the fae barrier collapsed.

He stepped through the downed barrier, turned around, and muttered under his breath. Magic flashed, resolidifying into a barrier spell that replaced the one he'd just destroyed.

All of that happened in the span of approximately one heartbeat—he was that fast.

That's...something.

EVIDENCE ROOM A was right by the door, so Noctus was able to slip inside without anyone noticing. I didn't even get a good look at the area beyond the secretary's desk.

Inside the evidence room were obsessively organized wire racks of cardboard boxes that went so deep into the room I couldn't see the end, and a plain desk with a single desk lamp on it, a laptop, and a brownie seated in a chair.

Brown haired, brown eyed, and brown skinned, the brownie's thick hair was pulled back in a ponytail, and she wore a white lab coat and had a newspaper spread out in front of her.

"Huh." She capped the pen she'd been holding and leaned back in her chair as she peered up at Noctus. "You're not with the department."

"Correct," Noctus said.

The brownie scratched her chin and studied Noctus for a few fear-inducing moments.

I clawed my way onto Noctus's shoulders as he turned in a slow circle. I would have jumped off and abandoned ship, but he reached up and gently rubbed my right cheek.

The brownie watched the interaction and shrugged. "I'll bite. What do you want?"

Noctus blinked. "You're willing to help?"

"That's my job."

"Even though I'm not with the department?"

"You've got a cat. You can't be bad if you own a cat."

"That seems ridiculous and easily disproven."

The brownie rolled her eyes and picked up her newspaper. "Fine, then I won't help you unless you help me solve the last two spots on my crossword puzzle: Who was the wife of the Greek god Hades? It's ten letters. Oh, and the last name of the famous American martial artist and actor Chuck—it's six letters, first letter is an N."

"You haven't sounded an alarm," Noctus said.

"Ah, you don't know them either, do you? That makes me feel a little better." The brownie put her newspaper down again.

Sitting on Noctus's shoulders like I was, I could feel the trickle of his magic stir. "Nor have you activated a spell," he said.

"Okay, let me be real with you." The brownie set her hands on her desk and leaned over it. "If you had bad intentions, you wouldn't sit around here ignoring my crossword puzzle questions —which, *rude*—you would have attacked me. You're carrying around a cat with a collar that's most definitely worth more than what I make in a month, so you're wealthy and not going to do anything stupid. You are drop dead gorgeous, and I'm realistic enough to admit that helps your case even if it is an unfair reflection of society, and finally...all the information in this room is public record. This is basically the parking ticket, fetching-kittens-from-trees section of the evidence department. There's not even one criminal case here. That means you badly need to see something in person for a case that is currently labeled non-threatening."

I could feel Noctus's surprise in the way he glanced over at me.

I was also surprised—not with the brownie, but with Noctus.

I'd thought for sure he'd strike the brownie down without a thought. It was more shocking to me that he was talking with her.

"I need to see a pocket watch—it's a recently broken artifact," Noctus said.

"Ahhh, yes, that case. The department is keeping it toward the front of the room since there's been an increase in broken artifacts and they're trying to figure out if there's a pattern to it, which might indicate it's a criminal case after all. Stay here."

The brownie jumped off her seat and grabbed one of the rolling ladders leaning against a rack—since brownies were a petite supernatural usually less than four feet tall, she'd need it—then disappeared behind one of the wire racks.

After a dangerous sounding thud, she returned a moment later, carrying a shoebox sized box. "Since you wanted just this one thing, I imagine that means you are not responsible for the artifact mess, but, all the same I texted my supervisor who will be on the way shortly," the brownie announced.

My tail puffed up at her statement—I hid it behind Noctus's head so no one would notice and wonder why a cat would get a spike of anxiety from something she shouldn't understand—but Noctus didn't seem worried.

He opened the lid of the shoebox. Inside was a typed report, and the busted remnants of the pocket watch inside a plastic baggie.

Noctus opened the baggie and peered inside.

"Don't touch evidence—you don't want your prints on that," the brownie warned.

He ignored her, and I felt the swell of his restrained magic as he used it to prod at the watch.

I could tell the magic in the pocket watch had left an impression, but I couldn't tell more beyond that. It must have made sense to Noctus, however, because he zipped the bag shut and tossed it back into the box.

"Thank you," he said.

"Yeah? You find what you were looking for?" the brownie asked. "Seriously, though, I'm going to need you to stay here a moment—woah."

While she was talking, Noctus had removed his sunglasses, revealing his oddly spiraled eyes.

When the brownie looked into his eyes her jaw went slack, and her eyes got a kind of glazed, hazy look.

Elf magic.

One of the many reasons why elves were so dangerous—as it would be good for me to remember.

Noctus replaced his sunglasses and walked out the door. As it started to swing shut behind us, I heard the brownie say, "What was I doing?"

Noctus passed through the department doors, and stepped back into the hallway of the Curia Cloisters.

Aristide was on his feet and was holding on to Ker's harness, though the secretary was still flitting around them while Charon was straightening up the velvet ropes and putting posts upright.

Noctus ignored them and strode toward the main chamber of the Cloisters, leaving the department behind.

He passed through the large crowd, then headed out a side exit of the building, following a sidewalk away from the Cloisters.

He walked approximately five blocks before the black SUV pulled up along the side of the road.

"Your Majesty," Charon greeted him from within the vehicle.

Noctus removed me from his shoulders, then got in.

"What did you find?" Aristide asked from the backseat where he was seated with Ker. "Ker, stop wagging your tail—you're getting fur in my face."

The werewolf had her head hanging out her open window and was wagging her tail—which was almost brushing the meticulous vampire.

"The person who imbedded magic into the pocket watch and the belt buckle are one and the same," Noctus said.

"There goes the random coincidence theory," Aristide said.

"This is likely proof that they were not trying to make cheap knock offs, but rather something that purposely self-destructs... but why? What would be gained by such a thing?" Charon asked.

"I don't know," Noctus said grimly.

Noctus spent the rest of his day in his study with Charon, Aristide, and Ker, poring over the evidence.

I avoided the area, and instead I tried to make some headway learning the Elvish alphabet with an Elvish cookbook left in the kitchen that I'd found one afternoon when I was attempting to break into the fridge in search of milk.

Yes, I was maybe a smidge addicted, but milk was a comfort drink to me, and Noctus was ruthless in his refusal to let me have even a sip of it.

My alphabet work was going very badly, because while I was starting to recognize some of the script, I didn't know what any of the letters meant.

I was left alone until nighttime, when Noctus tracked me down—probably using my collar—and carried me off to his room to eat.

He fed me bits of hard-boiled egg, some blueberries, and a few steamed carrots.

I was excessively pleased with this change in my diet, so I was still purring and happy when Noctus reclined on the chaise lounge and placed me on his lap.

I do not like this, but I did say you could pet my belly once for saving me from the tracker. This will be your even exchange experience.

I scooted higher up so I was sitting on his abs—which was doable only because of his lounging position. I was hopeful that if

I shed hair in his face, he'd maybe shoo me off and this wasn't going to turn into an hour of Chloe Cat Cuddles.

The blue and white flames flickered in the fireplace, reflecting on the pond, and I closed my eyes, still purring.

Noctus rested a finger on the top of my head. "I know you're not a cat, Amalourne."

CHAPTER TWENTY

Chloe

W*hat?*

My blood turned into ice in my veins. I flicked my eyes open and stared at Noctus's face.

He wasn't looking at me, but the fire. "I haven't figured out exactly what you are, but I can tell you have magic."

What is he talking about?

"It occurred to me you really could have been a fae's pet, and some of their magic has rubbed off on you, giving you greater intelligence. They might even be emotionally connected to you—which would explain your emotional responses and obvious ability to plot. You're not a shifter—Ker would have sniffed it out immediately," Noctus continued.

My eyes bulged as I listened to Noctus calmly discussing what I'd been trying so hard to hide.

"Charon has scanned you more times than you've eaten to make certain there's no listening spell on you, or anything that would implicate you as an accomplice to some other supernatural's scheme."

A meow was stuck in my throat.

I'd had no idea they'd been watching me so closely since the first few days they'd locked me inside Noctus's room. I guess it was a good thing I had never turned human inside the villa.

What do I do?

Noctus, thankfully, didn't seem to expect a response from me...

"It seems most likely you belong to a wizard or wizard subset —perhaps Chloe of Book Nookery," Noctus said.

All the air in my lungs left, and I suffocated for several seconds as my shocked body was unable to function.

I knew it. I knew he wasn't buying my "out for a walk" excuse when I met him at Shiloh's. This is bad—so bad.

Noctus continued, "There's no spell that I know of that is capable of transforming a human into a beast, or I'd say you *are* human."

Every muscle in my body tensed up.

He figured it out. He must know. I regret not getting more donuts this morning—I would have had no restraint if I'd known this was going to be the last day of my life.

"So I don't know exactly what you are. Except I do know you're Amalourne." Noctus finally looked at me, and pet me. "If you have an owner, I'll find them. I'll simply take them in, too, as I did with you. Whatever the situation is, I'll handle it."

...What?

Noctus scratched my chest for me. "No matter the truth of what you are, you're mine, Amalourne."

Does this mean you haven't put everything together, and I'm safe?

I sat stiffly on him for another moment or two, but he didn't reach for a weapon, didn't tap his magic, nothing. He just kept petting me.

I rested my head on his hand and watched him for a moment. *He's being honest. He really does care about me—or Amalourne.*

Maybe...maybe I could tell him?

If I didn't get out of here in the next few weeks, he was probably going to figure it out. If I fessed up, maybe he'd be more lenient given how much he loved Amalourne?

The Paragon is still a major "not happening" in my book. He doesn't love Amalourne like Noctus does, and he still has that glamour, and wants something from Noctus.

"High five," Noctus ordered, pulling his hand away from my head so he could hold it upright.

I automatically tapped my paw on his palm, so used to the trick it was now second nature to respond.

If I come clean now, Noctus might forgive me. He already knows I'm not carrying any harmful magic. He said he'd handle any situation. Maybe I could even tell him about the tracker since he's wary of Noctus.

Noctus's body had been relaxed, despite my weight directly on top of his stomach. Abruptly, he wrapped his arms around me and stood up. A few moments later, I felt magic ripple, as if it were playing on my whiskers.

Uh...what's happening?

Noctus walked across his room and stepped into the hallway.

What was that? What was going on?

Noctus headed for the staircase and was halfway down it when Charon came up the main hallway of the main floor, walking so fast it was almost a run. Charon's hood—which was pulled up again—looked ghostly in the night-darkened hallway and cast shadows on his face. "Your Majesty?"

"I felt it. Outside?"

"Yes."

Felt what?

"Thank you, Charon."

"Of course, Your Majesty."

Charon turned and walked with Noctus as they headed in the direction of the front door.

I wanted to move so I could see what was going on, but I couldn't really turn around while Noctus still held me. *It couldn't be the tracker, could it? It's not me—Charon wouldn't be so casual standing this close to me if it was.*

It appeared Noctus had decided to drag me out on this unexpected—and unwanted—field trip. When we reached the gate that led to the front lawn of the Cape Cod house, he shifted me to one arm and ripped it open, pushing through the hazy magic.

Noctus stepped onto the concrete porch and stared out into the dusty purple haze of twilight. His magic sharpened, growing more potent even though he didn't move a muscle.

I listened and peered through the darkness with my better than human night vision. There—I felt a tickle of magic, silky fae magic. I turned my head in its direction in synch with Noctus, who stabbed a dagger in front of us.

I hadn't even felt him pull the dagger—or noticed it. It glowed in the dim light, lighting up Elvish script that was carved into the blade.

Out in the darkness, someone shouted.

White magic dragged a body forward.

For a moment, all the air squeezed from my lungs—was it the tracker? Had he found me?

A body flopped up over the fence, rolled across the lawn, and came to a stop.

Charon turned on the front porch lights, illuminating the night-time perpetrator.

It was a man, slender built. He was halfway between a fae's flawless beauty and the sculpted looks of Noctus and Charon. He was dressed in gray, muted clothes that blended in with the shadows of the night, and his long brown hair was tied back in an elaborate braid.

He's half fae at least, and definitely not *the tracker.*

I caught the telltale gleam of metal, and peered at the sword strapped to his back.

For a moment the need to run screamed in my mind, before I realized that it didn't seem like he could move and his arms were pinned behind his back. The way he glared at Noctus was pure poison, and his jaw was clenched shut.

Noctus made a twirling motion with the dagger, and the fae was rolled closer—close enough to illuminate the swirling black tattoo at the base of his neck. It looked like Elvish script, but I couldn't tell for certain.

"Another gift from Auron, is it?" Noctus sighed deeply in aggravation.

"It would appear so, Your Majesty," Charon said.

Auron? Who is that?

"I thought he'd given up," Noctus said, bored. "Or gotten *better*."

"Do you wish to send him a message, Your Majesty?"

"How about a warning?" Noctus said.

He rotated his dagger, and the fae on the lawn screamed, hunching into himself as magic curled up and down his body.

My fur fluffed up, and I shed on Noctus's shirt as I shook in fear.

The fae kept screaming, and along the property line I saw an opalescent barrier glow. Someone—Charon, probably—had a barrier around the area, to keep the fae from being heard.

The fae's face was red with pain as he screamed, his voice raw and almost animalistic. His body shook, and I felt the pressure of the magic build.

Noctus frowned and looked down at his shackled wrist. "That will have to be enough, I suppose," he said.

"The shackles?" Charon asked.

"Yes," Noctus agreed.

He sheathed the dagger, and the magic cocooning the fae evaporated.

The fae still trembled and cried, his body broken.

"Tell Auron if he continues with these petty attempts at subterfuge, I will stop turning a blind eye and end him," Noctus said. "I ended the Mors royal family. If he pushes me, I'll get sanctimonious enough to end him as well."

He...he really did it? He was the one who killed his family? But...why?

The fae groaned as Charon hopped off the patio and approached the fae.

I sat, paralyzed, in Noctus's grasp as he casually turned around and headed back into the house.

As soon as we made it through the gate I leaped off him and ran down the hallway.

"Amalourne," Noctus called after me.

"Should I fetch her?" Charon asked as I kicked my running up a notch, eager to flee.

"No," Noctus sighed, his voice nearly out of my hearing range. "I should have known better than to handle a weapon in front of her..."

Whatever else he said to Charon was lost to me as I fled—heading to the kitchens since I didn't want to get caught in the elf king's study or bedroom.

No, I don't want to tell him what I am, I decided. *I can't risk it. He's gentle with those he cares about...but those he doesn't...if he was angry about my deception, he would end me without hesitation.*

He was King Noctus Mors, the Kingslayer. He had just said himself that he'd killed his own family—it was unlikely he'd spare the girl who had been masquerading as a pet, no matter how fond he had become of the pet.

BRIGHT and early the following morning, Noctus assembled his friends in his study for some minor furniture rearrangement that included bringing in a square table.

During the action, I was unwillingly carried into the study by Charon and placed in my bed on Noctus's desk with a catnip stuffed toy cactus to amuse myself.

"We know two of the artifacts—which were purchased from different sellers—had the same maker," Ker said. "But there've been over two dozen *reported* cases of faulty artifacts, which means there's got to be dozens more that weren't reported to the Curia Cloisters. Two artifacts are a terrible sample size." Ker picked up my toy cactus and wiggled it in front of me.

I batted at it for show, but what I really wanted was to put some distance between myself and the elf king who was probably mere days away from figuring out I was a human if the previous night's conversation was any clue.

He was leaning against his desk, less than a foot away from me, watching Ker play with me.

"We need to get our hands on more artifacts to confirm it," Aristide said. "But I don't know how we'll swing it—unless you want to go full scale and invade the Curia Cloisters, but that seems like overkill."

"Yeah, that should be our absolute last resort." Ker set my cactus down and frowned. "Unless you want to cut and leave Magiford. We could break the place open, but it would practically announce our presence."

"Leaving Magiford isn't an option." Noctus scratched my head, staring at me until I managed to produce a purr, then turned his intense gaze back to his friends. "And before jumping to an invasion, we should first see if there are any other patterns we can find in the information we got from the public records. Charon and I went over it and organized the incidents by the types of supernaturals that had purchased the artifacts, the location at which they were purchased, the location at which they broke, and so on."

"Did you find anything?" Ker asked.

"Using human computer programs we were able to organize the information, but I haven't looked over much of it," Noctus said. "Although Charon did map everything out."

"Here." Charon unfolded a map of Magiford that was dotted

with multi-colored dots and scribblings, and set it on the table that Aristide sat at.

"And for Aristide..." Charon fetched a separate map for the vampire.

It featured a much smaller area—mostly the downtown area with some of the suburbs supernaturals favored. It was inked out with the familiar streets of Magiford, then covered with tactile lines to mark out the streets with Braille that labeled the roads. Charon had also put different shaped pins into the map, so the vampire could feel the difference in the markers.

"The red stickers—the round pins, Aristide—are where artifacts broke. The blue stickers—or the triangle pins—are where the artifacts were bought."

Aristide felt out his map while Ker circled around Noctus's desk to look over the table.

"It looks like about half of the artifacts broke downtown," Ker said.

"Forty-eight percent, to be precise," Charon said.

I hunkered down in my bed, happy to be ignored for the moment, and began plotting how I could leave without anyone noticing—pleading ignorance if Noctus found out about me was a top priority, yes. But I was also starting to feel a little guilty about some of the secrets I'd learned while undercover, and I didn't want to add to that guilt.

Noctus tapped on one of the red stickers that was in a suburb. "Where the artifacts broke seems more scattered—particularly because there were about five or so that we couldn't map because they broke outside of Magiford."

"So it's not tied to the city, then," Ker said.

"The destruction? No," Noctus said. "But the purchasing definitely is."

"All of them were bought downtown," Aristide said as he touched the pins marking his map. "And many of them are centralized in a relatively small area."

Oh, that's not suspicious.

I *thought* everyone was distracted enough with the map, so I abandoned my bed and hopped off the desk. I intended to meander toward the door, but Noctus stared at me, so I had to abandon that idea and instead made myself wander over to him.

He, of course, picked me up and set me on the table.

This, I thought as I stared down at the map spread in front of my paws, *is the opposite of what I wanted.*

Noctus absently petted me, and Ker held her hand out for a high five, which I obligingly gave her as I settled in to bide my time before making my next escape attempt.

"I've made a spreadsheet of the dates the artifacts were purchased." Charon stalked past the line of stained glass windows, which cast shards of color across his dissatisfied expression. "Unfortunately they're rather imprecise estimates, so I don't know that we'll be able to pick out any pattern. The data is dirty since most supernaturals did not recall the hour at which they purchased the artifacts, and no longer had receipts."

Ker swiped a piece of beef jerky off the tray of snacks Charon had put out. "I'll take a look at the spreadsheet. Maybe I can find something. Do you have a copy printed out?"

I wrapped my tail around my paws, and glanced over the map while I waited for an opening I could take to leave.

Aristide and Noctus were right. Most of the sales took place in a several block section of downtown Magiford—and not an area I would have guessed as it mostly had boutique stores, the new clocktower, and other more human-focused places that wouldn't be great spots to sell magic.

But Prydwen did mention he found his seller online. Are they doing most of their business online and then just meeting to make the exchange?

"Here." Charon passed the paper over to Ker.

"Thanks." Ker winked at him, then strolled over to Aristide. "You want some jerky?" she asked the vampire. "It will help you think."

"Noise canceling headphones would help me think," Aristide said. "Then I wouldn't have to listen to your chewing."

"That's probably fair." Ker laughed. "But you do seem a bit peckish. Want a glass of blood?"

"Not yet," Aristide said. "That's for when we get desperate." He tapped the side of his map. "Charon—did the Curia Cloisters record *how* the artifacts were purchased?"

"About half of the cases, yes. The early ones—which would be the most helpful, I suspect—were not," Charon grimly said.

"The Cloisters likely didn't think anything dubious was going on at the time," Noctus said. "When more reports emerged, they recorded more information."

Charon folded his arms across his chest, betraying his irritation. "Yes, but we might have been better able to pick out a pattern when the maker was still new to their scam, and not as talented at hiding."

Maybe, except all of this has been done so fast. By the time Prydwen's artifact broke, the seller's website was down and their record removed from the Curia Cloisters. Whoever is doing this is very aware everything needs *to be temporary and that they should abandon it at a moment's notice. But...I still don't get why they'd do it since it's most likely not a cash grab.*

I started to forget the need to run as I studied the data points, my work brain kicking in as I tried mentally sifting through the possibilities.

I stood up and made a lap around the map, considering the area and going through a rundown of the specific shops in the area that had the greatest concentration of artifacts purchased.

What's down there that they could actually hide near?

"What's the current division of Magiford between the Seelie and Unseelie Courts?" Noctus asked.

"You think they have something to do with this?" Ker asked.

"I doubt it—whoever is organizing this is too clever for them," Noctus dryly said. "But it would be interesting to see if there's any change in the purchase patterns based on the territory lines."

"Downtown is a neutral zone," Charon said. "All the humans mean there's too much of a risk one of them would get hurt in a fight between fae. The territory lines begin around here—on Diamond Drive, Aristide."

"That's south of most of the purchase points," Aristide said. "So that doesn't help."

"The artifact selling began nearly four months ago," Ker said. "The clocktower was already being built before then."

"Correct." Charon's eyes twitched. "I do find it insulting that so many of the artifacts were purchased near the clocktower. It's insult to injury."

"It's proof no one has caught on about us," Aristide absently said.

I barely registered their conversation as I stared at the map some more and twitched my whiskers. *I wonder...*

I moved closer to the stickers so I was almost standing on top of them, my eyes tracing out the markings. *Four months ago, that's just before the donut shop opened up...but for the store to open, they must have done some refitting to it since it wasn't set up for an industrial kitchen.*

I'd seen the machinery they'd carried in and out—it was how I had realized the bakery was going in. There had also been a lot of noise—there always was a lot of noise in the store. The wizard said it was the oven...but what if it was something else making the noise? Like...magic?

I usually feel fae and some wizard magic whenever I go there, but I assumed they used magical baking methods.

Looking at the stickers, they all circled the bakery, and besides the clocktower, it was the only new store to go in that area for the past few years. Everything else was human built and run and had been around for a couple years. Whereas the donut shop had multiple supernaturals involved between the wizard clerk and the wizard *and* fae magical sensations.

It's the donut shop. I'd bet on it.

"Ama, if you would." Charon gently picked me up and deposited me on the side of the table.

I let him, my mind racing.

Do I try to tell them?

I wasn't involved in the case, I'd just been forced to live through it due to Noctus's doting pet parent ways.

But they were *elves*! And Noctus was a Kingslayer!

Elves or not...it's not right that they're getting hurt like this. Besides. Stopping whoever is doing this will benefit all supernaturals. I can't think of any downsides.

I flicked my tail back and forth as I thought.

I don't want Noctus to figure out what I am, but I wouldn't be able to live with myself if I let others keep getting hurt. I know what it's like to be powerless.

That thought alone made me stand up, impatience swirling in me. Yes, I'd do it. Not for Noctus, but for the powerless, like me.

But how do I tell these guys without talking? Or raising any suspicions?

"None of the artifacts were bought in actual brick and mortar stores, correct?" Aristide asked.

"Correct," Ker said.

"We don't have access to all of the individuals' testimonies, which would tell us reasons why they chose to buy from a seller instead of a location," Charon began. "But I imagine much of it was due to cheaper prices. Several of the reports included the original price of the artifact, and they are significantly under market price."

I jumped off the table and meandered over to my overflowing toy basket kept next to the giant fireplace.

I rummaged through it, picking out several mouse toys that tasted too much like catnip for me to suffer through holding in my mouth, and finally unearthed the cupcake shaped toy Charon had presented to me several days ago.

"We still haven't come up with a motivation, have we?" Aristide asked.

"You mean since we don't believe this is a money grab?" Noctus asked.

"Precisely."

"If they have a goal they're aiming for, it's beyond me." Ker frowned down at the map. "Besides injuring supernaturals, the scam doesn't accomplish much of anything else."

Carrying the cupcake in my mouth—which thankfully had no catnip at all and was stuffed with a squeaker—I went back to the table.

"Doesn't it accomplish quite a bit?" Noctus flicked his eyes up. "Supernaturals are starting to get upset, but the Curia Cloisters are most feeling the pressure from the humans witnessing this failure. There were humans watching when we met with Prydwen. If humanity is concerned enough, they might start to believe that magic is unsafe."

"Then the humans might start imposing restrictions," Ker said.

I edged closer to Noctus, purred when he petted me, then dropped my cupcake toy. I batted it over to the map, chasing it until I got it directly over the donut shop.

"While I can agree they likely have an agenda, I still think it's a bit of a flying leap to make it to that sort of conclusion," Aristide said.

Charon picked my cupcake up and put it on the side of the table.

Thanks, Charon. You're sooo helpful.

I went and got my cupcake again and put it on the donut shop's location once more, pressing down on it with my paw so it squeaked.

No one noticed.

Noctus rubbed at the shackle clamped around his right wrist. "It would be quite the 'flying leap' as you called it. Except Auron has persisted in sending me gifts."

Auron? He was the guy you talked about when you beat up that intruder. That guy has nothing to do with this. The donut shop does. Look at my cupcake!

I meowed and gave Noctus my cutest expression, which was a miscalculation because he picked me up and snuggled me against his chest.

No, no cat hugs! Look at my toy!

Too late, Charon was already picking it up—this time he tossed it into my toy basket.

"What an idiot. I can't believe he hasn't given up," Aristide groaned.

Noctus shrugged as I struggled out of his grasp. "I think now he sends them to check if I'm still alive. They're so infrequent—and *badly* trained. It would almost be an insult."

"Auron is twisted," Charon said. "It is possible he believes he is doing you a favor in assaulting you."

I sat down on the map and resorted to my final ploy. I rolled over on my back and presented my belly.

"He's crazy enough to think it," Aristide agreed. "And he's twisted enough that he probably wants as many elves to survive as possible—regardless of who they are. If he knew about your city, he'd have kittens."

No one noticed my rarely seen belly. Not even Noctus.

What the heck? Normally I can't get a moment's peace with you all running around the villa and carrying me around. Now when I actually want to communicate something important, you ignore me?

Charon bowed slightly to me, then reached for me. "Ama, I beg your pardon, but you must move."

I meowed angrily and sprang to my paws, darting across the table, away from his grasp.

"Do you want me to let her out in the hallway?" Ker asked. "She seems flighty, and I could use a snack."

Charon turned his back to me so he could scowl at Ker. "I prepared an entire tray of jerky and cheese snacks for you."

"Yeah, I ate them all."

"You should know after spending so many centuries with her, Charon," Aristide said. "If you want to satiate Ker, you'd better cook up a full feast."

I had been sneaking my way closer to the map, but I paused at that droplet of information. *Centuries? How can Ker have been with them for centuries? Werewolves aren't that long-lived.*

I wanted to think about it some more, but the *donut shop*!

One last try. If I don't get it across today, maybe I can try again tomorrow or something.

I walked over to the ring of stickers, then slammed my paw on top of the donut shop.

Charon rubbed his chin as he thoughtfully studied me. "Ama does seem dissatisfied. Perhaps she desires food as well. I shall take her—and prepare more food for you."

No, no, no. My paw, look at my paw! I batted at the map with my paw.

"Try giving her to me," Aristide said. "Maybe she just wants someone to hold her. We have been ignoring her."

I. Give. Up.

I drooped over, smacking the top of my head on the table. Obviously, I was not as cut out for this subterfuge stuff as I was starting to think.

"Amalourne?" Noctus's hands—which last night had nearly killed a fae—were gentle as he eased his fingers around me and picked me up.

It's no good. I've played my role as a cat too well. No one will listen to me.

Ker abruptly stepped back from the table where she'd been leaning over a corner of the map. "What did you call her?" she asked in a way that made me suspect there was something noteworthy about my nickname after all.

"Ama—that's her name," Noctus said in a tone that suggested he was worried for Ker's wellbeing.

I reluctantly let him tuck me against his chest, digging my claws around the collar of his shirt for a cat hug.

Ker tilted her head. "But I could have sworn—"

"Charon. What building is this?" Noctus tapped the donut store. "It's not labeled."

I stopped wriggling into a more comfortable position that didn't stretch my forelegs out so much, and peered up at Noctus.

Wait, did you actually notice?

"Let me check." Charon pulled his cell phone out and peered at the donut store, then tapped away on his phone. "Ah, it's not labeled because it is a relatively new shopfront. It's a donut store."

"It appears to be almost the epicenter of all the downtown sales," Noctus said. "And yet, no sales were done on its block."

Yes! Yes! You've got it!

I rewarded Noctus with a deep, throaty purr. In return he tried to hitch me higher up his chest, which I didn't want, please and thank you.

"That's the smart thing to do if you're trying to hide your location," Ker said. "And that does seem like an oddly *large* building for a mere bakery."

"You said it's relatively new, Charon?" Aristide leaned back in his chair. "When did it open?"

"Between three and four months ago," Charon said.

"If it was only three months ago the artifacts were already getting sold—the sketchy guy that kid from Queen's Court Café told us about was selling things around four months ago," Ker said.

"It's possible they could have started selling artifacts while the bakery was getting outfitted," Noctus said.

"We should visit it," Ker said. "And have a look around."

"Night would be ideal, but it will have to be midnight or thereabouts. Bakeries have early mornings," Charon said.

Well done, Charon! I take back my mean thoughts. With just a nudge, you lot are off and moving. You're very smart!

Noctus stood, cradling me in his arms. "Tonight, then. It might be nothing, but it's a lead. We can continue to look for additional patterns until then."

"Understood," Aristide drolly said.

"What made you notice the donut shop?" Ker asked curiously.

Noctus looked down at me.

Uh-oh. Time to play stupid.

I meowed at Noctus, then purred deeply.

Noctus slightly narrowed his eyes. "It was—"

A tremendous thump rattled the window frame behind Noctus.

CHAPTER TWENTY-ONE

Chloe

The elf king whirled around, treating me to the sight of the Paragon, his face pressed against the glass window of the Cape Cod house with his hands cupped around his eyes to block out the glare of the sun.

"*You* are *home*!" the Paragon declared, his voice muffled by the glass. "*Let me in—I brought tea! And some presents for Ama!*" He peeled himself off the window and strode off in what was probably the direction of the front door.

"I thought this window was charmed so you couldn't see in," Ker said.

"Do you really think a *charm* would stop the Paragon?" Aristide snorted.

"If we don't let him in, he's just going to camp out on the porch again and bother the neighbors," Charon said.

"But if we do let him in, there's a chance he could leave some kind of magical spell or device behind on the cul-de-sac to watch us, and then he'll know when we leave tonight," Aristide pointed out. "He's slippery like that, even if he does wear the guise of a fool."

Noctus sauntered toward the door, carrying me with him. "We can delay our trip until tomorrow. The donut shop isn't necessarily a solid lead anyway. We can spend our time searching for other possibilities and digging up more information on the bakery."

"Understood, Your Majesty," Charon said.

Excuse me, but could you put me down? I'd rather not see the Paragon again.

I tried to wriggle free, but Noctus didn't even notice.

Aristide stood and—using his walking stick—followed Noctus out of the room. Ker and Charon headed toward the kitchen, likely to get refreshments.

While I still tried to free myself from his arms, Noctus strolled up to the front door and nudged the gate open. He then nonchalantly reached through the portal magic and opened the front door, because seconds later the Paragon popped inside.

"Good afternoon!" The Paragon beamed as he stepped into the villa, bringing with him that ridiculously strong glamour that made me sneeze and my eyes water. "It's time for my visit. Might I come in, Your Majesty?"

I sneezed three times in quick succession. *Ick—it's filling my lungs.* I tamped down hard on my own magic so I wouldn't see through the glamour—I was determined not to make myself another potential, if not accidental, enemy.

Noctus glanced down at me, and I managed to hold another sneeze in. He waited another moment, then narrowed his eyes at the Paragon. "Yes, you can come in, but only because the Home Owners' Association informed me I cannot leave the elderly outside, crying."

"Rude! I'm younger than you are, elf!" Despite the brusque tone, the Paragon bustled in, rustling the paper bags he was carrying. "Ah, and hello to you, Lady Ama." The Paragon curtsied to me, holding out the sides of his tunic like a dress.

Um...hello? I flicked my tail from side to side and rapidly blinked as I tried to keep my magic from peeling the glamour back for me.

"This way." Noctus pointed down the hallway—where Aristide was already headed.

"Thank you, very kind," the Paragon said before he fell into step behind Noctus.

When I peered at the Paragon over Noctus's shoulders, the Paragon merrily waved to me.

I'm paranoid enough to wonder if he somehow found out about me, but my gut says he's just that much of a cat fan.

Aristide opened the door to the parlor the Paragon had been received in before. I was betting the Paragon had only ever seen that particular room.

"Take a seat," Noctus said.

"Yes, yes. And here is your tea—Aphrodite picked it out just for you!" the Paragon said.

"I'm not taking it," Noctus said.

"If it's because it's a gift, fret not. Consider it the polite thing to do—like a house warming gift. There is no need for you to reciprocate," the Paragon said.

"I'm not refusing to take it because it's a gift—a lunatic fae like you could never manipulate me into something I was unwilling to do, anyway. I refuse to take it because it reeks of charms, and I'm not drinking anything you've dabbled with," Noctus said.

That is probably a smart idea. I struggled to hold in another sneeze brought on by the overwhelming magic that made up the Paragon's glamour.

The Paragon plopped down in an overstuffed armchair that almost bounced him straight out of the seat. "I won't deny I plied a charm or two, but I assure you it's nothing harmful." He fixed the gold tasseled pillows arranged on the chair to make it more comfortable to sit in, then smiled.

"Let me guess. The tea includes a charm that encourages me to talk?" Noctus asked.

"*No*, it does *not* include a talking charm." The Paragon grimaced in a way that suggested he wanted to stick his tongue out at Noctus. "It's nothing of the sort! This is a potion designed to help you find true love!"

"Does that sales pitch work well on humans?" Aristide asked. He sat down in an armchair covered in a soft, crosshatch fabric. Based on the way he lowered himself into it, it was likely his chosen chair for the room—he liked textured fabrics. "Because I imagine they're the only ones stupid enough to fall for such a lie."

"It is not a lie! I'm a fae, I can't lie," the Paragon squawked. "Construed a certain way, it's very real."

Yeah...I might be able to avoid Noctus once I get this collar off, but I don't think I could ever match up against the Paragon in terms of wits and trickery. I'll try to grow fluent in Elvish before I reveal myself to him.

"I don't need to know—or want to know." Noctus sat down in the settee and let me down. I sat down next to him. When he glanced down at me I got to work licking my paw and grooming my face.

Yes, this is me. I'm just a cat. Totally a cat. Don't mind me!

"Well! Aren't you welcoming?" The Paragon sniffed and smoothed his long mustache.

"State your business, Paragon, so I can tell you no, and we can get on with our lives," Noctus said.

"In a rush, are you?" the Paragon asked. "What if I don't want to ask? What if I want to hang out for a few hours first?"

"Why do you have so much free time?" Aristide asked.

"You know, I get asked that question a lot," the Paragon said. "But, since you're both being so snippy. Noctus, where is she?"

"I have no idea," Noctus drolly said.

"Lies," the Paragon glumly said. "But at least you're consistent. Tell me this, then. Why are you in Magiford?"

"Why are *you* in Magiford?" Aristide asked, smoothly intercepting the question.

"Because *you're* in Magiford!"

"That's not very original. Can't think for yourself, can you?" Aristide asked.

"You, you...*vampire*!" the Paragon blustered.

I watched as Aristide and the Paragon—well, I mostly watched Aristide so my magic would stop trying to burn off the Paragon's glamour—bickered back and forth, Aristide making it so Noctus could neatly sidestep the question.

It's interesting. Aristide and the others aren't thrilled that Noctus won't tell them why he wants to stay in Magiford, but they'll run interference so Noctus doesn't even have to make up something to satisfy the Paragon.

Noctus curled a hand around my back, sliding his fingers through my fur. I peered up at him, but he was watching Aristide with the hint of a smile. He knew what Aristide was doing.

Their friendship runs deep. Years deep—or even centuries, going by Aristide's comment about Ker. But what could bind them so close to an elven king who killed his own family?

"If you won't satisfy my curiosity, the least you will let me do is play with your cat," the Paragon said, disengaging from Aristide. "Ama, I brought you some things!"

Everyone seemed to expect I'd react, so I reluctantly stood up, and Noctus's hand slid off me.

The Paragon rummaged around in one of his paper bags and unearthed a cardboard scratching post. "You need one of these—to keep your claws sharpened."

I hopped off the settee and went to inspect the scratching post. As a cat, my claws needed maintenance, particularly since I was spending so much time in this form.

Noctus frowned. "What is that?"

"It's a scratching post." The Paragon's smile was so smug, it was nearly scrunched up to his nose. "You didn't know she'd need that, did you? It will give her something to sharpen her claws on besides the furniture."

I got to work on the cardboard scratching post, stretching out my muscles in the process.

Noctus watched, his frown becoming more pronounced. "She hasn't clawed at any of the furniture."

"Probably because she's a good girl, aren't you, cutie pie!" The Paragon spoke to me in a baby voice.

Slightly disturbed, I yanked my claws free and backed up a few steps.

"Oh, don't you be afraid, you beautiful lady. Look—I also got you a tunnel!" The Paragon shook a circular mesh contraption at me, then ripped a few pieces of Velcro off it. The frame expanded, springing into a chute-like tunnel.

Wow. He goes all out for his pet—though Noctus is still probably worse. The Paragon hasn't given me anything covered in real gold or silver.

My nerves burned as Noctus and the Paragon stared at me.

I guess I should react.

I got up and wandered over to the tunnel, disappearing inside. It was like one of those plastic framed kid houses, except cat sized so I could comfortably walk down the whole length—which was maybe three or four feet.

Halfway down the tunnel, there was a hole for me to stick my head out of, which I did.

Noctus's frown eased, and his posture relaxed as he watched me so he lounged on the settee. "She seems to enjoy it."

"Yes. My beautiful Aphrodite used to enjoy such things as a kitten. Now she prefers to peruse teas." The Paragon slyly wriggled his eyes at Noctus. "I must say, I never pictured you as the doting pet parent."

Aristide snorted. "Doting is a mild word for it."

I ducked back into the tunnel and sauntered down it.

"You need not say it as if it's a bad thing—quite the opposite! It assures me of your character," the Paragon declared. "I didn't think there was a thing on this earth that could bring an elf low. Behold: the cat!"

I popped out of the tunnel just in time to see Noctus's indifferent shrug.

"You're being ridiculous," he said. "There are a great many things elves must be careful of."

"Hardly," the Paragon complained. "You are blessed by magic with so many unfair advantages. There isn't a supernatural that can defeat you—it's unnatural."

"Incorrect," Noctus said. "Shadows were quite capable of slaying any number of elves."

"Shadows?" The Paragon squinted at him. "They've been gone for so long, there aren't even stories of them, just myths! Be serious."

Shadows, what are shadows?

I sauntered across the room, hoping to sneak out the door, but Noctus caught me before I could get past the settee and picked me up.

"That doesn't mean the elves didn't fear them when they were alive." Noctus flicked his eyes to the Paragon as he stood up. "In fact, it should be a warning."

"A warning for what?" the Paragon asked.

Noctus was silent as he stepped around Aristide's chair, tapping the vampire's shoulder in some kind of signal.

"The shadows are gone because the elves killed them in their fear of them," Aristide said, "Much the same way the rest of supernaturals killed the elves because they feared *them*."

"History is doomed to repeat itself," Noctus agreed.

The Paragon's expression turned serious. "The war was waged not out of sheer fear, but because the elves had lofty goals that would have doomed us all. *You* of all people should know that."

"I do know that," Noctus said. We were almost to the door, now. "It's why I did what I did. But that doesn't mean the same terror won't be repeated, until we *all* learn our lesson."

It's why he did what he did? Is he talking about killing his family?

With that grim announcement, Noctus left, leaving the Paragon with Aristide.

He carried me back to his study and wordlessly buried himself in his work, with me sitting in his lap.

Before our visit with the Paragon, I would have been nervous to sit on his lap given how he was getting close to realizing my secret, and was a certifiable *killer*.

But...Aristide and Ker wouldn't stay with him if he'd killed his family in sheer bloodlust, and based on what the Paragon had said...did Noctus *agree* with supernaturals? Had he turned on his family because he knew the elves' ambition to fight humans would have ruined us all?

As I peered up at Noctus, I felt a sliver of sympathy.

There are so many layers to his life. How can he keep taking it?

LATE THE FOLLOWING MORNING, my electronic cat door opened for me and I escaped the house, trotting across the lawn as fast as I could go while still managing to look somewhat casual.

When I hit the sidewalk I took a left, heading deeper into the cul-de-sac to complete my "cover" as Ama.

Once I made it to the bush, I hid and changed into my human form—complete with my backpack and phone.

I'd changed shirts since the tracker had chased me in downtown just to make sure no one in the neighborhood saw me hanging around *too much* in the same workout clothes. I was hoping that between the backpack and athletic clothes everyone would assume I was training for some kind of hike or marathon, but I still had to wear a neck wrap to cover my collar, which kind of broke the image and was starting to get majorly uncomfortable as summer was starting to heat up the days.

After I extricated myself from the bush, I jogged down the sidewalk, checking my messages.

My parents had sent me some pictures from their travels, so I responded to them. I'd also gotten a message from Joy and Pat, as expected. Joy had sent me the day's cat photo—a white cat wearing a purple bonnet.

Pat, however, had sent me an actual text.

U OK squirt? Ur not talking much.

He'd only sent the text an hour ago, so I was responding at the perfect time.

I'm good! I recently checked out the Curia Cloisters again and have been reviewing my resume, trying to figure out what to do next.

It wasn't a lie—I still wasn't certain I could stay in Magiford, especially if Noctus found out Amalourne was a human. But I couldn't stay in any city that had a major supernatural presence, or I'd be risking my life. Maybe I could settle in a tiny rural village, but I wanted to learn more about what I was, and I wouldn't be able to accomplish that if I hid in the country. (Besides, werewolves were a major risk for the country life.)

I've told you, come live with one of us. No supernatural would mess with you.

That was Joy's text, and she wasn't wrong.

Pat had chosen to pursue law enforcement, and Joy had become a lawyer and worked for a large city. Supernaturals wouldn't risk doing anything that could damage our reputation with human branches of law.

Supposedly.

But my human family was my *only* family. I'd been abandoned by my supernatural one. I would sacrifice everything to keep my human family safe—I'd never be able to live with myself if something happened to one of them.

Until I had a better handle on my identity and got some allies, I didn't want to risk involving them. Especially now that I had become the pet of the last elf king. With that in mind, I bent my mind to the puzzle of replying in a way that wouldn't make either of them suspicious.

Thanks, guys, I appreciate your support, but I will figure this out! You'd be proud of me—I'm trying to come up with a five-year plan.

My phone beeped immediately after I sent the message.

You're right, I am proud. Five-year plans are the best!

Joy texted, and Pat was only a moment behind her.

U both need hobbies.

I laughed, but when Joy didn't say anything I exited out of the text message. Hopefully that would keep them satisfied until tomorrow morning.

"Hey, Chloe! Visiting your friends again?"

I looked up from my phone when I heard Shiloh.

She was trimming one of the bushes by her house, her blond hair tucked back into a ponytail and green smears on her shirt.

"Hi, Shiloh." I smiled at her and slowed to a stop by her white picket fence. "Yeah, I visit them as part of my training route."

"Neat! I admire your dedication to growing stronger." Shiloh set her hedge shears down, took her leather gloves off, and ambled up to me. "That's why I don't mind doing all this yard work. It makes me ripped!"

"Ripped in half, maybe!" one of the uncles next door chortled from his porch.

Shiloh wrinkled her nose at him. "I'm getting stronger!"

"Maybe." The uncle rattled his glass of iced tea. "But you still look like a middle schooler."

"Are you saying I look younger than I am? Aww, shucks. That's so sweet of you!" Shiloh grinned.

The uncles guffawed and elbowed one another.

At the same moment, my cell phone chimed and vibrated in my hand. I glanced at the screen and saw it was Ms. Booker, but the notification disappeared before I had time to read her message.

"So." Shiloh rested her hands on her fence and wriggled her eyebrows at me. "What do you think of Noctus?"

"Uh," I said as I internally scrambled for a reply. "He seemed...attentive?"

"Don't you think he's handsome?" Shiloh asked.

"Well, yeah," I said. "Is there anyone on the planet who *wouldn't* find him attractive?"

"I'm glad you think so," Shiloh said. "Because I want to set you up with him."

"*What?*" My voice pitched high into a shriek that would have made any neighbor dogs cringe.

"He hasn't had a girlfriend since he moved here," Shiloh said. "And you're both supernaturals, so you'll understand each other and have so much to bond over!"

"Uh, supernatural society is a little more complicated than that," I said.

"Come on. He's *really* nice."

"If he's so nice, why don't *you* date him?"

Shiloh's face scrunched up. "Ew, no! I've known him since before I was a teenager, and I'm almost twenty-two. He was one of the "adults" my dad used to tell me I should go to if there was a creeper skulking around the cul-de-sac or something."

"Oh. I guess I can understand that." I glanced at my cell phone and fought the impulse to look back at Noctus's house.

"He's also a little *too* pretty for me," Shiloh continued. "It just seems like it would invite trouble. And I would like to think I'm good natured, but I'm not sure I could ever suffer dating someone who has better hair than me *every single day.*"

"But you think I should?" I asked.

"Yes!" Shiloh's grin was back. "Because you can match him."

I stared at Shiloh in my mismatched clothes, with hair that I hadn't washed since I'd showered at my apartment, and a scarf tied around my neck to hide my collar. "In what kind of scenario do you *possibly* think I could match him?"

"Every day," Shiloh innocently said. "You're very captivating, you know?"

"You're one of those people who sees the beauty in everyone, aren't you?" I asked.

"You say it like it's a bad thing."

"It's not, except when it makes you overestimate me."

"I don't think it's overestimating. You should go over to his house and say hi—he'll be out soon anyway, his cat just came outside a few minutes ago."

"No, thank you," I said.

Though it's good to know Noctus isn't the only one I'm going to have to watch for in the future as a cat when I'm out and about in the neighborhood!

"Here, I'll go with you! It'll be fun," Shiloh said.

"Maybe later," I tried, hoping I could dodge the issue.

"No, we need to do it now," Shiloh said. "I need to be done with my yardwork anyway so I can get ready for class."

"Class?" I asked, desperately trying to distract her. "What kind of class?"

"I'm taking classes through Magiford's community college,"

Shiloh explained, her eyes briefly flickering past me. "I've got all my mandatories out of the way, and a bunch of basics! There are just a few more advanced classes left that I need to take to get a degree."

"That's great! Let me wish you an early congratulations," I said.

"Thanks. I wanted to make college as affordable as possible. Community college is so much cheaper!" Shiloh's relaxed posture said she wasn't going to try to move me anymore.

Why do I not feel relieved about that?

I felt a prickle of power tickle my back.

Dang it. Noctus is coming outside, isn't he?

I looked back, and sure enough, Noctus was crossing his lawn.

"You're a traitor," I said to Shiloh.

She laughed. "No, I'm sneaky! Especially when it's for something I approve of. Besides, I think he must be at least kind of interested. He doesn't come outside all that often. But you have to admit, he'd be fun to date, right?"

He was almost to the street by now, and chances were that he could hear her with his elf senses, so I shushed her like a librarian. "Shh, okay—whatever, just stop talking about it!"

"Hello Shiloh, and Chloe," Noctus greeted us, his sunglasses in place.

"Hi, Mr. Shade!" Shiloh happily chirped. "How are you today?"

"Fine. I hope you are well?"

"Yep!" Shiloh said.

Noctus nodded. "Remember if you need anything, just ask." His gaze flitted to Shiloh's yard. "As commendable as your care for your home is, I know it can be difficult to keep up with. There's no shame in asking for help."

"Oh, I know, but this stuff I can keep up with," Shiloh said. "When fall comes and I need my gutters cleaned, I'll call!" Her smile went from genuine to sneaky as she looked from Noctus to me. "Now if you'll excuse me, I'm afraid I've got to leave for class. But Chloe would love to talk to you, wouldn't you, Chloe?"

"No," I immediately replied, then hunched my shoulders up when I realized how rude I had just been. "That is, uhh, I smell from my training."

The uncles on the porch cackled.

"You'll have to try better than that, girlie!" one of them called.

Shiloh's eyes crinkled with her barely hidden amusement. "I have to get my shears put away, and go to class. Socialize—for Mr. Shade's sake!"

"Wait—and she's gone." I glumly watched her snatch up her shears and skip away with the grace of a gazelle, heading around toward the side of her house where her garage was.

Noctus watched her for a moment, then turned an expectant gaze on me.

CHAPTER TWENTY-TWO

Chloe

W*hat, is he expecting entertainment?*

"Uhhh, how's your cat?" I asked.

"Ama is doing quite fine—she's out here somewhere, exercising her independence." Noctus looked up and down the cul-de-sac, searching for me.

"You got her the cat door," I said.

When Noctus stared unnervingly at me, I lamely pointed at his house. "I can see it from here. She likes it, I assume?"

"She does," Noctus confirmed. "It was good advice, thank you."

Anything to avoid getting fixed. And chipped.

"You're welcome." I awkwardly adjusted my backpack, hiking it higher up my back.

I need to stop talking about cat-me, or I'll trip up. What else could I ask him? It took me a moment before I realized I shouldn't be asking him anything, I should be trying to extricate myself from this conversation as swiftly as possible.

"How is the Book Nookery?" Noctus asked.

I guess it was too much to hope he'd forget about me working there. "Working at a twenty-four-hour bookstore would be every book lover's dream, right?"

"That doesn't answer my question."

Why is it that he's not only sharp, he's confident enough to not care about social niceties?

"Uhhh." I nervously dug my fingers into the straps of my backpack. "The store is lovely as always."

Noctus tilted his head, and the morning sunlight caught his hair, making it more golden than usual. "I still can't get a read on you."

"Pardon?"

"You're not a wizard. Werewolf hunters don't typically live in large cities, and you don't have a vampire slayer's...*intensity*. You're not an oracle, are you?"

At that moment I was so glad neither Ker nor Aristide were around, because I instantaneously sweated through my shirt and my pulse jumped.

I need to calm down. It's not like he could guess right—no one knows what *I am after all. But I don't want him thinking about me! What do I do?*

Although my mind was frozen in fear, my body decided to go with the plan I'd been following for weeks: play nice with Noctus.

"Unless you intend to share what you are, isn't it kind of rude to try to figure out what I am through a game of ask twenty questions?" My voice was a lot more stable than I felt, and it took me two whole seconds to realize I was scrunching my nose at him. Noctus. The elf king that killed his family.

Noctus smiled—I couldn't tell if it reached his eyes or not because of his sunglasses, but it looked real enough. "I suppose that's true. Forgive me, it's just that I don't often see other supernaturals in my neighborhood."

Liar. You live with a city of them outside your window!

With that rebellious thought burning in my mind, I eyed

Noctus. Noctus stared at me for a moment before he burst into laughter—a deep, rolling laughter that seemed like it broke free from him.

I hunched my shoulders a little and sucked my head in like a turtle. "What?" I asked.

"It's nothing," Noctus said when his laughter subsided. "I merely didn't think another being was capable of making that face."

"What face?"

Noctus shook his head, dismissing my question. "You really should come to the neighborhood more often," he said. "Shiloh likes you, I'm certain Ama would, too."

"Is that our cue to get our barbershop quartet back together and sing love songs?" one of the uncles shouted from their porch.

I jumped in place—I'd forgotten they were there—and clutched my backpack straps.

"Although...there's only three of us. Hm, guess we need to hold auditions?" The uncle started to lift up his baseball cap, then immediately smashed it back down.

"There—got a picture," another uncle announced. "Shiloh might want to scrapbook it—the first time Noctus almost asked a gal on a date."

"Baby steps," the third uncle said. "You think we ought to applaud him?"

Noctus grinned at the uncles—this one I was certain was real because of the way he tilted his head.

"I should go," I decided.

"Very well. Then I'll look forward to our next meeting." He stepped off the curb, heading across the street and back to his house. "Because you are very amusing, Chloe of Book Nookery."

The way he said it was...odd.

It wasn't the same warm tone he used with me when he called me Amalourne, but it was still...caressing. Not gentle—his voice was too strong for that. But it called to me.

"Thanks?" I shouted back to him, my voice a little shaky.

He waved, then headed into his house. I watched as the door shut behind him.

Maybe I'm not as immune to elf powers as I thought.

Weirded out by the encounter, I hurried a little farther down the street, slowing down once I knew I was safe. I couldn't go *too* far, or Noctus might feel it through his little tracking spell, but I wanted to see what Ms. Booker had sent.

Hopefully she figured out how to get this thing off me!

My heart pitter-pattered at the thought, and I unlocked my phone and checked my messages.

Unfortunately...the text was just a request for me to call her when I was available. I needed to get back into my cat form soon, but I was willing to risk rousing Noctus from his yard for the promise of good news, so I dialed Ms. Booker and impatiently shifted from foot to foot as I stood on the sidewalk and stared at Noctus's home.

"Hi, Ms. Booker," I said when she picked up. "I got your text—"

"*Chloe.*" Ms. Booker's voice was tense and urgent. "*You're in far more trouble than you realize.*"

That doesn't sound good. Particularly because I didn't think there was any way this could be worse.

Immediately, I jumped to the worst-case scenario. "Will my collar kill me if I go too far away?"

"*No, no. Nothing like that at all.*" Ms. Booker sounded...upset, which was enough to make every muscle in my body tense.

She was never upset. Not even that night a troll accidentally busted an entire bookshelf.

"Then what is it?"

"*In all of my research, there is only one kind of elven magic that involves putting something on that cannot be taken off,*" she said.

"...Okay." I glanced up and down the street, but besides the uncles—who were talking among themselves—I was alone.

"If your collar was made using that magic, the only way you're ever going to get it off is if Noctus himself takes it off you."

"Is that really the *only* way?"

"I believe so, yes."

This is bad. This is so bad. I don't know what would possibly make him remove the collar—he's too responsible when it comes to Amalourne!

"No, there has to be another way around it." My voice shook, but I locked my knees and tried to organize my thoughts.

"If your collar has the magic I think it does, there isn't."

"What magic do you think it has?"

Ms. Booker was silent.

I licked my dry lips. "Ms. Booker?"

"I don't know for certain—it would be so strange*—but...the three jewels on your collar? I believe they might be a tie to his heart."*

"WHAT?" I yelled so loudly I made my own ears ring.

"Caution, Chloe dear," Ms. Booker warned me. *"This isn't something you want to draw attention to."*

"What do you mean—a connection to his *heart*!" I hissed into my phone, curling over it like an angry snake.

"The translation isn't perfect, so I can't tell if it's his soul, his heart, or the source of his magic—the elves weren't always precise with their language, and the texts I've found imply they are speaking figuratively, not literally. In this case I don't think the exact 'what' of it matters, as much as the meaning behind it. Those jewels contain pieces of himself. He tied himself to 'Amalourne' and gave a part of himself to her in exchange for an eternal connection."

"Who would want an eternal connection with a *cat?*" My voice rose again, and I felt my heart explode in my chest as I grew dangerously close to hysteria.

"I don't know," Ms. Booker said. *"He's an elf, dear. He's been around for centuries, seen empires rise and fall, and has been in hiding for a long time. Obviously, something inspired him."*

I raised a hand to my forehead and tried to forcibly calm myself. I needed to be clear headed. I couldn't afford to freak out when it was already hard to find a way to slip out and turn human.

When I felt slightly more controlled, I cleared my throat. "Maybe it's something he does with his inner circle."

"*Doubtful,*" Ms. Booker said. "*The exchange is dangerous, particularly since you can't reciprocate, which means he's given you an enormous gift with no hope of an equal exchange. The only reason he might have done it is because he believes you are a cat. A cat cannot take advantage of carrying a part of her elven owner with her.*"

But a human could.

Ms. Booker didn't say the words, but she didn't have to.

"He's going to kill me," I concluded. "There's no way I'll survive when he finds out."

"*I have equally bad news for you—there's no way you'll ever be able to live a normal life unless you tell him,*" Ms. Booker sourly said. "*No matter how far you run, he'll be able to find you. Your life as a human will be nearly nonexistent, because there's no way he's letting a cat he cherishes so much strut around town by herself.*"

She was right. Already I'd witnessed that Noctus would disrupt plans to come find me.

"Maybe you're mistaken," I said, a faint hope twinkling in my heart. "Maybe it's a different kind of magic. Some kind of subjugation spell?"

Ms. Booker sighed. "*I thought so, too. I investigated a great number of spells. But, Chloe, the most damning piece of evidence is you.*"

I breathed deeply through my nose as I struggled to control myself. "Me?"

"*If it were a spell cast on you, it wouldn't work. Your unique powers would cancel it. But what the elf king did wasn't a spell. He gave you a part of himself. That's not magic, that's personal, which is why even your powers can't wiggle out of it.*"

The world spun around me, and I closed my eyes to try to fight off the dizzying sensation. "Is this exchange something elves used to do frequently?" I asked. "Maybe there's historic precedence for getting it off."

"*Unfortunately, no,*" Ms. Booker said. "*The elves—though beautiful, talented, and intelligent—were power hungry and arrogant. They knew better than to trust each other with something so precious. There are very few recorded cases of it. Most of them are either between marriage partners, or battle comrades. Deep relationships that allowed for no doubts.*"

This was a worst-case scenario.

No, this whole thing has been a worst-case scenario since the day he took me in.

Yes, Noctus had come to adore his cat so much, he'd cast an ultimate magic to protect her, which doomed me to possibly live out the rest of my days as a cat.

But if I had revealed myself the moment Noctus had taken me inside his house, I wasn't certain I would have lived to tell the tale.

Now would be the perfect time to lose it.

The thought was tempting, but I didn't have that luxury.

If I fall apart, I won't be able to think of a way out of this—and there must *be a way out.*

With that decision made, I felt my magic flicker through my body, shoring me up.

"*Chloe dear?*"

"Sorry, Ms. Booker." I cleared my throat and slapped on a smile. Even though she couldn't see me, forcing myself to act calm made me feel better. "I was lost in thought. Thank you so much for your help."

"*Of course. I'll keep looking—there is a small possibility I could be wrong. Or perhaps there's a case of such a relationship fracturing. I will let you know if I find anything.*"

"I appreciate it," I said. "I'll see if I can do something. When I am a cat, Noctus might be willing to take the collar off if he thought something was wrong."

"*Good luck, Chloe dear.*"

"Thank you. Have a great day, Ms. Booker."

I hung up after our farewells and pointed my feet down the street. As I trudged off, I risked looking back at Noctus's innocent looking Cape Cod home.

I'll get this collar off. I'm not leaving my family to live as a cat!

CHAPTER TWENTY-THREE

Noctus

Chloe is connected to Amalourne. I'm certain of it.

I waited until the gate clicked shut before I started down the hallway, heading toward the staircase to the second floor.

With Amalourne still outside, this was a chance to open the closet of weapons in my room without offending her. I didn't strictly *need* anything from the closet for tonight, but the shackle locked me from all the magical weapons I'd normally use and tied me to regular ones. I'd feel more prepared if I had a chance to review what I was taking.

As I climbed the staircase, Chloe's look of disbelief flitted through my mind again.

The slightly narrowed eyes, the way her entire body hunched with her—the look was *so* like Amalourne's when I'd promised not to rub her belly anymore and she clearly hadn't believed me.

But it wasn't just the expression that made me so certain there was a connection. There was a similarity to how wild magic reacted to them.

Moreover, since Amalourne had her collar, I was connected to her. I swore I felt the same kind of connection to Chloe, which would have been impossible, unless Amalourne was directly connected to Chloe.

I need to figure out the nature of their connection.

I reached the top floor of my villa and slipped into my bedroom, crossing it as I mulled over the possibilities.

Figuring out the relationship between Amalourne and Chloe would be easier if I knew what kind of supernatural Chloe was. But as far as I knew, there wasn't a subset of wizards that was particularly skilled with animals. Unless she was only half supernatural? Fae sometimes had animal magic like my own. If she was half fae, Amalourne might have previously been her pet.

I bumped the wallpapered entrance to my closet, stepping in when it swung aside.

Blue flames ignited in torches as I stepped into my weapons closet and inspected the rows of swords, daggers, axes, lances, arrows, and more that lined the walls in carefully arranged displays.

It seems I should visit the Book Nookery again, to watch Chloe in her natural environment. I could bring Amalourne and see how they react.

I walked the length of the weapons closet and picked up the sharpening kit I left under the display of my crossbows.

It was suspicious that Chloe only appeared whenever Amalourne slipped out. Perhaps they were secretly meeting?

Whatever they do, it won't go on much longer.

I'd adopt Chloe into my inner circle, for the sake of keeping Amalourne.

It would be a risk, but a calculated one.

I was fairly certain Chloe didn't have many supernatural friends. Book Nookery was respected, but it was also an island unto itself. Ms. Booker didn't have allies—she didn't *need* them—and she only hired neutral employees as well, though I suspected that was mostly a sign of Ms. Booker's heart rather than an actual business practice.

If she really didn't have any true allies in Magiford, I could bring Chloe in as I had with Amalourne.

I sat on the sole bench left inside my closet and pulled my first dagger out of my boot so I could sharpen it, feeling more certain about the plan.

I am going to keep my cat, no matter what. And Chloe is interesting and amusing enough that she'd be worth the trouble to keep as well.

CHAPTER TWENTY-FOUR

Chloe

"Does your cat have fleas?" Aristide asked.

Noctus looked up from the city map he was studying. "What?"

"Does your cat have fleas?" Aristide repeated, not even missing a beat as he put a gun together with perfect familiarity, snapping the pieces into place. "She keeps scratching."

Ker was arranging parts of a gun into a specific pattern—probably so Aristide could put it together—but she looked up and peered in my direction. "She's been scratching ever since she came in from the outdoors. Maybe she picked up some fleas?"

No! The collar is uncomfortable and restrictive, can't you tell by the way I'm scratching?

Using my hind leg, I'd been scratching at my collar all afternoon. I was possibly overdoing it a little—I'd nearly given myself a bald patch—but I needed this thing *off*!

Come on, Noctus. Take the bait!

Noctus frowned as he walked over to me, crouching next to my bed that had been moved to the floor since every flat surface was taken up with weapons, maps, and other information for tonight's donut shop heist. "I suppose it's possible, but she's never gotten them before."

Ker made a clicking noise. "Happens to the best of us, I'm afraid. Even I've gotten a flea or two on occasion. Ticks are worse, in my opinion."

Noctus parted my fur, peering at my skin and completely ignoring when I clawed at the collar. "Her collar should have a healing effect on her, though."

"That will keep her from getting diseases, but she might need a bath to get rid of the fleas," Ker said.

Noctus slipped a finger under my collar.

Yes! Take it off! My heart leaped in my chest, and I meowed pitifully.

He slid the finger all the way around my neck, smoothing the hair, but didn't even try to remove it.

No! It's so close!

I tried to back out of the collar, but it stuck to me like a burr. That busted a loop I was hoping might work: I wouldn't be able to shimmy out of the collar if Noctus was holding it. He had to legitimately remove it.

"Maybe it's the weapons," Noctus said.

"Yeah, you said she didn't like them, but she was the one who joined us in the study, and she doesn't seem to care," Ker said.

"Her heartbeat isn't erratic, so she's not agitated," Aristide chimed in.

Noctus frowned. "In that case, perhaps it really is a skin problem."

"Preparations are complete, Your Majesty." Charon bowed as he entered Noctus's study. "Will you be removing the restraints for tonight's excursion?"

"No." Noctus released my collar and stood up. "I can't risk the Paragon noticing. The only reason he hasn't told the Curia Cloisters of my existence is because he thinks I'm leashed."

"I don't know." Ker scratched her cheek and stepped aside so Charon could view the three guns Aristide had assembled. "I think he hasn't said anything because he's trying to stay on your good side in hopes that you'll eventually break and tell him where 'she' is."

"Whoever 'she' is," Aristide grumbled.

So they don't know either? Interesting.

Charon frowned slightly. "It's a shame, Your Majesty. I thought you'd enjoy tonight."

Noctus shrugged. "I don't need access to my royal weapons to enjoy a good fight. But there is something I need to do before we head out."

"Oh?" Ker glanced back at the table in surprise. "But you already chose your sword, Aristide has his daggers, and we've got Charon's guns assembled."

"It has nothing to do with tonight," Noctus said.

Aristide tilted his head back and forth. "What is it?"

"Hold still, Amalourne." Noctus stroked the top of my head, then rubbed more conditioner in the fur around my neck.

Soaked from my nose to the tip of my tail, I sat in a plastic bin he'd put in the giant kitchen sink and glared up at him.

This is so ridiculous.

Not only had I failed in getting him to take the collar off—he wouldn't even remove it now that I was sopping wet—he'd been concerned enough about Ker's flea comments that he'd subjected me to a *flea bath*! He'd shampooed me in this harsh shampoo and thoroughly dosed me before moving on to a conditioner.

Noctus picked up my front left leg and rubbed conditioner into my fur, in my armpit, on the top of my paw—all over.

He crooned a few Elvish words to me which were pretty, and

kind of soothing because they sounded curly and sparked with magic.

The conditioner smelled like honey, and his fingers were gentle as he slathered it in the fur around my collar—where I'd been scratching. He hadn't gotten handsy with me, which was the only reason I hadn't used my claws.

No one can fault him for being a diligent pet owner.

Giving up my sour attitude, I sighed.

"That's my Amalourne," he said as he rubbed my other leg.

I looked away from him.

"Don't be like that, Amalourne," Noctus said. "This will make you feel better."

My ears twitched. *It will not!*

"It will," Noctus said, scarily able to interpret my body language. "You'll stop scratching so much."

It did feel like a spa treatment. My mom had taken me to a spa for my twenty-first birthday, and that hadn't felt quite as luxurious.

The conditioner probably has gold flakes and silk proteins in it.

"High five?" Noctus held out his palm.

No—no high fives! I purposely looked away.

Noctus chuckled, then thoroughly rinsed me so I resembled a large, sodden rat. Finished, he picked me up—not caring at all that I soaked his black shirt when I latched on to it—and wrapped me in cozy towels.

Bundled up like a baby, I could only meow pitifully when Noctus cradled me against him. "Good Amalourne." He looked toward the door, and I heard the familiar sound of Aristide's walking stick tapping the ground.

"How goes the cat bathing?" Aristide asked, pausing once he reached the open door.

"Done. She needs to dry," Noctus said. "Then we can head out."

"Neat. Preparations are pretty much finished—Charon is

doing his last check of the car. So, how badly did she scratch you up?"

Noctus left my makeshift bathtub in the sink and carried me over to Aristide. "She didn't scratch me at all."

"She bit you, then?"

"No." Noctus's smirk was audible in his voice. "It seems your and Ker's excuse for not helping me 'for fear of your lives' was unfounded. Ama is better than that."

Aristide tsked. "Or she just loves you." He held his hand out, and Noctus placed me under Aristide's hand.

Aristide stroked the top of my head with a gentleness that went against his sarcastic nature. "Despite your continued hurt that she won't let you pet her belly, I'd take her lack of clawing every last drop of blood out of you as a major sign of her affection."

"Perhaps," Noctus said. "But I don't believe she would claw you or Ker, either. And Ker isn't the greatest with cats."

"Noctus, that was one of my rare attempts to encourage you," Aristide said. "Just accept it—unless you would rather that I tell you 'yes, you just happened to adopt a magical cat who has the best temperament I've ever seen and she doesn't care about you at all'?"

Noctus laughed, a deep sound that made me jiggle in his arms.

I guess it's a good thing the elves made noises about conquering humanity when they did. If they'd waited until Hollywood and social media were a thing, they'd all be A-list celebrities and influencers and could just demand humans give up—and they would!

Together, the vampire and elf left the kitchen and meandered down the small side hallway before joining up with the main hall.

"Thank you, Aristide, for your unhesitating ability to cut me off at the knees," Noctus said.

"Of course. In that circumstance I am *always* at your service," Aristide said. "Shall I tell Charon you're ready?"

"Nearly. I'm going back to my room to change, get another towel for Ama, and to turn on the fire for her. Then I'll be out."

"Great. I'll let them know," Aristide said.

I meowed, which must have helped Aristide locate me, because he reached out and stroked the top of my head again, then peeled off and headed in the opposite direction.

Noctus carried me back to his room, dried me off with a towel, then draped me in a new towel.

He turned on the fireplace and set me in front of it, then retreated to his bathroom.

The blue and white flames dried me off, fast—faster than physics would have deemed possible, but that was the beauty of magic. By the time Noctus emerged—wearing his black utility pants and shirt—I had groomed myself into some semblance of order.

Noctus crouched next to me, frowning when he petted me. "You're still damp. Stay in my room until you dry—it's warmer in here." He rubbed me down with the towel, messing up my fur again.

Whatever. Once I turn human then back to cat, my fur will be perfect again.

Maybe I'd go outside and shift while everyone was gone so I wouldn't have to mess with it.

Noctus took my moment of preoccupation and shoved my head through an inflatable donut-pillow.

Wait...I can't scratch my neck like this. He put a cone on me!

By the time I realized what was happening, it was too late. He was fastening it to my collar with little strips of Velcro.

I meowed angrily and flicked my tail back and forth.

"This is for your safety, Amalourne," Noctus said.

No, it's not!

"I don't want you scratching your neck raw while I'm gone. I'll take this off when I return."

I growled. Normally I would have curled in on myself and

lowered my head, but with the pink frosted donut hanging around my neck, I couldn't do that.

"I won't be long. Nap, dry off—just don't scratch." He rubbed the top of my head, then was gone, disappearing through the door with barely a sound.

I got to work ripping at the Velcro. It was difficult to tear off because I didn't have thumbs and I couldn't see, but at least I knew how the cone was supposed to work, so after about ten minutes I was free—and grumpy.

I made sure I clawed the cone—poking a hole in it—before I slipped through the cracked door and headed for the stairs.

That's it. I'm going to go ruin some of his papers on his desk. I'll mix them up so they're out of order. That will teach him! There's nothing worse than disorganized paperwork.

My tail was high with righteous indignation, and I made it into his study, fueled by my irritation.

I hopped up onto his desk where, sure enough, there was a pile of papers, but I was aghast to discover that they were already out of order and weren't organized by date, topic—nothing!

No wonder he's working all the time. He probably can't find anything. Charon must hate it.

Still, I was angry, so I kicked a paper off his desk. It floated to the floor and slipped under a cabinet.

Okay, that's too mean. He'll never find it there.

I hopped off the desk, stuck my paw under the cabinet, and fished the paper out. It was a little crinkled and had a hole in it from one of my claws, but it served him right for sticking a *cone* on me.

Then I felt it: magic shuddered.

What was that?

I sat low on the ground and shivered when the sensation tickled me again.

It wasn't pleasant. It was like someone brushing against my whiskers when I was blind and couldn't see.

I could sense the magic rippling, but I didn't know what was causing it.

It feels like what I experienced the night Noctus trashed the trespasser. Noctus felt something then, because he knew to get up. He must have sensed something pushing the barrier spells on the house. But how could I feel that when I'm not connected to the spell?

Except, I was tied to Noctus through my collar.

If I was right and I could feel the spell because I essentially carried a part of Noctus with me, he was even more insane than I thought.

What could possibly compel you to give a cat *such a dangerous connection?*

I peered at the window that depicted the front lawn, but it was nighttime, so it was pitch black outside, and I could only see the glare of the lights on the glass of the window.

I jumped onto the windowsill, easily balancing, and peered outside.

It took my eyes a moment to adjust to the darkness, but between the streetlights and various house porchlights, I could see a man on the sidewalk in front of the house.

He turned, briefly casting his face in sputtering streetlight, revealing the tracker's craggy nose and face.

CHAPTER TWENTY-FIVE

Chloe

He rested his hands on the iron fence and leaned in, brushing against the barrier.

No—how did he find me? I've barely been outside! He—how?

Obviously, he was more powerful than I thought.

Based on the way he was studying the barrier, I think he was trying to figure out how to break in.

I crouched low on the windowsill and fought the impulse to run, to leave the room and hide deeper in the villa.

This is bad. Noctus is gone, and he won't be back for a while.

The barrier would hold—there was no way it couldn't. Noctus was insanely strong.

But as the ripple of magic touched me again, I couldn't help but worry.

The tracker stepped back and set down what looked like a leather computer case. He started pulling things out of it—a leather bound book, a handgun, a few glowing balls of magic.

It's officially worse than bad. If he starts wondering why *this place is so well protected...*

Noctus had managed to hide evidence of his elven city from the rest of Magiford—including the Paragon. If the tracker realized there was a city of elves within the house...

It would be my fault if anything happened. I can't even give them a warning...

I watched anxiously as the tracker tried to push a ball of magic into the barrier.

The barrier crackled and the ball of magic was repelled off it.

It would hold. Just until Noctus came back.

Maybe I should go out to the city and see if I can lure anyone inside the villa. Surely someone must have Noctus's cell phone number.

A light flicked on in Shiloh's house.

No—is he loud? If he attracts notice from the neighborhood—

As I watched in horror, Shiloh opened her front door.

She stepped out onto her porch, a frown tugging on her normally bright face. She called out to the tracker—though I couldn't tell what she said.

The tracker turned around and peered back at Shiloh. His hand strayed to where he'd holstered the handgun on his belt.

No!

I leaped off the window and bolted out of the study, skidding out when I hit the hallway. I made it to the front door in record time and jumped through a spot on the gate, then rammed my cat door and popped out on the front porch.

The tracker was starting to draw his handgun from his holster as I shot across the lawn and squirmed through the fence.

I growled as I ran past him, drawing his attention as I sprinted down the cul-de-sac sidewalk.

"Ama?" Shiloh shouted.

The tracker fumbled with his things before he ran after me, leaving Shiloh and the quiet neighborhood behind.

So that's Shiloh saved, now what?

I could try to lose him, but I hadn't been successful at that before without outside interference. I certainly didn't want to lead him to Book Nookery.

Noctus. If I can make it to Magiford Donuts, Noctus will stop him.

The decision made, I changed my course so I was pointed toward downtown. Now I just had to avoid the tracker long enough to get there.

As a cat, I was able to put distance between us. He didn't stand a chance at keeping up with me, and based on his steps I didn't think he could see in the dark as well as I could. Plus, the streets were quiet and abandoned. The only people I saw were a clutch of four Unseelie fae, who looked very lost as they were huddled under a streetlamp, peering at a cell phone.

But, as I knew would happen, when I was about four blocks from the cul-de-sac, I started to tire.

Without missing a beat—and risking breaking about twenty Curia Cloisters rules—I shifted from cat to human midstep.

In general, we supernaturals weren't supposed to use magic in public, but it gave me a fresh boost of energy.

I was wearing my backpack, which I flung off my back and tossed onto someone's front lawn. I couldn't risk carrying the extra weight of the backpack, but I clung to my phone.

My breath was calm and steady as I sprinted for blocks, fast closing in on downtown. However, now that I no longer had my cat speed, the tracker started catching up to me.

I tried to lose him by turning up a different residential street, but he was closing in on me too fast.

Time for drastic measures.

We were starting to hit the stores, so I waited until we reached the opening of an alleyway, then changed into my cat form. I scrambled up the alleyway, scooting around garbage bins. There was a brick wall at the back that was taller than me, but I was prepared for it.

I turned into a human as I ran at it, leaped, and switched into a cat midair. With my human momentum behind my cat body I was practically launched at the brick wall. I landed on the top, tapping into my cat agility so I didn't even hobble, then hopped down the other side, which dumped me into a tiny parking lot which I sprinted across as a cat.

I waited to change into a human until I slipped up another block.

By now I was only a few blocks away from the donut shop, but my lungs were starting to burn. I was good at running, but the grueling pace was getting to me.

I heard a clicking noise behind me. Trusting my gut, I dodged to the side as a crack echoed up and down the street. A bullet whizzed past, nearly grazing my ear.

Why is he trying to kill me? What did I ever do to him—I don't even know him! He must be a psychopath!

I turned into a cat again on the slim hope that Noctus would feel me coming through the previously seen as wretched but now potentially lifesaving collar and come for me.

I ran past the clocktower and turned down the block, keeping my sprinting pace even though it felt like my heart could explode. I could almost see the bakery. I just needed to get around the corner!

I heard the click of what I was pretty sure was a gun reloading behind me and started to panic, until I heard the voice of bliss.

"Amalourne." Noctus stood at the corner I needed to turn at, his hair glimmering in the faint light.

He crouched down, and I jumped into his arms, my heart beating frantically as I panted.

"What frightened you?" Noctus asked in a way that suggested he'd permanently eliminate the source of my fear.

Please, that would be so amazing.

Noctus stood upright and patted my back as he stared down the street.

When I turned around, I couldn't see any sign of the tracker, and I couldn't feel the dread and fear his presence inspired either.

Noctus, however, must have felt something. He flexed his hand and glanced down at the shackle on his wrist, staring at it in a contemplative manner.

He shook his head, then turned toward the shop, walking up the block.

Ker—in her wolf form—Charon, and Aristide were standing just outside the building, hidden by a glamour I could feel, but couldn't quite see due to my own abilities.

"Did he seriously find the cat?" Aristide asked. "I'm really hoping not, or he's going to be unbearably smug for weeks."

"I found her," Noctus said as we drew closer. "She was running here, absolutely terrified. She was trying to find me."

"Do we need to be concerned about how smart he thinks his cat is?" Aristide asked.

"It's a forgone conclusion Ama is not a normal housecat," Charon said. "Even if we don't know exactly what she is, she is obviously more intelligent."

Aristide leaned back and sighed into the night sky. "That's right, I forgot, you're an enabler."

Once we reached the group Ker happily crowded Noctus and smelled me, wagging her enormous tail in her joy.

I peered down at her so we touched noses, then immediately regretted it when she licked my face.

"Okay, Ama is here. We removed the three barrier spells cast on this place, and I nearly got my fingers singed in the process, thank you. *Now* can we go in?" Aristide asked.

That explains why they haven't gone in yet. It also supports the idea that the donut shop might be more than it appears to be. Who would cast barrier magic on a donut *shop?*

"We can," Noctus said.

"Do you want us to put Ama in the car first?" Charon suggested. "She'd be safer there since we are likely to encounter violence."

Noctus glanced back down the street. "I'm not certain she would be safer, actually. Something seems to upset her whenever we're apart."

I half expected Aristide to make a joke about it, but he was frowning. "She was that upset?"

"The tracking spell is more general than precise, but I could feel the path she took from the house to here." Noctus set me down. I sat close to his legs, like the very good pet that I was. "She was going as fast as she could and was very purposefully making her way here."

"Well." Aristide straightened up. I blinked, and suddenly he had a fistful of daggers. "It seems, then, that we'll be taking a cat in with us. Lead on!"

Noctus reached his right hand out, sighed in irritation, then retracted it and instead drew a sword from his left side. He glanced down at me.

I—not knowing what else to do—meowed.

Go on. I know how to stay out of the way in danger. And whatever you find, it's safer in there than out here with the tracker.

Noctus shrugged, turned to the side door, shifted his weight, then kicked the door in. With *one* blow!

He skulked in first, with Ker right on his heels. Aristide and Charon entered together, and I slipped in right behind them, sticking to the wall.

I couldn't see much besides boxes, table legs, and people legs from my vantage point. At least, I couldn't until Ker growled and launched herself on top of a table, and then onto a troll from there.

I didn't like being on the ground—it felt like it would be easy to sneak up on me, so I scaled a pile of crates and peered down at the bare bones room—brick with a cement floor and an industrial setup. There were tables littered with trinkets—jewelry, thumb sized statues, cuff links, belt buckles, hair accessories, knives, even a few pens—and there were stacks of books and magical equipment cast across other tables.

Clearly, this is the place. Why else would a donut shop have the equivalent of a magical arsenal in its storage area? I don't even see *a kitchen!*

Noctus was facing off against four werewolves in their wolf forms. The wolves looked pretty small compared to Ker, but four of them? That was dangerous.

Noctus's expression, however, was one of boredom as he kicked a wolf in the chest—sending it flying backwards—while cracking another in the head with the pommel of his sword.

While Noctus and Ker charged, Charon prepped Aristide.

"Open room," Charon said. "No walls, all machinery is hip height or lower with the exception of one workbench pressed against a wall."

Aristide tilted his head as he listened to Charon's description.

"Eighteen enemies. One shifter—a big cat, I think—four werewolves that His Majesty is taking on, four vampires, a troll that Ker is fighting, two dryads, three naiads, a faun, and two pixies. All are armed with bladed weapons. I don't see any firearms whatsoever, but there are daggers. And there's clutter on the floors, but there is a clear circle around you."

Aristide tilted his head up and narrowed his unfocusing eyes. "There's another enemy—a wizard. Two, actually. I can smell their disgusting blood."

"I don't see them, so they must be in the kitchen area," Charon said. "I'll inform His Majesty. Good luck."

"You too."

Instead of charging into the fray, Charon crept around the edge of the room, sliding his handgun from his shoulder holster.

Noctus caught the last werewolf when it tried to jump at him, and flipped it over his shoulder. It hit the ground with a splat, and Noctus turned to the vampires.

The biggest one tried to grab him, but Noctus slammed his

head into the vampire's, and the vampire let him go, wobbling on his feet as he clutched his head.

A female vamp tried to hit Noctus from behind. He ducked, and she slammed into the one he'd just brained, and they both collapsed in a heap.

Every move Noctus made was smooth and certain. He didn't react, he pushed his opponents into their reactions and then sprang when it suited him.

The alarming thing was, although his expression was watchful, Noctus didn't even seem to be *trying* that much. He scanned the cavernous room while dodging an attack from one of the pixies, but whenever he set his eyes on an opponent, he took them down.

After spying me on my crate, Noctus turned his attention back to the two remaining vampires. He jabbed his sword at the third vampire in a feint, then abruptly switched directions and popped the vampire in the throat with the flat of his blade.

The vampire grabbed at her throat and backed away from him.

He then grabbed the last vamp—who was attempting to flee—and slammed him to the ground with a painful sounding crunch. While he was staring at the vampire he'd just downed, he grabbed a knife from his belt and flung it, hitting the third vampire who'd been toddling away, knocking her to the ground.

Okay, I can understand how the Mors were able to dominate the battlefield. To take on four werewolves and then four vampires like they were nothing?

Ker was still facing off with the troll. They'd broken two tables, but the large fae creature couldn't even catch Ker, and whenever it tried to lumber away she'd drag it back.

Werewolf strength is scary.

A gun discharged, and the cat shifter—who'd been stalking toward Noctus's back—collapsed.

Ah, that would be Charon.

Aristide took down one of the dryads. He threw a dagger, nailing her in the back. I suspected he must have been tracking their heartbeat to anchor his aim, especially since he dispatched the second dryad with an equal amount of precision.

In the middle of the fighting, one of the wizards emerged from the front end of the shop. The woman was white faced, and I didn't see any coat of arms or emblem that identified her House —same as the clerk I usually saw.

Rather than jump into the battle, she crept to a workbench that was stacked with books, and summoned flames to her hands.

She's going to destroy those books. Why? Are they evidence?

I jumped off the crates and ran across the room, dodging the fallen werewolves and weaving between table legs.

By the time I got to the workbench, she was reaching for one of the books, the flames in her hand burning with her magic.

I launched myself at her back, digging my claws in as deep as I could through her thin t-shirt.

She screamed and bent backwards, and I clawed my way up her shoulders, spitting and hissing.

She tried to torch my fur, but her flames didn't harm me—I didn't feel anything besides the hum of magic from them.

"What the—" She dropped her magic and then tried to yank me off her by pulling my tail, but I was high enough that I could bite the back of her neck and dig my claws into her bare skin.

She shrieked then shuffled sideways and tried to ram her back against the workbench.

I bailed, so she only succeeded in jabbing herself in the spine.

As she groaned and struggled to stand, I jumped on top of the workbench, positioning myself between her and the books. My fur puffed up, and I growled deep in my throat.

"You stupid cat!" She tried to chuck a ball of lightning at me, but the lightning swept past me and extinguished. She tried to snatch me, and I savagely clawed and bit her arms. Despite the pain, she managed to grab me by the back of my neck.

"Got you!" The wizard triumphantly held me over her head. Gripping my scruff, she swung me down, aiming at the table.

She's going to try to beat me!

I tried to wriggle, but I couldn't. Fear spiked in my heart, and abruptly the world righted itself and all I saw was Noctus's shirt.

CHAPTER TWENTY-SIX

Chloe

The woman screamed and howled in pain, but with my face shoved into his shoulder, I couldn't see anything.

When Noctus finally relaxed his grip on me so I could climb up onto his shoulders, the wizard was passed out on the ground.

Charon emerged from the front of the store, dragging the unconscious wizard clerk behind him. "Clear," he announced. "Your orders?"

"Tie them up—put magic canceling bracelets on the wizards and fae." Noctus glanced at the unconscious supernaturals, then started paging through the books I'd protected.

Meanwhile, Aristide sat on top of a crate and whipped out a bag of what appeared to be homemade anti-magic bracelets.

Elf magic is scary.

Ker started dragging the injured over to Aristide by the collars of their shirts and dumping them at his feet.

Charon would then secure them, before Aristide tagged the wizards and fae with the anti-magic bracelets.

I jumped off Noctus's shoulders and landed on the table where I could study a few of the jumbled books myself.

This one is for power enhancements—that lines up with the magic cast on artifacts. But—hello, what's this?

Near the bottom of the stack was a book about *explosive* spells!

Noctus made a noise. "Hm," he said.

Charon looked up from the arduous task of tying up the troll. "What is it?"

Noctus held his book up by its binding. "All of the spells in this tome are timing-based spells. I'd say that confirms the artifacts' flashy expirations were intentional after all."

I enthusiastically rubbed against the stack of books, purring as I attempted to look nonchalant. I leaned into the books until I knocked the stack over, revealing the book about explosion spells.

"What was that sound?" Aristide asked.

"Ama was pointing something out to me," Noctus said.

"How?" Aristide asked.

Noctus didn't respond—or chide me for the mess I'd made. He petted the top of my head, then started looking at the titles.

Charon glanced in our direction as I sat and curled my tail around me. "She knocked over a stack of books."

Aristide frowned as he snapped the magic canceling bracelet on one of the wizards. "Seriously? Noctus, do we need to worry about you getting as fanatical as the Paragon? Or should we get you more cats so you have more targets to love?"

Noctus found the book on explosive spells and petted me again. "I've told you before that Ama is not a regular cat."

Aristide groaned. "I *know* you said that, which is why I thought we agreed not to let on about it, lest the information get back to whoever or whatever is controlling her!"

I uncurled my tail and felt markedly less proud than I had a moment ago. *Wait, all of them don't think I'm a normal cat? Noctus I knew about, obviously, but everyone else, too? How long have they guessed this?*

"Ama isn't being controlled," Noctus said.

"You can't know that," Aristide argued. "Charon, talk some sense into him."

"His Majesty says she isn't being controlled," Charon said. "So she isn't."

Noctus held my book up. "She found this spell book that is exclusively about explosions. I think it's safe to say this is the place—though we should question the workers before we notify the Curia Cloisters."

"What, you want to interview them to commemorate the first time you took down danger with your cat?" Aristide asked.

"No," Noctus said. "I want to make sure there isn't a second workshop hidden somewhere in this city."

"Oh," Aristide said. "Yeah, that makes sense."

"I believe one of the naiads could be roused," Charon said.

"Very well," Noctus said. "Let's go."

Go? Go where?

I was confused when Noctus picked me up, and we trooped outside, Charon and Noctus going first with Ker following behind, dragging the fae by the collar of her shirt.

Once we were outside, Noctus—still carrying me—led the way around the building. He stopped in one of the narrow alleyways.

While Charon knelt next to the naiad and administered some kind of potion, Noctus frowned at the brick exterior of the donut shop.

"Can you do it?" Aristide asked, his voice somehow softer than usual.

Noctus rubbed at the shackles on his wrist. "It will be a stretch," he admitted. "But I will force it."

"Don't overdo it. We can come up with a different method," Aristide said.

Noctus exhaled a breath of laughter as he pulled a dagger from his belt with his free hand. "No, I refuse to depart from a plan that has a history of working."

"I don't recall you being so *annoyingly stubborn* when we were younger."

"Well, you *are* a vampire," Noctus said. "The nostalgia for times gone by must be hitting you—"

Aristide squawked. "Not another word—not a word!"

What are they talking about—All My Donuts!

I puffed up in Noctus's arms as the whole wall of the bakery was engulfed in blue and white flames.

Noctus had done it—I could feel his invasive elf magic trickle from the dagger he was holding—his artifact, it would seem.

"It's fine, Ama." Noctus shifted his arm around me. "You're safe."

I'm not, actually, but I guess it's sweet that he cares?

His dagger glowed, and I felt the tickle of a glamour. I had to fight my natural immunity to magic to hear the crackle of fire and smell the sooty scent of smoke. As soon as I was distracted I lost the sensations, so this was definitely Noctus-made-magic.

Aristide twitched his nose. "Excellent work as usual. Is the fae ready, Charon?"

"Nearly," Charon said. He splashed the remnants of the potion on the naiad's face, and she awoke with a sputter.

"W-what—" She mutely cut herself off and shrank back when Noctus approached her.

"You have this one opportunity not to end up back in this building with the rest of your comrades." Noctus's voice was bitterly cold and biting, and the fae shivered in fright and hiccupped in her fear. "What Court do you work with?"

Woah! This is next-level mental warfare—too dark, Noctus! Too dark! She thinks the place is on fire and you're threatening to chuck her back in there!

"I-I don't have a Court." The naiad started crying—*really*

crying. Naiads can be beautiful, but she was ugly crying in her fear, her face turning red and scrunching up.

That Noctus could look intimidating enough to make her cry while he was holding a fluffy cat that clung to his shirt collar said a lot about the way he held himself.

Noctus glanced back at Ker, who took a few steps forward so the light from the blue and white flames made her eerie appearance almost spectral.

"Think *very* carefully about your answers," Noctus said. "As a naiad, you might be tempted to twist your words into something that isn't a lie but isn't the truth, but she can hear your heartbeat and smell your scent. We'll *know* if you're hiding something. I'll ask again, what Court do you work for?"

"N-not a Court," the fae cried. "I don't have a Court. Last year I was kicked out of the Summer Court for attempting to harm Consort Flora," she said, naming the wife of the Summer King. "I was exiled from all the large Courts."

"Then what were you doing manufacturing artifacts designed to harm their users, and potentially those around them?" Noctus asked.

"It was for money!" the fae blurted out. "All of us just did it for the money. The werewolves are all lone wolves, and the vampires are all unclaimed!"

That can't be a coincidence—whoever planned this must have known stragglers like them would be desperate for work.

"How?" Noctus demanded. "You didn't earn that much from selling the artifacts."

"No." The naiad emphatically shook her head, her eyes wild. "We were paid by a guy who set up the place."

The swirl in Noctus's eyes moved as he locked gazes with the fae. "What was his name?"

"I don't know," she squeaked. "I never met him. I didn't join until after the shop was already operational. I just know he mailed our paychecks and any additional instructions to us, which we then had to burn." With her hands and legs secure, the naiad could only wriggle backwards, until she ran into Charon.

This isn't a crime of opportunity; whoever created it put a lot of planning into it to hide his involvement.

"Who from your group has seen the supernatural who organized this?" Noctus asked.

"Um...uh..." She quivered in fear.

"Take your time," Noctus said.

I was pretty sure he meant it genuinely, but the naiad turned white and shook even harder.

"I, I don't think anyone?" she said. "Most of us started working here three months ago. The previous team taught us, hired even more people so the business expanded, then turned over management and left."

Aristide whistled. "That is some pretty nifty track covering."

The fae violently jumped at the sound of Aristide's voice—she hadn't seen him from where he was standing in the gloom, leaning against the next-door building.

"Are you aware of any other similar operations in Magiford?" Noctus asked.

"N-no," the fae said. "We didn't know why the guy wanted a shop of broken artifacts, either. We just did what we were told."

They were too desperate for money to care.

Lone wolves, unclaimed vampires, exiled fae—all of them were a specific kind of desperate that I understood firsthand. It was nearly impossible to live as a solo supernatural; they'd be frantic to find any way to stabilize their lives.

"Did you manufacture *and* sell the artifacts?" Noctus asked.

"Yes," the naiad said. "The other fae and I could put rudimentary magic in the items. The wizards helped. The others either purchased the items we enchanted, sold the new artifacts, or worked as security." Her lower lip quivered. "And a few made donuts—to keep up our storefront cover."

The best donuts! I still can't believe my favorite donut shop was just a cover. Noctus, find their recipe book!

Unaware of my thoughts, Noctus rubbed his thumb on the pommel of his dagger. "I see."

"Please, please don't kill me," the naiad cried. "I personally didn't harm anyone!"

"*Didn't harm anyone?*" Noctus repeated. His voice was dark and consuming. "Every artifact you made *hurt* people—supernaturals and even humans!"

"But I—"

"Yes, you did not physically harm them yourself, but their blood is still on your hands." Noctus took a step closer, and his hazel eyes were hypnotic in the pull of his icy anger. Behind him, the blue and white flames grew. "You will face the consequences of your actions."

"No—"

Charon struck like lightning, hitting the naiad in an instant knockout move. She slumped to the ground and groaned.

Ker padded forward, her nails clicking on the paved ground, grabbed the fae by her collar, then dragged her off.

"Right, then," Aristide said. "Who next? I vote for one of the wizards. Their kind usually screech a lot, but they're much faster to spill what they know."

Shocked by the deviousness of the entire operation, I hung from Noctus's shirt.

They're going to do this again!?

TERRIFYING. *They're absolutely terrifying.*

I sat huddled on Noctus's lap for the drive back, cowed by the intense brilliance of Noctus and his friends. It wasn't that I really thought they were scary in an "I'm going to kill you" sort of way, it was just their powers combined with their cunning made them a force of nature.

They "interviewed" both wizards and a vampire—handling each interview process the same way so they woke their target up and made them believe they'd left the others in the burning building.

They'd gotten matching answers, so they then called up the Curia Cloisters and left.

These guys...it's a good thing Noctus hates deskwork, or they could have taken over Magiford by this point.

Noctus spared me a glance—he'd been studying his cell phone for the past five minutes—and petted me. "It seems the Cloisters followed up."

"Already? That was fast," Aristide said. "Those little task forces of theirs are getting to be more efficient."

"How can you tell, Your Majesty?" Charon asked.

"They've closed all the streets down surrounding the bakery according to my cell phone map app." Noctus glanced outside—it was still pitch black since it was early in the morning.

I meekly stayed still, even when he curled his free hand around me.

I hope he doesn't feel like sleeping tonight, because that's all I want to do, and sleeping in the sink isn't very restful or cozy.

Charon slowed the car down as he turned onto their cul-de-sac. "Then the issue is closed," he said. "The broken artifacts will no longer be sold, our people will be safe, and the confusion charms will mean no one will remember us."

Yeah, that was the other scary thing about them—they'd used fae confusion charms on the entire lot. Confusion charms were a lot harder to reverse and were relatively simple to cast—unlike a spell that affected the memory. Fae magic didn't work on the wizards, but it wouldn't matter, because no one would have the same story—including the wizards, since Charon had knocked the second wizard out in the kitchen and he never saw any of the fight.

The Curia Cloisters task force would likely be able to tell it was a fae confusion charm, but that was the beauty of using a *fae* confusion charm—it wouldn't get traced back to Noctus or the others. (Not that I imagined the task force would overly exert itself to find whoever had taken down the illegal store...)

They think in layers. It's how they've avoided getting found this long, with so many heads—and varying abilities—working together, they're downright devious.

The car turned into the driveway and rolled to a stop inside the garage.

Noctus was out first. He tried to shift me so he could hold me balanced against his hip with one arm, but I hopped off him.

He let me wander off and instead offered Aristide an arm so he could get out of the car, followed by Ker.

"It's a bit disappointing that things will be back to normal," Aristide said. "I rather enjoyed our field trips of running around the city."

"Shut your traitorous mouth right now," Noctus said.

Aristide confidently reached out and poked Noctus in the chest, right over his heart. "Bore!"

Ker shook, shedding wolf hair all over as I strolled out of the garage.

Yep, I'm pretty sure Aristide uses a person's heartbeat to figure out where to aim for things.

I was heading for the front porch when I thought to glance across the street at Shiloh's house.

The lights were all off, so hopefully that meant she hadn't been too bothered by the tracker. But there was a sparkle of magic that made me...uneasy.

I should check it out, just in case the tracker came back and did something to her house.

I trotted across the lawn and hopped through the wrought iron fence.

I turned in a circle a few times before I was able to nail the magic sensation—it came from farther up the street. Shiloh's house was clear.

Although that reminds me, I flung my backpack onto somebody's lawn. I should probably check that out before the sun rises. It's got my wallet, and I don't need Noctus hearing about it...

I walked a little further down the sidewalk, considering how I could reclaim it, but Noctus wasn't having any of it.

"Ama," he called, his voice mellow but inflexible. "No. We're going inside."

"Have fun corralling your persnickety feline!" Aristide outright cackled as he whacked the porch step with his cane, stepped onto it, then let himself inside the house.

Ker woofed at Noctus as she passed, following Aristide inside.

"Do you want some help, Your Majesty?" Charon asked.

I passed a lumpy pile of trash bags—Charon was going to have to pick that up in the morning because the trash people only picked up trash in the appropriate bins—and again felt the sparkle of magic. When I peered back at Noctus and Charon through the spokes of the fence, Noctus didn't seem too worried.

"No, I think she's just exploring." He folded his arms across his chest and leaned against one of the porch's support pillars. "You can head inside, Charon. Thanks for your help tonight."

"Of course, Your Majesty." Charon bowed, then went inside, closing the door behind him.

"Amalourne," Noctus called—this time his voice had a toll of warning to it.

I stopped where the next-door neighbor's lawn began and craned my neck. *I guess I'll have to grab it first thing in the morning. I didn't drop it until I turned into a human, and that was after a couple blocks of running. I should probably wait to make sure Noctus is around in case the tracker is still skulking nearby.*

Guilt prickled my gut.

I had to tell Noctus—about me, and the tracker. I didn't want anyone on the street—much less any of the elves—to be hurt because of me.

There's not much that can make me risk my neck—I'm too used to acting on survival instincts to be brave. But if Shiloh or the uncles got hurt in the crossfire... Yeah. I must tell him. Soon. Once I can get enough courage worked up.

"Amalourne."

I turned to face Noctus, but when I heard frantic footsteps I peered back, curious.

A couple human-esque shapes were hurtling down the sidewalk. Fae—I could feel the silky sensation of their magic, but it would have been obvious when they passed under a streetlight. They were too graceful.

Why are a bunch of fae running around this late at night?

I rested a paw on the iron fence, watching with confusion as they bore down on me.

When I peered at Noctus, he seemed equally as confused, with a wrinkle spreading across his forehead.

"Amalourne..."

The pile of trash directly behind me moved, and something grabbed me by the belly. "I got her!"

I clawed and hissed, but whoever had grabbed me was wearing leather gloves that went past their elbows.

Within seconds, backup—the sprinting fae—closed in around the sentient trash heap.

My heart beat frantically in my chest, but as I fought my capture I realized it was a faun holding me, not the tracker, as he climbed out of the trash, reeking like moldy food.

"I got her," the faun repeated as he held me high over his head.

"Release my cat." Noctus's voice was quiet and seething.

The faun was smart enough to recognize the danger. He

gulped and lowered me—not to put me down, he held me by the armpits so I dangled at the same height as the fence, my heartbeat returning to normal now that I knew I wasn't in mortal peril.

"Sir." A naiad tried to bow at Noctus. I couldn't tell if it did anything, from this angle Noctus was a silhouette with the porch light behind him. "We have been sent by the Unseelie Queen of Magiford. She is done bargaining with you to join her Court."

Noctus was motionless. "Oh?"

The naiad gulped and spoke to the lawn, but she kept on going. "If you do not join her as a warrior under her services, there will be consequences."

Consequences? No! This is a stupid attempt at bargaining—you aren't just barking up the wrong tree, you're in the wrong forest!

I hissed and twisted in the faun's grasp, trying to get free, but he held me securely with his gloves.

"Consequences? Like the capture of my cat?" Noctus asked. His voice was so...different I barely recognized it.

"Y-yes," the naiad said. "If you do not swear fealty to Her Majesty, we are to take your cat."

Wow, yeah, even if they suspect he's an elf, they definitely don't know who he is. No one would try to coerce an elf king *like this. It's suicide.* I dug my claws into the faun's leather gloves and tried to thrash my way to freedom, but the faun clutched me tighter.

I wasn't too upset by the issue. *If the Unseelie walk away with me, I'll just turn into a human and squash the faun. I've escaped the Unseelie heaps before. They'll be infinitely easier to run from compared to Noctus: the overly invested pet owner.*

It said a lot about my life that I was calming down. But, hey, at least it wasn't the tracker!

Noctus exhaled—which sounded dangerously like snapping patience—and rubbed at his shackles. "I'm not joining the Unseelie Court, or the Seelie Court. Both factions are small, unimportant, and have nothing to do with me. If Queen Darina wants to save her people, she'd be better off throwing herself at the Night Queen's feet. Now, *give me my cat.*"

The faun tottered back a step or two at the pure malice in Noctus's voice, and the fae noble next to us shakily pulled an ax from his belt.

Noctus is really not happy about this. Don't worry, your insane collar means I'll be back. Can't risk you tracking me to my apartment even though I could really use a shower.

"I'm afraid we can't do that," the naiad said. "We will take her back to Queen Darina. If you change your mind—"

"No," Noctus said. The air crackled with power.

The fae started shuffling up the sidewalk, away from Noctus's house.

"Our queen looks forward to hearing from you," the naiad tried.

Noctus tilted his head, and his magic shackles—the supposedly unremovable chains—crackled.

They glowed from within like coals, then shattered into a million pieces that hung around Noctus, suspended in midair.

That can't be good.

CHAPTER TWENTY-SEVEN

Chloe

A glowing portal that bubbled with magic appeared, and Noctus thrust his right hand inside it. The air was so full of magic it made my bones ache.

Feeling every strand of fur on my body from the bone-jarring sensation, I puffed up, and my heart kicked back up.

I have a feeling I'm about to witness my first real usage of elven magic.

Noctus removed his hand from the portal, pulling out a sword —one unlike anything I'd ever seen.

The hilt was made of a shining gemstone that glowed like the moon, and the blade itself was clear like glass, but it looked like tiny stars that pulsed with power were captured inside it.

Once Noctus pulled it free from the portal, a ribbon of smoke curled around the sword, then engulfed Noctus. It hardened into a helm on his head—one that covered his skull and eyes, but cut off at the bridge of his nose. Razor sharp, metallic feathers were layered over the sides of the helm, giving it an angular look.

Next, the smoke created a chestplate that was so dark it was almost black, and an elaborate shoulder guard—all ornamented with the same feather-like design. A shimmering pale blue colored cloak flowed down from the shoulder guard, covering his left side. Chainmail covered leggings were next, followed by metal plated boots, and ending with metal gauntlets that sported the same metal feathers on the knuckles and specific edges—perfect for inflicting wounds on opponents.

As the smoke dissipated, Noctus pointed his sword at the Unseelie fae.

In that moment I understood why no one had stood up to the elves for so long.

He crackled with so much power my whiskers were numb, and the edges of his glass sword glowed with unrestricted magic. He was the pinnacle of supernatural society, and even though I swore I could feel the whispers of death come from him, there was something so painfully beautiful it was hard to breathe.

The fae with the ax took a few steps toward Noctus, raising the weapon over his head.

Noctus extended his free hand and clenched it. The ax collapsed in on itself, bending and smoldering as magic destroyed it.

The fae holding it yelled and dropped it.

The faun dropped me and held his hands high above his head.

I, thanks to my cat nimbleness, landed on my paws.

Concentrated magic flooded the lawn. I could feel it in my paw pads as I crouched on the ground.

"W-w-we're..." The naiad tried to speak, but magic was so thick in the air she couldn't force the words out. Her legs shook, and she collapsed to her knees, unable to move from the weight of Noctus's power.

I, with my anti-magic abilities, wasn't much affected. My hair puffed up, I wriggled through the fence and bounded across the yard, running past Noctus and bounding all the way to the porch. I meowed when I got there, to signal to Noctus I was safe.

He shifted the position of his sword, and white colored magic started to wrap around the sword.

He—what? Does he really intend to fire that thing off in the neighborhood? He could kill someone with that—or take out a house!

Every particle of my being said I needed to get out of there. It wasn't safe. Noctus was about three seconds away from blowing up the entire block.

I needed to head into the villa where I'd be okay—I could go get Charon. That would be the best plan for me.

But...there was so much at stake. Noctus had fought to be in this cul-de-sac. He hid his lineage, shackled his own magic, and protected his people.

I wasn't sure where I stood with him, but he'd saved me from the tracker several times, and I'd already endangered his home and neighbors once. I *owed* him...no matter how terrified I was.

I ran, my tail rail straight as I pounced on his feet. If I gave myself even a second to think I knew I'd bolt, so I tapped on his boots with my paws and meowed.

Either he couldn't hear me over the roar of his magic, or he was too far gone in his anger to notice.

Around us, lights were starting to turn on in the neighboring houses.

No, no, no! You can't reveal yourself now—not for me *when I've done nothing but lie to you!*

Frantically I tried clawing his leg, but I couldn't get through his chainmail.

Bolts of light were forming around his sword, and the Unseelie fae were collapsed on the cement, openly crying but unable to run from the force of Noctus's true power.

He's making a huge mistake, and he's going to hurt his neighbors in the process.

That, I knew, Noctus would regret.

I must stop him. No matter what it takes.

Before I could second-guess myself, I tapped my powers, shifting from cat to human.

As a human, his powers felt even stronger. The magic glided across my skin like water, surrounding me but unable to affect me.

I hope I don't regret this.

"Noctus, it's okay! I'm fine!" I shouted.

Noctus kept his sword raised, but he shifted his head slightly to look down at me. I couldn't see his eyes—just his chin and the set of his mouth, which didn't look promising.

Please don't kill me, please don't kill me!

Noctus was taller than me by *a lot*, but I could still throw my arms around his neck—mimicking what I did as a cat—and set my head on his shoulder. "You need to stop! You're going to blow the neighborhood up!"

I scrunched my eyes shut and braced, waiting for him to stab me in the back, or at least push me away.

Instead, I almost jumped out of my skin and nearly turned into a cat again when Noctus curled his left arm around my waist in a loose hug, the metal of his gauntlets brushing my back.

"Amalourne," he said. His voice had returned to a soothing timbre, and his arm on my lower back was gentle.

I'm safe, he's fine.

"They threatened you." Back was the flat, dark tone.

Okay, maybe he's not fine!

"They did, but they are very sorry now." I pulled back from his shoulder so I could peer up at him, but I kept my arms draped around his neck. I was kind of hoping it would kick in his Noctus: the overly doting pet parent part of him. "You can let them go."

"Let them go?" Noctus said as if I'd taken leave of my senses. "They *threatened* you," he repeated.

"Yes, I was there," I said. "But they didn't know not to mess with you. Now they know better."

"Yes..." Noctus adjusted his arm around my waist, but I was more impressed that he was still casually holding his sword aloft with one hand, as if it weighed nothing. "But they might be able to figure it out."

"Who you are?"

"Yes."

"That would be a problem." I absently rubbed my thumb on one of the feather designs on his chestplate as I tried to organize the churn of my thoughts.

Heading the race held inside my brain was the realization that Noctus hadn't seemed at all surprised to find out his cat was the Book Nookery clerk. *He didn't react. At all. Why?*

I glanced at him again. His face was pointed in the direction of the fae, and the set of his lips minutely tightened.

Later—worry later. I must focus on the current issue, or he's going to go overboard! I did my best to push the very important but not relevant at the moment thoughts back, and considered the issue.

We're dealing with fae—Unseelie fae specifically. They don't have access to the fae realm so they're starved for magic—that's what the war between the Seelie and Unseelie is over. How can I exploit that?

"You can make portals to the fae realm," I said.

"Yes."

"Can you pull magic from the fae realm and pump it through them?" I asked. "They're not a landed Court. They've been cut off from magic for so long, they'll get drunk off it," I said. "It will addle their brains. Or you could throw a confusion charm on them."

"It's a worthy idea," Noctus said. "But it's not the lesson they need."

"Have Charon tie the ruined ax to one of them," I suggested. "That will be all the communication you'll need."

Noctus was unnaturally still for a moment as he considered the idea. "Fine." He lowered his sword and pointed it to the ground.

The sidewalk under the fae swirled. The fae struggled for a moment, but when the magic hit them they sagged, their heads falling to the side or straight back. They swayed on their knees, and a couple of them even fell over.

"Woah," I said. "I was not expecting that strong of a response."

As I watched, the few who hadn't been pressed all the way to the ground flopped, landing face down on the cement sidewalk, their arms and legs spread in an excellent starfish impression.

"It was the superior idea to the confusion charm." Noctus pivoted toward the door. His arm at my back, he scooped me along. "They'll be addled for days after exposure to unfiltered, unadulterated fae realm magic."

Noctus carelessly tossed aside his glass sword—which evaporated into thin air—then opened the door, nudging me in first.

I passed through—barely noticing the head-spinning sensation of the portal magic.

Noctus came in after me. As he stepped free of the gate, smoke crawled across his armor—starting with his helm—and the armor turned into smoke and faded into nothing, leaving Noctus wearing the same dark, utility clothing he'd worn to Magiford Donuts.

The bits of his shackles that had been suspended in the air reformed around his wrists, recreating the supposedly unbreakable shackles.

Not only does he have enough magic to break them, he can hold the spell midair, and then make it reform?

I was starting to realize just how Noctus was able to overpower his entire family. He was a *king*. Not because of his blood, but his *power*.

"Charon." Noctus repositioned his arm so it was curled around my shoulders.

"Yes, Your Majesty?" Charon emerged from an inlet in the wall, half hidden by a grandfather clock.

"Relocate the garbage on the sidewalk—with their broken weapon."

"Understood, Your Majesty." Charon bowed to him. He eyed me as he headed toward the door, but didn't say anything.

Noctus let go of me so he could adjust the reformed shackles.

Without his arm around me I stopped moving, every muscle in my body tensing as I waited for whatever punishment he was going to mete out.

Noctus glanced at me. "Welcome to Calor Villa, Chloe of Book Nookery."

"I'm sorry," I blurted out. "I should have revealed myself when you took me from the Seelie fae but, but—" I stammered, unable to finish the thought.

I can't tell him I thought he'd kill me! That's—as Ker would say—not a way to win friends.

"But you're a shadow," Noctus said.

Confusion loosened my mouth. "I'm a what?"

Noctus slightly tilted his head back, making the black spiral in his eyes swirl. "You don't even know, do you?"

This is bad. I don't know what he's talking about, and we're already on severely uneven ground.

My mind whirled—how could I deal with this? I expected anger, not this...controlled intensity he was showing me. *I need to convince him that I'm nothing, maybe then he'll let me go.*

"I don't know what you're talking about," I said truthfully. "I'm no one. Just a freak of nature that even the Curia Cloisters can't classify. That's why the Seelie and Unseelie fae pick on me. Seriously, ask me again with Ker present—I'm not lying!"

Noctus watched me, his expression stoic.

At least he hasn't busted out his magic yet.

"I won't tell anyone what I know. Confusion charms won't work on me, but I'll take whatever vow you want me to," I babbled.

"That won't be a problem." Noctus started walking down the hallway.

"It won't?" I hesitated for a moment, then followed after him.

"No. You won't be telling anyone, because you'll remain here."

I what?

I struggled to keep my expression neutral. *Is that a euphemism for "I'm going to throw you into the dungeon"?*

The frantic beat of my heart made me suspect I was maybe right, but the stupidly optimistic part of me—the part that remembered the warm way he'd say "Amalourne"—nursed a tiny flame of hope that maybe he'd imprison me in a bathroom or something.

"What do you mean?" I asked.

"It's too dangerous to let you leave."

The problem is there are multiple ways to interpret everything he's saying, and I can't tell which meaning he's referring to. The lump in my throat made me suspect it wasn't a good way.

"Besides—I told you," Noctus added.

We reached the spiral staircase, and when Noctus started up it without adding anything, I followed him. "Told me what?"

"That whoever was connected to Amalourne, I'd handle." Noctus glanced back at me. "You are officially a member of my household."

A member of his household? What does that even mean?

"You stay here, under my reign and with my people," he continued.

Oh. That, I glumly thought. *It's an insurance policy for him. To keep me under his control. That's not good.*

"The extra caution is necessary, given that you are a shadow," Noctus concluded.

We reached the top floor, and Noctus led me toward his bedroom. "You think I'm a shadow?" I asked.

"I don't think. You *are*."

We passed Noctus's bedroom door, and I trotted to keep up with him. "If you don't mind my asking...what's a shadow?"

Noctus stopped at the next door and studied me. There was

something about the slant of his mouth and the slight crinkle to his eyes. I couldn't tell if it was rueful or...something else.

"Shadows," he said, "are the only natural enemy of the elves."

To be Continued in The King's Shadow: Gate of Myth and Power Book 2

For free short stories and more information about the Gate of Myth and Power Series, visit kmshea.com!

OTHER SERIES BY K. M. SHEA

The Snow Queen

Timeless Fairy Tales

The Fairy Tale Enchantress

The Elves of Lessa

Hall of Blood and Mercy

Court of Midnight and Deception

Pack of Dawn and Destiny

Gate of Myth and Power

King Arthur and Her Knights

Robyn Hood

The Magical Beings' Rehabilitation Center

Second Age of Retha: Written under pen name A. M. Sohma

ADDITIONAL NOVELS

Life Reader

Princess Ahira

A Goose Girl

ABOUT THE AUTHOR

K. M. Shea is a fantasy-romance author who never quite grew out of adventure books or fairy tales, and still searches closets in hopes of stumbling into Narnia. She is addicted to sweet romances, witty characters, and happy endings. She also writes LitRPG and GameLit under the pen name, A. M. Sohma.

Hang out with the K. M. Shea Community at...
kmshea.com

Made in the USA
Las Vegas, NV
13 May 2023